The Melon Boys

For Eleanor & Ethan —
Enjoy the story!

M.G. [signature]

The Melon Boys

❖

Michael George

Copyright © 2007 by Michael George.

COVER DESIGN: "Everybody in the Sun," by George Deem (1966). Collection of Michael Ottensmeyer

ISBN: Hardcover   978-1-4257-4433-5
          Softcover   978-1-4257-4432-8

All rights reserved. No part of this book may be reproduced or transmitted in any form or by any means, electronic or mechanical, including photocopying, recording, or by any information storage and retrieval system, without permission in writing from the copyright owner.

This is a work of fiction. Names, characters, places and incidents either are the product of the author's imagination or are used fictitiously, and any resemblance to any actual persons, living or dead, events, or locales is entirely coincidental.

This book was printed in the United States of America.

To order additional copies of this book, contact:
Xlibris Corporation
1-888-795-4274
www.Xlibris.com
Orders@Xlibris.com

To my father, who spent much of his life as a hard working farmer, and who taught me most of life's important lessons.

ACKNOWLEDGMENTS

I am forever grateful to my brother, Ed, for giving me the idea to write this story and for believing that I could.

* * *

I can never thank my daughter Shelby Mitchell, and my wife Joy enough for their encouragement, and for their assistance in editing the story contained in these pages. Shelby is a professional writer and former English / German literature major, and the kind of daughter any father would be proud of. Joy is a faithful companion with a keen eye for all the little things I never see.

* * *

My thanks also go out to the Watermelon, and especially the Crimson Sweet variety. According to one official website, "The Crimson sensation Hybrid Watermelon is bigger, better and earlier than standard varieties. Vigorous vines set handsome round fruits 30-35 lbs. apiece. Bright red flesh is incredibly sweet! Who needs dessert when you've got this incredibly sweet and juicy treat? Even small-space gardeners can grow compact varieties."

Mark Twain once said that watermelon was "*Chief of the world's luxuries, king by the grace of God over all the fruits of the earth. When one has tasted it, he knows what the angels eat.*"

Nutrition Facts

Serving Size 2 cups diced pieces,
1/8 medium melon (280 g)

Amount Per Serving

Calories 80   Calories from Fat 0

% Daily Value*

Total Fat 0g	0%
Saturated Fat 0g	0%
Cholesterol 0mg	0%
Sodium 10mg	0%
Total Carbohydrate 27g	9%
Dietary Fiber 2g	8%
Sugars 25g	

Protein 1g

Vitamin A 20% • Vitamin C 25%
Calcium 2% • Iron 4%

Courtesy of the USDA

1.

AP News Item: Montgomery AL, June 13, 1968

"Three Negro youths were arrested last evening for attempted watermelon theft on the farm of Clarence McMillan near Troy, Alabama. McMillan, owner of a large watermelon farm, told deputies he had been sitting in a small camouflage shelter on his farm, guarding his melon crops, when he observed the would-be thieves trespassing at approximately 11:30 P.M. McMillan suspected the intruders had come to steal watermelons, and surprised them by firing a blast into the air with his double barrel 12-gauge shotgun. The three suspects gave chase, provoking McMillan to fire a second round in the general direction they were running. One of the suspects, Willie Summit, age 19, was hit in the back by a shotgun blast and remains in satisfactory condition in a local hospital. The other two suspects, Bobby Kingsberry and Teddy Lumpkin, both 18, were uninjured and remain in a local jail on trespassing charges. No charges have been filed against McMillan."

2.

I decided to spend the summer of 1968 as a migrant worker in the South and found myself slumped over in the passenger's seat of a produce hauling truck driven by a fifty year old trucker named Doris. He was high on No-Doz. Doris Dickman had attended the same high school as my father, and Dad always believed Doris' parents gave him a woman's name because they wanted him to grow up to be a prize fighter.

I was in the middle of a bad dream in which long gray-green watermelons were flying toward me like oversized bullets off the end of the fast-moving conveyor belt. They came at me in such rapid succession that I was able to catch only one out of five or six. The others fell to the floor of the trailer and burst at my feet, leaving bright red "meat" and pools of slimy juice everywhere. Sticky melon juice oozed between my bare toes, and wet watermelon seeds accumulated in a slick-as-ice slime beneath my bare feet. I struggled to stay upright.

The watermelons I had started to pack into the trailer were slipping down toward me. A group of men—perhaps eight or ten—were laughing at me. I felt like someone had forced me to be a contestant in a sadistic game show with no host to stop the clock and declare me the loser.

A large black man howled with laughter and said; "This rookie melon packer ain't gonna' cut the mustard down south!" Then the other men laughed even harder.

I attempted to scream, but my mouth felt like someone had taped it shut. The melons continued hurling toward me until I forced myself to mumble; "You fuckers!" But my words were not loud enough to be heard through my tightly clenched teeth, especially when overshadowed by the rattle of the melon conveyor and the fiendish laughter of the other men. Finally, my mouth opened and I yelled in halting tones, "Stop it . . . . you mother . . . . fuckers! I'm working . . . my ass off here! I can't . . . work any . . . faster!"

Suddenly, the pointed end of a 40-pound watermelon struck my left shoulder. It hurt like hell, and I jerked awake from the pain. The truck driver seated to my left was laughing uncontrollably; his fat belly jiggling like a bowl of Jell-O atop what had once been his lap. His chubby hands rested at the bottom of an oversized steering wheel, and his sausage-like fingers were wrapped loosely around it.

"Sorry I thumped you on the arm to wake you like that, but what the fuck were you dreaming about young man? Sounds ta' me like them mother fuckers were givin' you a hard time!" He laughed harder. I looked at him in a stupor, and then I awoke enough to manage a reluctant smile. I was relieved that it had only been a dream. "Goddam," I said. "That was a fuckin' nightmare!"

Before the horrifying dream, I had been awake most of the night listening to the endless drone of the diesel engine, combined with country music tunes on the truck's radio. The heat inside the passenger compartment was intense, and I had started to wonder if hitching a ride with a trucker had been a good idea.

My follow-on plan was to catch a bus from Huntsville that would "carry me" (as southerners would say) to Holcomb, Alabama; a small town just north of the Florida panhandle and near the city of Dothan, Alabama. What Holcomb lacked in size, it made up for in watermelon production. My job for the summer would consist of packing watermelons into semi trailers towed by Mack diesels, White Freightliners, International Harvesters, and GMCs ("Jimmies"). Before I accepted the job, I was told that I would be able to pack two trailers every day six days a week over the course of the summer. I would earn $20 for every completed trailer, and a total of $40 each day.

* * *

As a college student, my socio-political awareness was appallingly limited. College students kept their noses in textbooks, took mid-term and final exams, drank beer, listened to popular radio stations and rarely picked up a newspaper. Sure, I knew Martin Luther King had been assassinated two months earlier in Memphis. I would never erase from my memory the tearful account of King's life that my black professor and friend, Dr. Andrew Harmon, had given in Social Psychology class the day after King was murdered. I would also have a hard time forgetting some of the bigoted comments of my fellow white dorm dwellers. "Thank God, they finally killed that fuckin' nigger . . . He was an instigator . . . that's all the fuck he was good for . . . maybe this will quiet them niggers down for a while!"

Had I been aware of the lasting impact of King's life on both black and white America, I might have decided to pack my bags and travel south as a civil rights worker, like a small percentage of well-informed college students had done over the past several summers. But for me it was too late. My eyes would soon be opened to a less publicized side of black American life. I was about to witness the incredible power whites had over blacks, and to learn the true meaning of institutional racism.

* * *

A week before my trip south, I met with Dr. Harmon and his wife, Rose. I was their dinner guest. I called ahead to let Dr. Harmon know I would be traveling to the South as a migrant worker for the summer. I explained to him that my job would be that of watermelon packer, and I would be working side-by-side with black migrant workers. He put the phone down and said something to Rose, and then he came back on the line to invite me for dinner the following evening. I accepted with great pleasure.

*   *   *

Dr. Andrew Harmon had grown up in Nashville, Tennessee, completed his doctoral studies at the University of Grenoble, France, and gone on to write his doctoral dissertation in the French language. Had Dr. Harmon been traveling with me that summer, he would have pointed out the highlights to make sure I was paying attention. But, much to my surprise, he *would* be traveling along with me on this journey because his voice would come to me on a regular basis over the next several weeks. I decided that I would not mind having him along as my imaginary traveling companion. He would speak to me periodically from his perch inside my brain, and I would be compelled to listen and sometimes to respond. I reasoned that anyone important enough to have burrowed his way inside my head probably deserved to be there.

Dr. Harmon, highly respected professor and Deputy Chair of Sociology at Elmwood State University, had traveled to the South as a civil rights worker during the tumultuous summer of 1964. It was known as "Freedom Summer," and all activity was focused upon the registration of black voters in the State of Mississippi. Fortunately, Dr. Harmon had not encountered the Klan "justice" that led to the deaths of three civil rights workers that same summer.

The reason Dr. Harmon asked me to his home was not only to share a good meal, but also to share his stories about his summer in the South. It was his way of preparing me for what I would likely encounter. I welcomed his insight, and hoped he could vaccinate me against some of the evils I might otherwise encounter.

Rose Harmon prepared a beautiful pot roast with mashed sweet potatoes and gravy, a side dish of okra, and pecan pie with vanilla ice cream for dessert. After the meal, Dr. Harmon offered me a cigar, and then he talked with me about some of his previous classroom lectures, "to bring a few things back into focus." Suddenly, those lectures seemed more relevant to me than they had before.

"Remember Montgomery, where Martin Luther King led a bus boycott in 1955 and 1956. This highlighted and brought national attention to black demands for the desegregation of the bus system, which finally came about when the Supreme Court ruled in November 1956 that segregation of public transportation was unconstitutional. Then, in 1957, Dr. King established the Southern Christian Leadership Conference to coordinate further civil rights action. During the summer of 1964, I was with a group of black and white students and professors in Mississippi. That was only four years ago, but it seems like yesterday, doesn't it, Rose?"

Rose looked at her husband and nodded her head in agreement.

"We worked out of a small Baptist church in a tiny Mississippi town, registering blacks to vote. Up until that summer, there had been moves to register blacks, but local white intimidation had been highly effective, so very few black folk were registered. Besides, they were harassed with meaningless written tests that contained unfair and discriminatory questions. Nobody could pass the tests that were supposedly 'required' in order to be enfranchised."

"Weren't you afraid for your life?" I asked. I must have sounded naïve.

"You bet your ass, I was scared to death every single day."

"How did you cope with the fear?"

"We drew a great deal of courage from heroes like Martin Luther King, and others who had been on the front lines. They would take a beating, get back up, and keep on keepin' on. When you knock a man down and he gets back up, it gets your attention. We felt if our leaders could do it, so could we if it became necessary."

That evening, I saw a side of Dr. Harmon I had not seen before in the classroom setting. He was a real person, not afraid to step up and make a difference. He and Rose understood the values they taught to young people every day of their lives. He, a university professor, and she an elementary school teacher, were genuine human beings who were making a difference.

The last comment Dr. Harmon made as I walked away from his home that evening was; "I will be right there with you all summer long. You can count on me. Listen for my voice."

3.

We arrived in Huntsville 15 minutes behind our 5:00 A.M. target. Doris Dickman's rig lumbered its way through tree-lined city streets, scraping against low-hanging limbs. Squared-off growth patterns of tree branches served as evidence that hundreds of trucks had preceded us, brushing their trailer tops against the same trees.

Dickman's diesel engine made its presence known in the sleeping city as he searched for the Continental Trailways bus station. He believed he was in the right part of town, because he'd heard from other truckers that the Trailways station was near the produce packing warehouse he would visit that same morning to pick up a load of peaches. The peaches were to have arrived from Georgia overnight. He would drop off his empty trailer, hitch up the refrigerated load of peaches and find a truck stop for breakfast before beginning his return trip to Indiana.

Despite his exhaustion, Doris Dickman never lost his intuitive feel for directions. Some drivers used maps, but Dickman preferred to feel his way through situations like this, bragging that he rarely missed his target destination. "It's good enough for gov'ment work," he would say.

I was surprised to see that Huntsville was truly a large city. The biggest city I had seen was Indianapolis, Indiana—capital of my home state. "Indy," as its natives affectionately knew it, was an overgrown farm town in the center of "The Hoosier State." But on this particular morning, I awoke to the realization that the South had big cities just like we had up north. I wondered, but only for a second, if my brother knew the population of Huntsville. Then I realized, *of course* he did. As a bare minimum, he would have a number in his head, say 200,000 to 250,000. Ben seemed to know everything there was to know about *everything*. If he had been making this trip, he would have looked up the statistics on population, major industries, square acreage, and the number of churches and taverns in every southern city he planned to visit. He would have spent hours in the Elmwood public library before crawling into Mr. Dickman's truck to begin his trip. I had done no research, with the exception of locating my destination, the tiny town of Holcomb, Alabama in a dog-eared family atlas.

I planned to drop Ben a postcard from the Huntsville bus station and reveal my ignorance by explaining that this city seemed bigger than I'd expected it to be. Ben would have a good laugh when he read my postcard, and he would be pleased at the thought of my writing to him at 5 A.M. on my first day.

* * *

"I reckon you thought the South was nothin' but a bunch of cow paths and one-horse towns, eh young fellar?"

Dickman was wide-awake, and he felt like talking for the few remaining minutes we would spend together. He obviously enjoyed acting smart around college kids. I had observed that truckers and factory workers shared this tendency—acting more educated than they really were in the presence of young people to compensate for their feelings of inadequacy. A friend of my dad's who worked in a local battery factory had a favorite saying; "I know a little bit about everything," he would say. Each time I heard him say it, I was reminded of the expression, "a little knowledge is a dangerous thing."

My ride with Doris Dickman was about to end, and I was happy I would not be traveling any farther with him. The bus ride I had ahead of me seemed an excellent choice compared with a free ride to the Deep South from Mr. Dickman. God only knew what babble I'd have to tolerate as his captive audience for another day on the road.

"I didn't think I'd see this many tall buildings in the South!" I replied. "I thought cities in the South were made up of short wood frames like in <u>Gone with the Wind</u>." I was playing along with Dickman's need to lord his knowledge over me. Why I chose to do this, I did not know!

"Well son, all this concrete, steel and glass you see around ya' kinda' changed all that!" He laughed, triggering his smoker's cough. "They couldn't make them wood frame buildings very tall back in the good ole' days. 'S'pose they woulda' toppled right over in the first big wind storm that came along. Now they can go up about as high as they want to, thanks to us truckers haulin' a shitload of steel and glass down here from up North. They don't seem to make things like steel down here . . . just a lot a' truck farms, cotton fields and paper mills . . . so they buy steel and glass from places like Pittsburgh PA and Gary, Indiana and we bring it down to 'em so they can have their big-ass skyscrapers just like we do back home. I suppose that's why I like the truckin' game . . . us truckers make a big difference in the lives of real people."

A faint memory flashed across my mind that Birmingham was sometimes referred to as the "Pittsburgh of the South" because of its steel production, but I dared not mention this to Dickman. Besides, he hauled fruits and vegetables, not steel and glass. The difference his work made in people's lives was that it helped a handful of farmers to make an honest living; and I was fair-minded enough to believe he deserved credit for that.

I noticed a sign that read, "Bus Station," next to a small sign that read "Continental Trailways." I stretched my shoulders and arms to demonstrate to Dickman that I was fully awake and ready to dismount as soon as he pulled up in front of the terminal.

I reached back into the sleeper compartment to grab the handle of my suitcase. In spite of the long night that had felt like a series of mild hallucinations, followed by an occasional blackout, I felt a sudden burst of energy. Surely the remainder of my trip would be more comfortable, I thought. Truck cabs were built for power and driver convenience. Busses, on the other hand, were built for passenger comfort. I imagined myself in the silver and red Trailways coach, being delivered in front of a produce packing shed in Holcomb after a few hours of much needed sleep. As my ride began, I would recline in my seat, listen to the quiet humming of the bus engine, and sleep peacefully for most of the ride from Huntsville to Holcomb.

Mr. Dickman stopped his rig about half a block from the bus station, and motioned for me to step out of the 10-foot high Mack diesel. It was more of a jump than a step. I literally leapt from the one-shoe-wide platform, just below the door on the passenger's side, and landed so hard that the soles of my *Converse All Stars* gym shoes slapped against the hard pavement below. The overweight trucker strained to lean outside the passenger door over his large stomach. After he dropped my suitcase into my awaiting hands, we waved to each other politely. I yelled, "thanks" from ground level, over the roar of his diesel engine. Absent any consideration for the sleeping population of Huntsville, Dickman blew his air horn twice as truckers do to the delight of kids who stand along highways in wide-eyed admiration of their powerful machines. He maneuvered his rig around the next corner and disappeared, leaving a trail of black smoke that mixed with the morning haze and hung 15 feet above street level.

I walked half a city block and entered the Trailways bus terminal, as if I was familiar with the station's layout. Once inside, I located the ticket window and walked over to purchase my one-way ticket to Holcomb, via Birmingham and Montgomery. The terminal reminded me of a badly misplaced Hopper painting, inhabited by me, a wino stretched out on a bench that resembled a church pew, and a few stray dust bunnies that floated across the black and white tile floor.

I handed a $20 bill to the man behind the ticket counter and asked for a one-way ticket on the "express" bus to Holcomb. The agent, who was holding a cigarette precariously between his lips with an inch and a half long ash dangling off the end of it, handed me a ticket along with a $10 bill in change.

"Sorry, but there ain't no express bus. You'll be changin' busses in Birmingham, and you'll buy the rest of your fare then. Have a nice day."

I was not yet aware of what it meant to travel the length of Alabama on a "local" passenger bus, but I had the feeling I would soon find out.

4.

The first leg of my bus ride, between Huntsville and Birmingham, seemed endless. I had expected the driver to proceed due west, toward the faster four lane roadway, then point the bus south for the relatively short trip to Birmingham. But this was a local bus that moved at a snail's pace along State Route 231, and it became obvious that the driver would be stopping at every wide spot along the road.

I soon noticed I was the only white passenger. I was not bothered by this realization, but I wondered if busses in Alabama were categorized "separate but equal," and whether I had boarded the blacks only bus. Most of my fellow riders traveled short distances, and then got off at factories, private homes or other wide spots in the road. There were no cars in the front yards of black-inhabited homes, not even broken down vehicles suspended on concrete blocks. These people had very little money to spend on personal transportation, so they had to be "carried" to their daily routines by the only affordable means of transport—The Continental Trailways Bus Company.

During the brief interlude between each new passenger's ascent onto the bus and their exit, I found myself looking into their eyes and studying them. Some people would return my looks, while others would not give me the opportunity to make eye contact.

Was this man drunk? What was that woman thinking? Were they all traveling to jobs, or simply escaping for the day? Were they lost, or trying to *get* lost?

I might have been bothered that I was the only white passenger on the bus, and the only person who was riding more than a few miles at a stretch, but as a student I had a fair amount of curiosity about human behavior. My mind was preoccupied with thoughts of the people who boarded the bus, as if they were subjects in my own behavioral study. The expressions of some of the passengers reflected abject poverty and the neglect that came along with it, while others bore no expression at all. Still others were inexorably cheerful, and made happy sounds as they climbed aboard.

A cheerful woman sat down across the aisle from me after greeting several passengers as she boarded. A few minutes after she took her seat, she couldn't help but comment on the fact that I looked entirely out of place.

"Y'all's is the only white face on 'da bus dis mornin'," she said. "We don't be seein' white faces on 'dis bus too offen."

Slightly surprised by the fact that she had spoken to me, I looked at her and smiled. I was not sure what to say.

"Oh, it be alright. I's jis' wonderin' where you be from and where you goin' is all. Jis' nosey."

"I'm from Indiana, and I'm on my way to Holcomb," I replied. "I have a job lined up with a produce shipping company out of Florida."

"Do tell," she said, and laughed. "I s'pose a big strappin' fella' like you could do a mighty hard day's woik. I bet you be gonna' woik in da' melons."

I smiled again. "Yes, I'll be working for the summer as a watermelon packer."

"My name's Clementine. I don't live far from here. Jis' goin' ta' see my daughter and grandbabies. I be back on da' lass bus home tonight. Jis' goin' fur today is all. Ain't never heard a' no place called Holcomb."

I noticed that the vegetation along the highways looked different from the summer vegetation I knew back in Indiana. It made for a distinctly brown landscape, which was populated by people who were a darker shade of brown than the landscape would ever become. I'd generally heard these people referred to as "Negroes," but as a semi-enlightened college student, I had learned a new term . . . "Black People."

My journey into the Deep South gradually introduced me to a vastly different world from the one I had left behind the evening before. I was reminded of one of my dad's favorite expressions, "You'd never notice from a gallopin' horse." While his expression was appropriate for most cases of drive-by observation, it certainly did not fit here. Even during rare intervals when the bus managed to get up a bit of speed, I found myself gazing outward from a moving picture window that revealed vast differences between Southern Indiana and Northern Alabama.

We passed countless tin-roofed shanties that had never been touched by a paintbrush. None of these rundown homes had lawns because chickens kept the front yards picked clean of vegetation and the seeds of potential plant life. I suspected that the chickens were more important than a pretty green lawn because of the eggs they provided, along with a delicious feast of fried chicken for Sunday dinners to mark special occasions.

* * *

Several hours passed, and I was well into my routine of observing other travelers and making them part of my secret study. Speculating about the lives of strangers helped pass the time, so much so that I had not even noticed when the bus entered the northern city limits of Birmingham. I emerged from my semi-hypnotic state when we entered the city center around 11:00 A.M. that morning. Suddenly, I realized that my bladder was badly in need of relief, and I had developed a hunger for a juicy hamburger with French fries.

After stepping off the bus and visiting the men's room, I decided the Birmingham bus terminal was not the place to look for my burger and fries. Judging from the lack of attention to hygiene in the men's room, I doubted that the kitchen of the greasy spoon at the far end of the terminal would be clean either. Besides, the 30-minute wait before my bus for Montgomery gave me time to purchase my next ticket and try out an attractive little diner I had noticed across the street. There was something intriguing about the look of the diner, with its lower level chrome exterior and rounded corners, like a Norman Rockwell illustration of a diner on the cover of the *Saturday Evening Post*. The only thing missing was a sweet old grandmother seated in the front window with her little grandson, both bowing their heads to say grace over a hot meal.

Besides the fact that the diner looked more attractive than the one inside the bus station, my grandmother had warned me against bus station food. As a young woman, she'd suffered a severe case of food poisoning while on a trip to St. Louis to visit her sister. The fateful stop had been in the town of O'Fallon, Illinois, a small town about 45 minutes east of downtown St. Louis. She remembered that the scent of hamburgers on the grill of the terminal's café was especially inviting, but by the time she had eaten her burger and completed her journey to St. Louis, she had fallen seriously ill with food poisoning and spent her entire visit in a semi-delirious state in an area hospital. I'd heard the story before, as one tends to hear such stories from older family members, but my grandmother made a point to repeat it as her contribution to the safety of my trip south. Her food poisoning story had achieved the status of family folklore, which gave it the power to entertain, instruct, and protect. The story's status as folklore also meant it could be repeated as often as needed, and especially when it related to a real event in the life of the family. While I had previously heard the story for it's instructional value, my summer travel plans qualified me to hear it once again, this time for protection.

I walked across the street and saw that my diner of choice was filled to the gills with early lunch customers, probably an indication that the locals liked the food. Many of the patrons were seated at an L-shaped lunch counter on round swivel stools, and the food was being prepared on the opposite side of the counter in plain view. The counter stools appeared to be preferred seating, and the men perched on them looked like they belonged there by birthright. Rather than a liar's table, this was a liar's counter. Some men at the counter wore white shirts and ties while others wore bib overalls, but they all seemed to know each other and all seemed to be tied into the ongoing conversation to varying degrees.

Non-counter diners were seated in four person booths around the outside perimeter of the room, next to the windows. To my surprise, the numbers of black and white customers were nearly equal, yet none of the men at the counter were black. I'd heard about racial strife and discrimination in the South, and the news media seemed to highlight cases of discrimination in eating establishments. It was fairly common to see news reports of restaurant owners like the infamous Lester Maddox, the restaurateur turned politician who wielded an axe handle at the front door of his all white establishment to demonstrate his dogged determination to keep blacks away like so many stray cats.

Conventional white wisdom held that blacks did not maintain the same standards of personal hygiene as whites. They did not bathe very often, and that made them unsavory dining partners. But the underlying significance was that blacks were socially "unclean." In any case, my education by way of TV news had not adequately prepared me for a time when I would walk into a diner in a major southern city and see blacks and whites dining together. It seemed almost staged. I wondered for a moment whether the TV newsreels had reflected a true picture of day-to-day life in the South? Then, I reminded myself that Birmingham was a very large city, perhaps the closest thing to a cosmopolitan center in the Southeastern United States, with the exception of Miami and Atlanta. For this reason alone, things might be different here.

Despite my initial surprise, the din of conversation inside the diner and the familiar clanking of forks against plates gave me a certain sense of ease. Thick cigarette smoke mixed with the heavy odor of fried foods, and this reminded me of a truck stop my dad and his friends frequented back home. White porcelain plates and stained coffee mugs added ambience, and customers didn't seem to mind using them even if a cup had a hairline crack or a plate had a chip out of it's outer rim.

Suddenly, Dr. Harmon's voice clicked itself on inside my head, as if someone had turned on a radio. The topic of his spontaneous monologue was blacks and whites eating together at the same lunch counters in Birmingham. What a surprise! He had popped in to tell me that what I was witnessing was miles apart from what was going on in the minds of the patrons.

"You can bet there is a degree of fear in the minds of the blacks. Don't be fooled! The visible signs of acceptance are little more than public politeness at this stage in the social development of the South, a form of peaceful coexistence. Notice that the blacks are coming and going through the back door of the diner."

Dr. Harmon's voice did not sound the least bit paranoid, nor did it sound conciliatory. His point was that I should not be deceived by what I was seeing inside the Birmingham diner. Perhaps he was right, I thought. Outward appearances can be deceiving.

Dr. Harmon's voice continued inside my brain: *"The Reverend Martin Luther King, Jr. directed a protest and became a national hero when he led voter registration drives in many of Alabama's cities during the early 1960s. His 'Letter from Birmingham Jail' in 1963 was written to local ministers after his arrest in a campaign to desegregate public facilities, just like the one you're standing inside at this moment. The culmination of King's crusade for black civil liberties was the five-day march from Selma to the State Capitol, Montgomery, that eventually led to passage of the federal Voting Rights Act of 1965 . . . a mere three years ago!"*

I had a mental picture of Dr. Harmon's broad, handsome, James Earl Jones smile, and I recalled the sound of his deep knowing laugh. It was almost as real as if I'd been sitting in a classroom listening to him, or sitting on the couch next to him in his living room. In the middle of his speech, his tone suddenly changed in my mind to one of hopefulness and optimism. *"You are getting a first hand look at a new kind of public experience (or, should I say 'experiment?'). Perhaps what you see on the outside is less than genuine, but it does reflect an important reality to come. People in Birmingham, and many other places are beginning to 'act out' what the future might look like in restaurants and diners across the South. And it remains to be seen what the future will feel like."*

Click! Dr. Harmon's voice was gone.

I waited patiently for about five minutes, and then caught the eye of one of the men at the counter. The man was motioning me toward an empty seat on one side of him. I nodded a polite "thank you," and then took a seat next to him. He then turned back toward the man who was seated on his other side and continued his conversation.

The waitress had a southern drawl as sweet as the glass of iced tea she laid on the counter in front of me. I noticed the looks I was getting from the other men at the counter, but sensed that I was in safe territory because one of their own had invited me to sit in their midst.

I finally sank my teeth into a juicy hamburger with lettuce, tomato, fresh onions and mayonnaise. As the men at the counter smoked, sipped their coffee and conversed, I devoured my burger, paid the waitress, nodded goodbye to the man who had earlier motioned for me to take a seat, and headed back toward the bus station. With only a few minutes left to buy a post card, I quickly picked out one that showed the front view of the Birmingham bus station. The vendors had been closed when I'd tried to purchase a post card earlier that morning in Huntsville, so this was my first opportunity to begin my summer correspondence with my brother, Ben. Cards and letters would be a poor substitute for having Ben along with me, but they would be better than nothing as far as I was concerned. At least I could carry on a one-sided conversation. I knew that Ben would be listening intently on his end, and he would write me back whenever he had a chance to do so.

* * *

"Ben—You're not gonna' believe this, but I just stopped off in Birmingham for a quick lunch before we took off for Montgomery and on south, and I walked into a diner that was at least half filled with black customers! From everything I've seen about the South on the evening news back home, you'd think that kinda' thing was impossible. But the people were all eating together in the same crowded place, and everyone seemed fine with the arrangement . . . as long as the white guys got to sit at the counter! (Including me.) Ha!

More Later,
Matt"

* * *

As the bus got underway, I looked out the window onto the streets of Birmingham, and the irrepressible voice of Dr. Harmon began to play inside my head again, like a tape-recorded version of a guided tour. I might have been on a city tour, listening to Andrew's voice through a set of earphones.

"*History was made here a few short years ago,*" said the voice of Dr. Harmon. "*Birmingham, where 'Freedom Now'—the slogan to recognize the Emancipation Proclamation Centennial in 1963—was the focus of national attention and Dr. King was leading a civil rights drive. The Birmingham authorities used dogs and fire hoses to quell civil rights demonstrators, and there were mass arrests. Less than five years ago, in September 1963, four black girls were killed by a bomb thrown into a Birmingham church.*"

Realizing I was remembering bits and pieces of Dr. Harmon's classroom lectures, I consciously turned his voice off for a moment to picture the pained look on his face as he spoke of events that carried such powerful emotion. I envisioned, as Dr. Harmon had, the screaming of black mothers looking helplessly upon their daughters' lifeless bodies. Surprisingly, the look on Dr. Harmon's face when he had spoken the words in the classroom conveyed no hatred, simply grief and understandable pain.

Ironically, these were the same events that evoked a fear of blacks among my own family and friends. It was true. Broadcast reports of acts of violence perpetrated by whites against blacks, caused white people to experience a fear of blacks where I came from. This fear stemmed from a belief that blacks in northern cities might retaliate against the violence visited upon their family members in the South, and that this black retaliation would spread from large cities like Detroit and Chicago to small rural communities. We were farmers, not generally prone to prejudice, hatred or violence, but people of all backgrounds were vulnerable to fear for the future of society and their way of life. Even people who claimed to be peace-loving had the capacity within them to turn violent once fear took over. Deep down inside was the basic human awareness not only of what outsiders could do to inflict harm, but what *anyone* of any *race* might be capable of when seriously threatened. The mere thought of what had come to be called "social unrest" frightened us, and people like my mother prayed that it would spare us in our little corner of the world.

* * *

Despite the lack of preparation I had put into my trip, I began to realize that Dr. Harmon had already prepared me for what I was seeing on my first day in the South. It almost felt like I was in a theater watching a 3D movie about one of the great battlegrounds of the civil rights war. The bus belched its thick black exhaust as I looked down upon the streets of Birmingham from my window. It felt like a high school trip I had taken to Gettysburg PA, and it (like Gettysburg) was far too serene to convey any real sense of what had happened here.

I recalled a point Dr. Harmon had made in a lecture about the war for civil rights in America. "Black people are giving their lives in the streets, like your white fathers gave their lives in the battle fields of Europe during World War II. Of course, you're thinking I'm unpatriotic, even ungrateful for the many blessings American life has afforded the people of my race. Your fathers fought a foreign enemy that posed a real threat against world freedom, but the tyranny of prejudice and bigotry right here at home has the same insidious power as any foreign enemy to destroy the American way of life if we don't destroy that tyranny first! And we *will* destroy it! And then, in the same sense that your fathers and mothers played economic and social 'catch up' after their sacrifices in World War II, people of color will be playing catch up in the 80s, 90s and well into the next century. When you reach the same age your parents have today, I predict you will see lots of black Americans buying big houses in upper middle class neighborhoods all across America. We will play social and economic catch up because, as sure as your parents' generation did after defeating Nazi Germany, we will rightfully take credit for winning the war on behalf of civil rights here at home. Then, we will succeed economically as black Americans, because we *are* Americans. This is who we are! Young ladies and gentlemen, it is too late to send us back to Africa! Get used to us and start liking us, because we *ain't goin' anywhere*!"

I suddenly had a pang of guilt because I had not come to the South to work on behalf of civil rights. "Damn you Dr. Harmon," I thought! "Stop playing back your infernal lectures inside my head, and let me enjoy my bus ride! This melon-packing job won't be a walk in the fucking park! Maybe I'll learn something about the plight of black people by osmosis this summer. But I'm not getting off this bus and signing up to work in a soup kitchen in Birmingham! Who would pay my expenses for next semester if I did that?"

I was suddenly aware that my mental conflict was a direct result of Dr. Harmon's influence on my social conscience, and I knew that a social conscience was an intended byproduct of higher education. Maybe that's why I felt a bit selfish that I had come all this way to take a job that involved mere physical exertion, and I momentarily felt it expedient to blame Dr. Harmon for my doubts.

"Dammit," I thought, "I'm not some rich kid who can take a summer off to save the fucking world like some students I know!" Up until now, my summers had been spent working on my father's farm to help the family pay for my education. Farm labor was cheap, but as far as my dad was concerned, kids were a source of *free* labor. Packing watermelons in the South was not only a partial escape on my part, but it would pay well, and the money I earned would be *mine*. Packing melons was no job for sissies, and it had taken me several years to achieve a skill level that qualified me to work alongside the packers from Florida. They were the *real* professionals. While most of my experience had come from packing watermelons on my dad's farm, I had ventured off part-time to other local farms over the past couple of summers to pack watermelons for a buyer who came to Indiana each year from Michigan. Because of that valuable outside experience, I was proud that I could now follow my dream. And although my summer employment lacked social significance, I wanted to think of myself as doing the honorable thing.

For a brief moment, I wondered why my friend Dr. Harmon was not spending his summer in the South, marching along with members of the Southern Christian Leadership Conference. Why was he not fighting on the front lines of the civil rights war *every* summer, not just the Freedom Summer of 1964 that he'd spoken to me about? After all, he was a university professor who had the summers off from his regular teaching duties. He could also chalk up his civil rights work as social research, and perhaps write a paper for a Social Psychology journal. But then it occurred to me that Dr. Harmon didn't need to leave Elmwood, Indiana to be a part of this particular war. The civil rights war was being fought on a variety of fronts, the most visible of which was the organized struggle involving a small percentage of black Americans whose faces appeared regularly on the evening news. But a much larger battlefront was the day-to-day lives of the majority of black Americans who were striving for equal participation in society. A black man did not need to make the Six O'clock Evening News to be a part of the action. For Dr. Harmon, being a black Social Psychology professor who dressed nicely, drove a nice car, and had the nerve to live in a white middle class neighborhood, placed he and Rose squarely on the front lines whether they had actively sought that position or not. As much as they would have preferred to go about their lives peacefully, a serene existence was not in the cards for them. Nothing illustrated this point more clearly than the story Dr. Harmon had told me about buying their first home.

Dr. Harmon and Rose had lived happily in a small apartment across the street from the Elmwood State University campus for their first several years as married professionals. To the outside community, they were university people and were not assimilated into the general population. Rose had started her career as a Kindergarten teacher at the University's "Lab School." To the local community, largely made up of retired coal miners, factory workers, farmers and a handful of professionals, Dr. Harmon and Rose were a model university couple, until they boldly decided to buy a home in an all-white neighborhood. The way Dr. Harmon explained it, he and Rose had found an affordable, three-bedroom ranch style home not far from the campus, and contacted a realtor to arrange for a formal showing. Some of the neighbors noticed the black couple coming and going with the realtor, and all were eventually notified by the realtor that a black couple was thinking of buying the home. The realtor intended to avoid panic, but the neighbors had promptly panicked.

As a student of human behavior, Dr. Harmon was fully aware of the social implications of his decision to buy in a white neighborhood. Therefore, as soon as he and Rose had agreed to make an offer on the house, they went door to door to introduce themselves. While becoming acquainted with would-be neighbors, Dr. Harmon and Rose invited them all to a meeting at their apartment near the university to discuss "matters related to the purchase of our home." As Dr. Harmon later told the story, the meeting was very painful for he and Rose, mostly because there would have been no need for a meeting had they been white. Neighbors would have sent the smiling people from "Welcome Wagon, Inc." to give them a proper greeting on moving day, and that would have been the end of it. But the situation *was* what it was, so they knew they had to confront it head-on. About half of the neighbors on the block came to the meeting. No sooner had the discussion began than one future neighbor asked; "What will happen to our property values after you move in?" Dr. Harmon's first reaction was internal rage, and a strong urge to throw the man out the window of his apartment.

Instead, he had smiled and calmly asked the man, "Are you wondering whether or not I'll keep up the lawn and paint the house when it needs a new coat?" Of course, the man's concern was not over the neatness of Dr. Harmon's lawn, but the fact that passersby and potential buyers might realize that the man mowing the lawn was not the hired gardener, but the homeowner.

As a student of Dr. Harmon's and a friend, I was almost ashamed to learn about the personal struggle he and Rose had endured in order to purchase their modest home. After all, Elmwood was my hometown as well as the hometown Dr. Harmon and Rose had adopted to pursue their professional careers. Although I lived on a farm outside of town, that was no excuse for the fact that I was oblivious to the racial climate inside the city limits. Having learned what the Harmons had gone through to purchase their home, I was certain that they were making a difference each day of their lives. There was clearly no reason for Dr. Harmon to travel south to join the more publicized struggle for civil rights. For he and Rose, merely living their lives without giving in to white bigotry was enough to keep them fully engaged in the cause of civil rights . . . on a very personal level. Each successful baby step they took to assimilate into the white community was a step in the right direction for other black families like them in the future.

* * *

As my bus to Holcomb lumbered onward, I closed my eyes to take a nap, and was suddenly aware that there was another reason white students from the North traveled south to take up the cause of black civil rights: *Vietnam*. Rather than losing their student deferments and being drafted into the Army, many remained in college and took up social causes in their spare time. Some continued to avoid service in Vietnam after graduating by sneaking into Canada, while others joined President Kennedy's Peace Corps, and still others declared themselves conscientious objectors and spent their conscripted years emptying bedpans in hospitals. But the pool of manpower created by liberal-minded white college students who were morally opposed to Vietnam became a formidable volunteer army on behalf of civil rights. The Civil Rights Movement led by Dr. King and others tapped into this source of free, educated, energetic manpower to swell protest marches and lend visibility to the fact that young whites supported the civil rights cause on behalf of blacks. It was not important *what* the college students were doing to help, but rather *that* they were helping. In this way, the historical juxtaposition alongside Vietnam was a fortunate coincidence for the civil rights movement. News coverage showing whites marching alongside blacks had a strong emotional impact on the middle class American psyche, particularly in the northern states. White parents sometimes saw the faces of their own offspring on television, participating peacefully in a predominantly black event. The impact of such events was real.

In addition to white students, young blacks were becoming more involved in the cause of their elders. For instance, the youth arm of the black civil rights movement known as the Student Nonviolent Coordinating Committee (SNCC) had grown out of sit-ins at restaurant lunch counters that refused to serve black people in the early 1960s. SNCC used the tactic that came to be known as civil disobedience in public places, including college campuses, to publicize the civil rights movement. White students joined black students in campus protests across the country. Student activists, black and white, were captivated by the courageous actions of young black leaders like John Lewis. Lewis, a black divinity student from Troy, Alabama, was instrumental in organizing Freedom Rides, an integrated "bus tour" of the South in 1961 that tested the Supreme Court decision to desegregate interstate transportation facilities. He was later involved as a leader of the "Bloody Sunday" march, during which mounted police beat and bludgeoned many blacks at the Edmond Pettus Bridge on March 22, 1965.

* * *

As my bus passed through the cities where high watermark civil rights events had taken place, it struck me that I was a mere spectator to the important social causes that concerned many of my own generation of Americans. My brother, Ben, was involved in activist causes as a college student at the small private college he attended. I was involved in mainstream student government, but I tended to shy away from political activity outside immediate campus boundaries. A coward at heart, I preferred to listen and learn from my brother as well as from Dr. Harmon, and occasional leaders of popular student movements who visited our campus as part of a monthly "Sociology Colloquium."

As president of the local chapter of Sociology Honorary, Alpha Kappa Delta, I had called the president of the infamous Students for a Democratic Society (SDS) and arranged for him to speak to the Colloquium. His speech was mostly show with little substance, but our ten or so "campus radicals" loved me for inviting him. He had them the moment he walked into the auditorium wearing his green Army field jacket, and accompanied by two similarly clad bodyguards. Olive drab field jackets, the same as those worn by soldiers in Vietnam, had become a popular symbol of protest against the Vietnam War. Most self-respecting anti-war protestors on the Elmwood State campus wore field jackets they had purchased at the local Army-Navy surplus store.

5.

Despite our apparent lack of progress toward Holcomb, the bus was moving at a reasonable pace until we were about 45 minutes south of Montgomery. Then, the driver made a stop in front of a Mom and Pop grocery store. The outside of the building was in desperate need of a coat of paint, with the noted exception being a multi-colored sign on the front of the store that read, "Molly Stegner's Grocery."

Immediately after the bus came to a stop, a black employee who appeared to be in his 50s emerged from behind the store and placed a stack of five brown paper packages beside the bus for the driver to load into the underbelly. Each of the packages was neatly wrapped in brown paper and bound with a heavy grade of twine. As soon as the driver climbed down from the bus, it was obvious to the most casual observer that he was irritated. He raised his voice and began shouting at the black man like an owner would shout at a disobedient dog. I cracked my window open just enough to hear his words over the steady rumble of the bus engine.

"Look here, boy, I've told you this before," the driver ranted. "I take three packages a day, and you damn sure brought five out here again! Now you get your sorry ass inside and fetch Miz Stegner. Tell her I want to talk to her! Hear?"

The clerk nodded and did not talk back to the driver. He rushed back inside to get the storeowner, limping noticeably but moving along surprisingly well despite his obvious handicap. As the black man disappeared into the store, the grouchy bus driver lit a cigarette, and then kicked the top two boxes off the stack the clerk had left on the ground. Next, he took the three boxes that remained in the stack and loaded them into the cargo bay of his bus.

"Fuckin' niggers," the bus driver yelled to himself. "You can tell 'em the same goddam thing every day, but they're too fuckin' stupid to learn! Shit! They don't *wanna'* learn, that's the problem! Maybe they're not stupid, but they just don't wanna' learn."

In less than two minutes, a handsome white woman in her early 60s emerged from the back door of the store wearing a long white apron. Like the store clerk, she too had a distinct limp, and she moved her elbows up and down like Walter Brennan did in his famous role as Grandpa Amos McCoy in a popular TV series. She carried a brown paper bag in one hand. As she approached the side of the bus, she glanced down at the two dusty packages the driver had kicked off the top of the stack before he had loaded the other three. She looked at the boxes and then at the driver, remaining calm as if this were all part of a well-rehearsed act. She was confident that the bus driver would not raise his voice at her.

"Mr. Langferd," she said, "this is all my fault. I can't for the life of me seem to remember that you only have room for three boxes each day. Maybe it's old age settin' in, but I told William to bring all five of these out to you. I'll have him come back out and get these two, and we'll send them tomorrow. I'll try to remember next time, I promise. Now you be on your way with Godspeed. Here's a salami sandwich, and I put in a can of the Vienna Sausages you like and a cold bottle of pop for all your trouble."

"Thanks, Miz Stegner," the bus driver replied with a smile. "It's OK. I understand. I'm sure you've had a hard day here at the store. I've had a long day myself. Now don't you bother, I'll pick up these boxes and carry 'em back inside for you." The bus driver was no longer playing the role of the nasty bigot who had kicked two boxes off the stack to teach the black store clerk a lesson. Miss Stegner had transformed him into a pleasant and deferential representative of the Continental Trailways Bus Company whose mother had taught him the proper way to act around an older lady. Nonetheless, he had enjoyed his momentary reign of power over the black store clerk.

From the vantage point of my bus window, I observed the scene as I would have observed an experiment in a Psychology Lab. I wondered if Miss Stegner had orchestrated the entire setup. Had she afforded the driver his fleeting moment of authority over the black man for her own benefit? Maybe the bus driver would do her some small favor the next time he stopped by, or in a future emergency when she really needed to send more than Langferd's arbitrary three-box limit. I didn't know, but I suspected that was the way the game was played.

As the huffy, self-satisfied driver climbed back into the bus and plopped into his seat of authority, I scanned the bus to see if any other passengers had reacted to what I had just seen. I had not looked for the reactions of others before, because I was preoccupied with what was taking place on the ground below my bus window. Now I expected to see a sideways glance or a raised eyebrow. Suddenly, I noticed the shoulders of the black passenger across the aisle from me moving up and down. He was laughing quietly, and although there was a mere hint of a smile on his face, I had no doubt that he was getting a kick out of something. Perhaps he was enjoying my reaction, because he turned and looked at me, and then sprouted a large grin that revealed an interrupted row of brown teeth. His gray stubble of a beard made him appear to be in his mid—60s.

"Dat Miz Stegner, and William. Dey knows how to woik dis driver." The man's shoulders bounced again, and his grin widened.

"What?" I asked.

"Dey use ta' put four boxes out, and da driver, he kick two off, sayin' he could only take two a day. Den dey starts sendin' William out wit' five boxes in da' stack, and da' driver still kick off da top two boxes. Now he be takin' three a day, but he gits him a salami san'wich from Miz Stegner to go wit' da' extra box."

"Amazing!" I replied. "Where does the driver take the boxes?"

"He done delivers 'em up along his bus route 'tween here an' Panama City. Free postage fur Miz Stegner an' a salami san'wich fur Mr. bus driver." The man laughed again, enjoying his explanation of what I had just seen.

"But what about William?" I asked.

"Oh, William? Miz Stegner takes care a' him. Fact is, he be my cousin. He done told me Miz Stegner gives him a slab a' fat back and a ham bone now and den ta' take home ta' da' Missus fur all his good woik. Y'all might say 'dis here bus driver thing is jis' part a' his woik."

I shook my head and smiled, then resumed looking out the window. The bus blew swiftly past several people who walked along the side of the road, carelessly stirring up large clouds of dust up beside them. I had seen very few rural pedestrians back home, but these walkers tended to stay close to the side of the roads as if defying the trucks and busses to hit them. The driver honked at each of them as he sped past, as if to remind them that he owned the road and they had no business walking so close to his bus. After the incident at Stegner's grocery, I was beginning to understand his little power game.

At one of our many stops, a cheerful black man got onto the bus carrying a large round watermelon that he used as payment for his bus ride. The bus driver nodded his acknowledgement of the large and juicy melon, and then impatiently gestured for the man to place the melon in a small jump seat opposite the driver's seat. After the man paid his watermelon fare, he trudged dutifully to the back of the bus with a satisfied smile on his face. He wore a dark wool sports jacket over his white shirt—rather out of place for a hot summer afternoon. I could tell by his rough and callused hands and the patches of field dirt on the thighs of his pants legs, that he'd been working in the fields. No doubt, he'd worked out a deal with his employer to take a less than perfect watermelon at the end of each work day and use it to satisfy his bus fare for the ride home. Melons that were less than perfect for sale to the public were often the best for eating. Some were slightly disfigured on the outside, yet plump and juicy and ideal for eating on the inside.

Just after the man paid his bus fare with the melon, I noticed a road sign that indicated we were ten miles north of Dothan. On the last stretch of highway before Dothan, I saw a roadside work crew of black men wearing bright orange uniforms with the words "Alabama State Prisons" written across their backs in large block letters. The bold black letters stood out sharply against the bright prison orange of their uniforms. The men, as dark as any black men I had ever seen, were bound together at the ankles by chains. They were bent over with bodies at similar angles, and swung crescent-shaped hand sickles in unison. The hand sickles reminded me of the one my dad kept in his tool shed. I used it regularly when I was home during the summer to trim around shrubs and trees after mowing our lawn on Saturday afternoons.

The sight of a chain gang, made up exclusively of black prisoners, was a first for me. I had seen crews of state and federal prisoners picking up trash along roadways, but the crews of inmates I'd seen up north had not been shackled together at the ankle nor were they made up exclusively of black men. I wondered, as I had earlier wondered about bus stops, whether prisons in the South were segregated. (Or perhaps prisoners in the South were mostly black men).

The voice of Dr. Harmon within me had fallen unexpectedly silent. He apparently didn't want to help me with this one. I wondered if the voice had fallen silent because I momentarily felt more at peace with myself. Yes, that was it! I suddenly felt OK about taking my summer job. God only knew I'd be suffering through many long days of hard physical work, and perhaps that would afford me a sense of spiritual absolution for my selfishness about *only* wanting to make money. The feeling of atonement born of physical work was a feeling I knew from my youth on the farm. Perhaps I would be liberated from my inner qualms if only by the sweat of my brow.

* * *

The stretch of road from Dothan to Holcomb consisted of 15 miles of narrow two-lane highway with no stops. This was my favorite part of the trip so far, because it felt like my own personal victory lap. When we finally arrived in the village of Holcomb, the Trailways coach slowed and veered to the left directly in front of the Holcomb melon-packing co-op. Dust swirled like a mid-June whirlwind as the bus rolled onto the edge of the sandy parking lot, and its brakes eased it to a metal-on-metal stop that sent chills up and down my spine. It was the same noise the wheels of the bus had made each time it had come to a stop over the past several hours, but this time it was almost music to my ears. I had told the driver before we left Dothan that the Holcomb farmer's co-op was *my* wide spot in the road. He said he was familiar with the co-op, and that it was the largest building in Holcomb and his *only* stopping point in the town.

My first glimpse of the co-op gave me a surge of unexpected energy. I moved quickly to the front of the bus and patiently waited for Langferd to open the door, then tried to pretend it didn't matter how long it took me to get off his bus.

My Midwestern politeness compelled me to be patient, even though every bone in my body was silently screaming to the driver, "open this fucking door or I'll wring your miserable neck!" I'd been taught that it wasn't proper to require another person to hurry the pace of whatever they were doing. There was a distinct disadvantage to this approach to life, in that it gave other people a certain power over me. Here I was, almost dying to dismount the ugly metal monster, yet allowing the bigoted bus driver a few more moments of power. In the big scheme of things, it didn't matter to me now because I had reached my destination. When I finally walked down the three metal steps of the bus, I was free but I forced myself to wait politely while Langferd pulled several parcels and suitcases from the cargo hold beneath the bus, and finally came to mine. I took a deep breath as he handed it to me, and then I offered him an insincere, "Thanks." I felt the same degree of insincerity as I had felt earlier that same day, when

The Melon Boys

Doris Dickman had said goodbye to me near the bus station in Huntsville. I had waved back to him, as if I'd truly enjoyed the overnight ride in his semi. I had not!

I turned around, and my back was now toward the bus. I savored my first good look at the co-op building, and knew without a doubt I was in the right place. There was no mistaking the large, gray, tin-covered complex. This state-of-the-art factory of watermelon packing looked like a cobbled house made of oversized corrugated playing cards. This was obviously not a proud example of southern architecture, nor was it intended to be. It had not been constructed for its beauty. One wing connected to another as if none of them had been planned. Symmetry and aesthetics were secondary to economy and utility, as each jutting extension had been added to accommodate more tractor-trailers, thus enabling the maximum number of watermelons to be loaded in the shortest period of time. The main co-op building housed a business office, denoted by a sign that read "Holcomb Co-Op Office." It was the only part of the structure that was made of brick, and it sported a slanted roof with real shingles. It was probably the original Holcomb co-op building. The rest of the looming structure was made of wood frame covered with corrugated tin sheeting, all nailed together to make up an insurance company's nightmare.

Conveyor belts loaded with logjams of watermelons snaked along in several different directions, like a labyrinth of early industrial technology. Each segment of conveyor found its way from a farm wagon or a small truck to the rear end of a semi trailer. I had heard that the melon business in Indiana was backward, and now I could see why. We had no high-speed melon moving technology back home. Every one of our melons had to be "conveyed" to the packer by human chain gang. This outdated method of loading had probably not been seen in Holcomb for years. Melon farming here was big business. Indiana's entire melon industry amounted to what the farmers of Holcomb would have called "small potatoes."

I tried to imagine what this farm co-op would have been like when it first opened, with nothing more than a shingle roofed office building in the midst of a sand lot and farmers hauling in wagonloads of watermelons. Kids would probably have been playing kick-the-can or stickball, and farmers would have pulled into the lot and parked their wagons or trucks at the rear of their assigned semi trailers. Then they would have begun tossing melons to the person standing at the back end of their designated trailers. That person would toss each melon to the next person in the chain gang, and eventually the melons would reach the hands of the packer at the front end of the trailer. That was the way we still did it back in Indiana.

* * *

Holcomb farmers were busily offloading melons onto conveyors in a strenuous but orderly process. Although it was very late in the day, there was no sign that the day's work was about to end. A man who looked like he was a member of the Quality Melon staff stood on a narrow platform at a strategic point on the catwalk. He was carefully examining watermelons as they sped past him on their way to designated semis. He quickly inspected each melon, touched some, and lifted defective ones off the conveyor to lay them aside. He was so focused that he never looked up from the conveyor, and he seemed oblivious to anything but the quality of the watermelons passing rapidly in front of him.

I started walking across the sand dune that served as the farm co-op's parking lot. The familiar warmth of sand shifting beneath my feet was the best thing I had felt all day. The parking lot looked the same as hundreds of sand lots back in Indiana, except for its slightly reddish tint. As my Converse All Stars sank in with each step, I felt the circulation gradually returning to my legs and feet.

The sound of the whining bus engine grew faint as it made its way through Holcomb. Although I'd grown to hate the cumbersome vehicle, it felt like an old friend bidding me a reluctant farewell. Trailways busses had been a poor substitute for a sense of place, but they had nonetheless served as my home for my long journey to Holcomb.

Suitcase in hand and baseball cap cocked toward the back of my head, I stood on the brink of a summer I had long anticipated and would never forget. At the age of 20, the shoulder, arm and back muscles of my 6'2" frame were well developed, but they didn't compare to those I would develop before the end of this summer. My build was athletic, and my thick blond hair and tanned face and arms gave me the look of a minor league baseball player reporting to his first major league training camp, yet each step forward felt tentative and unsteady, like the new territory that it was.

* * *

"Hey there," shouted a handsome ruddy-faced man in his early 40s. "Are you the packer from Indiana we've been lookin' for?"

"I guess that's me."

I was surprised to be recognized so quickly, but to the man who greeted me I might as well have been wearing a sandwich board that read, "*Watermelon Packer From Indiana.*"

"Matt Mayer," I yelled back. In spite of my weariness, I wanted my voice to sound upbeat, so I struggled to conceal my feelings of exhaustion.

The man walked in my direction with his back toward his new 1968 maroon Chevy Malibu, in which he had just placed a leather briefcase. As he drew closer, he looked more and more like the billboard image of the Marlboro Man. The only thing missing was the white Stetson hat. He was deeply tanned, had a cigarette dangling from his lips and a full head of light brown hair. The lengthy ash that clung to the end of his cigarette told me that he was a man with too much on his mind to be bothered with minor details.

"Hi. My name is Aubrey Jensen, co-owner of Quality Melon. Put your suitcase in the trunk of my car over there, and I'll introduce you to some of the boys. You'll be riding back to the hotel with me directly. We stay over yonder in Dothan."

"Directly" was a term that farmers in southern Indiana used. It meant "in a little while."

I took Aubrey's suggestion to put my luggage in his car, as if he had given me a direct order. Without hesitation, I pushed the chrome button in the middle of the trunk lid, watched the trunk fly open, then flopped my bag inside. Then I slammed the trunk down and checked to make sure it had latched securely.

"One step closer to a good night's sleep," I thought to myself. I would pretend to enjoy being at the co-op for a few introductions, even though I preferred to save the formalities until the next morning.

"What a bus ride! My ass has been asleep since we pulled out of Montgomery."

Although I had just met Aubrey, he struck me as a regular guy, and after traveling all this way I felt that I had earned the right to talk to him like a man.

"You ride all the way down here on that fuckin' rust bucket?" Aubrey asked.

"No," I replied. "I rode the first leg from Indiana to Huntsville with one of your drivers; Doris Dickman. He was deadheadin' to Huntsville overnight, and he didn't seem to mind having me along as company. He even let me drive his rig for a while. That was a hell of an experience!"

"You mean you never drove one a' those big fuckers before?" Aubrey said.

"No," I said. "Last night was my first time."

It was customary for people from Indiana to make a polite comment about any non-present third party whose name came up in conversation, so I told Aubrey that Doris Dickman was a nice guy.

Aubrey smiled. "Yeah, ole' Dickman's a nice enough fella', but he can be a real dumb fuck at times. But, come to think of it, what trucker ain't a dumb shit at times?"

I guessed that Aubrey was talking about the business aspects of dealing with truckers, who had a tendency to make bad decisions on the road from lack of sleep and too many "No-Doz" tablets to keep them awake.

Aubrey said, "A coupla' years back, ole' Dickman unhooked a trailer full of melons at a truck stop in middle Georgia, and then drove about 15 miles in his diesel cab to the next truck stop to get a massage at an 'Oriental' massage parlor he'd heard about from another trucker. I s'pose he figured a massage would do him some good after a hard day on the road. This little ole' Japanese gal specialized in what she called a 'Tiki Bath,' where the masseuse took off all her clothes, got into the hot tub with the customer, and gave him a complete bath and 'local' massage for $40. Dickman found the place and got his Tiki Bath, but when he got back to the truck stop he found that his open top trailer was about half as full of melons as it was when he'd left it. About 5 tons worth, stolen by melon thieves. I tell you, *nobody* made any money on that load! Dickman probably came out about $40 in the hole on the trip after payin' the little Japanese gal.

If there's one thing a melon buyer hates, it's a fuckin' head-up-the ass trucker who doesn't hire somebody to watch his trailer when he's out fuckin' around. If I didn't like ole' Dickman so much for his good points, he never would have hauled another load of produce for Quality Melon after that. Dumb fucker! Don't s'pose he told you about that little fuck-around, did he?"

"No," I said. "He didn't bring it up." I couldn't help but chuckle, and Aubrey laughed too.

"We expect ole' Dickman down here next week to pick up a load of melons. Maybe you can be his packer. You could give him a ration a' shit about where he's plannin' to get his next massage." Aubrey laughed.

"C'mon, let's climb up on the packin' shed and meet some of the fellas you'll be workin' with."

"Packin' shed" was a generic term used frequently by melon buyers and farmers. It didn't matter whether the building in question was a small lean-to on a farmer's private property, or an out-of-control tin covered pole barn like the Holcomb farmer's co-op.

My dad had a small barn he called his packin' shed, where we used to assemble "wire-bound" crates for packing cantaloupes. Once the crates were assembled, we packed them full of cantaloupes in the same building, and then pasted labels on both ends of each crate that read: "Indiana's Sweetest Melons." These labels were colorful, and pictured a beautiful cantaloupe with a fully developed netting on the outside and smooth yellow "skin" beneath the netting. Next to the whole cantaloupe was a picture of a delectable half cantaloupe with the seeds removed and its bright orange hollowed out center visually inviting the customer to grab a spoon and dig in. The enticing picture of the "Indiana Melon" on the labels had been so successful as a marketing tool that cantaloupe lovers from Ohio, Illinois, and Michigan were convinced that Indiana melons were better tasting than those grown in their own home states.

I was almost afraid to open the door of the packin' shed on our farm, because there was usually an enormous wasp's nest above the large double doors, which served as home to 10 or 15 wasps that crawled eerily around the outside of the nest on a hot summer's day. Nothing was angrier looking than a swarm of wasps on the outside of a nest, neatly tucked under the eaves of a farmer's outbuilding.

One hot July afternoon, when Ben and I were entering the building to assemble cantaloupe crates, he was stung by a wasp that made a beeline for his bare chest as we swung the door open. The angry insect stung him so hard that a welt formed immediately, giving Ben the appearance that he had a third nipple in the middle of his chest. He screamed bloody murder, and there was no doubt he was in terrible pain. Our dad heard the scream and came running for fear that one of us had been murdered. From that day forward, I was afraid to open the packin' shed doors because of what that angry wasp had done to Ben on that sultry July afternoon.

* * *

At the other end of the packin' shed spectrum was the large building owned by my uncle "Big Boy," who ran a wholesale fruit and vegetable business. Big Boy's packin' shed featured a 100 foot long canopied loading dock, a ten thousand square foot warehouse, and a two thousand square foot cold storage.

Uncle Big Boy's name was Charles Bean. He was a large man, the oldest of nine children, and the brother of my dad's mother. Truck farmers from miles around knew him as Big Boy because of his physical size, coupled with his larger-than-life personality. Ben and I liked uncle Big Boy because he was what our dad called "a real character," and I learned early in life that real characters were never boring people. Big Boy was larger than life. He always walked around his packin' shed with an unlit stogie in his mouth, and he sported what appeared to be a perpetual erection. Ben and I guessed that the package between his legs might have had something to do with his nickname.

Big Boy wore short-sleeved white shirts, and undershirts that you could plainly see through them. His undershirts were the kind with the thin strips of cotton material that went up over his shoulders. Big Boy always wore suspenders to hold up his 46-inch waist seersucker striped pants. The suspenders and pants together gave him the look of a Humpty-Dumpty with unusually long legs and a hard-on.

Packin' sheds like Big Boy's were places where young boys like Ben and me could learn things about men. For instance, Big Boy was the first man we heard using the word "fuck." He said it out of the clear blue one day, when we were at the packin' shed with our dad delivering a pick-up truckload of cantaloupes. Ben and I were caught completely off-guard by Big Boy's expletive. As usual, he was sharing a lament with a couple of local farmers over some sort of insect that was eating the leaves off watermelon vines. Farmers loved to hang around the packin' shed and "sing the blues" about the trouble they were having eking out a living. It didn't seem to matter if they were complaining about the weather, insects eating their crops, or the sorry-ass market price of melons. They just loved to complain!

On this particular day, the subject of the bellyaching was a pest called "Red Spider." This was an insect that gnawed away at plants so fast that, in a matter of days, they were bare and could no longer support the growth of income-bearing fruit. In sympathy with one of the farmers, Big Boy asked if "the fuckin' spider" was eating up his melons. The farmer replied that he thought it was that "motherfuckin' spider," adding the "mother" to up the ante on Big Boy.

Ben and I looked at each other and snickered in disbelief. It had never before occurred to either of us that adults used the word "fuck." We thought, as all kids did, that most "dirty" words were introduced to civilization by our own generation. As rebellious youngsters, we believed we were the only ones bold enough to use these words out loud. But uncle Big Boy proved without a doubt, our theory was flawed.

6.

I kept pace with Aubrey as he approached the packing shed, and I quickly formed the impression that I would enjoy working for him. Aubrey had been around melon farmers all of his life, and he didn't have a pretentious bone in his body. He seemed to be the kind of man who was busy with his own thoughts and couldn't be bothered with other people's trivia. His face twitched when he spoke, mostly around the mouth when he was thinking about the next deal he would make with a grocery chain for a few loads of watermelons. I had seen similar twitches on the faces of melon buyers before, and particularly the buyer from Michigan I'd worked for over the past few summers in Indiana. I began to think that nervous twitches were a common occupational trait of produce buyers.

The Michigan buyer, "Big Al," drank generous amounts of J&B scotch whiskey, and chased Elmwood waitresses on August evenings during his buying trips to Indiana. Like Aubrey, Big Al was a heavy smoker who took long drags off his cigarettes, and made a mouthful of white cigarette smoke look like the most satisfying taste sensation a human being could experience. Al, a man of routine, faithfully placed a phone call to his wife every evening from his hotel room, just before "going out to dinner." Aubrey would have done the same, but he had young sons who liked to travel with him during the summer, so he kept a low profile in the skirt-chasing department when one of the kids was traveling along.

Aubrey said, "We don't always keep our packers here this late of an evening, but we've got 'em all workin' tonight. It's peak season and we've gotta' get these melons packed out if it kills us. We'll be movin' to South Carolina in a few weeks, but don't breathe a word about that to the farmers around here."

The thought of "movin' on" didn't appeal to me in the least. I was only minutes into my stay in Holcomb, so Aubrey's mention of traveling to South Carolina depressed me just a little. I was completely exhausted, and the only thing that saved me from full blown despair was the realization that my next long distance ride would likely be in an air-conditioned automobile, not a semi or a bus. After a couple of weeks in one place, I might be able to tolerate that kind of journey.

Aubrey stopped at the back of a trailer and pointed to a black man inside. "This is Shorty," Aubrey yelled over the roar and clang of the conveyor system.

"Shorty, this is Matt Mayer, our new packer from Indiana. We've gotta' bring a few college boys from up north every summer. Company tradition, ya' know."

Aubrey smiled, and the corner of his mouth twitched. The way his mouth looked when it flinched, I imagined a long piece of straw dangling from the corner, accompanied by a clicking sound as if he were signaling a horse to "gee" or "haw." Somehow that image went along with Aubrey's Marlboro Man look.

Shorty looked like a character out of an Uncle Remus story. He was the "Br'er Bear" of watermelon packers, so dark that other blacks might have described him as "blue black." He stood about 6'1," and was built like a retired NFL linebacker whose stomach had gotten slightly out of control. Shorty had, in fact, played linebacker for Alabama State College for Negroes during his college days, but he had lost his left arm in an accident his sophomore year, and then dropped out of college. He had a powerfully muscled upper arm and a movable stub that extended a few inches below his elbow. Shorty, whose nickname had evolved from his shortened left extremity, had never become bitter over his misfortune. He figured he'd had his share of glory as a college football player, and academic pursuits would never have been enough to keep him at Alabama State. After his accident, he'd dropped out of school and taken a job packing melons when what was left of his arm had healed. He tried sharecropping at first, but he always preferred a greater challenge. He saw packing melons as a test of his physical strength, and an opportunity for an occasional change of scenery.

Shorty's smile was both friendly and genuine. I had always thought Indiana was the birthplace of the warm and well-meaning smile, but I had never experienced the southern black version. Shorty's smile defined the word "guileless." He was missing two of his bottom teeth in front, perhaps from his football playing days before the advent of the mandatory mouthpiece.

With the exception of one tooth of yellow gold, Shorty's teeth were the color of southern sweet tea; not brown but deep amber. I guessed they were discolored from years of smoking or chewing tobacco, combined with a lack of attention from the dental community.

Shorty's widely gapped front teeth slanted forward, giving him a deceivingly slow-witted look that was counter-balanced by a clever gleam in his eyes.

Perched nimbly atop a slope of perfectly stacked watermelons, Shorty stood 10 or 15 feet away from the rear end of the 40-foot trailer. He was working his way toward the conclusion of his final load of the day. With his right hand, Shorty doffed a sweat-soaked baseball cap in acknowledgement of my presence. Simultaneously, he caught a watermelon with his left upper arm, balanced the 25-pound lump of produce in the stubby curve where his forearm had once been, then cradled the melon between his bicep and left rib cage with minimal support from his right hand. He made it look so easy that it was hard to imagine how he might do it any better with a fully intact left arm.

As I watched Shorty manhandle one watermelon after another, I found myself staring in amazement. I had packed scores of trailer loads, but never had I built a stack so smooth across the top, nor had I put together a support structure of melons so symmetrical. It was rare to see such straight rows of watermelons from the front to the back of a 40-foot trailer; each melon lined up perfectly behind the one in front of it. This powerful, dark-skinned man wielded watermelons with his right arm as easily as Satchel Paige had used his left arm to groove a perfect curve ball over the plate during his prime years as a pitcher in the Negro baseball leagues.

Shorty's broad shoulders and upper arms were solid muscle from years of tossing watermelons as regularly as professional athletes lifted weights. He could handle a watermelon as easily as "Wilt the Stilt" Chamberlain could handle a basketball. When he caught a melon in his large and powerful right hand, he would bounce it lightly up and down for a split second to get a "feel" for it. Sometimes he would twirl a melon in the palm of his hand. After bouncing the melon a couple of times to establish a feel for its weight and size, he simultaneously found the perfect spot for it in his stack, then glided the melon gently into its designated space in a single motion. He never had to worry about damaging a melon or bruising it on the outside, because he instinctively applied the perfect touch so each melon landed softly in its place.

Aubrey and I were standing on the platform at trailer level, approximately five and a half feet above the ground, and looking into the rear end of the trailer as Shorty worked his melon packing magic. Maybe it was the angle of sight that made Shorty's stack of produce appear more symmetrical than any I'd seen before, but whatever the reason I was totally impressed. This one-armed man's technique for building a stack of watermelons could have been used in a training film on the art of melon packing.

Only another packer could fully appreciate Shorty's intuitive style. He eased the melons into the stack one by one, each nesting gently into its designated position.

"It's an art," I thought out loud, but nobody could hear me above the noise of the melon conveying machinery.

Shorty's bare chest with its sparse curls of tightly wound black hair dripped with sweat. The temperature and humidity that evening were almost unbearable. I knew from experience that 40-foot trailers covered with sheet metal on the outside, and a fair amount of insulation inside of their walls, would hold heat for hours at a time. Had Shorty been able to step outside the back of the trailer, just ten feet behind him, the cool evening breeze would have felt like the air conditioning in a whites-only hotel. But watermelons were still flying, one after another, from the end of the fast-moving conveyor, so Shorty had no choice but to stay inside the trailer and finish packing it before allowing the evening breeze to touch his overheated skin.

Aubrey said, "This fella's strong enough with one good arm to out work most men with two arms."

Shorty paused long enough to look back toward us with a smile. "Y'all gonna' have some fun tomorrow, young man! We gonna' make a packer outa' ya', we damn shore is!" He laughed. "But y'all looks like y'all can handle it! You play football up north?" Shorty panted slightly as he spoke.

"No," I answered, "but I've been accused of it a time or two. I guess I have the Indiana watermelons to thank for these shoulders." I laughed, and so did Shorty. His head shook and his powerful shoulders bounced up and down.

"Melon packin' is hard woik, but it's damn sure easier on you body than football playin'," he said. "At least in melon packin', ain't nobody on the other side of the ball tryin' ta' kill ya'!"

Aubrey gestured toward a second black man who was lifting melons off the end of the conveyor and tossing them one by one to Shorty. This man's skin was light tan compared with Shorty's. Aubrey introduced him as "Bobby Leeds." "He goes by both names," said Aubrey. "Only his close friends call him Bobby."

Bobby Leeds flashed a friendly smile, and nodded to acknowledge Aubrey's introduction. He was short and thin, but muscular. He had the look of a quick baseball outfielder compared with Shorty's bulky linebacker frame. I was suddenly aware that I was associating Shorty and Bobby Leeds with black sports figures. Maybe I was stereotyping, but they really did have the look of athletes, and I figured a stranger on the street would have made the same mental comparison. In Shorty's case, my mental stereotype was valid. He had been a college football player.

Bobby Leeds stood about 5'10" and looked tough and wiry. As a child I had seen the Disney cartoon movie entitled "Song of the South," a film that later become controversial because of its freewheeling use of black stereotypes. Nonetheless, I could not help but think of Bobby Leeds as the "Br'er Fox" of melon packers, compared to Shorty's "Br'er Bear."

The look in Bobby's eyes was friendly and intelligent. He spoke rapidly with a pronounced dialect that was nearly impossible for me to understand.

Bobby Leeds said, "please-ta'-meetcha', Matt." I understood that much, even though the four words ran together as one. Having spoken briefly, he then turned back to the conveyor, grabbed another melon off the end of it and tossed it to Shorty.

"Hurry-you-Nigga'-ass-up, Shorty! You gotta' be da' slowess muthafucker I know." Bobby's words sounded like part of a well-rehearsed routine between himself and Shorty. "Let's finish dis fucker and go git some supper! I'm fixin' to starve my ass off if I don't be sweatin' it off first."

Both men laughed. It was now obvious that they were putting on a show for my benefit. It was near the end of a workday when physical fatigue tends to take over, when mental stress dwindles, and levity comes easily.

7.

Aubrey didn't join in on the small talk with Shorty and Bobby Leeds, and I could tell by his body language that it was time for us to move on. As we walked toward the next group of introductions, I marveled at the sheer size of this watermelon packing operation. At every turn, there were more conveyors moving melons. Alabama melon growers had invented an effective method of attracting large scale produce buyers, and had created a buyer's paradise as well as a packer's dream come true! No time was wasted riding out to melon farms with truckers. I would suffer no bumpy rides in empty semis over unpaved roads; no searching for remote farm houses and no confusing verbal directions from locals like, "take a left just past where the old Baptist Church used to be." Farmers around Holcomb simply loaded their wagons and pick-up trucks to capacity at the farm, and brought them in to the co-op. Wagon and truck tires, many of which were tread bare from years of spinning in the hot Alabama sand, appeared nearly flat upon arrival at the co-op under the strain of the overloaded vehicles they supported.

I had visions of dollar signs clicking away and my college bank account swelling as the summer moved forward. As my father would have said, "this place has more watermelons than Heinz has got pickles." Although there were several experienced packers on hand, there would not be enough manpower to keep up with the workload. As a result, it would be easy for me to reach my quota of two or three trailers each day, and I would earn $40 to $60 dollars for every 10 or 12 hours of hard work.

"Shorty and Bobby are about to finish their fifth load of the day," Aubrey said. "They work together like that all the time, and split $100 to $120 bucks at the end of a five or six load day. Some days they'll knock out seven loads for a total of $140 in a day, so I'm sure they couldn't do any better working alone. Shorty is gettin' a bit long in the tooth for a packer, but ole' Bobby can pack like a sonofabitch when that skinny little bastard gets goin'. I've seen him pack four loads in a single day with Shorty tossing to him, then turn around and toss two more trailer loads to Shorty. If you think Shorty's packin' looked good just now, you should see a load Bobby has packed out. He gets 'em smooth as fuckin' glass across the top no matter what size and shape of melons he's workin' with! That little son-of-a-bitch is one of the best watermelon packers I've ever seen, and like you could see, Shorty ain't no slouch. I don't know what we'd do without the two of them, and I'll guarantee you that you can learn a few things from watching them two fellas."

I said, "I can't imagine how anybody could pack out a prettier load of melons than the one Shorty was just working on! Bobby must be super-human if he can beat that!"

Aubrey's mouth twitched. "Believe me, Bobby's better."

Convinced that Aubrey was telling the truth, I had no doubt that Shorty and Bobby were among the best in the business. Were they not top-notch packers, they would probably not have been Quality Melon regulars. Having briefly met the two of them, I was prouder than ever to have been called up to the "big time." Maybe this was not as prestigious as joining the Green Bay Packers, but I was certainly pleased to be one of the Quality Melon packers! By the time I worked my way to the Indiana crop in mid-August, less experienced packers back home would be coming around to see the loads of melons I'd packed. I knew this, because I had been one of them before. I had looked up to guys before me who'd made the trip south to pack alongside of the professionals.

After this summer, buyers like Big Al from Michigan would ask for me by name, and local farm boys would eagerly listen to my stories about the South while admiring my work. Every load I packed would be smooth across the top, rows of melons perfectly straight, and average pounds per melon exactly what the buyer ordered.

The truth about shipping watermelons from the point of loading to the marketplace was that no load of melons arrived at the market looking smooth across the top. No matter how skilled the packer, it was a miracle if scores of melons were not standing on end after the load completed its journey of several hundred miles inside a 40-foot box that was perched atop 18 bouncing wheels. When the back doors of the trailer were opened at delivery, the melons no longer lay neatly in rows pointing end-to-end toward the front of the trailer. Although packers took great pride in their work, nobody expected a delivered load of melons to look as good as it had at that culminating moment, when the last melon and the last handful of straw were carefully placed against the thick retaining boards at the back of the trailer.

Because the appearance of a completed load of melons was a matter of pride for packers, truck drivers took great pleasure in relating to packers how badly their last load of melons had looked when they were off-loaded at their destinations. Drivers took every opportunity to brag to packers about their driving skills, but they were never willing to take the blame when something went wrong with a load of melons.

A packer friend of mine in Indiana told me about a trucker who had returned from Detroit and demanded his $20 back, because the packer had "done him wrong." The driver claimed that a large number of melons had been broken in transit, and that it was a direct result of the packer's "piss poor job of packin'." Just as the trucker was telling his sad story and demanding his money back from the packer, another driver came up and asked the trucker if he was OK following the "scrape" he'd had on his way to Detroit. As it turned out, the trucker was sideswiped by another truck in the middle of the night along Interstate 75 in Northern Ohio. To keep his rig from turning over, the driver had taken to the shoulder, and then partially lost control of his semi and ended jackknifed in a ditch on the side of the highway. After being pulled from the ditch by a specially built tow truck, the driver had checked his load of melons only to find out that a couple of hundred had burst during the mishap.

The juice that dripped from the trailer in Detroit had nothing to do with a lack of skill on the part of the packer.

* * *

I followed Aubrey as he descended from the catwalk and walked toward the backside of the packing shed, where a thin white man was leaning against a deep blue 1963 Chevy Impala. The man, bare from two inches below the waist upward, was perspiring heavily. He was dressed in a dirty pair of black cotton dress pants with no belt. An unanticipated sneeze might easily have dropped his pants around his ankles. He wore an unpolished pair of black Wellington boots, with his left pant leg covering the upper part of its respective boot and his right pants leg tucked inside. At first glance, he looked to be in his mid to late 40s, but the look of his glazed-over eyes suggested he could easily be over 50 years of age. His thick black hair was slicked back close to his head, and sweat mixed with his natural body oil to give him the appearance that he had just stepped out of a shower. Central casting in Hollywood might have picked this man as a villain in a B-grade western movie. The cigarette that dangled from his lower lip completed the look to near perfection.

Aubrey introduced us. "Slick, this is Matt . . . Matt, Slick." It occurred to me that last names were not important around the farmer's co-op, Bobby Leeds being the possible exception.

Slick's sleepy eyes barely looked upward to see whom Aubrey had introduced, but an almost undetectable nod of the head acknowledged that an introduction of some sort had taken place. Slick met new people every day of each melon season for as long as he could remember, and most of them were farmers and truckers who came and went in a steady stream as he moved from place to place with the crop. In his migrant worker's mentality, he considered most new acquaintances as pointless. Besides, it was late in the day, and he was in no mood to socialize.

As Aubrey and I moved on, Slick looked up and mumbled, "Please to meet ya' fellar."

I turned around and smiled at the grizzled melon packer. "Nice to meet you, Slick." I was sure that I sounded a bit too cheerful, and I sensed that Slick saw through my eagerness to please.

"Ole' Slick is our most experienced packer," said Aubrey.

"I could have guessed that!" I said. "He makes Shorty look young by comparison."

Aubrey laughed. "The old geezer looks like death warmed over, but he can out work, out pack, out drink and out fuck any young man I've ever seen," said Aubrey. "He has two problems. He never met a bottle of cheap booze he didn't like, and he can't pass up a piece of ass. He flat don't care how cheap a bottle of whiskey is or what a woman looks like, as long as the whiskey is strong and the woman is willing to fuck!

You wouldn't think a guy that looks like him could get a woman in bed every night, but I've never known him to spend many nights alone when we've been on the road."

Aubrey paused to laugh his nervous half-laugh, almost surprising himself. "When it comes down to it, I don't give a shit about his personal habits, he's a damn good packer for a white man, and he rarely misses a day of work. Just don't count on him teachin' you a damn thing. You'll have to get that from Shorty and Bobby. Slick ain't interested in helpin' nobody; never has been. He don't see any point in it. He comes to work hung over every morning and he don't feel halfway human until noon. Hell, for all I know, he mighta' been drunk when he learned how to pack melons, and he's been packin' on instinct ever since! He just does it day after day on automatic pilot. If he knows you're tryin' to watch him and learn, it'll piss the ole' boy off, and he won't mind lettin' ya' know about it."

"I'll keep that in mind," I said.

Aubrey said, "One of our young packers got all impressed with Slick's packin' skills last summer, so he made the mistake of standing around for 10 or 15 minutes all wide-eyed, watchin' Slick at work. He couldn't help himself, so he finally said, 'Slick, I don't believe I've ever seen anybody pack melons as good as you do. How would you like people to remember you when it's all over for you in this business?' Ole' Slick looked the kid right in the eye and said, 'Young man, I really don't give a fuck!'"

"My advice is to leave Slick alone, just like you would a grouchy old dog. Talk to him only if he says something to you first. That way, the two of you will get along just fine."

Aubrey and I soon approached a group of young men who were standing next to a new Chrysler New Yorker. These four had apparently finished their last trailers of the day, and the phrase "smokin' and jokin'" described them to perfection.

"Fellas, this is Matt, our new packer, fresh out of Indiana."

I extended my hand and shook the hands of the other packers. Three of the four looked about my own age, and it was easy to tell that they were fellow college students. They were dirty from the day's work, but "clean around the edges," as my dad would say; neat haircuts, white teeth (none missing in front), shaven, and dressed in blue jeans and t-shirts. The fourth was a youngster, who could not have been more than 13 years of age. It was hard for me to imagine that he could lift a watermelon, let alone pack a trailer full of them.

"This is Lonny, William, Don Jr. and Danny. Don Jr. is my partner's son. His dad mostly stays up north in our Indiana office during the melon season, but he trusts me to keep an eye on this joker for him."

"Oh yeah," I said. "I spoke with Mr. Bartel in Elmwood. In fact, he offered me this job."

"That's him," Aubrey said. "He's one of the finest men you'll ever meet. He had major surgery to rip out some throat cancer last winter, and that's another reason he prefers to stay up north these days. Needless to say, he's quit smokin', but his energy level just ain't what it used to be." Aubrey laughed and began to cough. "I guess I need to think about quittin' too, but it won't be until after melon season. Too much pressure on me right now."

"Lonny comes down with his dad, who is one of our main melon buyers from the Schroeder grocery chain out of Cincinnati. He's the guy the rest of us REALLY work for. Since we linked up with the Schroeder chain, we've been able to move twice as many melons as we ever did before."

"I've heard Schroeder's produce is some of the best," I said.

"You damn sure heard right," said Aubrey.

"William here is my sister's son, from Florida. He's just learnin' to pack this summer, so maybe you and these other fellas can teach him a thing or two. And, oh, the skinny kid here is my son, Danny."

"Nice to meet all of you," I gave them my widest Indiana-style grin.

The car they were standing next to was the company car that was supposed to be driven exclusively by Lonny's father, but Lonny drove the other white packers around in it most of the time. His dad was usually late leaving the co-op in the evening, so he caught rides with a QM staff member or one of the truckers who would be passing through Dothan.

Aubrey looked at his watch and decided it was time to call it a day. "Fellas, I'm headin' to Dothan in a few minutes. Matt here has had a long day gettin' here, and I know you guys are tuckered out too. I'll take Matt up to Dothan and we might see you guys at the Holiday Inn later. If not, we'll see ya' here bright and early in the morning."

The packer Aubrey had introduced as William, from Florida, looked up from stomping out a cigarette into the sand. Despite his efforts to appear masculine, with the cigarette as his prop, he simply did not look the part.

"Hey Matt," said William, "if you think y'all have had a hard day ridin' busses today, wait 'til you work like a nigger all day tomorrow. We'll show ya' what a hard day feels like!"

Nobody acknowledged William's comment, and Aubrey and I walked away.

8.

I assumed that the hired help stayed in cheap roadside motels and had proportionate shares of daily room rates taken out of their pay. I not only expected to pay for my lodging, but I figured it would be fair for me to do so. But Aubrey told me I would be staying in a comfortable place in Dothan, and the company would be paying for my lodging. I would be sharing a room with two or three other packers, but the price would certainly be right! When Aubrey told me that the company paid for the rooms, I didn't think twice about the inconvenience of sharing a bed.

Having grown up with five siblings in a three-bedroom house, I was used to sharing a room with Ben and our younger brother, David, who was 10 years younger than Ben and 8 years my junior. Ben had an extra long bed, the rails of which had been extended by a local welding shop when he was 15 years old to accommodate his 6'6" frame. David, who shared a double bed with me, was at a clear disadvantage because I commanded more space than he did. He frequently complained to our parents that I was "crowding" him. Unfortunately, his complaints fell on deaf ears because there was not enough floor space to accommodate a third bed, nor enough money to buy one.

* * *

As we got into his car, Aubrey said, "My son Danny will be sharing the hotel room with those three college boys for a couple more nights, so I'll need to ask you to spend your first night or two with our accountant, Monty. Monty has been with us for years, and he runs the business end of the operation. I don't think he'll bother you, much!"

Aubrey laughed in his slightly nervous way.

"Danny will be heading back to Florida the day after tomorrow, so you can start bunking in with the other three packers in a couple of days. We'll stick with that arrangement for the rest of the summer."

I had no objection to the sleeping arrangements for the first two nights, and I'd read nothing into Aubrey's joking comment that the company accountant would not bother me, "much." I was simply grateful to look forward to a clean, air conditioned,

Holiday Inn room for my first night's sleep on the road. I needed to stretch out on a bed so badly that I would have agreed to share a room with a half starved alligator.

Aubrey pulled up to the Dothan Holiday Inn, and I immediately recognized it as the same hotel I had seen from the bus window as the Trailways bus had passed by it earlier that evening. My journey had begun nearly 28 hours before, and now I could finally stop counting the hours. I got out of the car, stretched my arms high into the air and arched my spine forward. Keeping my knees locked, I reached down as far as I could and touched the toes of my shoes with my fingertips.

Aubrey motioned toward one of the first floor rooms of the hotel, room number 53. "Let's check in on Monty. You can put your stuff in his room, then we'll get something to eat; I'm buying. I figure you've earned a good meal after the trip you've had, and the burgers and steaks here are pretty decent."

"Thanks, I'm starved," I said. Dinner sounded like a great idea, especially in a Holiday Inn restaurant. I anticipated the aroma of a grilled steak and the look of it on my plate, along with a pile of deep fried onion rings and a bottle of ketchup on the side. To my surprise, the raw onions I'd eaten with my hamburger at lunch in Birmingham had not bothered my stomach as I'd expected, so I assumed an order of cooked onion rings would agree with me as well.

I was wearing the same clothes I had worn when I first crawled into Doris Dickman's truck the evening before, and I was eager to get back to the room after dinner to change. I would take a long cool shower, then change into sleeping clothes and start my first letter to my brother. Writing to Ben would help me relax and wind down. The process of writing down my thoughts had that effect on me, like a therapy session that brought the daily monologue in my head to its logical conclusion. That process seemed especially important at the end of a day like this one, in which I had chalked up many miles and a list of new experiences.

Aubrey knocked on Monty's door, and a portly man in his mid-40s answered after a few seconds. The man stood about 5'11," and was clad in a pair of pants with an elastic waistband and a white undershirt. He wore thin, wire-rimmed glasses that rode a bit low on his oily bulb-like nose, and he smiled as he extended a friendly hand to greet me. "Hi. I'm L. V. Rosemont! The guys call me 'Monty.' You're Matt from Indiana, right?"

Not waiting for a reply, Monty continued. "I'm the accountant for this outfit, and my job is to keep this guy," pointing to Aubrey, "and his partner out of jail."

"Nice to meet ya', Monty. I guess you're doing your job, because Aubrey appears to be a free man. I understand you don't mind if I stay here for a night or two."

I stepped into the room and looked for a place to put my suitcase. The couch next to the window looked like a good place. It also looked like it might be a sofa bed. Bed or no bed, it seemed like the most logical place for me to sleep for a night or two.

Monty looked at Aubrey and smiled. Aubrey smiled back with a nervous twitch, and motioned with his head for Monty to follow him to the restaurant. Aubrey seemed to be running on the power of his own nervous energy, and it was obvious that he was eager to get to the restaurant and get on with his evening. In addition to his two or three packs of cigarettes a day, and several cups of black coffee, Aubrey enjoyed a medium-rare t-bone steak with a large Coke, topped off in his hotel room by a pint of Scotch whiskey, just before he passed out into his bed. There were a few high rollers among the ranks of produce buyers who insisted on filet and Chivas, but Aubrey was satisfied with his t-bone and pint of J&B Scotch. With the exception of the steak, which he customarily inhaled, food wasn't very important, and it didn't deserve much of his time. After devouring his meal, he would head back to his hotel room to make a few late evening phone calls, then toss down a few glasses of whiskey on the rocks and smoke his last four or five cigarettes before turning in for the night. His final act before turning out the lights each evening was to pick up the empty cigarette pack and feel inside it with an index finger to make certain he had not left a cigarette unsmoked. Following this inspection, the crisp, crinkling sound of paper and cellophane was exactly what he needed to hear before closing his eyes.

Each morning, Aubrey arose at 5:30 AM and started his routine all over again by sitting on the edge of the bed and tapping the top of a fresh pack of cigarettes against the heal of his hand to tighten up the tobacco. He then removed the red cellophane ring from the top of the pack and ripped off a piece of the foil paper that held the cigarettes inside. Taking out his first smoke, he then took his Zippo lighter and flicked the wheel against the flint to watch the flame leap forward and light his cigarette. He eagerly inhaled as much smoke as he could with his first drag. From that point in the day, all was well in his world, and life was able to move forward.

There was something very manly about a daily routine that began with a cigarette and ended with a pint of J&B in a hotel room, followed by the wadding up of the exoskeleton of an empty cigarette pack. The key ingredient in a routine's manliness was the single fact that it was automatic. Aubrey's subconscious took care of the details, while his conscious mind was occupied with more important matters. If it was true that successful men did things un-self-consciously, then the way in which Aubrey went about his routines was evidence that he was a successful man.

* * *

Monty put on a loose fitting, even tailed sport shirt. The shirt was neatly pressed and extended approximately three inches below his ill-defined waistline. It was a Panama style shirt, not meant to be tucked in, and it gave him the casual look that seemed to be reserved for middle-aged fat guys. The three of us left Monty's room and walked through a passageway under one wing of the hotel, then through a well-groomed courtyard with a large blue swimming pool surrounded by white plastic lounge chairs. Just past the courtyard, we entered through the glass door of the air-conditioned Holiday Inn restaurant. As we went inside, the smell of charcoal broiled steak hit me instantly. The hostess knew Aubrey and Monty, and she seated us without delay. A waitress appeared at out table immediately to take our orders, and we received our meals in less than 10 minutes.

Finishing his meal with minimal small talk, Aubrey excused himself and headed for his hotel room. Monty announced that he was going to the hotel bar for a nightcap before coming back to the room. He invited me along, but I didn't feel like giving him a speech about the fact that I was not yet 21. And besides, my instincts told me that I would be carded if I tried to order a drink in an Alabama bar. It was almost a guarantee in the midst of a "dry" county, with no liquor stores for miles and alcohol sold only in a handful of legally sanctioned bars that were connected with high volume restaurants.

Eager for a few minutes of privacy, I declined Monty's invitation and asked him for a room key. Without argument, he handed me a key with the familiar green Holiday Inn logo and room number connected to it. I started toward the room in ever-growing anticipation of a cool shower, after which I would begin a letter to my brother, Ben.

On my way to Monty's room, I again walked past the swimming pool and momentarily considered putting on my swim trunks and taking a cool evening dip. But I remembered that the water in swimming pools tended to retain its heat well into the night. In spite of a mild evening breeze, I knew that the water in the pool would probably feel like bath water, so I stuck with my original plan to enjoy a cool shower in Monty's room.

As I arrived at Monty's hotel room, I noticed an enormous powder blue 1968 Buick with a white convertible top, parked directly across the parking lot from the room door. The car had probably been there during my introduction to Monty, but my tired brain cells had not registered its presence. Whatever the reason, I had not paid attention to the massive hunk of steel and sheet metal on wheels, but I had a feeling that the bona fide "Detroit Barge" *must* belong to Monty.

* * *

After my shower, I put on a purple fraternity jersey with the large gold Greek letters "Sigma" and "Pi" on the front of it. I stepped into a pair of tan shorts, and sat at the table next to the sofa. Before starting my letter, I lifted the cushion from one side of the sofa to make sure that it doubled as a full sized bed. It did. I opened the drawer of the desk and found a complimentary ballpoint pen along with an ample supply of hotel stationery and envelopes with the pre-printed retutn address:

Holiday Inn
Dothan, Alabama
Heart of Dixie

It occurred to me that if I asked Ben to keep my letters, I might reclaim them later as a sort of diary of the summer of 1968.

* * *

"*Dear Ben—*

I finally got to Holcomb about 5:30 this evening, after the goddamndest day I've ever spent on a bus! In fact, I can honestly say I have never before spent an entire day on a bus! As soon as I arrived, my new boss (Aubrey) introduced me to the rest of the packers I'll be working with, and then he gave me a ride back to Dothan where they're putting me up in a really nice Holiday Inn. Not bad for a lowly watermelon packer, eh?

Ole' Doris Dickman (can you believe that fuckin' name?) was a pain in the ass to ride with as far as Huntsville, but the cool part was that he let me drive his big-ass semi part of the way down highway 41, when traffic was almost non-existent in the middle of the night! He caught a nap while I drove.

I wrote you a post card earlier today, so if you get it before you get this letter, you will already know about my lunch in the diner in Birmingham on the way down. I don't know why, it just shocked me to see whites and blacks eating together in the same Alabama restaurant. I thought whites down here were still making blacks eat in separate places, drink out of their own fountains, and piss in separate urinals. Everything I've seen on the news made me feel like this was an unfriendly as hell place if you were black. Oh well, it probably still is, but it was encouraging to see whites and blacks eating together in at least one city diner.

OOPS! I hear my roommate opening the door. Yes, they've got me sharing a room for my first night or two with this older (fat) guy who is the company accountant. I hope he doesn't fart too much or talk in his sleep. I can really use a good night's rest. (I'll finish this later.)"

* * *

I got up from the desk and placed my partially written letter inside my suitcase as Monty turned his key inside the doorknob and entered the room. It was 9:30 PM, and I was relaxed and ready for bed. I knew if I got a good night's sleep, I could handle the workload that faced me the following morning. Two loads of melons was the most I had ever packed in one day back home, but that included travel time from one farm to another. Three loads on my first day would be a challenge, but having seen the co-op, I knew it was entirely possible.

"Do you drink alcohol, young man?" Monty was in good spirits after his nightcap. I assumed that he'd had several drinks. Nobody ever had just one drink, even though that's what they always said: "Let's get together sometime for a drink." In Monty's chubby hands were four small, airplane-sized bottles of gin he had brought from the bar. Apparently, he was now ready for yet another nightcap, and he seemed even more determined than before to share with me.

"I really don't drink much," I answered.

Monty gave me a look of disbelief.

I said, "Don't get me wrong. I've had a few beers in my day. I don't suppose I'd be an honest fraternity member if I didn't admit to drinking now and then." I laughed nervously when it dawned on me that I was alone in a hotel room with a slightly drunk man I had known for a total of 2 ½ hours, and about whom Aubrey had left me a bit uncertain when he'd said . . . . "I don't think he'll bother you, *much*!"

"Well, imagine that," said Monty. "A studly college kid like you that doesn't just *love* his booze. Surely, you must use a little of the firewater to warm up your girlfriends now and then. But that's all right, I'll take your word for it that you're not a big fan of the drink. You do seem a bit sheltered compared to some of the college kids we get down here. I'll just put these on the dresser next to the TV, so you can help yourself if you change your mind. There's ice in the bucket here and mixers in my small fridge, in case you didn't notice it at the end of the dresser. I bring my little fridge along with me during the melon season, and the hotel folks in the places we stay are real nice about letting me plug it in. Anyway, I've gotta' take a shower and get myself ready for bed. 5:00 AM gets here damned early, you know! In the Army, they called that 'O-Dark-Thirty.'"

Monty let out a silly giggle as he headed into the bathroom, still dressed with his white terrycloth bathrobe draped over his arm and two small bottles of gin in his hand.

"After a couple of night caps, a man needs his 'shower cap,'" I thought to myself.

I pulled out the hide-a-bed across the room from Monty's queen-sized bed, and prepared to ease my tired body under its covers. I hadn't appreciated Monty's comment about my seeming a bit sheltered, but I chalked it up to his state of mind after his trip to the hotel bar. Shortly after I'd gotten under the covers, Monty emerged from the bathroom wearing a loose-fitting white robe. His street clothes were draped over his arm. Not enough time had elapsed for a man of Monty's size to take a proper shower, but I had heard the water running and the toilet flushing, so I guessed he had taken the traditional shit and shower.

Monty pulled down the covers on his bed, and then he glanced at me from across the room with an expression that looked like fake surprise. "Whoops, young fella! Sorry to tell ya' this, but don't get too comfortable in that couch bed over there. Aubrey might have a lot of money, but he ain't stupid. This room here is priced out as a single. I suppose I could pay the extra out of my own pocket if the hotel management finds out I've had a second person in here, but I'd rather not do that, and I really don't mind sharin' my bed. It's only for a night or two, and I don't snore too much. Know what I mean?"

"Oh," I replied. "Sorry, I didn't think about the hotel charging you for another person. I suppose I could take half of your bed. It looks big enough."

Completely naïve and without suspicion, I got out of the hide-a-bed and put it back together, then went over to Monty's queen sized bed. I pulled down the covers on what would be my side, and reluctantly crawled under the sheets. Monty's side of the bed was the one closest to the wall and the bathroom, and farthest from the door to the parking lot. He had slipped under the covers and turned off his table lamp, which left the room in total darkness except for a narrow sliver of light that leaked in between the curtains on the parking lot side of the room. I felt a certain need to stay close to the outside edge on my side to make sure Monty had plenty of space. After all, it *was*

Monty's bed. He was shorter than I, but he was a man of considerable girth. I guessed that he weighed in at around 240 or 250, a good 50 to 75 pounds heavier than me, so he clearly needed more than half of the available real estate.

* * *

As I lay in bed with Monty, eyes wide open, I was suddenly reminded of a story one of my uncles had told me about his experience during WW II. Although wartime circumstances were considerably more austere than mine, my uncle's story had also involved an over-crowded bed. While stationed in France, my uncle and a close Army buddy had been invited to stay overnight on a cold winter's weekend in a farmhouse that belonged to the family of his buddy's French fiancée. According to the story, when it came time to sleep on Friday night, my uncle was invited to share a large "matrimonial" bed with his friend and the friend's fiancée. My uncle politely declined, but when he learned that the only alternative sleeping place was the hayloft of the barn behind the house, he agreed to share the bed with the engaged couple. He situated himself as closely as possible to his own edge of the large bed, and the attractive young French woman took her place in the middle. His buddy cuddled up to his soon-to-be bride on the opposite side of the bed.

In the middle of the night, my uncle awoke to the sound of the couple making passionate love inches away from him. He lay perfectly still and continued breathing loudly, pretending to be asleep. He even faked a light snore.

Shortly after the couple finished making love, the young French woman tapped my uncle on the shoulder and asked in broken English, "You want fucky-fuck?" According to my uncle's version of the story, he graciously declined. In his words, "It was tempting as hell, and I had never questioned my buddy's generosity. But I'm sure if I'd accepted the favor, it would have changed our friendship forever."

* * *

Monty's bed was firm and the sheets felt cool against my skin. Without a doubt, it was more comfortable than the hide-a-bed would have been. The feeling of the sheets against my skin was the best feeling I'd had all day. Monty obviously believed in cranking up the AC to the "meat locker" setting, so I pulled the covers up to shoulder level. I closed my eyes and tried to doze off, in case Monty was about to start snoring, farting, or carrying on with some other noisy habit that older men were likely to have.

Suddenly, I felt something warm against my jockey shorts, immediately below waist level. It was moving. It was Monty's left hand. He was gently patting my ass!

"Hey there young fella," Monty whispered. "If I don't hear the alarm in the morning, make sure you wake me up, OK?"

"OK," I replied. I was suddenly beyond uncomfortable that Monty had felt the need to touch my ass. "Christ," I thought. "I just met this guy, and he feels it's OK to play with my ass to get my attention!" I knew I was in the hospitable South, but this would have seemed weird to me in *any* region of the country! Suddenly it felt really strange to be in the same bed with this corpulent company creep. Men probably patted their wives on the ass to get their attention in bed, but I assumed such a tactic was generally used with sex in mind.

"Hey, fella, I really mean it now!" Monty began patting my ass again, but this time there was something new in the motion of his hand. It lingered, then suddenly began to migrate toward the sharp tip of my pelvis as I lay on my side with my back toward him.

"If I don't wake up on my own, make sure I get up early. I've had a bit too much to drink this evening, so feel free to shake me if you need to in the morning."

"Fuck this!" I thought. The confusion inside my head was such that I was almost certain I'd said, "fuck this" out load. I wasn't sure what the acceptable ass-patting limit was, but I was pretty sure Monty was on the verge of exceeding it. Besides, the thought flashed across my mind that a responsible company accountant would most likely have no trouble hearing his own alarm in the morning, even after several drinks the night before.

For me, it came down to this; Monty was probably doing a bit of reconnaissance work on my sexual preferences and sleeping habits. I suspected that I already knew where this was headed. He was testing out the fresh meat, and if the fresh meat stayed in bed with him after a few well-placed pats on the ass, then it was meat that could probably be had! Once he'd established that he had a chance, Monty would wake up in the middle of the night, or wait in his semi-drunken state until I dozed off (hoping I was a quick and heavy sleeper), and then begin fondling more than my ass!

Talk about springing from the bed to see what was the matter? I nearly leapt from the bed 'cause *I knew* what was the matter!

"You know what, Monty?" I said. "This bed isn't big enough for the both of us after all. I'm going back to the couch bed. I'll sleep on top of the covers, and then fold everything back up in the morning. The maids will never have a clue anyone has used it. I don't think that'll be a problem, do you?"

Monty said, "Just don't open up the bed and crawl inside it." He saw no way of objecting over my sleeping on top of the hide-a-bed. He could tell my mind was made up.

"Night, Monty," I said. I found a blanket in the closet and pulled it over me, hoping to protect myself from the cold air that poured out of the air conditioning unit underneath the hotel room window next to me. A couple of nights of being too cold would not hurt me, as long as I would soon be a safe distance away from Monty.

"G'night, young fella'," Monty grunted from the other side of the room, a few seconds before emitting his first prolonged snoring sounds.

Thanks to the company accountant, my first night in Alabama afforded only sporadic periods of rest rather than the deep sleep my body craved. In spite of my disgruntlement, I lie awake and chuckled to myself when I recalled a story from Herman Melville's *Moby Dick*, about the rookie whaler, Ishmael, who was forced to share a bed in a cold and crowded Whaler's Inn with a smelly harpooner named Quiqueg. The large and unsavory man smoked a tomahawk-shaped pipe in bed, woke up in the morning with his arms locked in tight embrace around Ishmael, and shaved his beard with the pointed end of his finely sharpened harpoon. Melville's masterful introduction of the character Quiqueg went on for the better part of two chapters with great detail about the bizarre bedding down experience.

Perhaps my experience in Monty's bed had not been so bad by comparison. And perhaps I had misread Monty's intentions. Was I completely paranoid? I was too tired to think about it any longer.

* * *

In the middle of the night, I lay on my back looking up toward the ceiling, afraid to give in to my need for sleep. Suddenly, I heard something in the bathroom. Could it be that Monty had gone in for a piss break? The toilet flushed, the door cracked open, and the bathroom light shone through momentarily. There was just enough light that I could see the outline of a young woman wearing a teddy style negligee. She reached back and turned out the bathroom light before I got a look at her face, yet I could still discern the outline of her body as she slowly walked past the foot of Monty's bed and toward the sofa bed I occupied. I hoped the small amount of light that leaked in from the parking lot through the drawn curtains behind me was enough that I could get another look at her after my eyes adjusted.

She came slowly towards me, and I felt her sit down on the edge of the sofa bed next to me. I still could not see her face, but I could tell that her long hair was draped over her left shoulder, and it nearly reached down to her breast. Without a hint of shyness, she leaned over and kissed my lips softly. I reached up instinctively, put my hands on her shoulders and returned her kiss. Her body slipped effortlessly under the flannel blanket I had draped over myself.

I must have momentarily fallen asleep, so soundly that I hadn't noticed when this lovely woman had entered the room. I hoped that Monty hadn't been awakened either when she came in from the outside, nor as she emerged from the bathroom and walked past his bed towards me. She didn't seem concerned about the presence of a third person in the room as she continued to kiss me, her tongue soft and wet, easing into my mouth with a velvety smoothness that made me want her with every living cell in my body. Aware that my penis was becoming erect, she eased her right hand down and began to stroke me gently, cupping my balls in the palm of her hand between slow, gentle up and down strokes. I wanted to explode, but feeling my extreme arousal, she removed her hand and slowly started to kiss her way down my quivering body. Her kisses were warm and moist on my abdomen.

Who was this amazing goddess? Was this yet another initiation surprise, after the unpleasantness of Monty's attempts to fondle my ass? Had Monty felt guilty, and decided to make up for his antics by calling for this gorgeous young woman to pay me a visit in the middle of the night? "No," I thought. Surely that could not be. I had been awake most of the night, so I would have heard Monty making a phone call.

The thought suddenly occurred to me that Monty might enjoy watching and listening as couples made love, so he might have been lying in his bed masturbating at that very moment. But I couldn't have cared less whether Monty was lying in his bed playing with himself while listening to us in the darkness, as long as he didn't interfere with the pleasure I was feeling.

My penis felt like a hot steel poker as the beautiful mystery woman eased her way under the covers and pulled down my jockey shorts with her soft feminine hands. Wasting no time, she gently kissed the head of my cock. I sighed with absolute pleasure, trying to keep the sounds muted as she took me in and began to suck ever so gently. I wanted to cum, but she was so good at this that she knew how to make it last. Her mouth was hot, wet and slick, and her tongue was as soft as silk as she eased back toward the head of my penis, her tongue moving gently up the sensitive underside and back down again. I would cum very soon, despite her intuitive efforts to forestall my orgasm. Suddenly, she began kissing her way back up my torso as slowly and gently as she had kissed her way downward a few heavenly minutes before. She made sensual kissing sounds that sent shivers through me, and she caressed my throbbing cock with her hand as she had done before. This time, she was careful not to touch the head, but stroked the lower shaft, then wrapped her fingers firmly around the base to hold me off a bit longer. Her kisses eventually moved upward and reached the level of my nipples. She stopped to brush her soft lips against them one at a time to tease me. I squeezed her soft, feminine shoulders with my hands, and rubbed the soft skin of her back. This no longer felt like Dothan, Alabama; I was in heaven!

I had yet to get a look at this wonderful creature's face, but every cell of my excited body was eager to look into her eyes. Suddenly, the top of her head crested outside the blanket, and moments later I saw a face. To my absolute horror, it wasn't her face at all, but Monty's large grinning face peering down at me like a fat, sexually aroused Cheshire cat. I sat up in the bed and yelled, "*You fucking bastard!*"

My heart was pounding so hard that I thought it would come out of my chest any second. I reached over, turned on the lamp next to the hide-a-bed, and looked over at Monty, who was sound asleep as an innocent choirboy.

No sensual goddess had visited me at all. It was only a dream born of complete physical exhaustion! I turned off the lamp so I would not awaken Monty, then slowly felt my way to the bathroom to relieve the pain in my throbbing bladder. My heart was pounding so hard as I crept past the foot of Monty's bed that I was afraid it would awaken him. I wasn't sure whether my dream had been triggered by my need to urinate, or the result of my fear that Monty would try to molest me during the night. All I knew for sure was that the dream might have been the wettest and stickiest of my entire life had it not been for a seriously distended bladder!

* * *

Despite my encounter with Monty and the bizarre dream that followed, I survived my first night's initiation as a member of the QM team. I passed my first test, and I had not overreacted by screaming my way out of the hotel room like a teenager being pursued by a sexual predator. Monty might have been a bit overly friendly, but he did not strike me as a sexual predator!

9.

My first day on the job as a Quality Melon packer couldn't have come soon enough. After my night in L.V. Rosemont's hotel room, I was more than ready to be away from him, regardless of how little I'd slept. I was confident that my body could recover from the lack of sleep, and I would be able to face a hard day's work.

I got out of bed and brushed my teeth at the vanity sink outside the bathroom while Monty was taking his morning shower. I then finished dressing, and slipped out into the Alabama morning that greeted me with a bright blue sky above and hot asphalt underneath my feet. I stretched to relieve the stiffness in my joints and muscles. As I left the hotel room behind, I noticed that Aubrey Jensen was just coming out of his hotel room. He paused to light his first outdoor cigarette of the day, then walked toward his car and began to cough. I guessed that he had already smoked a couple of cigarettes while he was getting ready, yet I knew that his first drag outside would make him cough. Sure enough, it set off a coughing spasm; the telltale sound of a serious smoker. His coughing ended with a deep gagging sound that heralded the early stages of emphysema. I walked toward Aubrey's car and greeted him just as he spit out a disgusting ball of phlegm. Aubrey must have wondered why I was so eager to get out of Monty's hotel room and begin my first day of work.

Aubrey nodded in my direction and mumbled something that vaguely sounded like, "mornin'." Then he explained to me that I would be riding to Holcomb with his foreman, Joe Harper, who would be out in a few minutes. Aubrey said he had some phone calls to make, so he wouldn't be driving to Holcomb until later. He had pointed Joe out to me the evening before at the farmer's co-op, but only from a distance. Joe had been busy performing his quality control over the melons as they passed in front of him on the co-op's conveyor system, so Aubrey had not interrupted him to make an introduction.

It wasn't long after Aubrey went back to his hotel room that Joe Harper came out of his room and greeted me.

"Hi, name's Joe Harper. Aubrey tells me you're the new guy from Indiana. Let's get in my wagon here, and we'll be on our way to the salt mines. Hop in, I don't keep it locked."

The Melon Boys

Joe Harper opened the driver's side door of his 1964 Ford station wagon. The wagon was maroon with fake wood grain trim, the kind of station wagon that my friends and I called a "woody," because it resembled the older wagons from the 1930s and 40s that were decorated with real wood trim. I opened the front passenger's side door and got in.

Joe Harper, aged 55, was a portly but strong looking 5'10" and 225 pounds. Not flabby in the least, he sported a full head of silver hair that was fashioned into a perfectly groomed flat top haircut. The shape of his head and the texture of his hair made it appear that he had been born with that hairstyle. I was envious of men who could grow good flat tops, because I had tried growing them as a young teenager but could never get it right. After applying what seemed to be a ½ quart of butch wax to make my hair stand up straight, I would look into the mirror 15 minutes later only to find that my would-be flat top had reattached itself to the contour of my head. While other guys had perfectly "trained" hair that resembled the top of a birthday cake, my hair clung to an anti flat top growth pattern that left each of my feeble attempts looking like buzz-cuts with a bald spot on top of my head.

As Joe started his car engine, he looked at me and smiled. His friendly face and ruddy complexion put me instantly at ease.

"So, what got you all fired up about comin' down here to pack melons? The money, like most of 'em?"

I nodded in the affirmative, and Joe continued.

"I bet you were hopin' I was the quiet type, so you could close your eyes and catch a few more winks on the way to Holcomb. Well, I hate to tell you, but I'm just the opposite of Aubrey. He's a man of few words, kinda' keeps his thoughts to himself. But me, I'm just happy to be alive every morning and I'm ready to greet the new day the second my feet hit the floor. It's in the evening that I get quiet. I'm not much of a night owl, I guess you might say."

Joe looked over in my direction and smiled, but did not slow down.

"You don't seem in the mood to talk, so let me tell you a few things about myself. I started out as a packer and truck driver, and played the watermelon haulin' game to the hilt like most of the old timers in this business did. I owned my own fleet of trucks, 12 big rigs in all, and had dreams of owning a lot more and building a produce trucking empire, then branchin' out to all kinds of hauling besides produce. But after a really bad year, when two of my rigs were wrecked by drivers who went to sleep at the wheel—one of those drivers was killed—I sold out of the trucking business and took this job as field supervisor for Quality Melon. My job description is as broad as I am." Joe laughed. "I guess you could say I'm a jack of all trades, and master of none."

As Joe talked about his past, I realized that truckers in the 1960s were relatively pampered compared with the hard driven men in the early days of the interstate watermelon hauling business. Old produce men like Joe had to be everything, from buyers to packers and haulers. According to my dad, the "melon boys" in the early days of the business were "men's men," who were not afraid of backbreaking work and thrived on very little sleep. They went out to the farms and determined when the melons were right for picking, then they cut deals with farmers. They packed their own trailer loads, and after the melons were loaded, they crawled into the cockpits of their semis and drove all night to deliver the melons to northern markets. In the pre-supermarket era, truckers either sold their melons to wholesale produce handlers at a discounted price, or went store-to-store and peddled them to locally owned groceries.

The old time melon boys could be favorably compared to the old timers of major league baseball. They did what they did for the love of the game, and did it without an elaborate support staff, and for a modest rate of pay.

The melon business in the 1930s and 1940s was built on the sweat of a handful of over-achievers. These men were strong of character and dynamic personalities; men about whom stories were told. Some burned out early and failed to make it, but others paid their dues and went on to build successful wholesale produce companies.

My own uncle Big Boy built his wholesale produce business literally by the sweat of his brow. In 1935, Big Boy purchased a Chevy straight truck that could legally haul up to 10 tons. As a young man, he worked day and night packing loads of melons, then taking to the road and driving for 8 or 10 hours at a stretch to deliver the melons to Chicago, Detroit, and other northern cities during the month of August. Eventually, he built up enough capital to construct the first wing of his produce wholesale warehouse, and by the mid 1950s, he began contracting with other independent truckers to take over the packing and hauling. From that point on, Big Boy stayed home and brokered the sale of produce to fledgling grocery store chains for a middleman's commission. Ultimately, as the supermarket phenomenon began to grow, he became the owner of the largest packing shed in Southern Indiana, and ran a year-round operation. During the summer months, he bought and brokered locally grown truck crops such as sweet potatoes, sweet corn, tomatoes and melons. In the winter months, he purchased bulk tomatoes, lettuce, and citrus products grown in the South, then repackaged them for shipping to local groceries and supermarket chains in the northern states.

As was the case with old time baseball legends, Big Boy and his melon-hauling cohorts had plenty of war stories to tell about their early days in the business. One of his favorite stories was about the night his truck was hijacked at 2:00 A.M., while he was driving across southern Illinois toward St. Louis on old interstate highway 50. A car passed him going in a westerly direction along the two-lane highway, and another pulled up close behind him. The driver of the car in front of him began to apply his brakes, and when Big Boy flashed his lights at the car, it sped up again and widened the gap. At the same time, the car behind him stayed so close to his truck's rear bumper that Big Boy was hardly able to see its headlights. Eventually, Big Boy became so irritated with the repeated slowdown and acceleration of the car in front that he pulled off the highway onto the narrow gravel shoulder. This was exactly what the occupants of the two cars wanted him to do.

Immediately the car in front of him and the car behind him closed ranks. Before he could get out of the truck, Big Boy saw that the two drivers were brandishing handguns. They quickly flanked his cab, one standing on the running board of the driver's side and the other on the passenger's side. Both men had donned half masks like those worn by the Lone Ranger, and the one on the driver's side of Big Boy's truck demanded that he step outside.

Big Boy always kept both doors of his cab locked, and his cab windows were rolled up that evening because it had turned cold out. Pretending he had not heard the command from the highjacker on the driver's side, Big Boy slowly rolled down his side window with his left hand. With his right hand, he reached for an open Thermos of hot coffee that lay on the seat between his legs. The engine of his truck was still running, and the hijacker screamed at him to turn off the engine and get out of the truck immediately. There was no doubt that Big Boy could hear his command through the partially opened truck window.

"OK," Big Boy yelled back. But rather than reaching for the ignition key to shut down the engine, he secured his grip on the Thermos with his right hand, and as the highjacker on the passenger's side of the cab watched, he dowsed the man outside the driver's window with hot coffee. As the other hijacker pounded on the opposite window with the butt end of his pistol in hopes of breaking into the cab, Big Boy slammed his right foot down on the accelerator of the powerful Chevy engine. The vehicle lurched forward, ramming its front right bumper against the left rear bumper of the car in front. The enormous cast-iron truck bumper nearly destroyed the rear end of the car in front of it, as it knocked the vehicle to the side. The stunned would-be hijacker on the driver's side of the semi fell backward, but managed to land on his feet, his face and eyes still burning from the hot coffee. The man on the opposite side leapt off the running board. Both men recovered to watch Big Boy's tail lights move away and grow smaller. The looks on their faces were similar to the looks of the stupid bad guys in a Roy Rogers or Lone Ranger episode; foiled again by the clever hero. The two would-be bandits gave up their attempt to rob Big Boy of his precious produce cargo that night, and he never saw them on highway 50 again. "Rank amateurs," Big Boy would forever call them each time he repeated the story.

* * *

"Anyway," said Joe, "part of my job as a jack of all trades for this company is directing traffic at the co-op; backing semi's into their proper spaces to be loaded. After the trucks are in place, I assign a packer to each one. Once I've got things running smoothly at the co-op, I go out to the farms around Holcomb and make sure the melons are ripe, ready to be picked, and free of disease before I authorize farmers to collect them up and haul them into the co-op for loading. That's the hardest part of the job. A fella' really has to keep an eye on these farmers. This is their livelihood, and they'll do almost anything to get rid of their melon crop when prices are high, like they are right now for Holcomb melons. Ever tried to tell a farmer his crop can't be sold because of anthrax? Believe me, you don't want to! I've had a couple of farmers so pissed off that they damned near shot me; and these ole' boys all have gun racks in their trucks so they wouldn't have to go to a whole lot of trouble to shoot you. It's bad enough to negotiate with them over the price of melons, but that's a whole lot easier than telling a farmer he's sittin' on a total crop failure!"

* * *

At dinner the evening before, Aubrey had referred to Joe as the company "strawboss," "the real deal," and a "good ole' boy" from Florida. "I don't know what the fuck we'd do if we lost him," Aubrey had said. "Farmers and truckers respect him, and that goes a long way when you're runnin' a company like ours! He directs traffic, keeps our packers in line, and runs the public relations end of the operation with the farmers. Joe is the most salt-a'-the-earth guy I've ever met. He's lived through every angle of this fuckin' business, and he knows it better than me and my partner put together. He ain't never moody; just the same every goddam day as he was the day before. Ya' gotta' have that kinda' guy around to keep everybody happy. Never seen anybody like him. You'll get along with him just fine. If ya' don't, it'll be your fault."

* * *

As we continued our journey toward Holcomb, Joe suddenly changed the subject away from his own job duties.

"Probably the best man we have on the packin' crew is the fella' called Shorty. I don't mean he's the best packer, but he's the best man we've got, all around. I'm sure Aubrey introduced you to him last night. His name is Samuel Williams, from Ocala, Florida. He was born somewhere in the late 1920s, and raised by sharecropping parents. Shorty was too young to serve in one of the all black Army units during WWII, and he missed out on the Korean War because of the accident that cost him a good piece of his left arm."

"How did he lose his arm?" I asked.

"Bad car accident," replied Joe. "Most people don't know anything about it, but Shorty told me the whole story once. It seems there was a logging truck, his car, and a second automobile involved. A broken log chain caused a payload of several tons of timber to roll onto Shorty's car. A family of three from Ohio was following close behind him, and Shorty and the Ohio car were both passing the timber hauler when the big logging chains broke loose. Before Shorty realized how bad he was hurt, the adrenaline rushing through his body took over."

"What did he do?" I asked.

"Well, Shorty is a helluva strong man," said Joe. "He freed himself from his own car and rushed toward the vehicle with the Ohio folks in it. The car was in flames, but that didn't slow Shorty down at all. He pulled the family out, one at a time, and dragged them each a safe distance away with his one good arm. Just before their car exploded, he placed the third one (the father of the family) on the ground next to his wife and daughter. Then Shorty collapsed from his own loss of blood."

"Jesus Christ," I said. "That would qualify a person for some kinda' medal where I come from!"

"It'd qualify a white man for a medal here in the South too," said Joe.

Joe continued with his story.

"By the time ole' Shorty regained consciousness in the hospital, the white family he'd saved were safely back home in Ohio, and Shorty was missing most of his left arm. He never heard a word of thanks from the Ohio family he'd saved. Not a single fuckin' word! When the trucker who had been driving the load of logs reported to the police what Shorty'd done to save those folks, the police made a notation in the official accident report. It read: 'One of the injured at the scene (a Negro man named Samuel Williams) assisted an out-of-state family in escaping a flaming vehicle.' You might say the recognition Shorty had coming, well . . . never came."

"Damn, makes you wonder why blacks aren't more bitter than they are towards whites." Joe didn't respond.

"When Shorty recovered, he moved on with his life right away. In spite of losing a football career and the chance to complete his college education, he rose above disappointment and bitterness and returned to the only thing he knew before college—sharecropping. He moved back to the farm in Florida and, in no time, taught himself to handle a watermelon with the same strength and coordination as could any man with two good arms. When Aubrey met him, he immediately offered Shorty a job packing melons full-time for the summer, and Shorty's been with us ever since."

"What does a guy like Shorty do when he's not packin' melons?" I asked.

"In the off-season, he goes back home where he's active in his local community in Florida. He cares about his people, and he dedicates himself to helpin' the less fortunate. His status as a former college athlete opens a lot of doors where he comes from. People listen to what he has to say, and most of what he has to say is based on strong convictions: 'God heps them that hep theirself,' Shorty likes to say. He's never relied on handouts and has little sympathy for people of his own race who do. Even those with certain disabilities can learn, like he has, to make it on their own. Shorty has a real passion for showing the way to others."

"Shorty doesn't talk about his background or the things he does in the off season. As far as most of the QM staff is concerned, he's a melon packer and a damned good one, but that's the extent of his talent. Aubrey has the citrus season back in Florida. Johnny, Don Jr., William and you have colleges to go back to, and Monty has the QM business office to run year-round. But what men like Shorty do in the winter is a mystery to most people in the company, besides Aubrey and me. Maybe it's best that way. Like I said, Shorty's not one to advertise when it comes to his private life."

10.

When Joe and I pulled into the dusty parking area next to the packing shed, I noticed that the other packers were already there, and empty semis had begun to arrive. The drivers knew that Joe Harper would try to load them in the order of their arrival at the co-op, so they tried to be there early in the morning. Even though most of the drivers were exhausted from driving all night to arrive in Holcomb, they would not earn another red cent until they delivered their next load of melons up north. As a driver once told me, "If them wheels ain't turnin' and my eyes ain't burnin', then I ain't earnin!"

Most of the trailers that arrived that morning were the closed box type, but a few were open tops, normally used for hauling bulk grain such as corn and wheat.

Local farmers were also arriving early, wagons overflowing with loads of shiny dew-covered watermelons. Soon, the melons would be offloaded onto the fast moving conveyors to begin their journey toward designated trailers.

The atmosphere at the co-op felt like the opening scene of a Hollywood movie; a saga that traced a wealthy southern family from the Civil War era when cotton was king, to modern times and the advent of more diverse cash crops including the watermelon. While the Confederate Army boiled down watermelon as a source of sugar and molasses, interstate trade of watermelons was almost non-existent until the advent of the interstate highway system, which allowed the fruit to be transported rapidly over great distances.

It felt good to be a part of this scene, and I had butterflies in my stomach as I got out of Joe Harper's station wagon. As Joe and I walked across the sandy parking area, I saw Lonny, William, and Don Jr. standing in front of the co-op building. Shorty and Bobby Leeds were sitting in Shorty's Buick with the radio blasting and the two front doors flung wide open. They smiled as I walked past with Joe. I gave them a friendly wave, and Joe glanced over toward Shorty's car and nodded "Good Morning" to the two men.

Slick had arrived on time, and was leaning against his Chevrolet just as he had been the evening before, only this time he was fully clothed. A cigarette barely held on between his wrinkled lips. He appeared hung over, as I'd been told he would be every morning, and his body seemed limp like the scarecrow in the *Wizard of Oz*. His eyes were glazed over and the whites looked an unhealthy reddish-yellow. They were deep set in their sockets, like two cigarette burns in a pinkish gray blanket. I couldn't decide whether he looked worse after a hard day's work, or a hard night of drinking.

"Mornin' Slick," Joe said as he walked past Slick's car. "Girlfriend keep ya' up last night?" Joe always made it a point to say good morning to Slick, even when he was preoccupied with the business of the day. Perhaps Slick's advanced age had earned him a measure of respect if for no other reason than his continued survival.

"Shit yeah," said Slick. He looked numb, but he smiled a surprisingly toothy smile out of the corner of his wrinkled mouth. I could not understand how his cigarette kept from falling on the ground as he spoke.

Joe turned back to me and said, "This hooligan's got a different woman in every town along the trail, and most of 'em are fat and ugly! I swear to Christ, they're not the kinda' ladies a self-respecting fella' would take home to momma." Although Joe's comment was intended for my benefit, he looked directly at Slick and smiled broadly as he spoke.

Slick's shoulders shook in a silent laugh, triggering a wrenching smoker's cough that lasted 10 or 15 seconds and made my lungs hurt in sympathy.

"Shit, Joe, you're just jealous," Slick said. He laughed audibly this time, and his laugh triggered a second coughing spell that lasted longer than the first. I could have sworn his lungs were about to collapse any second.

"You better believe it, you wiry old fart," Joe said. Slick's comment about Joe's jealousy was the first thing that made Joe belly laugh that morning. Joe said, "These skinny little guys can out-screw any big man any day of the week. Slick is living proof of that theory." Then Joe smiled. "Well, it looks like he's still alive, but I haven't checked him for a pulse lately."

Slick smiled this time, avoiding laughter that might set off another coughing spasm.

I had now heard of Slick's sexual prowess from both Aubrey and Joe, so I accepted it as the truth.

I kept pace with Joe, who was all business the second his feet hit the co-op steps. He was ready to direct the trailers against the building and assign packers to their first loads of the day. As Joe ascended the platform, he went straight to the electrical power switch that started the noisy conveyor system. As soon as he pushed the switch to the "on" position, the noise grew like a symphony of clanging metal parts, reaching a crescendo and sustaining it for hours on end. The only words that seemed appropriate to describe the occasion were the well-known words of Tony Hulman, as he started the Indy 500 race each year: "gentlemen, start your engines."

Joe handed oilcans to Lonny and Don Jr., and told them to check for squeaky spots along the conveyor line, and squirt some oil on them as needed.

I climbed up the concrete steps and onto the platform behind Joe. He told me to go inside the office and wait for Monty who would provide me with some papers to fill out. As I walked toward the office, I noticed a tall, red vending machine just outside the co-op office door. Had the machine not been directly in my path, I would not have felt the urge to drink a cold bottle of Coca-Cola for my breakfast. But there it was, and I happened to have 25 cents in my pocket. "What the hell?" I thought, "my mouth feels dry, and a cold Coca-Cola would be just the thing!" I put my money into the machine and it dispensed my first bottle of cold Alabama Coke. I located the opener on the side of the machine and inserted the neck of the bottle, then lowered the bottle until I heard the pleasing sound of the cap popping off. I wondered if the nickname "pop" that we used for soft drinks back in Indiana had come about because of that sound.

After filling out my W-4 form, and completing the rest of my paperwork to become an official employee of the Quality Melon Corporation, I would report back to Joe for my first work assignment. In the meantime, Joe would meet with the rest of the packers to get them started on their assignments for the day.

11.

Monty arrived at the Holcomb Farmer's Co-op with his usual flourish, and parked his enormous Buick Electra 225 convertible in front of the packing shed office, like he owned the place. He got out of his car and glanced around the parking lot, focusing for a second on Shorty's black Buick Electra, as if to reassure himself that his Detroit leviathan was prettier, cleaner, shinier, and more expensive than any automobile a black man could afford. If anyone on the planet would begrudge Shorty's ownership of a fine automobile, it would be Monty.

Neither Joe Harper nor the other packers greeted Monty as he walked past them on his way up to the Quality Melon temporary office. Monty didn't care about the formalities because he was preoccupied with the dust on his maroon alligator wingtips. He stared down disgustedly at the light tan stains that had been left by the sand of the parking lot. The look on his face spoke volumes as he stomped his feet up and down like a spoiled little boy. When he was satisfied that the remaining sand particles did not pose a threat to his fancy footwear, he walked over to open the office door and begin his work day.

Motioning with authority for me to step inside, Monty unlocked the office door, looked me in the eye, and greeted me as if nothing had transpired between the two of us the night before. I politely greeted him back, then went inside his office and sat down in the Grange Hall style folding chair that was situated in front of his desk. Perhaps nothing *had* happened between Monty and me the night before. But as much as I wanted to believe that, I still felt that Monty had truly wanted something to happen.

Monty's office was cold and clammy like he kept his room at the Dothan Holiday Inn. He had left the window air conditioning unit turned up to full blast before leaving the office the evening before. The aging unit had kept the air cold but had not removed enough moisture. Without looking up from the desk, he handed me some papers to sign, and then he lit a cigarette. He smelled as if he had dowsed himself with English Leather after-shave lotion before leaving his hotel room. I liked English Leather, but the thought of Monty drenching his pallid and corpulent carcass in it nearly made my skin crawl.

We were the only two people in the office, but Monty still looked around as if to make sure nobody was listening. Then he checked the office door to make certain it was shut. "Jesus H. Fucking Christ, I'm so goddam hung over. Why did you let me drink so much last night?" He gave out a silly giggle.

I couldn't think of anything to say, but it didn't matter because Monty was not expecting an answer. All he hoped to accomplish was to convince me that he had not been fully in control of his faculties the night before. He wanted to plant the notion in my mind that he was not fully responsible for the little ass-grabbing incident. I thought it was a very clever tactic on his part. He was smart enough to stay several steps ahead of others, and clever enough to cover his tracks when necessary. All it took was a single allegation by the wrong person, and Monty's future employment as an accountant could have been in jeopardy. Since the night before had been my first night in Alabama as a QM employee, I probably was not the person who could get him fired, but he was covering his bases nonetheless.

"Now listen to me young man. You watch out for those nigger packers." Monty seemed to be skipping the business part of my in-processing in favor of providing me with a bit of avuncular advice. "Don't get me wrong, our niggers are nice boys, like Shorty, but they still go out and drink up their pay the way all niggers do. When they come in on Monday, they're hung over real bad, and broke. They might take a notion to pick your pocket if you're not on your guard. If they take a likin' to you, they might not take your money, but they'll damn sure hit you up for money come Monday morning after pay day. Once you loan a nigger money, he'll come back at you with a whole raft of excuses, but he ain't never gonna' pay you back. Mark my words, and just be careful, is all I'm sayin'. Don't put your wallet down where you can't keep an eye on it, and for God's sake, don't loan a dime to a nigger!"

I tried to stay focused on the papers in front of me, and tried not to react to Monty's so-called advice. If there had been a problem with Shorty and Bobby, Aubrey or Joe Harper surely would have mentioned it to me right away. I felt sure of that. But Joe Harper had said nothing but good things, especially about Shorty.

"Oh, another thing you need ta' keep in mind. Don't go runnin' around with Bobby Leeds and Shorty in your free time! I don't know how they treat nigger lovers where you come from, but they don't take kindly to that down here. If anything goes wrong and you find yourself mixed up with these niggers, you come to me right away . . . hear? I just happen to have a cousin who is an Alabama State Trooper, and around these parts that's as good as gold. Anything that happens when it comes ta' niggers can be handled, as long as you've got a relative who's a lawman. Shit, you could kill a goddam nigger and never spend a day in jail if you've got trooper connections. You know the old joke about the Alabama State trooper that found a dead nigger down by the river with 15 feet of log chain wrapped around him, and 10 bullet holes in the back of his head?"

I kept my eyes on the paperwork in front of me, but I could tell that Monty was not prepared to go on without some sort of response from me.

"No, I don't believe I've heard that one," I said.

"Well, the trooper looked down at the dead nigger, then looked over at his partner and said, 'Damndest case of suicide I ever saw'!" Monty laughed.

I didn't respond.

"I don't suppose I'll have much chance to hang around with anybody after work," I said. "I plan on going back to the hotel and resting after my work's done here. That way, I figure I'll keep my nose clean."

"That's probably a good idea. This God forsaken place don't have much to offer you after workin' hours anyway, except trouble if a man ain't careful. They have a saying around here, and I think there's a grain of truth in it: "Nothing good ever happens after midnight." So you're better off keepin' a low profile. The other white packers are good boys, so stick with them and you'll be OK for the most part. You'll have some time off, mostly on Sundays, since the farmers down here in the Bible Belt don't believe in packing melons on 'The Lord's Day.' Me, I ain't into all that Baptist crap, even though my momma raised me as a Southern Baptist. Anyway, when you young fellas have some time off, you should head on down to the beach at Panama City or somethin,' or find a place to play some golf. You play golf?"

I didn't respond to his question because he handed me more papers to sign. I wondered how many more papers he was going to give me before we were finished.

"I asked if you played golf," Monty said.

I said, "No, I haven't played anything but miniature golf back home, usually for something to do on a date. Drive-in movies and miniature golf. 'Putt-Putt' is the big excitement in the town I come from. Regular golf is mostly for guys with money, like doctors and lawyers who can afford to join the Elk's Club. It's not really that popular with farm boys like me. We're more into baseball and stuff like that."

"Well, maybe you can talk Lonny into gettin' his old man's car, and drivin' some of you fellas to the beach at Panama City. You should see the ocean while you're down here, or 'The Gulf' as it's called in this part of the country. I don't suppose you've seen a whole lot of water, coming from a land-locked place like Indiana. They say the white sand beaches along the Florida panhandle are some of the prettiest in the world."

I wondered why Monty was being so friendly and talkative. Perhaps he was afraid I would say something to Aubrey about the pats on the ass he'd given me the night before. If I reacted in a halfway friendly way to his small talk, he would conclude that I was the forgiving type, and all would be OK in his private world. I was beginning to think he walked a fine line.

I left Monty's office, and I was back inside the main co-op building where I found Joe Harper and the others. To my surprise, Joe was still talking with Lonny, Don Jr., and William. Slick, Shorty and Bobby Leeds had already started to work. The three of them required very little instruction.

"Hey there, new guy," said Don Jr. He was the first to acknowledge my return from Monty's office.

"Hey Don," I said. "How's it going?" I greeted them with a smile.

Don Jr. said, "We're all just fine and dandy here." He had a mischievous look in his eye. "Did ole' Monty get any last night? Seems like you spent a lot a' time in his office. The two of you gettin' along pretty well so far?"

The three could hold it in no longer. They simultaneously burst into out-of-control laughter. I was suddenly aware that my first night in Alabama had been a pre-planned initiation rite.

"Thanks a lot, you fuckers!" Suddenly I was not amused over the fact that I'd been set up to spend the night with Monty as part of a prank. Having been through fraternity initiation, I was familiar with hazing rituals, but I was not a big fan of them.

I said, "I thought it was my cute ass that got Monty all excited! By the way, any of you fuckers let him blow you on your first night in town?"

The three packers laughed harder than ever, but this time their laughter was not at my expense. They were actually laughing *with* me. My quick retort had caught them off guard, and I could tell that I had passed my first test. Any show of weakness on my part would probably have guaranteed additional tests of my manhood. But they could tell from my reaction that I was man enough to take it, and that was what they'd wanted to find out.

"I've gotta' tell ya' dude," laughed Lonny, "Aubrey said he'd let you stay in the extra bed in his own room last night, but the rest of us made him go through with the 'Monty Ritual.' Ain't a new packer in this crew that's gonna' get out of Monty's rite of the first night! That's just the way it is! Now you're one of us. Put her here, partner," Lonny said, extending his right hand towards me.

"Thanks!" I said, as I shook Lonny's hand. "You fuckers are real pals!" We all laughed.

Joe walked over and placed his large, thick hand on my shoulder and pointed to the back end of a trailer. He then repeated the action, placing his hand on Lonny's shoulder, then on Don Jr.'s, signaling to each of them which trailer was theirs for the morning. He didn't assign a trailer to William, but asked him to come along with me and toss melons off the conveyor.

As we walked toward our respective trailers, William and I went past the trailer to which Slick had been assigned. Slick swung into action as soon as the first melon had flown off the conveyor, like Joe Namath on a Sunday afternoon. The analogy to Joe Namath was not far off, because it didn't matter that Slick had been awake most of the night making sloppy drunk love to his local girlfriend. He had shown up on this morning, as he did every morning, and he was ready to sling watermelons faster than any two packers could. Slick was a professional, and when the conveyor was powered up he knew it was show time.

* * *

I had the feeling that William would be my least favorite member of the Quality Melon staff. Don Jr. obviously had a good sense of humor, and Lonny was quiet, quick witted, and a regular guy. Lonny seemed to enjoy hard work, in spite of the fact that he was a rich kid who could have stayed home in Cincinnati and spent the summer playing golf with his buddies. William, on the other hand, had a sinister look about him and seemed overly defensive, like he didn't feel that he belonged. It was easy to see he didn't want to be a part of the melon-packing scene. Nonetheless, he and I would be working together for at least one morning, and as we made our way toward our assigned trailer, it occurred to me that we could probably hit it off. At least, I would make the effort to get along with him, because I had no choice. My genetic make-up, combined with my small town background had programmed me to "get along," even when the person I was getting along with was a spoiled, bigoted southern boy.

It was obvious that William lacked the muscle power to succeed as a watermelon packer. He was very thin, 5 feet 11 inches tall, and the typical 150 pound weakling. He looked like the "before" pictures in the ads on the back covers of comic books; the classic milquetoast who dreamed of being pumped up into a "He-Man," if only he would mail in $100 for a revolutionary diet supplement and a set of dumb bells. But in William's case, I wasn't sure whether he wanted to build up his body if it meant having to work to do it. He seemed more the type who would hire somebody else to work out *for* him!

As William and I approached our assigned semi trailer, I saw two farmers standing next to the conveyor system. Above the noise, I could tell they were discussing the watermelon crop in Holcomb. They seemed in good spirits, which was typical of farmers in the early morning hours. The first wave of physical tiredness and melancholy didn't come until late morning when their hearty breakfast began to wear off. Then they would lament the lackluster melon prices, the cool weather in northern states, the impersonal treatment they were getting from Aubrey, and whatever else came to mind. There were definite emotional patterns to a farmer's day, but at day's end, they always wished each other a good night and returned home to a decent evening meal and the dream of better things to come. Farming was a profession of hopes and dreams, and when a farmer lost his ability to dream of a better day, he would cease to be a farmer and trade in his dream for a steady paycheck at a factory in the nearest large city. Many smalltime farmers where I came from had already abandoned their dreams and gone to work "for the other guy."

One of the two farmers who were standing near our trailer had brought along his small son, who stood next to his dad watching William and me as we prepared ourselves for the task at hand. When we got closer to the two farmers, the little boy (I guessed he was about 6 years old) started talking to us. He looked me directly in the eye as if he were a grown man, and asked; "How much y'all git paid when y'all gits paid?"

"Oh, on a good day they tell me I can make $60," I replied to the boy.

"Y'all think that's' 'nuf fur y'all when y'all gits paid?" The boy asked.

"Oh, I guess it's enough," I replied. I couldn't help laughing at the small boy's pure southern dialect, and his unabashed adult-like boldness. It occurred to me that the little boy was completely comfortable in this environment. At his age he was already certain he would be in this place, like his father, earning a decent living and talking about the watermelon business for the rest of his life.

* * *

Before and after each semi was loaded, truckers would drive their rigs across a truck scales so the empty and loaded weights could be established. These gargantuan truck scales were usually located at grain storage elevators, where bulk grain was hauled in by growers for sale on the commodities market. But watermelons were big enough business in Holcomb that co-op owners had invested in their own truck scales. This was an expensive piece of equipment that had to be housed in its own building, a large pole barn approximately 50 feet in length. Drivers pulled their rigs through the building carefully, so each of their axles could be weighed individually. A weigh master who sat inside an elevated booth waved drivers forward three separate times; once to place the steering axle squarely on the scales, a second time to position the drive axle, and a third time to weigh the trailer's rear axle. From his perch above semi level, the weigh master had a clear view of each tractor-trailer as it inched its way through the building. After the trailer was fully loaded, a final calculation was made to determine the weight of the melons on board. The driver would be compensated based upon the net weight of the produce, provided he delivered it safely. Each farmer who had been a party to loading the semi was compensated according to the number of melons he had contributed to the completed load.

The cooperative process of loading melons was more efficient than the system we had back home, which left each farmer to fend for himself. Farmers in Indiana were locked into a friendly competition with one another, as opposed to the "co-op-eration" here. Most farmers back home made certain they planted enough acres of melons to fill a semi-trailer each time they picked through their crop. Occasionally, when a melon farmer could not fill an entire trailer alone, the buyer would locate a smaller "straight truck." In case a straight truck could not be located, the buyer would send a full sized semi to the first farm to be partially loaded, and then the semi would be weighed in transit to the next farm so the contributing farmers could be accurately paid for their portion of the completed load. When partially filled trailers were sent to our farm, my dad would usually be a little perturbed. In his opinion, melon farmers should plant enough melons to pack out their own semis without the help of others.

From a melon packer's perspective, the process of hauling partially filled loads from one farm to another was a nightmare. The only load of melons that could be moved with any degree of success was a fully completed load with straw and boards packed tightly against the tail end of a fully loaded trailer. A partial load of melons in transit was like a one-sided pyramid, and the slightest movement of the trailer caused melons to shift and slide toward the back end of the trailer. After a partially loaded trailer was driven over a few miles of country roads, the tenuous pack was usually ruined. The best method of damage control during transport was to secure the partial load with trailer-width boards, lain on the floor of the trailer immediately behind the stack of melons and bolstering them from behind with several bales of straw weighing about 100 pounds each. The best bolstering job on the part of the most experienced packer was not enough to prevent the melons from shifting backwards as the semi moved from one farm to another, oftentimes crossing potholes and railroad tracks.

* * *

The driver of my assigned semi on my first morning in Holcomb was already snoring away in the sleeper compartment of his diesel-powered cab when William and I arrived. Compared with southern Indiana on melon packing day, there was not much interaction between farmers and truck drivers at the Holcomb co-op.

In spite of the reputation of the South as a place of friendly conversation, the businesslike atmosphere at the co-op was less personal than the almost festive atmosphere back in Indiana, where new loading technology had not been introduced. In fact, my parents were on a first name basis with every truck driver, packer and buyer who visited our farm. The mood of anticipation on melon packing day in Indiana mirrored the mood of primitive cultures known as "airplane people" in the Amazon, where entire tribes would stand on a hill and await the arrival of the airplane that periodically brought food, medicine and supplies essential to their basic survival. When the airplane was heard approaching in the distance, a great celebration ensued.

My family reacted much the same as the airplane people when a tractor-trailer rig approached our farm during watermelon season. A thrill of excitement shot through every stomach when we heard the roar of the powerful diesel engine approaching from a half mile away. "He's comin,' he's comin'" was the cry, as we scurried to get my dad. The power of the diesel and the size of the rig were awe-inspiring. For my father, it was not a quasi-religious experience that pumped up his adrenaline, but the realization that a long awaited payday had arrived. In addition to the money, the next most satisfying part of the process was that the fruits of his works would be hauled to a far away place for somebody else to enjoy. For this reason, his satisfaction did not end with the paycheck from the buyer, but extended to the nameless and faceless consumer on the other end who would enjoy what my father had nurtured and grown from a tiny seedling a few short months earlier.

* * *

Once William and I were inside our trailer at the Holcomb co-op, I took out my Barlow knife and cut the twine that bound two bales of straw. The co-op provided straw for padding material, so our trucker had stopped off next to the enormous stack of hay bales behind the co-op building and picked up six bales before Joe Harper had guided him into his assigned slot.

William's voice had a classic southern tone and cadence, and he projected an attitude of disdain for hard physical work. His family breeding had given him a sense of privilege that rendered him a clear misfit in this labor intensive environment. As we began our day's work, William felt the need to provide me with a bit of education about the South as he saw it.

"You know anything about the South?" William asked.

I was caught off-guard by his question.

"No, not a lot," I replied. "That's one of the reasons I wanted to come down and spend a summer here," I said.

"Well, there's a lot more to it than what your liberal college professors teach you up north. It's all a matter of historical perspective, I s'pose."

"What do you mean?" I asked.

"I mean, on things like slavery. What do they teach at your Midwestern College on the subject of slavery?"

"The usual stuff I guess. That it was a terrible institution because it took away the dignity of millions of people who were brought here from Africa against their will. Maybe it wasn't on a par with Hitler's mass murder of Jews during WWII, but it lasted a lot longer, and was evil in its own right."

William rolled his eyes to convey his disbelief over what I had just said.

"Damn! That's exactly what I'm talkin' about! Your liberal professors have a way of twistin' the truth around to where it's no longer anyways *close* to the truth. The truth is, Matt, that the slaves in the South were not all that unhappy with their place in life. Most of 'em had it better here than they *ever* had it back in Africa, and they were grateful to be here. Oh sure, they had to learn a new language and adopt a new religion, but the language was far superior to the ones they left behind, and Christianity was a whole lot better than the hysterical, pig-god-worshipping crap they left behind."

I didn't know how to react, and I was almost certain that the noise from the machinery would soon make it impossible for William to continue his yakking. But much to my surprise and disappointment, he increased the volume of his high-pitched voice and persisted in spite of the loud clatter of the melon conveyor.

"I'm tellin' you Matt, and you can take it to the bank . . . black people had it better in the old South than they've had it since you Yankees came down here and messed things up. If you keep your eyes opened and notice what goes on around here, you'll see that most of the blacks are lost and misguided, and they have very little purpose in life. That wasn't the case in the good ole' days. They knew who they were, and they knew their place."

Joe Harper turned on the directional switch to our section of the conveyor, and melons began making their way toward William at a rapid pace. He had no choice but to shut his mouth and get to work.

I said, "Make sure I'm looking at you before you toss these melons to me. I might be grabbin' a handful of straw or something, so make sure I'm ready for the next melon. If you need to stop the melons, all you have to do is throw that lever at the end of the conveyor, and they'll stop coming." I knew the feeling of being hit in the thigh or calf by the blunt end of a watermelon tossed by an inexperienced daydreamer, and it was not pleasant.

"Yeah, I think I can handle that," William replied loudly in a snotty tone of voice.

When the melons started passing from William's hands to mine, the art of packing came back to me without thought or effort. "Like riding a bicycle," I thought. I was a little surprised at how graceful the motions felt when the melons began passing through my hands. My only problem was William's lack of strength, because some of the melons he tossed fell just short of my hands, causing me to strain my back and arm muscles in order to reach back and catch them. I thought of how Slick might deal with a greenhorn like William. There was little doubt that William would be *wearing* the first melon he threw short of Slick's hands.

William attempted, all too successfully, to babble over the sound of the conveyor equipment for most of the morning as he clumsily tossed melons to me. He yelled until he became hoarse, but he kept chattering on. I tried to tune him out. An occasional nod in his direction was all I could manage.

"My great, great, great granddaddy was a proud slave owner," said William. "He had over 100 slaves on the family plantation in South Georgia before the Civil War came along. My great granddaddy, who knew a little bit about the situation, told me that the slaves on the family cotton plantation were very well cared for and most of them didn't want to leave after they had been declared 'Free Men.' They stayed around and became sharecroppers, living happily on the family plantation for the rest of their days. Great granddaddy said, 'it was the slaves' home and they thought of it as *their* plantation too.' They were more than welcome to stay as long as they saw fit."

The conveyor slowed down for a minute to accommodate a lull in the flow of melons, and suddenly I could hear myself think again.

"Well," I replied, "I guess that's the only life they knew. Probably woulda' made them insecure to pick up and leave."

William said, "That wasn't it at all." A hint of anger was in his voice. "They liked their lives and they knew they had it made. Nobody else would have provided for them as well as my ancestors did on the plantation, and they didn't want anything to do with the phony Yankee freedom y'all came down here and forced on them."

Once again, I didn't know what to say. Mercifully, the conveyor sped up again and William and I literally had our hands full of watermelons. I wanted William to focus on his work, not on teaching me about the glory days of the old South. While he seemed to be well versed in his point of view, he was not properly tending to the melons as they came off the conveyor belt. I thought out loud, "Is the rest of your family in denial about slavery too, or is it just you?"

"What?" William asked. He turned a bit pale and had the look of a man who had been sucker punched with a frying pan.

"You seem to have a closed mind on the issue of slavery," I said.

William said, "No sir, it's you Yankees who have closed minds! We know what it was all about, and it was not that bad. The slaves hated to see it go as much as their owners did. The ones who are honest will admit it, even today. Ask a few of the older niggers around here. I bet you dollars to donuts that most of them will tell you plantation owners tended to their welfare far better than their relatives are tended to up north by your phony government welfare system. In fact, I'd go so far as to say your Federal Welfare is just another way of keeping them in their place—but without the dignity they had in the South in the old days. In that regard, your government welfare is worse than slavery ever was."

I yelled back, "You gotta' be shittin' me!" I was beyond the point of disbelief. The suggestion that black people were happier as slaves and unhappy with no longer being someone else's property, seemed utterly ridiculous. The welfare issue was a sidetrack that William was using to throw me off. The real issue in slavery was one of personal freedom versus a lifetime of bondage to a master. Despite William's attempts to make it sound like a good deal for blacks, the fact remained that slavery was a violation of the rights of human beings to basic self-determination.

"It's true, I shit you not," William replied. "By the way, you seem to know your stuff when it comes to packin' watermelons," William changed the subject. "How'd a Yankee white boy like you learn to pack melons like that?"

I hadn't noticed Joe Harper in my peripheral vision, but he had apparently been watching my work from the back end of the trailer. I had no idea how long he'd been watching and listening to our banter about blacks and slavery.

"Looks like you're doin' a good job, young man, and it sounds like William is settin' you straight on the slavery issue?" Joe smiled at me, not even looking at William. "I don't know about you, but I always thought it might be nice to come from one of them southern aristocrat families like William's. I s'pose that would cause me to take a different view about these sharecroppers down here. Maybe they really appreciate the little shacks they live in out in the melon fields. Who needs windows and wood floors, anyway?" Joe was still smiling and his eyes never left mine as he spoke.

Joe said, "Hey fellas, how about we take a break and go get some dinner?"

12.

William's morning lecture on life in the South had taken my mind off my work enough that I lost track of time, and that was probably a good thing. He was doing everything he could to convince me that the South had never accepted the outcome of the Civil War and, given their druthers, former slaves would have continued to live within the institution that brought them to North America in the first place. His rosy depiction of happy black sharecroppers willing to remain on his ancestors' plantation, struck me as almost surreal. Perhaps he had a point, but then I remembered the stories I'd heard about the Underground Railroad, and slaves who hungered so deeply for their freedom that they had courageously risked their lives to migrate northward "illegally" before the institution of slavery ended. William would no doubt have said that the slaves who took to the Underground Railroad were the rare few who had suffered under the hands of the occasional bad slave owner.

William tossed melon after melon that morning, but his un-calloused palms, his long skinny fingers, and his manicured nails reminded me more of a pianist than a man who knew the value of hard work. Despite his lack of physical prowess, I had to give him credit for showing a measure of courage. Two thousand watermelons averaging 22 lbs each had ridden across his palms and into mine. I was sweating profusely, but I felt exhilarated. William was beginning to look pale and gaunt.

As my first loaded semi pulled away from the platform, I had a sense of pride in the fact that Joe Harper had noticed my finished product and approved. "Not a bad morning's work," I thought to myself. If I kept up the pace, I could make three loads by the end of my first 12-hour day, but I didn't believe William would last until mid-afternoon. In fact, I hoped he wouldn't.

As I passed the other trailers on my way to the parking lot side of the co-op building, I looked into each one to see how the other packers were coming along. When I walked past Lonny's trailer, I could see that his packing style was much as I'd expected it to be; deliberate and precise.

"C'mon," I yelled. "Let's go to lunch."

I was really hungry, and I had been brought up in the tradition that no good morning of farm work should go un-rewarded by a generous helping of meat and potatoes. In passing along that tradition, my dad loved to tell stories about how local farmers around Elmwood pooled their community resources and helped each other to bring in the wheat harvest in "the good old days." Every able-bodied man and boy would meet at the designated farm at dawn, and begin to cut the wheat and gather it from the fields. They would then haul it to a central location in the field, and there it would be run through a steam-powered thrashing machine. The work was hard, and by mid-day the men were tired and hungry. When the lunch break was called, the men proceeded to the farmhouse to enjoy a feast of fried chicken, roast beef with potatoes and gravy, along with coleslaw and sweet corn. They would eat their fill and drink gallons of sweet tea, then top it all off with a large slice of warm apple or cherry pie. When my dad told the story, he made it sound like it was a wonderful time to have been alive, but more because of the delicious food than the hard work.

Lonny said, "I've set aside some nice melons here to put on top. Could you toss these last 15 or so to me?"

"Sure," I replied, as I hopped across the foot wide gap between the platform and the rear end of the semi. Joe Harper had already shut the conveyor down, so we no longer had to yell over the noise. I said, "Get these damned things packed so we can go eat."

"Hell," Lonny replied. "Don't get too excited, big fella'. The place we go to eat around here is no prize, unless you like greasy meatloaf and soggy okra with black-eyed peas and grits, all smothered under a shitload of gravy! It's called Smitherman's. I don't think we'd go if there was anywhere else to eat, but there isn't!"

I said, "Well, I guess I'm in for a new experience. I've never tasted some of the shit you just mentioned, but I've always heard that southern cookin' was supposed to be good." I shrugged. "You know, juicy fried chicken, mashed potatoes, gravy, and the best pecan pie you've ever tasted."

"You're in for a real treat!" Lonny laughed. "But not the kinda' treat you just described. This place doesn't have what I'd call good cookin' of any kind, so don't get your hopes up. The best thing they have is the sweet tea, and it's pretty hard to fuck that up. Let's go, and you can see for yourself."

"I'm hungry as a fuckin' bear," I said. "I'm sure they'll have something I can eat. Us Hoosier farm boys aren't known for being real picky."

In 1968, fast food chains had not yet warmed up to markets the size of Holcomb, Alabama. The industry was new and feeling its way along. Market analysts had yet to envision its future popularity compared with that of local mom and pop restaurants. Because of this uncertainty about its future, the minimum requirement for cities that wanted a burger franchise was roughly 50,000 residents. Holcomb didn't come close to qualifying for a McDonald's. Even my hometown of Elmwood, with its population of 25,000, was not large enough for fast food chains to be interested in setting up shop in the 1960s. We had a McDonald's look-alike, known as Charlie's Burger Barn, but most locals didn't trust it as a "real" eating establishment. Teenagers, on the other hand, loved to hang out at Charlie's, and it was a good source of part-time jobs for high school kids. A friend of mine who worked there told me that his favorite pastime during summer slack periods was catching grasshoppers in the bushes surrounding the Burger Barn, and frying them on the griddle that was intended for cooking burgers. He said it was hilarious to watch the grasshoppers jump around on the hot metal plate until they suddenly stopped in their tracks, stuck in place, and quickly fried to a crisp. "Extra protein for the customers," he said.

Lonny and I jumped down from the trailer and walked toward the far end of the farmer's co-op building, where William and Don Jr. waited for us. Joe and Aubrey had already departed for the restaurant, and Bobby Leeds and Shorty were about to pull away from the co-op in Shorty's car.

"Lunch" was the wrong word to use in Holcomb to describe the noon meal. It was referred to as "dinner," and the evening meal was "supper." The proper order was "breakfast, dinner and supper."

Even though Aubrey had arrived at the co-op in mid morning, he took a noontime break to have "dinner" with Joe Harper. The midday hour was the best time for Aubrey to catch up with Joe on how things were going with the local farmers and how the melons were looking out in the fields. For Joe, it was a good time to catch up with Aubrey on how melon prices were looking in the northern markets. Supper would be their next opportunity to talk, but there was no guarantee that their paths would cross at that time of the evening.

While it was plain to see by looking at Monty the accountant that he'd seldom missed a meal, he rarely joined Aubrey and Joe for their noon meal. Only after the rest of the crew had returned to the co-op did Monty climb into his Buick and drive over to Smitherman's. He had joined us for supper at the hotel the evening before, but he had only done that because Aubrey had wanted him to meet the "new guy" who would be staying in his room for the first couple of nights. It had made sense for Monty and me to meet each other over a meal before we bunked in together.

Lonny drove us to Smitherman's in his father's company car, despite the fact that it was no more than a 10 minute walk from the co-op. I crawled into the back seat next to William, and Don Jr. got into the front seat with Lonny. The second Lonny started the engine, it struck me that this would be our only chance for a few moments of air-conditioned comfort until we returned to the hotel in Dothan that evening. "Max-air" was a new feature in many American cars, and it was designed to cool down the driver and "shotgun" seat occupant within seconds. The driver would use Max-air when the inside of the car was, in my dad's words, "hotter than hammered hell." Unfortunately, the two of us in the back seat felt nothing but a blast of warm air after it had blown past the two overheated bodies in the front seat. When we arrived at Smitherman's restaurant, hot air still swirled around in the back seat and there had been no relief from the misery of our sweat-soaked shirts.

Lonny parked the New Yorker in front of Smitherman's, just next to Aubrey's Malibu. The parking lot was nearly full, and it was only 11:40 AM when we got out of the car and walked toward the front door. We were greeted by the smell of deep fried food oozing from the busy restaurant, and the thought of sinking my teeth into a plate of fried chicken made me hungrier than ever in spite of Lonny's warning about Smitherman's lack of healthy dining choices.

Fully aware that I could be bringing up a topic that was better left alone, I felt the need to say something about Monty. I also knew from my fraternity experience, that the opportunity to interject a few good one-liners would almost always help a newcomer to establish himself as one of the guys. Besides, wise cracks aimed at a non-present third party were always safe territory. Smart remarks aimed at someone present showed chutzpah, but I wasn't ready to try that just yet.

As we got out of the car, I said, "You know, that Monty guy is one bigoted son of a bitch. He tried to convince me in his office this morning that Shorty and Bobby are a couple of thieves, just because they're black, and I need to keep a close eye on my wallet when they are around."

Don Jr. said, "Don't pay him any attention, big fella. He's harmless. My dad and Aubrey wouldn't have kept him around all these years if he didn't have his good qualities when it comes to the business side of the operation. I'll admit, he's a fucking bigot with strong fairy tendencies, but he has never caused any serious trouble. Kinda' keeps to himself, ya' know? I don't think he'd really try to get inside of your jeans, unless he thought you wanted him to."

We all had a good laugh.

"So you bastards talked Aubrey into putting me in the same hotel room with Monty for a couple of nights, eh?"

Lonny and Don Jr. laughed, and William shook his head.

Don Jr. said, "I know my dad and Aubrey have offered truckers a free night in many a hotel room with Monty and his one-eyed trouser trout, just to check out their 'tendencies.' The ones who 'like' Monty—or maybe I should say the ones who are *like* Monty—never say a word the next morning. But you should see the looks on the faces of the others when they come to work after a night with Monty! If I were Aubrey I'd be careful because a lot of these truckers carry handguns. I've told Aubrey more than once that he's gonna' get one of them truckers pissed off, and ole' Monty is gonna' get his ass shot. Or worse, Aubrey's gonna' get his nuts shot off!"

We all had a laugh at the thought of a trucker going berserk because of Monty.

"Don't worry, big guy," said Don Jr., "You passed the test. We know you're not a homo!"

"That's good to know, because I'm absolutely *sure* I'm not a homo. At least I knew better than to fall for his little tricks last night, plus I'll be moving in with you guys tomorrow night, so all will be well . . . I hope!" Everyone laughed.

* * *

When approached from the front, Smitherman's had the look of the general store from the TV series *Gun Smoke*, despite the fact that southeast Alabama and southwest Kansas had next to nothing else in common.

There was no blacktop pavement surrounding the frame building, and no gravel, but plenty of loose sand that shoes and sneakers sank into as people walked from their cars. I stepped gingerly to keep the sand from sifting inside my low cut Converse All Stars, and I wondered why the modern miracle of paved parking lots had not yet reached Holcomb, Alabama. Perhaps it had, but the locals decided to ignore it because asphalt was too expensive, and it held in too much heat on a summer afternoon. Besides, tires on cars, wagons and pick-up trucks could almost melt from the kind of heat that asphalt could absorb.

The gray clapboard on Smitherman's building looked like many old buildings in the South, and the large wooden sign on its façade was weathered so badly that the word "SMITHERMAN'S" was badly faded, as well as the three words underneath the name; "Kwick Kwality Kookin'." I couldn't help commenting on the unusual spelling of the three words.

Not allowing my naiveté to go unpunished, William chimed in. "I can tell you're not from the South!" He laughed with a laugh that gave him more pleasure than was called for. "Haven't you heard of the KKK; the Klan?"

"Well, yes," I said, "we have them up north too. In fact, Indiana has had more than its share of activity from those bigoted fuckers. Evansville, not far from my home town, used to be a hotbed of Klan activity around the turn of the century, from what I've heard."

William said, "Ole' man Smitherman's a Klan member and proud of it. The three Ks on the sign of a business goes back to the early 1900's, when owners wanted to advertise that they were part of the Klan. It was good for business. It was kinda' like a fraternity, where your brothers bring you repeat business. Customs die slowly in the South, especially in a place like this that's off the beaten path. You don't find ole' Martin Luther King marching through places like Holcomb; it's too small to make the Six O'clock News. But if he *did* come here, you better believe that sign would end up on Walter Cronkite's CBS news in a heartbeat. Those Yankee liberals would have a heyday with something like that."

"I wonder if the Klan had some other code words for advertising lynchings," I said. "Maybe a few posters around town that said; 'Tree Decorating Party . . . Sunday Afternoon . . . 3 P.M.'"

"Come off it!" said William. "You're just proving what southerners already think about you Yankees. You're so god-awful self-righteous when it comes to the way we treat our niggers. If you look into it, you'll probably find that lynch mobs were pretty common up north, too. Southerners weren't the only ones who took the law into their own hands when niggers got out of line."

"Funny how you say that, William . . . 'Out of Line,' as if there was some sort of imaginary line blacks had to walk, but only whites knew for sure when the blacks stepped over it."

"Be careful big guy," Don Jr. said. "You'll get ole' William worked into a frenzy, and he won't be any good all afternoon."

I said, "The way he looked when we finished our first load of melons, he won't be much good anyway." Lonny, Don Jr. and I laughed, and William shook his head in disgust. I was already repulsed by William's attitude. Since I couldn't get away with punching him in the nose on my first day at work, I opted for humor as the next best method of getting back at him.

The poplar planks that bedecked the front porch of Smitherman's were timeworn and shaky. I noticed that many of the nails were gone, leaving larger than necessary holes behind as evidence that they had once been there. The screen door leading inside looked like it had once been painted green, but the paint was badly faded and what remained was flaking off. The screen was detached on one side and along the bottom of the door, so flies and other insects had no trouble gaining entry.

As we walked inside, I could see that Aubrey and Joe Harper were already seated and working on plates piled with cooked sweet corn, okra, grits, and what seemed to be a mound of fried chicken pieces. The two men reminded me of hungry dogs devouring a coveted prize, and ready to attack anyone who interrupted. This was clearly a place for devouring, not dining.

I looked around for Shorty and Bobby Leeds, but the two black packers were nowhere inside the dining area. In fact, there were no blacks at all inside.

"Hey, Lonny, what happened to Shorty and Bobby?" I asked. "Come to think of it, I didn't see Shorty's car outside in the parking lot, but I saw him driving away from the co-op right before we got into your car. Were they going somewhere else?"

"No," replied Lonny. "Blacks have to park behind the restaurant and eat in their cars."

"You're shittin' me, right?" I said. "I guess the rules are different here than they were in Birmingham where I saw whites and blacks in the same diner."

"I wish I were shittin' you, but this is not Birmingham. This is the *real* South! There's a 'blacks-only' door they can access from the lower level parking lot. It's one of those half-doors, like Mr. Ed sticks his head through when he's talking to Wilbur. Bobby and Shorty get their meals on paper plates, and then they sit in Shorty's car and eat with plastic forks. William wasn't bullshittin' when he said old man Smitherman is a card carryin', dues payin' Klansman. He'll serve blacks, and gladly take their money, but he doesn't appreciate their business one bit. It's like he's almost afraid to hand them their food, for fear that some of the color will rub off on him, and he won't wash and re-use anything a black man has touched. I was surprised too at first, but you sorta' get used to their bigoted ways around here. You're only gonna' be around here for a few weeks tops, so you'd best let it slide. Besides, what the fuck is one person gonna' do to change it?"

"Damn," I said, "It still doesn't seem right to treat people that way!"

Lonny laughed at my naïve comment. "Just because you hear stuff up north about things changing, doesn't mean the real world down here is changing."

"Damn is right," said William! "There you liberals go again."

A mere halfway into my first day on the job, I had begun to dislike William in direct proportion to the frequency with which he opened his mouth. I'd been caught off guard by his morning-long apologetics on behalf of slavery, but now I began to see the true extent of his deeply ingrained bigotry. His defense of slavery was based on a whitewashed view of black history, he was very comfortable with the notion that blacks had their "place," and he took great comfort in the fact that his place was noticeably superior to the place occupied by people of color. I wondered how a man of William's youth and inexperience in the world could become so bigoted, but then it struck me that his attitudes toward black people, like the attitudes of millions of socially programmed bigots, had been programmed into him since birth.

The four of us packers lined up and waited for a sweating 250 pound woman behind the counter to ask us for our meal choices: "fried chicken with okra and grits, or chicken fried steak with corn and grits?" She had a soggy toothpick in her mouth, which made her look like the female version of the short order cook from the Dagwood and Blondie comic strip, absent the tattoo on her forearm.

Flies and gnats avoided the serving line because of its intense heat, but they feasted freely on the sweaty skin of the woman serving the food, who had long since given up on fanning them away. Her lack of concern over this little detail of personal hygiene didn't seem to discourage the hungry men who were lined up waiting for their plates to be filled.

I looked around to get the layout of the place, and to locate the silverware, napkins and iced tea. Suddenly, I caught a glimpse of the rear parking area through one of the windows at the back, and then I saw Shorty and Bobby Leeds carrying their paper plates from the back door of Smitherman's to Shorty's car, where they would listen to the radio while eating their meals with plastic forks.

After we had gotten our meals, drinks, and silverware, we picked out a table close to Aubrey and Joe Harper. The interior of Smitherman's was as dingy as was the outside. The dining experience bordered on depressing, but was salvaged by the sheer volume of food and the abundant sunlight that streamed inside through the windows on both sides of the dining room. Locals said the look of the place didn't amount to "a hill a' beans," because you can't live on atmosphere. All they wanted was a hot meal that would stick to a man's ribs, and Smitherman's never let them down in that department. Trouble was, Smitherman's food also stuck to their arteries.

Two large ceiling fans churned precariously above the dining area, swaying back and forth as their paddles rotated and threatened to fall on diners any second. The wooden tables looked like they had been purchased at yard sales because no two were alike. The chairs were a hodge-podge of chrome kitchen chairs with plastic upholstered seats of varying colors, alongside folding Grange Hall chairs. With the exception of the chrome dining chairs, everything inside the restaurant might have fit into an 18th century Western motif. Had Marshall Matt Dillon walked in wearing his seamless pants and low-slung gun belt, followed by his limping deputy Chester Goode, it would have seemed entirely fitting.

The serving line at Smitherman's was partitioned off from the rest of the dining area by an unpainted wall made of thin wooden planks. Just behind the serving area was another wooden plank wall that concealed the kithen, where Mr. Smitherman worked his dubious culinary magic. The planks that made up the two interior walls were in far better condition than the ones on the outside of the building because they had not been subjected to the hot summer sun and drizzling winter rain.

Customers who entered the restaurant headed toward the serving area through a large opening to their right. Immediately to the left behind the partition were two folding tables held up by rusty metal legs. These tables, which looked like they had come out of a church basement, were covered with serving trays, stacked drinking glasses, pitchers of sweet tea, a large wooden box full of silverware, napkins, salt and pepper shakers, and a large glass bowl filled with lemon slices for the tea. After gathering up their trays, drinks, napkins, and silverware, diners turned about face and made their way toward the food serving table.

The kitchen could be accessed through a small door with a tiny round window that looked like a ship's porthole. From behind the building, the kitchen could be accessed through the door where Shorty and Bobby Leeds were served. Once in a while, Mr. Smitherman would come into the serving area with a replenishing supply of meat or vegetables, but he never stayed to socialize. He appeared to be a humorless man who did not enjoy small talk.

The food was served cafeteria style, with a long steam table standing between the customers and Sadie Smitherman, who stood with her back to the kitchen wall. Her rose colored porcine face was covered with perspiration that occasionally dripped next to the metal serving vessels. She looked like she could explode at any minute. It was easier to imagine this 5'5", 250-pound woman falling over dead of heat stroke than to understand how she withstood the physical strain of her daily routine.

Each customer who stopped to get a plateful of food was greeted by an unpleasant grunt, which "Miss Sadie" dispensed as her social greeting. Customers greeted her with slightly more cheerful grunts, and sometimes a "G'day Miss Sadie," then watched as she filled their plates. Next, they moved one at a time to the end of the serving line and placed their $1.50 in a shoebox that served as a cash register. Payment was on the honor system, and those who needed change reached into the box and took out whatever they had coming back.

A hot meal on a hot day with complete lack of ceremony was a Smitherman family trademark. Having lived in a college dorm, I was used to unceremonious cafeteria-style service, but even Elmwood State University's relaxed health standards would not have tolerated Sadie Smitherman's "hands-on" serving methods. Diners pointed out what they wanted, and Miss Sadie picked up the meat, a few pieces of deep fried chicken or a chicken fried steak with a bare hand. After dropping the meat onto the plate, she used the same hand to wipe her forehead, and then grabbed a large serving spoon to dish up the vegetables. Sadie used one large serving spoon that appeared to have come from an Army / Navy surplus store, and she used it for everything that could not be served by hand. The spoon was the perfect size for dishing up servings of green beans, okra, corn, or black-eyed peas, and it had neat little holes in it to let the juice drip through. Her serving sequence went like this: step 1) take a plate in one hand, 2) reach for the meat course with free hand, 3) release the meat onto the plate, 4) wipe sweat from brow, 5) dish up vegetables, and 6) reach for another plate while staring at the next customer while new beads of sweat formed on forehead. This sequence was repeated over and over again, as automatic as the melon conveying system back at the farmer's co-op.

This mind-numbing routine made up a significant portion of Sadie Smitherman's life. The first time I saw her reach her hand into a serving tray of fried chicken, or dip her oversized spoon into a vessel filled with okra, I had no doubt that her physical dimensions were a direct result of her miserable lot in life. Food not only represented her livelihood, but it was also her consoling friend. No matter how many customers she fed during the noon meal hours, there was plenty of food left for later in the day when the restaurant closed and the customers were gone. Then, she and her overweight husband sat down and quietly ate to their heart's content, before washing up and returning home until it was time to prepare for the evening meal.

After making my first trip through Sadie Smitherman's lunch line, I joined the others at our randomly selected table. It was the first one on the right, just inside the front door and next to Joe and Aubrey.

As I sat down I said, "You know, it's a shame those guys have to eat in their car. I mean, this place isn't the greatest, and I can't get over the fact that they're treated like that. It's the 1960's for God's sake, not the 1860s."

"Jesus Lord a' Mercy," said William. "Here you go!" William looked at Don Jr., then at Lonny, hoping for some sign of support. "Like I mentioned before," said William, "I come from a genuine southern family, and I'm here to tell you that blacks and whites had a better lifestyle before liberals like you," gesturing in my direction, "started coming down here and screwing' things up! I tried to explain that to you this morning. Life in the Old South had style, class and dignity for whites *and* blacks. I swear I know what I'm talkin' about!"

I suddenly had the feeling that William was showing off for Lonny and Don Jr., and I sensed his need to sell himself on his own idealized view of life during slavery.

"Yes," I said. "Here I go again. You've said it enough already, and I get your point, but believe me I didn't come here to ruin things for you. I just came to work a summer job like you did. Don't blame me for upsetting your little apple cart!"

"I didn't come here for the same reasons you did, Matt. My mother insisted on it. She said something about my need for a little dirt under my fingernails, and to see how the other half lives. You know what I mean by 'the other half,' don't you?"

"No," I said. "But I'm sure you will enlighten me."

"I always figured the other half was made up of people like you, who *have* to do physical work for a living," said William. "But what I'm tellin' you is true, and I'm not pissed off at you personally, or any of my northern friends. Hell, I met Lonny at the University of Florida, and we run into each other once in a while on campus. He and I hit it off, don't we Lonny?" William paused and looked toward Lonny, who was chewing on a mouthful of food, and didn't provide the reassurance William was hoping for.

"OK," I replied. "Give me one example of what you're talking about, so I'll be properly enlightened."

William jumped right in. "There are lots of examples of what I am talking about. First off, when the South was a world economic power, people had lots and lots of money. To build up their fortunes, they needed productive power to get the work done, and physical labor was the state-of-the-art technology of the time. Like my daddy always told me (God rest his soul), 'most rich men are generous by nature, and wealth works its way down to benefit the less well-to-do.' Successful business men in the South provided employment, and eventually land and houses for their slaves. Blacks were treated like family more often than not. After slavery ended, a lot of black people were given part of what their plantation owners had, and there were plenty of blacks who ended up living well, don't think they didn't! Many of them saved up considerable sums of money and were not only happy, but proud, and they never cared about moving into white people's neighborhoods, riding to work in the same busses with white people, or using the same public restrooms as white people. They appreciated what they had been given, and all of the so-called symbols of equality didn't matter to them until this modern era came about and rabble-rousers like Martin Luther King came along and convinced them they were deprived. Damn him and his Southern Christian Leadership Conference! It's just a big front for a good old-fashioned Communist revolt! It doesn't have a blasted thing to do with Christianity."

Emotion was dominating Williams' speech. He began to breathe heavily like a Baptist preacher on Sunday morning. I almost expected someone in the restaurant to yell out, "Amen Brother!"

"King's whole purpose was to convince blacks they had it bad down here," said William. "Before he came waltzing into the picture, the niggers were happy enough with their lives! Ain't it amazing what a good white man's education on the East Coast, surrounded by a buncha' liberals, can do for an uppity nigger?"

"Do you really believe this shit?" I asked. "I mean, do you believe all of this crap about how black people enjoyed being slaves? Do you think slaves got a kick out of being sold away from their families, and young slave girls enjoyed being raped by their owners?"

I knew I had an audience this time, so I kept going. "And now, you believe that free blacks could have gone on forever enjoying their poverty stricken lives, if it hadn't been for Martin Luther King?"

Lonny laughed so hard he almost fell off his chair onto the wooden plank floor. "We've had several of these kinda' talks in the coffee shop at the University of Florida," said Lonny. "I try to tell William he's a bigot no matter how you slice him, and he tells me I'm a flaming liberal who came to school in the South on a special program to infiltrate 'his' state university with liberal 'commie' ideas! Just take him with a grain of salt, Matt. You're not gonna' change him."

"What was your motivation for coming to the South for college?" I asked.

Lonny said, "I read in *Playboy* that the University of Florida was the biggest party school in the United States. I picked it because of that, and it hasn't disappointed me one little bit, and I'd put our women at U of F up against the co-eds on any campus you can name."

Don Jr. said, "I bet there's something you'd like to put up against those women too!"

Lonny, Don Jr. and I laughed.

* * *

Suddenly, I heard a loud disturbance from behind the restaurant. It sounded like a fight was breaking out, so I quickly walked across the dining area to get a view of the parking lot out back. As I peered through the window, I caught a glimpse of the restaurant owner for the first time. It was obvious that he was confronting Shorty. From the words I could make out, I knew that Smitherman was laying down the law because of something Shorty had done.

"Look here nigger," I heard Smitherman yell, "I don't care if you want more fried chicken. We're runnin' low on chicken today, so if you want more to eat you'll pay extra and get the chicken fried steak. If you don't like it, get the hell outa' here and don't come back! Hear me, boy?"

At that, Shorty stopped in his tracks, turned around to face Smitherman, and dropped his plate in the sand upside down.

"Pick that up, you stupid nigger!" cried Smitherman at the top of his voice. Shorty ignored him and kept walking toward the car. Smitherman kicked the sand with his left foot, like a major league baseball manager who was having a fight with an umpire over a close call, and then he walked over and kicked sand over Shorty's discarded plate.

"I don't ever wanna' see your big black ass again, hear me boy? Your little buddy there will have to come up and get your dinners from now on if you want to eat here. You keep your fuckin' ass in the car, or don't come here at all, hear?"

By this time, Shorty had already reached his car and the music from his radio began to drown out Smitherman's tirade.

"Jesus Christ," I said as I walked back toward our table. The others had kept eating. "Looks like ole' Shorty really pissed Smitherman off," I said.

"What happened?" Lonny asked.

"Best I can make out, Smitherman went fuckin' ape shit over something Shorty said!"

William looked up from his plate. "Look, Matt, Shorty is a nigger. It's not your fault he's a nigger, and it's not my fault either. But the sooner you get used to the realities of life down here, the better off you'll be. Just give your bleedin' heart a rest."

"You know, William," I replied, "the fact that he's black can't be changed, but it's your kind of thinking that relegates him to the status of 'nigger'."

William was getting the edge over me because I was becoming emotional. He calmly shrugged off my remark and continued eating while several heads turned toward our table and eyes fixed on me.

Don Jr. patted my forearm and said, "Steady now, Big fella'. You're gonna' get us all in trouble."

Lonny said, "Matt, you'd better get used to William being a southern aristocrat. You're not gonna' change him one iota." Lonny lowered his voice and leaned toward me. "I think what Don here is saying is that it's not just William who feels the way he feels, if you get my meaning. Just look around you."

My attention to the distraction from outside had caused me to fall behind the others in eating. As I looked down at my plate, my mind suddenly blocked out everything with the exception of one voice, and it was the voice of someone who was not even present: Dr. Andrew Harmon.

* * *

"As much as I hate to admit it," said Dr. Harmon's deep voice, *"your buddy William has a point. Blacks are beginning to see the light about many things, and they are beginning to acquire new expectations, but whites in the Deep South think that most blacks were more or less content with slavery. It's a tough one to swallow, but there it is. If I were there with you right now, I'd wanna' run out into that parking lot and strangle that restaurant owner, then come back inside and kick William's ass, but I'd end up the loser. So, take the advice of Dr. King, and say a silent prayer for peace and understanding. Remember, peace and freedom begin inside a person's own heart."*

I continued my secret conversation with Dr. Harmon as I finished my meal, and blocked out the noise and clatter around me.

"How can whites be so blind as to think that blacks were EVER happy with slavery?" I asked Dr. Harmon. I was searching every brain cell to find something I had learned that might be a positive aspect of slavery, but I found nothing!

Dr. Harmon's soothing voice said, *"They share a different history down here, which gives them a different set of beliefs. The eyeglasses through which they view the world are different from yours, and neither of you can focus with the other's lenses. Besides, as is the case with any ruling class, they want to believe that their captives are pleased with the treatment they receive. To feel otherwise would create cognitive dissonance, and we all strive to avoid that. Whites like William, who are the grandchildren and great grandchildren of former slave owners, are completely sold on the notion that slaves were the benefactors of relatively humane treatment."*

"I can see I have a lot to learn," I thought. "But I don't want to learn any of it from William!"

Dr. Harmon's voice broke into laughter. *"Just keep in mind,"* he said, *"there is a certain synergy that exists between blacks and whites in the South that you will never understand. People of color have always found ways of adapting to their plight before and after the civil war, and not all whites are villains."*

* * *

Aubrey and Joe Harper paid little attention to the ruckus in the back of the restaurant, and I was surprised that neither of the men felt the need to stand up for a valued employee. Sadly, William's comment seemed accurate. From the indifference of the white customers, including Aubrey and Joe, it was apparent that confrontations between white restaurant owners and black patrons in this part of Alabama were commonplace, almost to the point of being accepted as part of the ambience.

As soon as Aubrey and Joe finished inhaling their meals, they got up from their table to return to work. Although we were not yet finished, we took their sudden motion toward the door as a signal that we should hurry it up, but Aubrey looked over and signaled with both hands that we should take our time.

"We're gonna' head back to the packin' shed," said Aubrey, "but you fellas worked hard this morning so take it easy here for a few minutes. Don't worry, we'll save plenty melons for you this afternoon." With that, Aubrey's mouth twitched, and he walked out to the front porch where Joe was impatiently pacing back and forth.

13.

As we arrived back at the farmer's co-op following my first dinner at Smitherman's, we saw Slick leaning against his car and taking a nip from a pint of cheap whisky. The aging man's stamina in the face of his own demons was impressive. He was thin and wiry, but he still sported a muscular six-pack in his abdominal region.

I said, "How does that guy stay alive, much less pack watermelons, day in and day out?"

Don Jr. said, "That old bastard is pickled, big guy. His liver probably outweighs him, and he says his doctor told him to keep it filled up with booze and everything would be alright!"

The rest of us nodded as if Don Jr. had given a serious account of Slick's medical status. For a second or two, it seemed to make perfect sense.

I added, "From what I've heard, his dick is as stiff as his liver. I wonder if the booze helps with that, too?"

"That's what his girlfriends seem to think, since they buy most of his booze for him," Don Jr. verified. "His wife must think his one-eyed trouser snake is worth keepin' around too. She's a real nice lady, and not bad lookin' either. You'll probably have a chance to meet her before the summer is over. She'll show up in South Carolina to spend some time with ole' Slick. She doesn't drive, so Slick sends her money for train tickets to come up and spend a week or two with him every summer. She's a waitress, and probably has a 25 year old boyfriend back home."

"If I were that boyfriend, I'd make sure she got a stiff shot of penicillin after every trip to see her husband!" Lonny said.

"Does Slick's wife know about the women he hangs out with in these watermelon towns?" I wondered out loud.

"Hell, she's met some of 'em," said Don Jr., "and it doesn't seem to bother her one bit that they keep Slick entertained when she's not around. She loves ole' Slick to death and wants him to be happy, even if that means an occasional case of the crabs during melon season. I've heard that when he's home during the off-season, he's the perfect husband. Strange world we live in, eh?"

I nodded my agreement.

Following our noon break, Joe Harper brought us together for a quick stand-up meeting in which he assigned me an open top trailer to start my afternoon's work. I was less than delighted to learn that William would be working with me again. I wondered if this was some other sort of newcomer's harassment. Joe asked me to let William pack part of a trailer after I'd gotten things set up for him, but packing melons in open tops required more experience than packing in box-style trailers, so I talked Joe into holding off on William's training until the next closed trailer came along.

* * *

Once William and I got started in the open top trailer, we made faster progress than we had in the boxed-in one that morning. Open top trailers were usually shorter and slightly narrower than their cavernous box-style counterparts. They were by far more difficult to pack, but I felt refreshed after the noontime pause and there was a slight breeze that eased the discomfort of the hot afternoon sun.

I had taken off my t-shirt and it presently dangled from my right hip pocket. I reached for it occasionally to wipe the sweat from my face, and it occurred to me once or twice that I should put it back on as protection for my reddening shoulders. But knowing from past experience that most good tans started with a serious sunburn that peeled away to reveal a new generation of darker skin, I reasoned that the worse the burn on the first day and the greater the pain, the faster the peeling and tanning. I would achieve the Coppertone look through a combination of sun and sweat, without wasting my money on coconut scented lotion.

I took a couple of breaks inside the co-op building early in the afternoon, mostly to get large gulps of water from the cooler near Monty's office. I noticed that Shorty and Bobby took occasional breaks under a large elm tree next to Shorty's car, and they took turns drinking from a gallon-sized glass jug that Shorty kept buried in the cool sand under the tree. The sand was hot in the sunlit parking lot, but under the shade tree it was cool. If a person dug down just a few inches, the slightly moist sand was dark in color and very cool to the touch.

Shorty and Bobby might have gotten away with using the water cooler inside the co-op, but only to refill their jug and not to drink from it. As demonstrated earlier at Smitherman's, they were well accustomed to the social realities of eating and drinking in public places.

While William was taking a breather of his own under the shade of the co-op building, Shorty paid me a visit to see how I was doing with my first open top trailer. He agreed with me that open tops were the hardest trailers to pack because of their rounded front corners, and he wanted to see how well I was handling the challenge. While packers started open trailers the same as others, carefully laying a row of melons end to end parallel with the front end, the rounded off corners of open tops required larger handfuls of straw to build a padded foundation. Many a truck driver of open top rigs told horror stories of juice dripping from under their trailers, and almost gushing out the back end by the time they reached their points of delivery. Their paychecks were reduced in proportion to the number of bad melons, or "juicers" offloaded, so drivers of open tops tended to be picky about the packers who were assigned to them.

Shorty looked over my progress and nodded his approval. "Y'all seem to know what you doin' there, fella! Only thing I'd do different is the way you paddin' them rocks along the sides."

Shorty and Bobby referred to watermelons as rocks, and I had no idea where that bit of slang had originated. Perhaps by the end of the day, each melon began to feel like it was as heavy as a stone of similar size.

"Mo' straw," said Shorty. "Y'all can't be afraid a' usin' straw, and y'all damn sure don't want that fuckin' driver ta' come down here next week all up in your face and lookin' ta' kick you' ass 'cause he done lost a hundred dolla's or so on y'all's packin'! No sir, you gotta' do dis man right, den he be askin' fur ya' to be his packer da' rest a' da' season."

I said, "Now that's a good deal! Maybe I'd be better off to screw this load up, so I don't get any more of these open-tops!" I looked at Shorty and smiled.

"Y'all jus be fuckin' you'self if ya' does dat," said Shorty. "Open-tops is only 35 foot long. Five foot is damn near a ton a' rocks, so you gots a ton less to handle. Y'all still git da' same 20 bucks fur packin' one a dees here fuckers! Jis git damn good at it, and y'all be makin' easy money!" When Shorty laughed, his belly shook and he wiped the spit off his mouth with the back of his hand.

Shorty jumped over the side with the agility of a man half his size and landed inside the trailer in a single smooth motion. He grabbed a huge handful of straw and tucked it under his stub of a left arm, and then he took several more small sections (or "flakes") from an open bail and began strewing all of it along the floor of the trailer. He gave out another deep laugh, as he always did when making a point that tickled his sense of humor. He didn't stop strewing until the straw was so deep that I could barely walk through it to start a new row of melons. "OK, Matt, that should be about 'nough." With that, he turned and flung his large body back over the side of the trailer, landing briefly on the narrow ledge on the outside of the trailer to get his balance. Then he hopped down into the sandlot below him.

"Thanks," I said. "Appreciate the help."

"Ain't nothin'," Shorty said as he looked back over his shoulder. "You seem ta' be gittin' da' hang a dis shit! You doin' fine!"

I continued to look over the side of the trailer as he walked away.

"Hey, Shorty," I shouted. "What was that shit over at Smitherman's today? I heard the yelling, and couldn't help looking out the window."

"It weren't nothin'," said Shorty.

"It sure as hell looked like somethin' to me," I replied.

"Dat man don't like me and Bobby eatin' at his place, but we gits used to that kinda' shit when we on da' road in melon season. When I be back home in Flawda, and Bobby be back in Sow Calahna, we knows where ta' go so we don't run inta' his kind a' people. Round here, we jus' want a plate a' hot food. We figger a fella' gonna' run inta' some asshoes like ole' man Smitherman, who wanna' take it out on ya' 'cause you gots black skin. Like I say, Bobby and me gits use to it."

With that, Shorty shrugged his shoulders and laughed as he headed back toward his own trailer.

"But it's not about the food, Shorty! How can you stand the way that bastard talks to you?"

Shorty turned around.

"Matt, I see y'all gots a lot ta' learn 'bout life in da' South. Shit, you might even have a lot to learn about life up north, where y'all comes from!"

"What do you mean?" I asked.

Shorty laughed. "You been white all you' born days, and I been a black man a lot longer than you been a white one. When you be a black man, white folk don't like ya' eatin' wit' 'em. An' somethin' else I can tell ya' 'bout bein' black."

"What's that, Shorty?" I asked.

"Bein' a black man down here, you gots to close your eyes to da' white man takin' your women when he please. If'n a white man see him a good lookin' black woman he want, den a black man better damn well stay outa' da' way an' keep his mouth shut. Like me and Bobby, we stay outa' da' way and don't say nothin' when ole' man Smitherman come knockin' on da' door next ta' where we be stayin' in Holcomb, ta' see his black honey. I bet dat fat chick he be married to don't know nothin' 'bout dat!" Shorty laughed. "If'n she did, she might be after his sorry ass wit' a big ole' butcher knife, gonna' cut his stubby dick off!"

"You think ole' Smitherman doesn't like you comin' around to his place for dinner because you and Bobby know too much about him?"

"Could be," said Shorty. "Could be."

"Maybe Bobby an' me can teach ya' a few things 'bout how da' black man live. Even in y'all's neck a' da' woods up in Indiana, it ain't no picnic bein' black. Bobby and me, we gots a few Church folk up in Indiana we stays with. Ain't no hotel or boardin' house fur no black folk. I 'spose a fella'd have to drive all da' way down ta' Evansville to find a place ta' stay, like a hotel, and dat ain't da' most friendly place I ever did see. Still lotta' Klan left ova'."

I was taken aback at what Shorty said about my "neck a' da' woods." Because there were so many more blacks in the South, the discrimination was more visible, and we were much better at sweeping our racial bigotry under the rug back home. But, with the exception of what I'd learned from Dr. Harmon, I had failed up until now to see the truth of racial discrimination where I had grown up.

14.

It was around 9:00 P.M. when we got back to our hotel at the end of my first day on the job. I used a key Monty had loaned me to let myself into his room. I took a quick shower, and then changed into a clean pair of blue jeans and a clean t-shirt. I then walked down to the room where the other packers were staying, and we got back into the car and drove to a fast food place for a late evening meal. It occurred to me that this felt almost like Marine Corps boot camp, or late summer "two-a-day" practices for a college football team.

By the time we had eaten our burgers and returned to the Holiday Inn, we felt a little better, and I felt a slight surge of energy. This was surprising because part of me was still numb from a serious sleep deficit over the past few days.

The other three packers decided to put on their swimming trunks and catch a few minutes of relaxation in the pool before it closed for the evening. It was already past 10:00, so I decided to pass on the lukewarm pool water for the second time in as many nights. I went back to Monty's room to finish my letter to Ben.

* * *

Letter to Ben . . . Continued

I really don't know how to begin this part of my letter, but here goes. Just after I wrote the first part last night, the company accountant (Monty, the guy I'm sharing a room with for the first couple of nights) tried to feel me up! Yes! You read that correctly! He tried to play with my ass! At first, I didn't really know what was going on, but when he tried to grope me a second time, I knew things were going in a direction I didn't want to go, so I bounced over to the hide-a-bed, and slept with one eye opened and a blanket over me. This guy, Monty, convinced me at first that I had to share his big bed with him, because he'd supposedly have to pay extra if I opened up the hide-a-bed. I guess when I bought off on that load of crap, he took it to mean I was either a naïve farm boy or I might be interested in playin' around. Of course, it was the naïve farm boy in me that caused me to buy off on his line of shit. (Stop laughing, dammit!)

At the co-op on my first day of work today, the other packers gave me a ration of shit about my night with old Monty, so I knew the whole thing had been a big set-up. Ben, this fucker tried to grab my ass, and these other guys knew he was gonna' do it! It was like some kind of fuckin' initiation rite, and most of the other packers had had their own experiences fighting Monty off. I guess you live and learn! I thought I was hip to the way things were in the real world. I mean I have a few friends back in the dorm who prefer the company of other guys. (Most of them belong to the campus chapter of the Young Republicans! Ha!) They leave straight guys alone, and have their private parties on weekends. But ole' Monty seems to prefer pot luck with every swingin' dick that comes along, thinking he'll get lucky every now and then.

Changing the subject to my job, which is what I really wanted to write you about, my first day was pretty good. I packed three truckloads, and made a grand total of $60 bucks! Not bad for a bush league packer from Indiana, eh? One of the black packers gave me some pointers on how to pack those god-awful open top trailers, and it really helped. This packer's name was 'Shorty.'" According to him, it's not a bad idea to get good at packing open tops, since you get the same amount of money for packing a 35 foot long open top trailer as you do for a closed 40 footer. I never thought of it that way before, but I'm sure you already knew it! Boy, I'll be packin' circles around your ass before I get back to Indiana, especially with you sittin' on your lazy ass in your air conditioned office, and gettin' outa' shape!

Well, I'm about to doze off. I have one more night in Monty's room, but I pretty much think he'll leave me alone tonight.

I'll close this now so I can get it in the mail to "y'all" in the morning. More soon!

Matt

P.S.: I gotta tell you about the place where we eat lunch down here. It makes the worst places we have back in Elmwood look like 4 star restaurants! I shit you not! I'll fill you in on how the redneck owner treats blacks. It's not quite the same as the integrated diner I mentioned in my post card from Birmingham."

15.

As I finished my letter to Ben, Monty came back to the room. For the second evening in a row, he had joined Aubrey for supper in the Holiday Inn dining room, then Aubrey had adjourned to his room and Monty had gone to the hotel bar.

"Well, how do you feel after your first day on the job, young man?" Monty's face looked tired.

"Not bad," I replied. "I'm sure I'll feel stiff and sore in the morning, and even more the next day. I always get the worst soreness on the third day, for some strange reason."

"Did you say 'stiff'? What muscle group are you talking about?" Monty giggled at his attempt at sexual innuendo. "Must be that it takes your muscles a couple of days to start stretchin' and growin'." Now he was attempting to be a regular guy.

"I think I'll like workin' with the rest of the crew," I said. "The three white fellas are ok, even though William is a little hard to take at times. But Shorty and Bobby are about as nice a' guys as you'd ever wanna' meet."

"Just be careful where you keep your wallet, like I told you this morning. I don't know where we'd be this summer without you and the other three white boys. We're short of experienced packers this season, but I think you guys will take up the slack." At that, Monty tossed his robe over his shoulder and disappeared into the bathroom. I was asleep a few seconds after my head hit the pillow.

16.

I slept well and the night went fast. Once again, I woke up earlier than Monty and got into the shower right away. After I showered and dressed, I stepped into the parking lot to meet Joe Harper for the ride to work. As we began the trip to Holcomb, Joe was his usual talkative self.

"I noticed you were a bit upset yesterday at dinner time, when old man Smitherman jumped all over Shorty. That bothered you, didn't it?"

I wasn't sure how to react, or where Joe was going with his question. Thinking back on the incident, I could have sworn that Joe had been deeply immersed in business talk with Aubrey, and he hadn't paid the least bit of attention to Smitherman's rant against Shorty.

"Well," I said, "I saw something like that during my trip down to Holcomb. A black grocery worker got a real tongue lashing from the bus driver. Maybe I am overly sensitive, but it shook me up a little when I saw Smitherman yelling at Shorty yesterday. What is it with these white guys down here, Joe? They seem to enjoy treating blacks like dogs. I don't see you and Aubrey acting that way toward Shorty and Bobby, or even toward the black farm hands that come in to the co-op with the farmers."

Joe said, "It's not all smooth sailin'. We get our share of truckers that come down here and try that shit. We know who they are and we try to keep a close eye on them. I've even seen a few local farmers lay into a black packer from time to time over a close call on culling out a melon. You'd be surprised how a farmer can get up in arms over one stupid watermelon, especially when it's a black packer that culls it out of the load."

"Believe me, I know," I said.

"How do you handle a situation like that when it involves a black packer?"

"Simple," Joe said, "I stick to the old adage that the packer has the final call, and I couldn't care less if the packer's skin happens to be green, blue or black. Some farmers try to go over my head, but Aubrey always backs me up on the way I run things. That's one of the reasons I work for QM. I know they treat people fair and square, so I work for them because I figure I'll be treated that way too. It's that simple." Joe smiled.

"Have you ever seen a farmer lay into one of his black farmhands at the co-op, when one of the black kids gets tired and drops a melon?"

"Oh sure," Joe replied. "I've seen farmers jump all over black workers, callin' them all sortsa' names like 'lazy little nigger' and 'worthless black bastard.' It always makes me half sick to my stomach when I hear it. Decent farmers generally keep that kinda' thing in the family, if you know what I mean."

"I'm not sure if I do," I said.

"Well, most farmers tend to be kinda' quiet around outsiders, and what they say and do to their black farmhands and sharecroppers is not meant for anyone else. They like to think what happens on the farm stays on the farm. We don't see much of it, and that's the way they want to keep it. It's like a secret society. Some farmers treat their black sharecroppers pretty good, but others treat 'em like dogs. And I know for a fact that some farmers in these parts belong to the Klan, so that's always a factor in the way they deal with their black farm workers."

"What do you think these white guys get out of treating blacks like shit? I mean does it give them some feeling of power?" My question was slightly rhetorical.

Joe smiled and kept his hands steadily on the steering wheel in the ten and two o'clock positions. I noticed his fingers moving slightly, as if he gripped the wheel a bit tighter, and then he relaxed his grip. "You know that's the reason as well as I do. You're a smart college kid, and I've seen how you act around Bobby Leeds and Shorty. I know you respect them and you have nothing to lord over them. But let me give you a little perspective on these folks down here, and maybe it'll help you understand them a bit better. The average white in these parts runs a grocery store, restaurant, farm or what have you. They're small business people and they all play their part in making the community tick. They make their beds, and they lie in them. I guess a fella' could say their bed is made for them in most cases, like when they inherit their daddy's farm and have no training in anything else, so they farm. The same thing happens with local store and restaurant owners. The young ones who are lucky have money to go off to college, and you don't generally see them back in a place like Holcomb after they finish their studies."

"So, tell me more about the ones who are stuck here," I said.

"A lot of fellas who stay around here ain't all that happy with the cards they've been dealt, but they're stuck here anyway. Sometimes I don't know if they even realize they're unhappy. At the end of the day, they go home to a wife who bitches at them non-stop because she can't scrape two pennies together for the new Sunday dress she's had her eye on. First thing you know, the man of the house is looking for folks to blame for his misery, and it doesn't take him long to run across a black man who's got it worse than he does. So he decides to take out his frustrations on the black man. It's like the fella' in the joke who comes home at night and slaps the wife around, then she slaps the kid, and the kid walks over and kicks the dog. Down here, they tend to spare the wife and kids, and the dog that gets kicked is the black man who doesn't have a damned thing to do with the white man's problems in the first place."

I said, "My favorite college professor is black, and he says blacks are guilty until proven innocent in American society, especially in the South. It's kinda' like the dog who gets kicked by the kid. He says blacks are always on the front lines of the racial struggle."

"I don't suppose I'm as smart as your professor friend, but I've been around for a few years, and I can tell you he makes a good point. I'm not sure about the front lines, but I'd say blacks in the South are down in the trenches, and the front line isn't far away. I'm tellin' you, one of these days blacks are gonna' bite back, even in backwaters like Holcomb!"

"Seems to me that they're within a stone's throw of the front lines," I said. "And I think Martin Luther King was sounding the bugle to charge."

"Well, young man, I think you've got your head screwed on right. But let me give you a bit of advice. Always try to stay focused in your mind on what's important to you, and don't let anybody distract you from that. With a bit of luck, you'll be able to figure out what it is that's important to you, and then go after it with all your power."

I said, "Makes good sense to me, Joe."

* * *

I closed my eyes for a few seconds, and Dr. Harmon's voice suddenly popped into my head.

"I like the way this Joe Harper thinks," said Dr. Harmon. *"Sounds like you can learn a great deal about life from this man. From what I've heard him tell you this morning alone, he seems to be a real salt-of-the-earth fellow. He knows a lot about life, and he has a 'live and let live' philosophy, similar to yours. Maybe he's not as good a mentor as I am, but he's not bad either."* I could see Dr. Harmon smile.

17.

My third day as a melon packer in Alabama started out with another ride to work with Joe Harper. Lonny had offered me a ride since I was now staying in the same room as the other three packers, but I wanted to talk to Joe a bit more about Shorty and Bobby Leeds. And, much to my own surprise, I woke up in a talkative mood.

Shortly after Joe and I exited the motel parking lot I said, "Bobby Leeds seems a bit quiet, but his laugh is so damned contagious. I can't help but like him. I'm even getting used to seeing him in that black bandana he wears all the time."

"Funny, ain't he?" said Joe. "He wears the bandana to protect his straightened hair when he's workin'. I suppose his hair has so much gunk in it he's afraid to get dirt in it too."

"I've seen that kind of head gear before, but mostly in photographs of black women in *National Geographic*, or on boxes of Aunt Jemima's pancake mix."

"Bobby's proud of his Geechee background," said Joe. "He talks about his family a lot. Like Shorty, he's a man with a story and a family history that he don't mind talkin' about. He'll tell you all about it one a' these days, after he gets to know you a little better."

"When Bobby and I were introduced by Aubrey a couple of nights ago, he told me he had grown up on Saint Helena Island. His dialect is a lot different from Shorty's, and that laugh of his is very unusual. His speech and his laugh kinda' flow out like water. And his whole body gets into the act."

Joe Harper continued. "Bobby is 'good people,' as we like to say in the South. It means he's a good guy on his own, but it also means he comes from a good family."

"Funny," I said. "I know a little about the Geechee people from books and lectures in school. I wrote a paper in a Black History course about the Gullah and Geechee people. Can you believe that?"

"Damn," said Joe, "are you one a' them smart guys that'll end up bein' a professor?"

"I don't know. I like some of my professors a lot, and I look up to them. Maybe I could do that for a living some day. It doesn't get you as dirty and sweaty as packin' melons." I laughed.

"It seems like a real coincidence that you came down here and met Bobby Leeds," said Joe. "I think it was meant to be!"

"I know. It really surprised me when Bobby said he was a Geechee. The only Geechees I'd seen before were in books, and most of the pictures were from many years ago."

Joe said, "St. Helena is part of what they call the Sea Islands. It's a beautiful area. If you ever get a chance to go there, you should. The people have a different way of talkin' there, for sure. I can guarantee you that if Bobby spoke to you in pure Geechee, you wouldn't understand a damn word he was sayin'." Joe laughed.

I looked out of the side window at the small houses we drove past on our way to Holcomb. I thought about the reading I'd done for my paper about the Geechees, and how they lived in small farming and fishing communities on what Joe called the Sea Islands. Their ancestors in West Africa were known for their skills in growing rice, in places I knew nothing about, like Senegambia and the Sierra Leone. Apparently the climate of the Sea Islands made Georgia and South Carolina perfect locations for growing rice, so these West Africans were highly prized in slave trading.

In doing the research for my term paper, I had been fascinated with the fact that life on the Sea Islands, isolated from outside influence, enabled the Gullah/Geechee communities to retain their cultural links to Africa. While many cultural characteristics were lost because of slavery, the Gullah/Geechee people were the exception. They had retained more of their African heritage than most other slave populations on the mainland.

18.

As the hot days of Holcomb summer moved forward, my suntan took hold and my broad shoulders and biceps continued growing like a thriving cactus with each sweltering summer day. We slept late on Sundays, but always made it to the local pancake house before the hoards of local Baptists were released from church services.

On Sunday afternoons, we stayed around the hotel swimming pool.

Slick stayed drunk in his cheap roadside motel between Holcomb and Dothan, and wallowed between sweaty bed sheets with his sweetie du jour.

Shorty and Bobby stayed at their boarding house in Holcomb, but none of us knew what they did on their Sundays off. We were pretty sure they didn't go without female companionship and a fair amount of cheap wine to help them sleep through the steamy Alabama nights.

* * *

My melon packing skills steadily improved and much to my own surprise, the trailers I completed looked almost as good as if Shorty had packed them. Try as I might, I could not duplicate the magic of Bobby Leeds or the skeletal alcoholic Slick. Their work had an intuitive quality that no other packer could duplicate. I thought it was ironic that Bobby Leeds and Slick were physically the smallest among our crew. Had I passed either of them on the street without knowing what they did for a living, I would never have imagined either of them doing this sort of work. Nonetheless, they were clearly masters of the trade.

Night after night, we drove back to Dothan following 12 to 14 hour workdays. Night after night, we took showers and went out for late evening meals at local fast food joints. Night after night I closed my eyes exhausted. Despite my state of exhaustion, I was not able to fall asleep because of the steady stream of watermelons that kept coming at me every time my eyes were shut for more than a second or two. As I stared at the insides of my eyelids, indelible copies of watermelons flew toward me in fast forward mode. The more fatigued I became, the harder it was to stop my brain's motion. I talked about this with truckers, only to learn that the phenomenon was common. They experienced it too, but when they closed their eyes at night, they saw endless stretches of concrete highway coming toward them. Although the melons were packed for the day and the trucks had been parked for the night, the brain's momentum continued. In the case of truck drivers, their brains were often impaired by high doses of caffeine and No-Doz, so the impact of the nightly highway "re-runs" was almost psychedelic, with winding highways becoming colorful *Alice-in-Wonderland* spirals.

* * *

Shorty was the best coach I'd ever had, and he seemed to enjoy watching my work and lending his advice. I sometimes watched Bobby Leeds during my breaks, and learned that he didn't mind having an audience. In fact, he rather enjoyed it.

Shorty and Bobby eventually confided in me that they were staying in a boarding house in the small black neighborhood of Holcomb. Shorty said the black neighborhood was off the beaten path. Nobody else on the QM staff asked the two men about their living arrangements, and Quality Melon was not paying for their lodging. The two men tolerated Holcomb, but Bobby made it clear that he was looking forward to the move to South Carolina, where he had friends and family. Most of his family had eventually migrated away from the Sea Islands, and only a handful of them remained on Saint Helena. Bobby called himself a "home body," so the time he would spend in Harkensville, South Carolina would be the highlight of his summer.

Bobby made sure that Shorty was fixed up with "Carolina Ladies" whenever he wanted to go out. He knew the lay of the land, including card games and brothels, so it was easy for him to keep Shorty entertained and out of trouble.

19.

Sunday evening before my third week in Holcomb, I went to bed feeling refreshed. I was now in excellent physical condition, and my earlier sense of fatigue was gone. I fell asleep around 1:00 A.M., and awoke at 3:00 A.M. following a disturbing dream. In my dream, Bobby, Shorty and I had been out together for an evening, and found it impossible to get served for dinner. We were in a small town that looked like it could be Holcomb. The three of us were dressed up for the evening. Shorty wore a white broad-brimmed felt hat, a white shirt with open collar, green dress pants, and white patent leather shoes. Bobby wore a red hat, a red silk shirt with open collar, white pants and black patent leather shoes. I wore my Sunday best suit of green stretch cloth, white shirt, red tie, and black leather wingtips. In my dream, I felt like a rich white kid out on the town with two black pimps.

During our search for a meal we walked up to the door of a nice looking restaurant and noticed a sign that read, "Dining Club—Members Only." I boldly led the way inside, and Shorty and Bobby followed. The three of us knew the establishment was designated a private supper club for one reason: it was whites only. Nonetheless, we entered the establishment with the greatest confidence and played it like we were long-standing club members, a farce to anyone who was not legally blind. As we approached the registration podium, the kind a choir singer would stand behind, the hostess greeted me. When she saw my companions behind me, she looked down at her reservation book and appeared to study it in earnest. I looked over my shoulder at Shorty and Bobby, and they nodded in the direction of the hostess to signal that I was doing just fine. I moved slightly forward, and the hostess looked up from her book.

"How may I help you, sir?" The hostess greeted me as if I were the only one standing in front of her.

I knew in my dream that her smile, though inviting, was not intended to convey a genuine welcome. I would have been welcome had I been alone, but only on the condition that my two black bodyguards did not intend to join me for a meal. I grew tense and my forehead and neck broke out in a sweat. I could feel the perspiration gushing down the sides of my body from underneath my armpits, like my under arm deodorant had given out. Despite my earlier attempt to exude confidence, I now spoke in a wavering voice.

"Three memberships for dinner," I said.

The hostess looked at me as if I had stepped off a spaceship from another planet.

"Three?" She asked, as if Shorty and Bobby were still invisible. I looked back over my shoulder, and both men were still there.

"Yes, three memberships for dinner," I repeated.

"Wait a moment, sir. It appears that our membership roles may be full. I'll get my manager."

I turned around as the pretty, hoop-skirted Southern Belle departed from her appointed station. I glanced back at Bobby Leeds and Shorty with a fake look of confidence, and neither of them spoke. They looked at me as if they were determined to become members of the club, no matter what it took. No longer smiling pimps, they had both assumed a demeanor that was characteristic of gangland hit men.

I looked back toward the registration podium, saw the manager walking toward me and suddenly felt a stifling lump in my throat.

"May I help you?" The manager smiled. He was trying his best to remain calm and businesslike, while appearing to be genuine.

"Yes, we need three club membership cards, and we'd like to stay for dinner," I replied.

"I'm so sorry," said the manger, "but it appears that our membership roles are full, and we cannot take in any new members at this time."

Before I could reply to the man, Bobby Leeds and Shorty leapt around me like two agitated Bengal tigers, grabbed the manager and knocked him to the floor. While Bobby pinned him down, Shorty pummeled the slight built man with his only fist. Suddenly, Shorty was not the mild mannered giant I knew from the farmer's co-op, but a one-armed Mohammed Ali. Bright red blood gushed from the man's nose, and a steady stream poured from his eye sockets and ears, as well as from the large gashes that spread across his face with each of Shorty's powerful blows. Having turned the man's face into a bloody pulp in a matter of seconds, Shorty stood up and began kicking him about the head until the man's head came off, rolled across the carpet, and bounced against the wall ten feet behind him.

I was petrified and speechless!

Suddenly, a large white man came around the corner behind the guest registration podium. The man was brandishing a double barrel sawed-off shotgun. He pointed the weapon directly at Shorty and blasted him with both barrels.

I awoke suddenly, shaking with fright and out of breath as I sat up in bed. In the dream, I had been trying to form the words to tell Shorty to duck to avoid being shot. But, as in most of my nightmares, my mouth would not open wide enough for the words to escape. All I had managed were a few muffled sounds of a man whose mouth was filled with cotton balls and taped shut.

I was not accustomed to remembering my dreams, but so far this summer they had been both vivid and memorable. First was the one in Doris Dickman's semi as we neared Huntsville a few weeks ago, then my nightmare in Dothan after being assigned to share the room with Monty, and now Shorty kicking the dining club manager's head off just before being blown away by a powerful shotgun blast. I hoped there would be no more, and I sincerely hoped this one did not foretell Shorty's demise.

20.

When Shorty predicted that the word would get around about my skill in open top trailers, I had not given it a second thought. But everything he'd taught me about extra straw to make open top loads look and ride smoothly was paying off. Joe Harper lined up a full week's worth of open top trailers for me, and he arranged for farmers to bring in melons no later than 6:30 A.M. Just my luck! He'd promised the drivers that he would bring a good packer along with him early each day. I didn't mind, because my respect for Joe had grown steadily over my first few weeks on the job. He was not only a good businessman and a straight shooter, but I appreciated the fact that he was a self-taught student of human behavior. For a man who had never set foot in a college classroom, his insight into the produce market and it's complexities, as well as his understanding of the people around him was truly amazing. Some may have seen Joe as a glad-hander who knew how to manipulate people to get what he wanted, but I saw him as a man of innate business savvy and emotional intelligence, qualities that could not be taught.

Joe and I started our Monday morning trip to Holcomb as we had on my first day on the job. As expected, he was wide awake and talkative, and on this particular morning I was back to my old self, wishing Joe would be quiet and let me grab a few winks of sleep in the car.

"I take it you don't care much for William," Joe said.

I was somewhat surprised that Joe brought up William's name again.

"How did you guess?" I said, smiling.

Joe chuckled and said, "Well, it's not hard to notice that he's been getting on your nerves from the first day on. He's the kinda' kid who has to have all of his ideas in a neat little bundle, and you seem to be the type that can deal with the changing times. I could see from the beginning that he was kinda' pissing you off when he tried his little routine on you about the South and slavery. As you can imagine, a lot of folks around here agree with his line of bullshit, so that kinda' takes the fun out of it for him. You got annoyed and he knew it, and that's why he's keepin' after it with you."

I said, "It was kind of a shock to me at first, and I didn't know how to react. But after a few days, I started ignoring most of it. Lonny told me the best way to handle

William is to ignore him and he'll eventually go away,' but somehow he keeps luring me back with his obnoxious little comments."

"Well," said Joe, "you won't have to worry about that little prick for much longer."

"What do you mean?" I was surprised, but nonetheless pleased to hear Joe call William a "little prick."

"Aubrey and I talked it over. We thought he would show some potential as a packer by the time we wrapped things up here in Holcomb. If he did, we'd take him along with us to South Carolina and turn him loose to pack on his own. God knows we could use the extra set of hands. But it's clear he won't make the grade, so we've decided to send him back home to his mama. When it comes right down to it, we're paying him to toss melons off the conveyor to packers, and there are more than enough farm kids to toss melons to our packers for free."

I couldn't help laughing. "You mean his shit is flaky?" My dad had taught me that expression, which he'd learned in the Army, and it had stuck with me.

"That's about the size of it," said Joe. "He can't handle hard physical work, and that's the long and the short of it. He'll soon be on his way back home, where he can sit around in his mother's air conditioning and eat bonbons and play tunes on the baby grand piano, or whatever he does all day." As Joe chuckled, his head, which sat directly atop his broad shoulders without a neck, bobbed up and down.

"I can't say I disagree with your decision, Joe," I said. "William doesn't measure up to some of the farm kids around here. In fact, I've let some of them help me with packing a few times, and they're far better at it than William is. That includes 12 and 14 year olds! You wouldn't want to keep him on the payroll if the original idea was to turn him into a packer. Like you said, that just isn't gonna' happen."

Joe said, "I can see you've been paying attention. It's a simple business decision. We're only paying him $2.25 an hour, but we don't like the idea of carrying him as overhead when everyone else is earning their keep. If you figure it takes about four hours to pack a load of melons, and a packer gets $20 out of the driver's paycheck, it just doesn't make sense for Aubrey to pay William almost half that much to do a job that takes no skill at all. I mean, if he helps with three trailers a day, that's $27 of QM's money wasted every day, and it adds up to $162 every week. Aubrey and Don Sr. are good businessmen, and I learned a long time ago that good businessmen pay attention to the little details. That's what makes them successful in the end. William is a little problem, but enough little problems, and all of a sudden you've got yourself a big problem."

Again, I nodded agreement. I had no idea how to run a business, but what Joe said was making sense.

Joe smiled his broad, friendly smile. "I wish William no harm. I just hope there is some kinda' talent inside that skinny body of his. So far, it looks like he's got enough bullshit that he might do well at politics." Joe laughed.

21.

Wednesday morning of my third week was hot the moment the sun rose above the horizon, and no clouds could be seen except for one wispy little fellow who looked as though he might evaporate any second. The minute I stepped into the parking lot, I felt the heat beating down on my back. The dew was heavy on the grass surrounding the parking lot, and the air was thick with humidity that would soon become stifling. Even though we were still packing out 15 to 20 semi loads of melons each day in Holcomb, it was the morning that Joe Harper would tell us the crop in South Carolina could wait no longer. We would have to move on because the quality of melons in Holcomb no longer measured up. This was part of the normal crop cycle. The inevitable aging of melon plants in the fields reduced their ability to give birth to large and juicy melons, and melon vines were run over week after week by tractors and wagons causing them to become weak and frail.

The idea of migrating held little appeal, but daily scouting reports Aubrey received from South Carolina convinced him that Charleston Grays and Crimson Sweets in South Carolina were the best anyone had seen in recent memory. While exaggerated reports about new watermelon crops were commonplace, it had been a perfect summer in South Carolina, with many hot rainy days and cool dewy mornings . . . perfect for growing high quality melons. Farmers in South Carolina were growing new hybrid varieties of melons, and first pickings were being touted as "outstanding shippers."

Lonny's father had made a scouting trip to South Carolina the previous weekend to get a first hand look at what the rave reviews were all about. He had been around watermelons most of his adult life, and heard similar reports hundreds of times before. But this year was different. His weekend in South Carolina provided all the proof he needed . . . it was time to move on! The farmers of Holcomb would be unhappy at best, and feel abandoned at worst. But business was business, and the higher price of Carolina melons meant greater profits for everyone, from buyers in the South to supermarkets up north.

Farmers in Holcomb would complain for a few days, and then they would get on with the work of finishing their melon crop, and move on to late summer grain and autumn corn. All would be forgiven long before the Schroeder and QM buyers pulled into town early next summer.

As soon as we had arrived at the co-op, Aubrey gathered us up for a quick meeting to tell us we would be moving to South Carolina at the end of that same day. After completing our normal day's work, we would begin our trip. Our only stop would be the Holiday Inn in Dothan to grab a quick shower, and then we would pack our bags and turn in our room keys. None of us relished the thought of a long ride without a shower and a change of clothes, so we appreciated Aubrey's generosity in allowing us the time to freshen up. Little did I know when I joined the traveling squad that the watermelon business would resemble the military when it came to moving from one place to another. It felt like we were in the Marine Corps, being told by our unit commander of an overnight deployment, and informed that we would be on the ground at a new battlefront the next morning.

Aubrey explained to us that once the decision had been made to move on, it was not a good idea to hang around. "Farmers get irritable," said Aubrey. In a small town like Holcomb, the economy felt the impact immediately. The greatest surge of economic activity for local businesses took place while melon buyers were in town. Along with it came a short term feeling of general well-being, and the community came to life when wagons, pick-ups and semis began coming and going. Local merchants held "watermelon season" sales, and farm wives came into town to spend some of their husband's melon money before it became earmarked for other purposes. But once the word reached northern markets that a new crop of melons was ready for picking in another part of the South, prices shifted and buyers moved on. Having enjoyed their time in the watermelon trade's equivalent of ground-zero, Holcomb farmers would now have to settle for a lesser price for the remainder of their crop, because South Carolina melons would now be the darlings of northern supermarket produce departments.

Upon breaking the news to us, Aubrey gave us strict orders to keep our mouths shut. He, Joe Harper, and Lonny's dad were the only men authorized to break the news to farmers, and they would handle the damage control. The three men had been coming to Holcomb for many melon seasons, and only they knew how to deal appropriately with the locals. Farmers were an independent breed, and each one had to be dealt with a bit differently from the others. There would be no general meeting, but the three buyers knew the right words to use with each farmer. By the time they departed the co-op that evening, the word would be out and we would be on our way to South Carolina. The farmers would be assured that sufficient rolling stock would be sent to finish out their crops, and a fair market price would be maintained until the final load of Holcomb melons was packed out. Holcomb farmers would accept the fact that their new price would not be top dollar, but they would be OK with that as long they knew that their last marketable melons would not be left to rot in the fields. Buyers had to do right by all of their growers, especially after the decision to move on to greener melon fields was announced. To do otherwise would break a bond of trust that had been carefully nourished over the years, and the long-term consequences could be negative for both sides.

Joe Harper assigned us to our trailers and we worked fast to load as many melons as possible before the morning was over. I finished my first trailer by 10:00 A.M., and Joe assigned me a second, an open top. The morning flew by, and it seemed like no time until Joe made the rounds to inform us it was time to knock off for dinner. From the sounds of Aubrey's little pep talk that morning, I was not certain we would be making the daily trip to Smitherman's. Perhaps, I thought, Aubrey would send Joe to see if Sadie Smitherman could put together some pork tenderloin sandwiches for the packin' shed crew. But, on second thought, I realized that any change in our daily work routine could be taken as a sign that QM was pulling out, and the last thing Joe and Aubrey wanted was a flash message on the Holcomb grapevine, put out by the likes of Sadie Smitherman.

* * *

On his way to the parking lot, Shorty stopped for a second. He was carrying his gallon sized water jug back to his car, but I noticed it had been emptied and the wet sand had been rinsed off the outside of the jug.

"Mr. Aubrey done say me an' Bobby s'pose ta' take off for Sow Calahna 'sevenin.'"

I knew that 'sevenin' meant any time after noon, a bit of dialect that was familiar to me from back home.

"Soon as me an' Bobby goes over to dat fuckin' cancer kitchen and git somethin' to eat out da' back door, we's headin' off ta' God's country! Bobby's so damn excited he even went and axed Mr. Aubrey dis mornin', and Mr. Aubrey say 'yeah, you and Shorty jis' git on outa' here 'sevenin.' 'Dis be my 40th birfday, if'n I remember right. So Bobby says he gonna' show me a good time over in his home place tonight!"

"40! You don't look a day over 30" I was being honest. Looking at his muscular physique and ignoring the belly, he looked like a much younger man.

"I damn shore is 40! My momma always say I'ze borned back in 1928, so dat means I's 40 right now!"

"Jesus Shorty, for a man who claims to be 40, you're the spittin' image of a prize fighter in his prime!" I laughed, and so did Shorty. I reached over and squeezed one of his firm and youthful looking biceps.

"Thank ya', big fella," Shorty said. "I guess maybe ole' Shorty likes to hear dat kinda' talk!"

We climbed into our respective vehicles and headed off toward Smitherman's. I wondered why Shorty and Bobby had chosen to eat their final meal of the Holcomb season at Smitherman's rather than hit the road right away. But my thoughts shifted away from Shorty and Bobby when William admitted to the rest of us in the car that he had told one of the farmers this would be QM's last day in town. He tried to make it sound like he'd done the farmer a favor. In his words, "Aubrey and Joe Harper seem to think these farmers are a bunch of dumb fucks! Don't you think they've figured out that we're minute-to-minute with all the talk about the South Carolina crop? Hell, everyone around here has been talkin' about the new crop of melons in Harkensville and Bamberg for the past week. I'm sure it came as no big surprise to the farmer I told."

I looked at William in disbelief, and for the moment I was mesmerized by his appearance. His lower lip protruded like a pouting child, and his expression reminded me of a little boy who'd been sent to his room without dinner. I knew the second I looked at him that Joe had told him his employment with QM was finished, and he would not be moving to South Carolina. With this in mind, I assumed that William was the kind to seek revenge for his hurt feelings, so he'd decided to blab a company secret to one of the farmers. I wondered if Joe might have been better off to wait until the last second to break the news to William that he was being let go. Telling him in the morning had erased any miniscule sense of company loyalty William may have had, effectively turning him into a loose cannon.

"I hope you don't live to regret spilling your guts, William!" I said.

"What the hell are you talking about?" William leered at me as he slowly measured out his words. His mouth had a repulsive snarl to one side.

I interrupted. "Joe and Aubrey know what the fuck they're doing here. They didn't fall off the goddam turnip truck this morning, you know. When Aubrey told us to keep our mouths shut about this move, I figured—and I think everyone else in this car figured—QM was trying to finesse this thing as best they could. Among other things, that probably meant waiting until this afternoon to start breaking the news. I'm sure the last thing they want is a bunch of whiny and pissed off farmers and farm hands getting together for dinner at Smitherman's, bitchin' to each other about fly-by-night melon buyers."

Lonny looked at William through his rearview mirror and said, "I agree with Matt on this one, William. You obviously don't know the first thing about dealing with farmers. You really stepped on your own crank this time."

As the son of one of the QM owners, Don Jr. couldn't help but speak up in agreement with Lonny and me. "William, you stupid fucker!" Don Jr. said. "If I were Aubrey and Joe, I think I'd kick your slimy little ass all the way back to your mommy in Florida."

William's eyes welled up with tears and his mouth began to quiver. "They *are* sending me back to Florida!"

"What?" Lonny said.

"They *ARE* sending me back to Florida! You heard me." William nearly yelled it this time.

Despite the way I felt against William, I couldn't help but feel sorry for him at this moment. His announcement about being sent home was no surprise to me, but I suddenly felt badly for him. And then I thought of how worthless he was on the job, and of the trouble he could cause in South Carolina, particularly if he went against Aubrey's instructions on a matter of importance to the company. The remainder of our short trip to Smitherman's was silent. Nobody in the car said another word. We pulled up in front and located a parking space with some difficulty, then we saw Shorty and Bobby Leeds driving past us toward the back of the building. They parked just in front of a wooded area that formed a lush green backdrop to the ugly gray restaurant building. It didn't seem to matter to Shorty and Bobby that they had to park in back, as they had more spaces to choose from than those of us who were privileged to park in front. But this day was different. The front of the restaurant was packed tight, and there were only a few spaces left in the back. I thought to myself, this was proof that William's deliberate slip of the tongue had made an impact. Something was obviously different.

22.

Geneva county Sheriff, Rufus Lane, and Deputy Tommy Evans were returning to Holcomb after investigating a grocery store robbery in a neighboring village, when their mobile police radio crackled and the voice of dispatcher Elsie Gruber came on.

"Sheriff Lane, do you read me?"

Lane picked up his handset. "Roger that. What is it, Elsie?"

"Suspected drunk driver in a 1957 Chevy, spotted a few minutes ago by an eyewitness in downtown Holcomb. The caller said the man was drivin' about 60 miles an hour through the heart of downtown. That's a 30 mile an hour zone, ain't it Sheriff?"

"You got it, Elsie, as of this year! Used to be 35. Which direction was the guy headed when the witness saw him?"

"Northeast. Toward the farmer's co-op."

"Thanks, Elsie. We'll get there as soon as we can. Over and out."

"Sounds like it might be Teddy Braslow, one of Clarence Dillon's farmhands," said Deputy Evans. "He drives a '57 Chevy and has a speeding record as long as your arm. Has a keen taste for the firewater too."

"I bet he's headed over to Smitherman's for dinner," said Sheriff Lane. "What do you think, Tommy? It's about that time of day, and even drunken farm hands take time out for dinner. I'm gittin' right hungry myself. What say we head on over to Smitherman's and check it out? We might could kill two birds with one stone; take the keys away from our little drunk drivin' buddy, and stay around for some dinner. Miss Sadie is pretty good about givin' a free dinner to an officer of the law.

"Dinner sounds like a winner!" said Deputy Evans. He smiled at his accidental poetic lilt, and Sheriff Lane simply shook his head.

Rufus Lane reached under the dashboard and flipped on his siren, then sped toward Holcomb, destination Smitherman's restaurant.

23.

After Shorty parked his car behind Smitherman's, Bobby got out and went to the back door to purchase two paper plate meals. Mr. Smitherman, who had banned Shorty from approaching the back door, did not charge extra for the hostile looks he gave to Bobby each day as he tossed the food onto the plates with his oversized spoon.

Just after we'd walked inside, the roar of a powerful car engine drew my attention to the side window of the dining room. I saw an eight cylinder 1957 Chevy with two white passengers, roaring into the parking lot. The way the driver threw sand with his oversized tires, he was either drunk or insane, perhaps both. The Chevy's radio blasted loudly enough that it could be heard inside the dining area, and the two men inside the car were laughing. Otis Redding's voice could be heard singing . . . "Sittin' on the Dock of the Bay . . . ." After spinning his tires for a few seconds in the sandy front parking area and stirring up a large cloud of dust, the driver pointed the heaving hulk of steel and sheet metal toward the rear parking area, then quickly disappeared from my line of vision. I glanced at my watch, and noticed it was 11:40 A.M.

As Bobby made his way back toward Shorty's car with two lunch plates, the Chevy pulled up within 5 feet of the driver's side of Shorty's Buick. The driver opened his door and practically fell into the sand. His passenger exited from the side of the car closest to Shorty, then the two men staggered around like two high school kids in a carnival fun house.

"Hey, would ya' lookie here," Teddy Braslow said as he zeroed in on Shorty and Bobby Leeds. "If it 'ain't a couple of big shot nigger melon packers, all the way from Florida!" The drunken man had already noticed the Florida plates on the back of Shorty's car.

"Nice car you got here, nigger. I bet you mother fuckers still got jobs, don't y'all? We done heard y'all are pullin' up stakes and headin' yonder to South Calahna 'sevenin.' Well, fuck you nigger bastards and the black-ass horse you rode in on! We're out of jobs 'cause our bossman says he can't sell any melons after y'all mother fuckers leave town."

Shorty laughed nervously. "Hey man, we jus' woiks' here, ya' know! Boss man say move on; we move on!"

"Shut the fuck up! Did I tell you niggers you could talk back to me? What I'm tellin' you here is my buddy and I just lost our jobs, but you two flat dicks just fall back on that fuckin' same ole' nigger talk; 'da' bossman—he say we gots ta' go, so we gots ta' go!' Well, fuck both a' you worthless mother fuckers! And by the way, who the fuck told you ta' come here and eat white people food anyway?"

Billy Matthews, who had been Braslow's passenger, hadn't opened his mouth except to hock a large ball of saliva-soaked snuff from between his brown stained lips, but there was no doubt he thought his friend's unprovoked rant was funny. After wobbling back and forth on his feet and laughing loudly in support of Braslow's asinine tirade, he pulled a large knife from a leather sheath attached to his belt. "Teddy, I'm gonna' cut me up a couple a' nigger bastards, just for the fun of it! Ain't no nigger gonna' drive a big-ass car like this and leave town with his good payin' job, while we can't even put food on our tables!"

Braslow turned and looked at Matthews, said nothing, then began to laugh hysterically. "Fuck it! If y'all gonna' stick 'em, then stick 'em good, Billy!"

Suddenly, Matthews lunged clumsily toward Bobby Leeds, and the 6-inch knife blade sunk deeply into Bobby's left shoulder. Normally, Bobby would have been too quick for the drunken man to score a direct hit, but he was still holding two plates of food, one in each hand, making him a relatively easy target.

* * *

Inside the restaurant, two farmers were standing next to Joe and Aubrey's table. One of the farmers, a man named Clarence Dillon, could be heard complaining. "This is the first goddam time y'all have pulled out without botherin' to come to us and tell us. Pretty damn tacky, I'd say. What's this goddam bidnuss comin' to, anyway?"

Aubrey smiled and his mouth twitched. Joe, always the diplomat, explained to the farmer that there was no choice, and that it was common knowledge that the melons in South Carolina were ready. "Most buyers have already settled in there. We've stayed here as long as we can to make sure you fella's got the best deals for your melons."

"Well," said Dillon, "I've never known you fellars to treat us this way. You usually come to us man-to-man and tell us when you've decided to move out. This time I had to hear it from one of your snot-nose packers."

24.

Bobby and Shorty were first introduced in South Carolina. Shorty had already been working with QM for several years, but it was Bobby's first summer as a packer with them. Up to that point, Shorty had worked alongside another packer from South Carolina named Richard Saunders, who most people knew as "Nigger Rich."

Saunders stood about six feet tall and was slight of build, but not as thin and gaunt as Slick. In his earlier years as a melon packer, he was known simply as "Rich," but after a particularly good season in 1959, he purchased a shiny new Ford Fairlane, and one of the buyers in Florida dubbed him "Nigger Rich" when he reported to work the following spring in his newly acquired ride.

Blacks in the South in the 1950s were accustomed to smiling and going along with racial humor visited upon them by white "bossmen," so the nickname stuck without protest from Rich. After a while, other black packers were calling him by the nickname. His favorite reply was, "You can call me anything you wants, jis' don't be callin' me late fur dinner."

Shorty always remembered the first day he met Bobby Leeds at the Harkensville, South Carolina farmer's market, where melons grown for miles around were loaded for shipping. His first impression was that Bobby was physically too small to survive a summer as a packer. But Shorty soon learned differently. Bobby not only had the strength and stamina to handle the work, but he had a natural ability to "find the hole"—as Shorty liked to say. Each melon Bobby handled seemed to end up in exactly the right place in his stack, and the end result of every load he completed was the closest thing to melon packing perfection. After teaming up with Bobby for a couple of truckloads when Rich was not at work, Shorty realized he'd found a new partner for the inevitable day when Rich decided to retire and move on to less strenuous pursuits.

What Shorty liked most about Bobby, besides his natural ability as a packer, was Bobby's quick wit. Bobby had the ability to make Shorty laugh. Even when Shorty was having a bad day, Bobby could have him laughing by mid-morning and suddenly his problems seemed to fade away. It was like the friendship I had with my brother, Ben. I could always make him laugh, and he relied upon me for that.

After becoming good friends, Shorty and Bobby could not imagine packing melons without being side by side. And there was something else; Bobby had saved Shorty's life. It was not Shorty's first close call, and thanks to Bobby it turned out much better than the car accident that cost Shorty his arm. In the summer of 1964, the two packers were working out of the Holcomb farmer's co-op, when the tail end of a semi trailer came within inches of crushing Shorty against the concrete loading dock. It was a potential accident like hundreds across the United States each year that result in loss of life or permanent disability. Shorty was leaning against the concrete platform with his back to the sandy parking area. He was busily sharpening his favorite pocketknife against a slender gray flint stone, and he just happened to be in the driver's blind spot—directly behind the semi. The driver could not see Shorty through either of his large side mirrors.

Bobby had just come out of L. V. Rosemont's office following a conversation about his paycheck, when he saw the rear end of the semi approaching Shorty. The trailer was just about to crush Shorty between its own rear end and the loading dock. Knowing that Shorty's hearing wasn't the best, yet desperately hoping to get his attention, Bobby yelled out Shorty's name as loud as he could. At the same time, Bobby pointed toward the approaching semi. Fortunately, the high pitch of Bobby's voice pierced through the roar of the co-op's conveyor system. At that instant, Shorty looked up to see Bobby frantically pointing, then turned to see the rear of the trailer no more than two feet away. Reacting with lightening speed, Shorty dropped to his stomach; face down in the sand, avoiding certain injury or death. There was little doubt in his mind that the impact would have killed him, or left him an invalid for life. Had Bobby not warned him with his high-pitched scream at the last possible instant, Shorty knew he would never have packed another melon.

Upon learning of the incident, Joe Harper severely scolded the trucker for backing up to the packin' shed on his own, without a ground guide. Joe told the driver in no uncertain terms that if he were *ever* to jeopardize the well-being of one of QM's packers by repeating the "bonehead move," the driver would never haul another load of produce for the company.

25.

Shorty reacted quickly and instinctively to the sight of the knife tearing into Bobby's shoulder. Grabbing Billy Matthews' arm, he twisted it behind the man and applied massive pressure to Matthews' torso with his short left arm. Shorty's powerful stub pressed hard against Matthews' sternum, causing him to gasp. He felt that his lungs were about to cave in. Shorty saw the knife fall to the ground as Matthews screamed in pain. Shorty's closest friend in the world was bleeding profusely, and the sight of Bobby's blood threw him into a panic. He quickly let go of the man's torso and reached down to pick up the knife. His next reflex action was to bring his powerful left shoulder upward, and with the knife firmly in the grip of his right hand, he buried the blade squarely into the man's abdomen. The drunken man staggered and fell backward as blood spurted from his midsection and a slight trickle of crimson appeared in one corner of his mouth. He landed on his back, and his body began to shake convulsively as blood spurted with each heartbeat. A massive volume of blood trickled downward and eventually mixed with the sand beneath Matthews' body to form a small puddle of purple mud. From his mouth came a gurgling sound, then his head jerked back and his eyes appeared to be fixed on the wispy summer clouds that floated peacefully across the Alabama sky. Shorty had lacerated the man's aorta, and he bled out in a matter of minutes.

Bobby screamed in pain, and blood continued to gush from his severely lacerated shoulder. Shorty had no idea how badly Bobby was really hurt, and he felt a rising sense of panic at the sight of the man bleeding on the ground next to the car. He feared that Bobby would soon be joining the man in a swift and bloody death.

Shocked into what could have passed as sobriety, Teddy Braslow got back into his car, started the engine and jammed the car into reverse. When he slammed his pride and joy into first gear, the Chevy engine roared louder than ever as the car heaved forward. Braslow threw a cloud of dust three times the size of the one he had stirred up during his grand entrance into the parking lot a few minutes earlier, and he sped away with the wild look of a frightened fugitive.

Shorty could only hope that Braslow was going for an ambulance to help his fallen friend, and that whomever responded might be willing to help a gravely injured black man as part of the bargain. Experience had taught him, however, that ambulance crews sometimes ignored black victims if a white person at the scene needed urgent care. On the day he had lost half of his left arm, Shorty awoke in the Negro section of a county hospital following the accident, to the face of a friendly black nurse in his hospital room. She explained as much as she could about what had happened to him, and then a few sketchy details about the accident came back to him. The nurse had pieced together the story of Shorty's heroic actions, along with many facts he could not remember. When the ambulance arrived at the scene, the superficial wounds suffered by the white family Shorty had rescued were treated immediately. Meanwhile, Shorty was left unconscious and unattended long enough that there was no chance for doctors to save his crushed left arm. When the emergency room doctors looked at him, they concluded that the circulation had been cut off below the elbow for a sufficient period of time that amputation was the only means of avoiding serious complications and gangrene.

Now, Shorty's brain blocked out everything except his fear that Bobby's life was in grave danger. He even blocked out the fact that he'd stabbed a man, that he still held the hunting knife in his hand, and that the blood up to the elbow of his right arm gave him the look of an enraged killer. All he knew was that Bobby Leeds lay in the back seat of his Buick, quivering and nearly in shock. Bobby had stopped screaming, which Shorty took as a bad sign.

Shorty looked toward the back of the restaurant and saw only a bolted door. As soon as Bobby was handed the two paper plates, Smitherman had locked the rear door and gone back inside to prepare extra rations for the larger than usual crowd. Smitherman routinely locked the door after he'd dispensed with Shorty and Bobby. He would never have left the rear end of his establishment unsecured with two black men on the premises.

The clamor inside the jam-packed dining room overpowered most of the noise from outside the building, making it impossible for Smitherman or his patrons to hear what had just taken place outside. In a panic, Shorty ran to the front of the building, still unaware that he carried the knife in his right hand. All he knew was that he needed help if Bobby's life was to be saved, and he needed it now!

* * *

Sheriff Lane pulled into Smitherman's front parking lot just in time to see Shorty opening the door and entering the restaurant from the white's only entrance. The sight of the bloody knife in the hand of the large one-armed black man prompted Deputy Evans to radio Elsie Gruber for backup. "Possible homicide in progress at Smitherman's restaurant! Call the State Boys to come at once! Repeat, AT ONCE!" Rufus Lane flung the car door open and reached into the back seat of the cruiser for his 12-gauge shotgun. The Sheriff and his deputy were on Smitherman's front porch in less than one minute, poised to deal with whatever might be happening inside.

A terrifying memory flashed across Lane's mind. A black man about Shorty's size had robbed Holcomb's only small supermarket back in 1965. When Lane arrived at that scene, the black man had fatally stabbed a cashier and the owner of the IGA store lay bleeding to death on the floor. At this moment, Rufus was ready to use the double barrel 12 gauge shotgun without a second thought, because this felt eerily like that fateful morning at the IGA. Two incidents of deadly violence involving blacks in less than five years would probably cost the most popular of southern Sheriffs his job.

As the Sheriff burst through the front door, deputy Evans was right on his heels. Rufus Lane feared the worst, and the scene inside was chaos. An agitated black man wielding a bloody knife was back in the food service area and could not immediately be seen from the dining room.

Oblivious to the patrons inside, Shorty had raced toward the food line where Sadie Smitherman, red-faced and sweating, was serving her would-be diners. Shorty needed a large towel or a piece of cloth material before he rushed back outdoors to apply pressure upon Bobby's gaping wound. Mrs. Smitherman looked upon Shorty with terrified, bulging eyes. She was horrified at the sight of the large, bloody black man with a stub for a left arm and a knife in his right hand. His appearance was freakish and grotesque to Sadie. Although Shorty had only come inside seeking help for Bobby, the woman let out a scream as if she herself had been stabbed. As she screamed, she dropped the large spoon that was filled with a heaping serving of mashed potatoes, and fell backwards. She lost her balance and continued falling until she was on the floor. In the process, she knocked a pitcher of hot gravy onto herself. This caused her to let out a sharp wailing sound like a wounded animal. Just behind the gravy, a bowl full of dark red ketchup had fallen onto her grossly oversized abdomen. Her husband was inside the kitchen, but he could not help hearing his wife's desperate cries from the opposite side of the flimsy plank wall.

Shorty saw the woman fall backwards, but his mind was still focused on what had happened outside. He scanned the room for anything he might use to stop Bobby's bleeding: a first aid kit, a kitchen towel to use as a tourniquet, even a large wad of paper napkins. From his health science class in college, he knew that a gushing wound could be helped by applying pressure with a sufficient amount of cloth, held tightly against it. Bobby was running out of time. The bleeding had to be stopped soon, and Shorty was desperate to do anything he could to save Bobby.

Suddenly, Mr. Smitherman burst through the swinging doors that separated the serving area from the kitchen, brandishing a double-barrel, sawed-off shotgun. His eyes were filled with terror when he saw his wife screaming and wallowing on the floor in a puddle of hot gravy, and what appeared to be blood on the front of her Moo-Moo style dress. Until now, Shorty had not given a thought to his own safety, but the sight of Smitherman with the shotgun in his hands shocked him into the realization that he had a death grip on a bloody lethal weapon. He instantly dropped the knife, but Smitherman's fear combined with his own survival instincts had kicked into high gear. Without hesitation, and at point blank range, he blasted Shorty directly in the abdomen with both barrels of the overpowering weapon. Smitherman was literally knocked backward by the recoil action of the shotgun. Shorty staggered backward, just as Sheriff Lane rushed around the partition that separated the dining room from the serving area. The force of the shotgun blast hurled Shorty backward, his midsection a bloody mess and his body transformed into so many pounds of careening carnage.

As the Sheriff rounded the partition between the dining room and the food service area, he held his powerful shotgun in the ready position with his sausage-like finger on both triggers. He reacted out of the same fear that had possessed Smitherman, along with his overwhelming desire to protect a white business owner against a black intruder. Sheriff Lane contributed two barrels of his own buckshot to the back of Shorty's head. Blood spattered everywhere as Rufus Lane's shotgun blast removed the back of Shorty's skull. Pieces of blood-soaked bone, brain and hair flew like shrapnel, some of it landing on Smitherman and a handful of customers who had sought refuge under food serving tables. As if the entire scene were unfolding in slow motion, Shorty's body continued falling backward. The momentum of Smitherman's initial blast to the torso, combined with Shorty's weight, could not be reversed by the counter-explosion from behind that snapped his head forward and blew it apart. Shorty lay dead at Sheriff Lane's feet in a matter of seconds. Despite the sickening feeling Rufus Lane had in the pit of his stomach, he was fully aware that he would now be considered a hero, and his job would be safe through the upcoming fall elections.

Sheriff Lane wheeled around immediately and barked out orders for all patrons in the dining room to clear the area at once. The last thing he needed was a bunch of nosy customers gawking at the scene and lending their own interpretations to what had just happened. Many had already bolted from the dining room and made a beeline for their cars, while others cowered under tables as if they were expecting the roof to cave in any second.

Responding to Elsie Gruber's call, a State Trooper had pulled into the parking area as people rushed outside to the safety of their own vehicles. He turned off his siren, left the flashing red lights on above his cruiser, and followed Alabama Trooper procedure for sealing off the scene of an investigation. His lawman instincts told him that no vehicles must leave or enter the area until the situation could be sorted out. Just then, however, an ambulance, which Teddy Braslow had summoned from a phone booth after fleeing the scene, screamed into the front parking lot. The Trooper had to make an exception for emergency vehicles, so he stepped aside and waved the vehicle through. The driver stopped in front of the restaurant to confer with the law enforcement officer about the situation.

Now that Shorty was dead, nobody knew that a white man lay dead behind Smitherman's, and that Bobby Leeds lay bleeding in the back seat of Shorty's car. Braslow reported over the pay phone that a disturbance had taken place in which "a man was stabbed by a nigger." All anyone had witnessed was Shorty storming into the restaurant carrying a bloody knife. They also knew that he was dead, and no longer a threat to a living soul.

The patrons who had been herded outside ran for the safety of their automobiles. As I ran along with the others, I wondered why people thought of their cars as personal safety capsules. My parents had always herded our family into the car whenever there was a threat of an electrical storm, or a National Weather Service tornado warning. Perhaps the automobile, with its heavy metal frame and potential for speed, represented the ultimate personal security shell that satisfied the human instinct to run from imminent danger.

Smitherman followed his customers into the front parking lot, waving his shotgun in the air like he was Davy Crockett, King of the Wild Frontier. I caught a glimpse of the proud look of victory in his eyes, and it sickened me. He was a sorry little man.

Suddenly I felt a heavy hand on my left shoulder, as Joe Harper grabbed me and shoved me into the car where the other three packers were waiting. In a voice more agitated than I had ever heard from him, Joe said, "OK boys, clear out! This establishment is off limits. We need to get outa' the way and let the lawmen do their job. Now get the hell outa' here, and get back to the co-op!"

I wanted to defy Joe's order and stay behind to tell the Sheriff to check on Bobby Leeds, who still had to be somewhere behind the building. I felt that I knew Shorty well enough that he would not have come into the restaurant unless something dreadful had happened, and that he was desperate for help. I had seen the look in his eyes, a look of abject terror, not anger. If his terror was over something that had happened to Bobby, then Bobby needed help.

The Sheriff took jurisdiction, overruling the State Trooper, who now agreed to clear out rather than seal off the parking lot. The Trooper wasted no time posting himself in the middle of the blacktop road that ran past Smitherman's, where he began waving a flare and attempting to speed up the customer exodus. Lonny pulled his dad's car out of the parking lot at the direction of the Trooper's hand signals and onto the main road that would take us back to the co-op.

"I swear to God," I said, "Shorty wasn't capable of hurting anyone, except in self defense. There *has* to be a good reason why he came inside! How the fuck did Shorty end up with all that blood on him?"

William sat silently next to me in the back seat, slowly shaking his head. I could tell he wanted to say something, but he knew better than to open his mouth. We made it back to the co-op in a few short minutes. I was reeling from the tragedy we had just witnessed, and yet had no idea what happened to Bobby Leeds. As each minute passed, I feared more and more that Bobby was in serious danger.

26.

Once the dinner patrons had all cleared away from Smitherman's parking lot, Deputy Evans accompanied the ambulance driver on foot to the rear of the building. The driver said his dispatcher had reported a stabbing at Smitherman's restaurant, so the entire scene had to be searched for possible victims.

Bobby Leeds was still screaming for help, and in addition to his own pain he was screaming out of panic over what he suspected had happened to Shorty. He had heard the gunfire coming from inside of the restaurant several minutes earlier.

As the deputy followed Bobby's screams to Shorty's Buick, he nearly tripped over Billy Matthews' dead body. Matthews had died in a pool of his own blood, and the sticky mud underneath his corpse was now drying in the hot midday sun. Hundreds of flies swarmed to partake of the sweet tasting nourishment.

The ambulance driver sprinted back to the front of the building and jumped into his vehicle, alongside the emergency technician who had accompanied him to the scene. "Jesus Christ, we gotta' hurry," the breathless driver yelled to the technician. "There's a man that looks dead back yonder, and a nigger bleedin' like a stuck hog in the backseat of a car!"

Deputy Evans came running to alert Sheriff Lane about the gruesome scene he and the ambulance driver had just witnessed. Evans was on the verge of vomiting as he attempted to speak.

"Rufus! Come around back! You ain't gonna' fuckin' believe this!"

Flashing a look at Evans like Andy of Mayberry would at Barney Fife, the Sheriff broke into a slow jog toward the back of the restaurant, with Smitherman right behind him. Sadie Smitherman, who seemed to have come back to life after her husband had helped her off the floor, waddled behind the others. Her tent-like dress was still soaked with warm gravy and ketchup.

Sheriff Lane looked down at the dead man, and said, "Well, I'll be a goddamned monkey's uncle!" He then heard Bobby Leeds let out a scream, just as the ambulance arrived in the rear parking area of Smitherman's.

"Fuck! This don't make any goddam sense," said the Sheriff. "What the hell went on back here? Didn't anybody see this happen?" Lane, at a complete loss to make sense of the scene, realized the situation would now be complicated. He also realized that the only other man who might be able to explain what had happened behind the restaurant was Teddy Braslow, who had fled the scene and would have to be tracked down. Not only would the Sheriff have to deal with the dead black man inside the restaurant, but he would also have to sort out what had happened to Billy Matthews and the wounded black man in the back seat of the Buick. There would be paperwork, which Rufus despised. In addition to himself and Smitherman, who had both applied deadly force to uphold the law, other white men were involved. One lay dead at his feet, and the other was probably outside of Alabama by this time.

Now Rufus was painfully aware that he would have to explain away the death of another white man at the hand of a black man on his watch. A twinge of anxiety brought beads of sweat to the back of his neck, when he suddenly realized that his upcoming reelection would not be a sure thing after all.

"Looks to me like these two niggers started some kinda' fight, and this fella' here took the brunt of it," said Evans, in an obsequious tone. "That dead nigger inside the restaurant probably started the whole goddamned mess. I ain't got much use for Teddy Braslow, and I had even less for Matthews, but it's usually the niggers that start this kinda' shit, especially when there's knives involved. That's their trademark. They like to stick people with big knives."

"Who the fuck knows?" Sheriff Lane was not in the mood for his deputy's sycophantic comments. "I can't charge that little nigger in the car with anything unless he's got a weapon on him. We've got one murder weapon from the hand of the dead nigger inside, and that looks like it was enough to do all of the damage I see here in front of me. But just in case, check out the back seat of this car to see if he's got a knife or a gun, and check underneath of him too. After that, we'd better get him on his way to a hospital before he goes ahead and dies on us. Two dead bodies is enough for one day. Plus, we might could use this one's story to sort this fuckin' thing out."

The Sheriff looked at Smitherman. "I'm damned glad I wasn't here earlier for dinner. No offense to your cookin' boss, but I don't think I'd be able to keep my dinner down if I'd already ett. No matter how long I'm in the Sheriffin' bidnuss, I never get used to the sight of blood, guts and brains."

Bobby Leeds was rapidly fading into a state of semi-consciousness. After what seemed an eternity, he was finally placed inside the ambulance and sent on his way to badly needed medical treatment. As the ambulance sped away, its siren shrieked ominously in the hot Alabama sun for all of Holcomb to hear. Besides getting the help he urgently needed, the best thing about the ambulance ride for Bobby was the fact that he had just made his final visit to Smitherman's restaurant.

Sheriff Lane said, "While we're still here, Tommy, call and fetch a tow truck to come for the dead nigger's Buick. Have 'em carry it down to the county storage lot. I reckon we'll need to hold it for evidence, at least for a while. Damn nice automobile for a nigger melon packer," he said as if talking to himself. "Too bad the fuckin' back seat is full a' nigger's blood!" He paused. "Oh, by the way, radio Miz Gruber and have her call the coroner. Then she'll need to call Holcomb funeral home, and the nearest black funeral home. We ain't got one here, but there's one in Dothan. I'm sure she knows that."

Sheriff Lane turned to the young State Trooper, who had spoken only a few words since he'd arrived at the scene. "You might wanna' radio in and put your State Boys on the lookout for a 1957 Chevy. Tell 'em to look for blood in the car if they find it, or some evidence that the driver was in on this shit here. I was lookin' for that Chevy when I came here a little while ago. Now a buddy of the guy that drives it is dead. We're gonna' need ta' get to the bottom of this fuckin' mess as soon as we can! If Braslow was in on this, it sure as shit don't look good for his ass; leavin' the scene while his buddy was dyin' and all. He musta' been spooked by that big nigger, or just too fuckin' drunk to think straight!"

The black funeral home would send their own ambulance to Smitherman's to pick up Shorty's body once the medics and the coroner had verified the obvious: "He's dead." Shorty's lifeless body would be taken first to the county morgue for examination as to the cause of death, and then transferred to the funeral home in Dothan. The coroner's death certificate would eventually read, "massive trauma," and would contain no mention of gunshot wounds. With this official cause of death, the coroner would essentially guarantee that no future review or analysis of Shorty's demise would implicate Smitherman or Sheriff Lane.

27.

Aubrey and Joe brought us together at the co-op for a crisis session. Immediately taking charge, Joe said, "Here's what we're gonna' do, fellas! You're all gettin' in the car *right now* and headin' for Dothan where you'll stop off at the Holiday Inn and gather your shit together. Sorry there's no time for showers, so just put up with the stink for the trip. It's best if you get on the road to South Carolina within the hour! If people around here start choosin' sides, you never know who could be waiting for you when you get to the hotel. You could be faced with an angry mob of farm hands because a white kid is dead, or a black sniper because of what happened to Shorty and Bobby. I doubt it'll be either one if you get outa' the area fast, but it's just not worth the risk of having you fellas hanging around."

We all nodded in agreement.

"I'll ask the co-op to line up some farm hands to finish these loads here, and some of the farmers and truckers can help with the packing," said Joe. "I'll make sure Monty pays you all for the loads you were working on when we broke for dinner. Don't concern yourselves with anything here, just do as I say and get yourselves on the road."

"Any word on Bobby?" I asked.

"We know nothing more than you do, Matt," said Aubrey. "This all happened too fuckin' fast, and there's a lot to sort out. But that's the Sheriff's job, not mine. All we can do is say a fuckin' prayer to ourselves that he's OK. We'll try to find out what's happened to Bobby so we can give you fellas an update when Joe and I catch up with you in South Carolina. That'll probably be tomorrow morning, if we're lucky enough to get outa' here this evening."

Joe Harper interjected that he and Aubrey had a brief conversation with a farmer who'd been eating dinner at Smitherman's. Joe said, "According to this ole' boy, one of the packers at the co-op said something about QM leavin' town at the end of the day, and he had no choice but to let a couple of his farm hands go. Any of you boys know who might have opened his mouth about us pullin' out 'sevenin'?"

At that instant, my intense dislike for William boiled over, and I could not contain my rage over the role he might have played in Shorty's death. To my own surprise and everyone else's, I threw an elbow squarely into William's left rib cage with enough force to knock down a man twice his size. He went stumbling across the parking lot for 15 feet or more, and fell flat on his face in the hot sand. Without thinking, I followed up with a deep kick in his direction, which sent a cloud of sand and dust in the direction of his sprawled out body. He rolled over and squealed like a pig that had been hit in the rear end by an electric prod. I kicked another cloud of sand directly into his face. "That's for Shorty, you bastard."

"Help me!" William yelled out, still squealing." Nobody helped him up. Lonny and Don Jr. looked on in total silence.

I looked back towards Joe and Aubrey. "This worm-ass fucker told that farmer this morning that we would be leaving for South Carolina at the end of the day."

"What the fuck?" Joe yelled as he looked down at William who was lying in the hot sand, whimpering like a terrified puppy in a thunderstorm.

"Is Matt telling the truth, young man? Did you tell one a' these farmers about our plans to move?"

Sobbing now, William nodded. "Yes, sir, I couldn't see as though it would cause any harm."

"Well, I hope you can see now that it did a *great* deal of harm! We've got a dead packer on our hands, and we don't even know what's happened to Bobby Leeds. This could all be your fault for opening your big mouth. I told you boys this morning that these folks around here get all jumpy when they find out we're leaving. That's why I also told you to keep quiet about this, dammit! If I find out any of this was caused by you letting the cat out of the bag this mornin', you'll have hell to pay, even if you *are* Aubrey's nephew! Do you hear me, young man?"

Aubrey stood silently, looking at William with disgust and disappointment in his eyes. The corner of his mouth twitched nearly out of control. "My nephew," he thought to himself. "My own nephew!"

William did not attempt to answer Joe Harper, but went on whimpering as he lay on his back with tears leaving dark trails of wet sand down his face.

* * *

I could tell that Joe and Aubrey would gladly have left along with us if it were not for their obligations as businessmen to complete the partially loaded semis before leaving town. Their relationship with the melon growers association of Holcomb had been solid for many years, and they hoped the farmers wouldn't blame QM for what had just taken place at Smitherman's. Had it been anywhere else, it might not have had the same impact, but it had happened in front of a large group of farmers in a public establishment. Events that took place in eating establishments had their own way of gaining emotional momentum and causing a ripple effect throughout the community.

Aubrey, a nervous type in any tight situation, was more anxious than Joe was. Joe's experience in the Marine Corps had given him a view of the world in which there was very little a man should fear. The death and destruction he had lived through as a young man during World War II had vaccinated him against most of the daily fears that affected other people, but it obviously had not taken away his humanity. His stern lecture to William stood as proof enough that he was deeply human.

28.

Our trip to South Carolina was long and tiresome. Somewhere along the way, the three of us realized how close we'd come to mortal danger when Smitherman and the Sheriff had blasted away at Shorty. The powerful blasts had gone off no more than 20 feet from the table where we had been seated. A slip of the weapon in Smithermans' hands could have brought serious harm to us. I had seen a demonstration in a gun safety class that showed how a shotgun blast at close range could easily penetrate a wooden or sheetrock wall, and even travel through it. In a few notable cases, people had been killed by errant gunshots from adjoining apartments. Smitherman's flimsy partition was made of a single layer of wooden slats, each 1/4 inch thick, leaving little doubt that a barrage of close-range buckshot could have passed through it. It would be a long time before the three of us would forget the deafening sounds of consecutive double-barrel blasts from the two powerful weapons; and perhaps even longer before we would feel their full emotional impact.

* * *

I was grateful for the long daylight hours of summer, mostly because there were enough of them left for me to write a letter to my brother. I knew that the trip to Harkensville would be more tolerable if I got out paper and pen and started a letter to Ben about the feelings that were now tormenting me. With the exception of a few older relatives who had passed away, I had been sheltered from close encounters with death. But my friend Shorty had been alive just a few hours before, and now he was gone. The events that led up to his death suddenly weighed heavily on me.

* * *

"Ben,

Things have turned sour in watermelon land! The way I feel at this moment, I could come home and would not miss this bullshit at all! One of our packers, a big black guy named Shorty, is dead. I have never dreamed I would witness anything like this. During our lunch break today, the owner of this little greasy spoon killed Shorty. The local Sheriff also got into the act, and before anybody knew what was going on, Shorty took four 12 gauge shotgun shells, all within a couple of seconds of each other and all at very close range.

Shorty and Bobby Leeds, the only two black packers in our crew, were eating their lunches behind the restaurant according to local custom, and I knew something really bad must have happened when Shorty came rushing in the front door of the place. He wouldn't have done that if it were not a major emergency, because he always went along with the rules about what blacks can and cannot do in public places.

We couldn't see everything that happened from our table, but when the owner's wife saw Shorty (his skin black as coal except for blood on his one good arm), she screamed like a stuck pig! Then her husband came out from the kitchen with his shotgun in his hands. At that point the husband was already in a panic mode, so without asking any questions, he blew ole' Shorty away. Apparently he either thought his wife was in serious danger, or he assumed that Shorty had threatened the fat old bitch. Then, just as the restaurant owner blasted Shorty, a big ass Sheriff came running in through the front door, and blasted Shorty again. As big and powerful a man as Shorty was, he didn't have a fuckin' chance! I didn't see him after it happened, but I know he musta' been a bloody pulp.

Ben, one thing I've learned is that a black man down here is never innocent if he's around when trouble breaks out. Any black man who gets mixed up with any kind of trouble is guilty for being AT the scene! I think all this shit with civil rights marches and bus riding protests over the past few years has gotten whites down here more pissed off than ever at blacks. The blacks are perfectly right for wanting things to be changed, but the whites want the good ole' days back when their Steppin Fetchit "niggers" smiled and went along with the program. I guess whites felt they could trust blacks in those days, and now nobody trusts anybody.

I gotta' tell ya', our white-bread upbringing back in Elmwood left me totally unprepared for a tragedy like the one I saw today! I guess I haven't been around this sort of prejudice and racial hatred for one simple reason: I haven't been around black people enough to learn how things go when blacks and whites bump into one another on a daily basis. When whites feel threatened, all hell breaks loose. I know a lot of white guys who talk about how black people in the South are trying to ruin things for all of us, and how they should all be sent back to Africa. But I didn't have a fucking clue what life was like for blacks down here. I'm tellin' ya' Ben, this day has pretty much fucked up this job for me! I hope things will be better in South Carolina, but I doubt if I can expect anything different. And even if it is different, it'll be fucked up without Shorty, my big league packin' coach.

I'm writing this in the car because we're on our way to South Carolina right now, and we don't even know at this point if Bobby Leeds, the other black packer who always hung out with Shorty, is OK or not! Nobody had located Bobby by the time we left the restaurant in Holcomb. We'll probably find out in the morning when our bosses arrive from Holcomb. Hopefully we'll learn that Bobby is all right. Take care, you big Hoss.

More soon!

Matt

29.

Before leaving Dothan, Aubrey and Joe received word that Bobby Leeds would remain in the hospital there, and that his life had been saved by a young emergency room intern. Without regard to the color of Bobby's skin, the young white doctor had performed an unconventional surgical procedure to stop the bleeding, and then applied 75 stitches to close the gaping shoulder wound Bobby had suffered. Joe Harper stopped by to visit Bobby before departing for South Carolina, and learned that Bobby would need at least two to three weeks of rest and recuperation, one of which would be in the hospital.

Bobby, under heavy sedation, explained to Joe how the stabbing incident behind Smitherman's had developed. With a heavy heart, he admitted that he thought Shorty was better off dead. "Joe Harper," Bobby had said, "If Shorty wouldn't a' got killed today, dey damn shore woulda' kilt him in da' muthafuckin' 'lectric chair, or let him rot away in jail da' rest a his born days fur killin' dat white man!"

After visiting with Bobby in the hospital, Joe had driven back to Holcomb to pay a visit to Sheriff Lane, who had also sent his deputy to the hospital in Dothan to complete some paperwork on Bobby's injuries, as well as to obtain a statement from Bobby.

"Are you gonna' press charges against our packer?" Joe asked Rufus Lane point blank.

"No, buddy, we ain't. Seems like your boy that got himself stabbed in the shoulder was not armed, so far as we could tell. The one that allegedly started the fracas, ole' Billy Matthews, is dead. We know he was the owner of the knife. Damn shame, he was a good baseball player when he was younger. I know his daddy and the kid weren't all that bad as long as he stayed off the hootch. By the way, the State Police boys picked up Teddy Braslow, the kid who was drivin' the 1957 Chevy. He says he took off like a bat outa' hell as soon as Matthews got stabbed, and in his statement he said Matthews started the whole thing by pullin' out the knife and stabbin' your little melon packer in the shoulder. We're chargin' Teddy with drunk drivin' and leavin' the scene of a crime. I'm chalkin' the whole thing up ta' these two fellars bein' piss drunk over the trauma of losin' their jobs. Just so's you know, I gotta' tell ya' that these local white boys around Holcomb gits all crazy when they see a couple a' niggers they don't think s'posed to be someplace! They kinda' fly off the handle when they've been drinkin', like these two white boys did when they saw your nigger packers grabbin' a meal at Smitherman's. And like I said, these two were hurtin' over losin' their jobs that morning. I ain't blamin' you folks for that, 'cause I know that's the way the melon bidnuss works. Far as I can tell, this thing is over and done with, but you and your boss might wanna' ask your black boys ta' find someplace else ta' eat dinner when y'all come back to Holcomb next summer, hear? By the way, sorry you fellas lost one a your packers. I hear that Shorty fella' could sling a load a' melons with the best of 'em, even with one arm missin'."

"Just between you and me, Sheriff, I don't think I'll ask any black packers to come here with us next summer," said Joe. "This shit that happened here today ain't the kinda' thing they're gonna' forget any time soon. I've known these two packers for a long time, and they'd never start any trouble with local white boys. I can damn sure guarantee you that much. It had to be the white boy's fault, pure and simple, and you've pretty much admitted to that. If I was you, I'd have that kid that was drivin' the Chevy behind bars right now, charged with accessory to murder. And there's something else I wanna' get off my chest, Sheriff."

"What's that?" Rufus Lane asked.

"It's about ole' man Smitherman and you haulin' off and shootin' our packer like you did. Didn't it bother you just a little bit that you blasted a man from behind like that, after he'd already been shot? For Christ's sake, man, neither Smitherman nor you had the time to figure out what was goin' on, but as soon as you saw a black man was involved, you pulled the fuckin' trigger like you were at a Sunday afternoon turkey shoot. Don't you feel just a little bit bad about that, Sheriff? Especially, now that you know the whole mess was probably started by a couple a' drunk white boys?"

Rufus Lane looked at the papers on his desk for a second, then he looked Joe Harper squarely in the eyes. "No," he said. "I was just doin' my job. A Sheriff in this neck a' the woods has gotta' protect his citizens, and when niggers gits involved, he damn sure better handle the situation, if you know what I mean."

Joe Harper shook his head in disgust. "That's what they always say, isn't it? I was just doin' my job! Well, congratulations Sheriff, you sure as hell did a bang up job of it today!"

Sheriff Lane ignored Joe's comment. "By the way," he said, "the funeral home in Dothan will put your dead packer on a train and ship him back to Florida tonight. We need to keep his car for awhile though."

"How long will you need the car?" Joe asked.

"Not sure. I guess the best answer to that is, as long as it takes to complete our investigation."

"Well," said Joe, "I think my other packer who's laid up in the hospital will want to come over and pick up the car at some point."

"I don't s'pose we'll be needin' ta' hold it for more than a few weeks. Just tell him to give us a couple of weeks to get the investigation done, then he can come on over and we'll see about releasin' it to him if he has a valid driver's license."

Joe Harper left the Sheriff's office with a sick feeling in his stomach. Although he and Shorty had been a world apart socially, they made their permanent homes not far from each other in Florida, and Joe had talked Shorty into traveling with the melon crops after he'd observed Shorty's packing skills years ago in the main Quality Melon co-op. Now, Joe felt partially responsible for the fact that Shorty lay dead, and it didn't help at all to learn that the Sheriff who had blasted off the back of Shorty's head felt no remorse. After all, it was all a "big misunderstandin', and misunderstandin's happen all the time." And besides, the Sheriff had only been "doin' his job."

30.

Lonny, Don Jr., and I departed Dothan early that afternoon as Aubrey and Joe had instructed. No angry crowds awaited us at the Holiday Inn, in Dothan. Once we were on the road toward South Carolina, we progressed into Georgia and across the wide lower half of the state; destination Harkensville, SC. The trip was more than 350 miles and we estimated it would take 7 to 8 hours. We would travel along two-lane state routes with two exceptions: a leg northward along I-75, and another leg eastward on I-20 into the Augusta, Georgia area. When we arrived at our destination, we were to check in to a motel near Harkensville, South Carolina.

Lonny had worked for QM during the South Carolina tour of 1967, so he had a good idea where the motel was located. He also had an excellent sense of direction, so Don Jr. and I were relying on him to get us to our destination without complications.

I was exhausted after finishing my letter to Ben, but writing it had helped me to deal with an internal firestorm of random emotions. My mind began to wander, and I found myself re-living Indiana melon seasons past intertwined with inevitable cameos of Smitherman's restaurant and Shorty's death.

* * *

Despite my exhaustion, Dr. Harmon had something important to say to me about the day I had just been through. Or, perhaps it was *because* of my exhaustion that he had something to tell me. Suddenly, a light came on in one corner of my brain, and there stood Dr. Andrew Harmon. This time I noticed his clothing . . . a black suit and white shirt with a minister's collar. It was as if he was ready to deliver a sermon.

"*Now, are you beginning to appreciate what black people have to endure? Are you beginning to understand what Dr. King's message was about? You have seen today that a black man who asserts himself, though he is of good heart and without malice of intent, is assumed to be evil. Such a man, a kind and gentle man, can suffer the most exacting judgment and his undeserved punishment is often administered in the absence of due process.*"

"But, what about the white man's fear of a blood soaked black man carrying a knife?" I asked. "Could that not be described as legitimate fear? Could the fear Smitherman's wife experienced upon seeing Shorty have been enough to justify a strong reaction, even if bigotry were not a factor?"

"Perhaps it might have been," said Dr. Harmon. *"Fear is a powerful force, tied directly to self-preservation. But I contend that in this case the reaction was excessive and criminal. I'm telling you that if a white man had done the same thing Shorty did today, Smitherman might have gotten the shotgun out, but would probably not have used it."*

"I suppose you're right," I thought.

"By the way," asked the voice of Dr. Harmon for the sake of argument, *"did you even think to stop Shorty yourself when you saw him storming into the restaurant with fear in his eyes?"*

"What do you mean? It all happened in an instant. There was no time!"

"Maybe a true friend would have jumped up and grabbed him, taken him back outside and tried to sort out what was happening. You must have sensed that he was in grave danger simply by the fact that he had come inside. For God sakes, the man was not even welcome outside, so he clearly was not welcome inside under any circumstances!"

"Hell, Dr. Harmon, aren't you getting a bit theoretical here? This isn't a Hollywood movie, where the good guy reacts quickly and always does the right thing. This is real life, and smothering me with guilt over what I might have done won't bring Shorty back."

"You're absolutely right. Nothing will bring Shorty back. But the next time something happens that puts a friend of yours in danger, maybe you should react a bit differently."

For the first time, I truly enjoyed turning off that light in my brain and quieting Dr. Harmon's voice. Like everyone else in the dining room at Smitherman's that day, I had been shocked at the horrific sight of Shorty with blood on his arm and a knife in his hand. Like the others, I had cared most about my own personal safety. And yet, Dr. Harmon's voice haunted me. I might have done more had I possessed true courage. I might have jumped up and grabbed Shorty, as Dr. Harmon had suggested. I could have taken him back outside by wrapping him in my arms and applying every ounce of force I had in my strong young body. Smitherman and the Sheriff would probably not have blasted us both with their deadly weapons. After all, I was white. I might have been the hero, who not only saved Shorty's life but also legitimized a black man's right to self-preservation.

* * *

We arrived in Harkensville, and then drove back outside of town for a short distance to locate our motel. As Lonny had predicted, we reached our destination at approximately 8:30 P.M. The flashing neon sign next to the highway read, "Motel—AC—Swimming Pool." At least, I thought, it didn't read "Kool Komfortable Klimate." Smitherman's restaurant had already given me more Klan-friendly ambience than I would need for a lifetime. The motel's sandstone façade was familiar to Lonny from the year before, and he remembered the large swimming pool that was in clear view as we pulled into the motel parking lot. Around the pool's perimeter was a white wrought-iron fence, a common feature for many southern motels. What better advertising than the image of a cool dip in the pool as motorists drove past? Many a carload of family vacationers drove past, only to turn around when the kids in the backseat begged to go back so mom and dad could check into a room and they could take a swim.

Lonny parked his dad's company car in front of the motel, and then got out and walked toward the door underneath a flashing neon sign that read "Motel Office." He registered the four of us under the name of Quality Melon Produce, Inc. We would have two adjoining rooms with a common door between, and two large double beds in each room at a rate that was less per night than the single room the four of us had shared at the Dothan Holiday Inn. This, we thought, would please Aubrey and Monty. Once we had checked in, the three of us agreed that Monty had better not complain about QM paying for two rooms. In our giddy and exhausted state of mind, we vowed that if Monty said anything to Aubrey about the cost of our sleeping arrangements, we'd haul his fat ass into the motel parking lot late one night and treat him to a college style "blanket party!"

Blanket parties were normally reserved for campus adversaries who got out of line. The group giving the so-called party would gather around the squirming, blanket-covered body of the "guest of honor" and proceed to pummel him through the blanket, leaving the victim with no way of identifying individual attackers. It was a punishment frequently joked about at fraternity parties, but almost never administered. We were fully aware that we would never treat Monty to such a cruel punishment, but given our feelings about him it was fun to fantasize about it.

After deciding on bed assignments, we were too exhausted to consider going out for dinner. Even if we had been interested in a late bite to eat, we would not have been likely to find an open restaurant within miles.

Don Jr. took one of the beds in the larger double room, and Lonny took the other. I got the slightly smaller adjoining room, with two double beds to myself. I felt lucky to have a bit of privacy for the first time since I left home. We agreed to rotate bed assignments, so each of us could have the adjoining room to ourselves, sans roommate, for a week. Three weeks would be our maximum stay in the Harkensville area, so we could each expect to enjoy a week in a semi-private room.

31.

Dothan Daily Herald, June 30, 1968

"Billy Matthews, age 27, was stabbed to death in Holcomb yesterday. The stabbing took place during the noon meal hour in the parking lot behind Smitherman's Restaurant, following an altercation with two Negro men who were both employed by the Quality Melon Corporation of Florida. The incident was said to have been provoked by an argument that broke out between Matthews and the two Negro men, Samuel "Shorty" Williams of Ocala, Florida and Bobby Leeds of Harkensville, South Carolina. Williams reportedly stabbed Matthews to death, then went into a fit of rage and was shot and killed by the owner of the locale, who was aided by Geneva County Sheriff, Rufus Lane.

Leeds, Williams' companion, was stabbed in the shoulder in the melee. No charges have been filed against Leeds in the incident. A fourth man, Theodore Braslow of Holcomb, fled the scene, and was later apprehended by the Alabama State Patrol who charged him with drunk driving and leaving a crime scene."

32.

The next morning, Don Jr. arose at approximately 6:30 A.M., found his thick glasses, and peered through the motel room window into the parking lot. He saw at once that Aubrey's Chevy Malibu and Joe Harper's Ford station wagon were parked out front. Monty's car was not in view, and Don Jr. thought that Monty had probably stayed behind in Holcomb to close out the books and make certain that farmers and drivers were properly paid. Don Jr. could tell that the two cars had not been parked for more than an hour or two, because the small pools of water that had dripped from the cooling coils of their air conditioning units had not evaporated.

Don Jr. wondered if the presence of the cars signaled good news or bad news about Bobby Leeds, but there was no way to tell. Had Bobby been OK, Aubrey and Joe Harper would not have felt the need to stay in Holcomb, so their presence here was probably good news. On the other hand, had Bobby died, the two men would still have come to South Carolina because a dead man would no longer need their help. Only if Bobby were in serious condition would one of them (probably Joe), have stayed behind for a day or two. In the end, Don Jr. realized the two cars could not give him any information about Bobby's condition, no matter how long he stared out the motel window. As much as he wanted answers, he knew that Aubrey and Joe Harper needed to sleep for an hour or two before they would give us any news about Bobby. In the meantime, he decided to awaken Lonny and me so we could go out for breakfast.

*   *   *

The scouting reports about the beautiful watermelons in South Carolina were not exaggerated in the least. Our drive to breakfast took us past melon fields that were larger than any I'd seen before. Every field we drove past was adorned with lush green melon vines, well above knee level to a fully-grown adult. Not as much as a tiny postage stamp of earth shone through to disrupt the dark green canvas for the passerby. Besides the perfect stand of melon vines, only the occasional misplaced corn stalk or tall nettle weed could be seen sticking its head defiantly above the sea of deep green. I was reminded of my dad's lifelong dream of having a melon crop like this, so other farmers around Elmwood would enviously drive past and stare. All farmers drove past and spied on each other's crops, usually as part of a leisurely Sunday afternoon ritual that was carefully designed to gather intelligence about the competition.

But dad said the information gathered through drive-by observation was not always accurate. There was more to a good melon crop than beautiful vines. He claimed he had seen the occasional perfect looking drive-by melon crop, only to find out later that the vines had taken over and the melons themselves did not amount to much of anything. This did not appear to be the case in South Carolina, because we could see an abundance of tall "pyramids" built of gorgeous watermelons that had been picked in the cool of the previous evening and stacked in perfect symmetry across the fields. These harvested melons were ready to be loaded into wagons and transported into Harkensville for packing and shipping later that morning. They would probably represent a good part of our workload for our first day in Harkensville.

Watermelons were usually picked in the evening, well after the heat of the day had subsided. They were stacked neatly in pyramids along straight rows, so they could be picked up easily the following day. Early the next day after the dew had formed on the melons, farmers drove their wagons and pick-up trucks through the fields as farm workers loaded the harvested melons onto the passing vehicles.

Watermelon fields in southern Indiana were generally situated on small, hilly truck farms of 50 to 200 acres. They were called truck farms because the vast majority of crops were literally hauled by farmers to local markets in small trucks with less than 5-ton capacity. The crops consisted of "truckable" fruits and vegetables like watermelons, cantaloupes, tomatoes, strawberries, sweet corn, cucumbers and a few odd pumpkins for local kids to enjoy during the autumn season. By contrast, these South Carolina fields of splendor would have dazzled the melon growers of southern Indiana. I longed for my dad to see them. While casual tourists might slow their cars to take a quick look, melon farmers like my dad from up north would have stopped, looked, gotten out of their cars, breathed in large gulps of sweet smelling air, and waded out into the fields. Then they would have bent over to feel the cool surface of a few of these plump melon specimens. Without a doubt, most Indiana melon farmers would have paid money for a trip to see what I was seeing.

The idea of a watermelon "plantation" came to mind, although I had no clue if there was such a thing. I had heard only of cotton plantations in the old South, but in modern times it seemed that these farmers had put most of their resources into growing melons. This would not have seemed a good idea to the farmers back in Indiana, because our growing season was short and made it impossible to rotate crops in and out the way farmers could in the South.

33.

To the farmers of South Carolina, Shorty and Bobby Leeds were no more than a couple of expendable black watermelon packers who had gotten themselves into trouble. But this was certainly not the case for me. Shorty had taken the time to help me improve my packing skills, and he and Bobby had used their humor to bolster our entire crew's morale during long workdays that lingered well into darkness on many occasions. But now, the reality was sinking in. Shorty was gone forever and Bobby might also be dead. We were on our way to breakfast, and suddenly I didn't feel like eating.

* * *

After Lonny and Don Jr. ate their breakfast, and I drank a glass of milk in hopes of settling my stomach, the three of us got back into the car and headed for the Harkensville farmer's market to check out our new worksite. Lonny told me at breakfast that I would be surprised at the sheer size of this co-op compared to the one we had left behind in Holcomb. He also said that, while the overall layout was larger, the South Carolinians hadn't invested in the modern technology we'd had in Holcomb. Some packers were still sent out to the larger farms with truck drivers to load melons the old fashioned way, via human chain gang like we did in Indiana. Several farmers lived far away from the co-op, making it difficult and dangerous for them to haul their crops into Harkensville along narrow county roads in wagons and farm trucks. The farmers who hauled their melons in had to bring additional workers because this co-op lacked the conveying equipment to load trucks rapidly.

It was about 8:30 A.M. when we pulled into the farmers market, and there were already dozens of farmers arriving with melon-laden vehicles. "Jesus Christ!" Lonny remarked. "I never saw anything like these babies last summer! These things are huge! I'm not sure if my dad's company in Cincinnati will even want melons this big."

Don Jr. said, "Damn, I've never seen anything like this either. Not even Raquel Welch has melons like these! We'll probably have to ship these to Detroit and Chicago, where the black folks like these giant sized melons! No offense guys, but I don't think your white relatives in Ohio and Indiana can truly appreciate a jumbo sized melon when they see one. Middle class folks in the Midwest want a melon they can cut open and save the heart in the fridge in Tupperware. Blacks in the big cities appreciate a big ass melon they can bust open when 50 people are together for an inner city picnic."

I had to agree with Lonny and Don Jr. that these were not only the biggest but also the prettiest melons I'd seen. I was ready to get to work because the redeeming quality of hard work might help me to deal with the inner turmoil I felt over Shorty and Bobby's fate.

The physical layout of the co-op, or farmer's market as it was called in Harkensville, resembled a southern fortress from the Civil War era, surrounded by a red brick wall roughly the dimensions of one city block. There was a small blacktop "ring road" that circled along the inside perimeter of the co-op grounds, and at least 30 gravel "slips" for long semi rigs to park for loading. Each of the quadrangular slips was wide enough for a tractor-trailer rig and a farm wagon or pick-up truck to park alongside for loading. Each had a makeshift roof resembling a gigantic carport that provided shade for the farm hands that tossed melons up to the semis during the heat of the day. The remainder of the farmer's market property was grass covered, and most of the grass had turned brown under the hot summer sun.

A dozen tiny cinder block buildings stood in a row along one side of the market, about 30 feet away from the brick wall that surrounded the co-op grounds. Melon buyers rented these pastel painted structures, and set up their business operations for the duration of the Harkensville melon season. These so-called "office buildings" looked more like concrete toilet facilities one would find in a camping ground. Inside each building was a single wooden desk, two phone lines hooked up to separate phones, four or five odd chairs that looked like early Salvation Army, and a miniscule room in one corner containing a toilet and a sink. The melon buyers who rented these structures couldn't have cared less about furnishings or decor. They cared only that the telephones worked and the toilets flushed.

The Harkensville marketplace had a traditional look about it. The 10-foot ivy-covered brick wall around the compound looked like the outfield wall in Chicago's Wrigley Field, and gave the structure a touch of old world character in direct contrast to the ugly but functional co-op building in Holcomb, Alabama. I was nearly as impressed with the market as I had been with the enormous fields of watermelons in the local area. Something inside of me said this town was more like the *real* watermelon capital of the world! How could any other farmer's co-op match its authenticity?

Although my hometown boasted its status as "The World's Watermelon Capital," I now understood that the whole thing back home was contrived by local business owners. Elmwood's city fathers had obviously invented the Watermelon Capital story as a way of attracting tourists who would stay to visit the National Memorial Park that had been dedicated in person by President Lyndon Baines Johnson, and take tours of local historical sites that were not famous enough to draw crowds on their own merits.

After our introductory drive around the farmer's market, Lonny parked in front of a pale green cinder block cottage, roofed with bright green shingles. The three of us got out of the car and slowly walked toward the front door. The building had no air conditioning, but cinder block buildings with screen doors and windows tended to stay several degrees cooler than the out of doors when afternoon breezes passed through them. At the front of the building next to the door was a gold colored plastic nameplate that read, "Quality Melon, Inc." Ready or not, we had arrived at our new work place.

Lonny rapped his knuckles against the flimsy screen door, more to get the attention of somebody inside than to gain entrance. A man dressed in an expensive looking *Arrow* dress shirt and dark-green suit pants came to the door. His perfectly shined brown and white wing-tipped shoes looked like they had come out of the box for the first time that morning. Apparently happy to see us, the man smiled and motioned us inside.

"Hey Lonny! How's it hangin', Don?" Extending his hand in my direction, he said, "My name's Melvin, Melvin Jones, cousin of Aubrey Jensen of Quality Melon. Ole' Aubrey called yestady ta' say y'all flat dicks would be comin' in this mornin'. Sorry to hear 'bout your nigger packin' buddy, ole'—what the fuck was that boy's name?"

"Shorty Williams," I answered. "Shot and killed on his 40th birthday."

Melvin nodded toward me, completely oblivious to his racial slur. Changing the subject, Melvin looked at me and said, "Did these yahoos put you up to spendin' your first night in the same room as ole' Monty?" Melvin had an evil smile on his face.

"Oh yeah, they sure did," I said.

"I bet that fat fucker tried ta' git lucky with ya like he does with everbody else?"

"I think he tried, but I'm not sure. I was pretty tired and I coulda' misread what happened."

"I'll take that as a yes," said Melvin. "That horny bastard tries somethin' with every swingin' dick," he laughed. "Well, y'all packers won't have ta' worry about ole' Monty anymore this season. I just got off the phone with him a few minutes ago, and he said Aubrey done gave him the OK to go back to Flawdy and work outa' the company headquarters for the rest a' the summer. Seems like his mother is sick again, and you can imagine how close he is ta' 'mother!' Y'all will have ta' turn in your weekly packin' tallies ta' me, and I'll call 'em in ta' Monty, then he'll do up the payroll and mail the paychecks to us, or send 'em with a driver who happens ta' be passin' by here. Don't worry, we'll take good care a' y'all. Ain't nobody gonna' git fucked outa' their pay, and that includes the pay y'all had comin' from Holcomb."

Melvin continued. "Anyway, gittin' down ta' bidnuss, you boys is fixin' ta' rake in some serious green here in Harkensvul. I ain't never seen a crop a' melons like this one here, and I've been comin' here with Aubrey since Jesus Christ was a corporal. Ain't never been a shitload a' Charleston Grays and Crimson Sweets like these ole' boys been haulin' in here the last coupla' days! The rest a' these brokers here have got their packin' crews workin' full time, 10 or 12 hours a day. They been turnin' on the floodlights at night, and this place has looked like a big league ballpark at a late night double header. These packers have been keepin' their heads down and not comin' up fur air. All I been seein' is assholes and elbows, and I know they all are takin' home some damn fine paychecks. I've been tellin' ole' Aubrey he's needed ta' git your sorry asses over here so we can git into the fuckin' ballgame. This is damn sure the big leagues here, fellas!"

Melvin changed the subject. "By the way, is that ole' boy Bobby still comin' over from Holcomb? I don't remember what Aubrey told me yestady about him, but that little ole' muthafucker can pack him some goddam watermelons! I believe he's from these parts over here, ain't he?"

Lonny said, "We hope he'll be here! Aubrey and Joe Harper will probably be here in an hour or two, and they'll know the latest about Bobby, at least up to the point when they left Alabama last night. We think Bobby must have been hurt in the fracas in Holcomb yesterday, but we just can't be sure. We hope he's OK."

I could hardly look at Melvin because I could tell that he had all blacks neatly categorized as "niggers" or "boys," or some other white man's term that came to his mind in the middle of a sentence. Melvin was like a crude adult version of my least favorite packer, William. And like slave owners of old, he had his personal favorites and Bobby Leeds one of them.

"It's too bad 'bout them two nigger packers. They's good boys, but out-a-state niggers gotta' watch their asses down in Alabama. Folks down there is pretty jumpy 'cause that Martin Lucifer King raised all kinda' Cain fur so damn long. Can't say I blame the white folks fur gittin' tired a' some a' the shit goin' on in their back yard. It's a fuckin' Communist plot, I tell ya'! You college boys don't know it, but ole' King had all kindsa' money comin' in from Russia and that Castro fellar down in Cuba, ta' support him in overthrowin' the American Gub'ment. He kept all them niggers and college kids stirred up, talkin' bullshit about peace and 'love your neighbor' and all that crap. The Commies loved his ass, and they hated it when the CIA had him bumped off! Thank the good Lord the niggers over in these parts is a bit more laid back about things, and the white folk is more relaxed when it comes ta' dealin' with their niggers. Don't git me wrong, this here ain't no fuckin' love fest between yer niggers and yer whites, but it's a little more like the old days. You can have your Alabama and Georgia. As long as I got my Flawdy and Sow Calahna, I'm OK. Ole' Aubrey, he says he don't want my ass over in Alabama. He's scared I might smart off ta' somebody and cause some sorta' riot. Hell, maybe he's right."

Melvin walked over to the desk in the middle of the block building, where he had placed an unopened bottle of Cutty Sark scotch whiskey, his drug of choice. Melvin was 5 feet 10 inches in height, and slight of build. His thick, jet-black hair was slicked back on the sides with generous amounts of Brill Cream, and parted neatly down the middle. The eerie mono-brow that extended the width of both of his eyes was as thick and dark as the hair on his head, and it was obvious that he thought of himself as a smooth operator—perhaps even a ladies' man.

"How's that sexy lookin' wife a' yours, Melvin?" Don Jr. asked.

"Shit man, she's mean as ever," said Melvin. "But she damn shore gives a helluva blow job, just like always. Listen ta' me when I tell ya' boys, you marry a whore and treat her like a lady, and you'll never have to leave home to get a piece a' pussy! Seems like the drunker I am when I go back to the hotel at night, the more she wants to hummmmm a tune on my crank. Maybe that's the reason I drink so much fuckin' whiskey. A man can't never git too much of a good thing, ya' know."

Don Jr. laughed. "Shit, I can see you haven't changed one little bit since last season, Melvin."

"Now, what the fuck would be the point a' me changin'," said Melvin. "I got the world by the fuckin' dick, baby! Easy job, good lookin' blonde wife that's an only child, and a pappy-in-law that's got money drippin' outa' his ass! Made all a' his money sellin' cheap black market stag films. In fact, he starred in some of those films in the old days."

On the table next to the bottle of scotch sat a black dial telephone, two small drinking glasses, a pair of dice and a deck of playing cards; the tools of Melvin's trade. The room had the look of a cheap, one act stage production about a backroom gambling operation. A heated argument on the subject of cock fighting would have seemed more appropriate in this setting than the business of buying and selling watermelons. On second thought, the gambling atmosphere seemed appropriate because every load of melons that pulled away from the market was a result of some broker's willingness to take a risk. The broker was the middleman who paid the farmer up-front at the daily market price, assumed the risk that the load would arrive safely in a far off northern market, and tried to sell every load of melons to a grocery chain at an agreed-upon price. While in transit, every load was at risk. Sleep-deprived drivers were accident prone, and there were occasional thieves along the way who enjoyed the sport of highjacking a load of watermelons now and then. Added to the risks in transit, the weather could change overnight and rob grocery shoppers of their appetites for cold and juicy watermelon. The occasional load of produce that had not been sold prior to shipping was subject to the fickle influence of temperatures in Cleveland, Detroit, and Chicago, where potential consumers might cancel picnics and outdoor barbecues after a cold front passed through.

Comparing the watermelon market to a crapshoot added a certain context to Melvin's early morning bottle of whiskey, as well as to the pair of dice on his desk next to the poker deck. Men like Melvin began by masking their stress with alcohol, and ended up hiding their alcohol addiction behind a stressful job. Most buyers I had known were like Aubrey, who dealt with his stress in the privacy of his hotel room at night; smoking, staring at the TV screen, drinking second-rate whiskey from a half-pint bottle, and talking on the phone with potential buyers until he passed out in his bed. Melvin, the exception to every business rule, was known among buyers as a fully functioning alcoholic who never appeared drunk. He could sell a truckload of melons on a 65 degree day in Cleveland, then hang up the phone and take your hard-earned cash in a hand of poker or a quick roll of the dice across the concrete floor of his so-called office. Unlike most heavy drinkers, he also had the uncanny ability to remember every penny he'd won in craps, and every deal he'd made, no matter how much Cutty he'd tossed down.

The Melon Boys

* * *

Melvin grabbed the full bottle of scotch by its neck with one hand, and simultaneously reached for an 8-ounce whiskey glass with the other. He opened the bottle (it was 9:30 A.M.) and poured himself about half a glass straight up. Looking at the glass with fondness, he picked it up and tossed its contents toward the back of his throat like a cowboy in the saloon of a Hollywood Western movie. He then put the glass back on the table and filled it to the halfway point again. Replacing the cap, Melvin left the bottle on the desk and walked over to the front doorway of the tiny building to have a look through the loose-fitting screen door, as if he were expecting company any minute.

"Well I'll be goddamned if it ain't ole' cousin Aubrey and his sidekick, Mr. Joe Harper! Ya' hardly ever see one of them ole' boys without the other . . . kinda' like Deputy Dawg and Musky Muskrat."

Lonny and I moved quickly toward the screen door and nearly tripped over each other as we brushed past Melvin to get outside. Once outside, I jogged toward Aubrey's maroon Chevy Malibu to get the news about Bobby Leeds. Aubrey and Joe looked tired, but their even-tempered demeanor was the same as every other day.

Before Aubrey had shut off the car engine, I said, "What's going on with Bobby?"

"Looks like he's gonna' make it OK," said Aubrey. "He was stabbed pretty deep in the shoulder, but the ambulance that carried him away from Holcomb got him to an emergency room in Dothan just in time for some patchin' up. They decided to keep him 'cause he lost so much blood, but we saw him last night before we took off, and he seemed to be doin' OK. Only thing is he's mighty tore up over Shorty gettin' killed and all. As soon as they let him out of the hospital, he'll be headin' to Shorty's burial service in Florida. They were real close, them two."

Suddenly I was no longer concerned about the background or details of what had taken place. I was simply pleased with the news that Bobby would be all right.

Lonny, on the other hand, wanted to know. "Any details on what really happened? I mean, about how Bobby and Shorty got into that mess in the first place?"

Aside from the background Joe Harper and Aubrey had gleaned during their brief visit in the hospital with Bobby, and Joe's meeting with the Holcomb County Sheriff, few details were available. Joe said that he'd telephoned the farmer who had spoken with him and Aubrey at Smitherman's just before the two laid off farm workers confronted Bobby Leeds and Shorty behind the restaurant. According to the farmer, the drunken farm hand who fled the scene had driven around for some time in his 1957 Chevy, trying to sober up so he could consider his options, until the State Troopers eventually apprehended him near the Florida state line.

Joe said, "The farmer also told me that the first thing the two did after he told them they no longer had jobs, was to stop off at the Holcomb liquor store for some cheap whiskey. Then they sat in the car and got as drunk as a coupla' skunks."

Joe continued, "By some miracle, the cops decided to believe Bobby's version of things. Maybe because they knew the white fellas had both been drunk, and the one that was still alive had fled the scene. You fellas pretty much know the rest, because you were right in the thick of it. I mean you saw how it all played out once Shorty got inside. It's too damned bad you all had to see it. What a goddamned waste! I knew Shorty for many years, and I never knew a man, black or white, that was more well-meanin' than he was."

Joe Harper, the ex-Marine, became tearful as he continued talking. "I called Shorty's wife and told her I'm payin' to bury him. I wouldn't be able to rest any other way. Ain't nobody gonna' talk me out of it. I've got a little nest egg in the bank back home, and I feel that's the least I can do to help Shorty's widow. When I think about that little punk William and his big mouth, tellin' that farmer before dinner time that we were pullin' out, the whole thing makes me wanna' quit the melon bidnuss."

Aubrey said, "QM's payin' for Bobby to go down to Florida for Shorty's burial, and to get him back up here to Harkensville. He's in no shape, in mind *or* body, to pack any watermelons right now, and he damn sure needs to be there when they put ole' Shorty in the ground."

"The Doc in Dothan says they had to work fast to save Bobby from bleedin' out, and they found that the knife had cut deep into a tendon. There was a lot of muscle damage too, and that'll slow Bobby down for a while. The least we can do is to pay his way to say goodbye to his best friend, and to make sure he's there to give his respects to Shorty's wife and family. After that, he wants to come home to South Carolina to see his own family, and let them see first hand that he's OK. Joe and me called his wife here in Harkensville this morning, and told her what's happened and that Bobby's gonna' be fine; just a bit delayed gettin' home. We also told her that Bobby was not in any kind of trouble with the law, and that calmed her down a lot."

Joe smiled and said, "Yeah, I think that calmed her down about as much as finding out that Bobby was gonna' live!"

Aubrey's mouth twitched, and he smiled just enough to show that he appreciated Joe's attempt at humor.

Joe said, "Knowin' ole' Bobby, he'll wanna' be here packin' melons in a couple of weeks. He'll go stir crazy if he can't finish out the crop with us here in South Carolina. We'll just have to see how fast he heals."

After downing his glass of Cutty Sark, Melvin slowly sauntered out toward Aubrey's car, wiping his partially puckered lips with the backs of two fingers.

"Hey, cousin Aubrey. You sorry ass fuckers gonna' stop blubberin' over that dead nigger and git these strappin' young men to work here? I've got trucks comin' in this mornin', and farmers chompin' at the bit with big-ass wagonloads of these beautiful melons. Or did you buncha' pussies even notice? All these farm boys need is an empty semi and a packer, and they'll be tossin' us some a' these big juicy grays! I done lined up enough melons for 6 loads here at the market today. We damn sure fixin' ta' make us some mean green today, once we git these sad younguns off their asses and busy loadin' some melons!"

Lonny, Don Jr., and I did our best to ignore Melvin. Even Don Jr., who normally showed very little emotion, was visibly annoyed by Melvin's remark. Lonny and I looked at each other like two actors in a B-Western movie who were ready to signal each other with the slightest nod that it was time to pounce on the bad guy. Nothing would have made us happier than to have acted on that impulse, but our polite midwestern upbringing rendered us incapable of any such action.

Joe Harper gave Melvin a look that did not hide his feelings of intense dislike for the alcoholic bigot.

Aubrey said, "I see you're the same asshole as always, Melvin!" Partially for the benefit of Lonny and me, Aubrey gave us a look out of the corner of his eyes that was halfway between shame and disgust. Working alongside Melvin for three weeks at the Harkensville market did not exactly stack up as the highlight of Aubrey's summer. But Melvin's deceased father, one of the early pioneers of the melon brokering business, had asked Aubrey to give cousin Melvin a job "for as long as he needed it." The "as long as" would depend upon how long Melvin's wealthy father-in-law was still alive.

Given his druthers, Aubrey would have sacked Melvin years earlier, but there was something else in the back of Aubrey's mind. Despite Melvin's drinking, fowl mouth, and unmasked bigotry, he had a nose for the watermelon market and his nose had frequently been an asset to the company. Some men knew instinctively when the market was about to take a turn in one direction or the other, and Melvin was one of those men. It was an unconscious knack, like a sixth sense, and possibly linked to his innate gambling prowess. Like a dog that becomes restless and begins to whine just before an earthquake, Melvin's uncanny ability to forecast subtle market changes had saved the company enough money over the years to pay his salary. One could say, in a certain sense, Melvin's services to QM had come free of charge.

Aubrey said, "Melvin, these fellas here just lost a friend and co-worker, and I just lost a damned good melon packer, so back off! I've got half a mind to put your sorry ass to work packin' melons. On a good day, your scrawny little ass might live through half a semi load, but most days, a full 40-footer would be enough to put you outa' your fuckin' misery!"

"You gotta' be bullshittin' Aubrey! You know I'm half in the tank b'fore the first truckload a' melons pulls outa' here in the mornin'. B'sides, what would the rest a' you buyers do for fun all day if I wasn't here to swindle y'all outa' your walkin' around money?" Melvin laughed. "I'll make a lot more than these packers, and I won't pick up nothin' heavier than a couple a' pretty little ivories inside this building here!" Melvin let out another one of his evil laughs, and his sinister-looking eyebrow lowered in the middle, forming a "V" shape between his eyes. The first couple of belts of scotch were kicking in, and Melvin was feeling good as he settled into his morning groove.

* * *

Joe Harper had no use for Melvin, and was in no mood for a confrontation even though his blood was about to boil. Joe knew that curing Melvin of his bigotry would be more difficult than curing him of his drinking, and life would not be long enough to accomplish either one.

Joe motioned to me, Lonny and Don Jr. "Come over here with me, fellas. We've gotta' face up to the work before the day gets any futher away from us." Joe used "futher" instead of further or farther, and he did it so often that it sounded like proper English usage.

"We're all tired from the trip over here, and we're sick to death about Shorty, but Shorty wouldn't want us to sit around feelin' sorry all day, and besides, it damn sure wouldn't bring him back if we did it." Joe stopped for a moment, almost broke down, and then regained his composure.

"Matt, I'm sorry to do this to ya', but I need you to go out to a farm with that trucker over yonder." He pointed with his right hand, index finger extended, toward a huge rig with the tallest Mack diesel tractor I'd ever seen. The rig was fire engine red with shiny chrome diesel exhaust stacks, and looked like it had just been driven off the showroom floor. Hitched up behind it was a silver 40-foot trailer that looked as if it had just emerged from the factory as well. It occurred to me that in another place and time I might have been fascinated by this monstrous piece of machinery. Guys were generally into trucks, cars, and motorcycles, and those who grew up on farms were into pretty pieces of farm machinery. But on this particular morning, I would have preferred to be alone rather than crawling into the gargantuan melon-hauling machine.

Joe called out to the other packers. "Lonny and Don Jr., you fellas each pick out one of them five rigs lined up against the south wall. This morning, it's packer's choice. Every swingin' one of them puppies has to be packed out before the day is over, and it don't matter to me which one leaves here loaded first. The two of you will stay here, and Matt's goin' out to a farmer. We've got this one farmer who grows a shitload of Crimson Sweets, and we can't get the ole' boy to bring 'em in here to save our asses. He's a cranky ole' bird, and thinks he's better than the rest of us, but we can market his crop in the big cities up north so we send the trucks and packers out to him."

I was less than delighted that I'd been chosen to meet the farmer whom Joe had just described, but I trusted his judgment and felt the change of pace might get my mind off Holcomb. Besides, I was now part of the team, so I had to step up and act like it.

As QM faced the demanding workload in Harkensville, it also faced a serious shortage of skilled labor. Nobody knew for sure when Slick would show up in South Carolina, and when he was back in action, Aubrey and Joe would need at least one more packer to keep up with the volume of melons that Melvin had lined up.

For Slick, the long drive from Holcomb was a bit more than he cared to handle in one sitting. And besides, he had "somebody to take care of" (Slick's exact words to Joe before he had departed Holcomb the afternoon before). Once Slick arrived in Harkensville, he would work as hard as anyone else. In fact, he would probably stay sober and not miss a day's work, because his wife would be visiting for a week or two during the Harkensville tour. Staying off work could mean a dreaded day of shopping with "the warden," as he called her, and Slick would rather take a beating than go shopping with the warden.

* * *

After assigning the three of us to our respective workstations, Aubrey and Joe focused their attention on scaring up an additional packer or two. Joe remembered that Shorty and Bobby had an old friend in South Carolina who had retired from the melon packing business, but Joe could not remember the packer's name.

"Aubrey," Joe said, "Do you have any idea what that fella's name was, who used to hang around with Shorty and Bobby a few years ago when we'd come here to Harkensville? I think he used to team up with Shorty before he quit, and Bobby started up with us. You know, the colored fella' who had kind of a strange name?"

Overhearing Joe's question to Aubrey, Melvin said, "Wasn't that ole' Nigger Rich?"

"What?" said Joe.

"You heard me," said Melvin. "I'm damn sure it was Nigger Rich. In fact, I'm sure as all fuck that was the fellar's name. He was the ole' boy that used to hang out with Bobby and Shorty. In fact, he's the one that used to pack with Shorty before he retired and y'all hired Bobby Leeds."

"You know, in spite a' hell, I think he's right," said Aubrey.

"I don't know what the fuck the ole' boy's doin' these days," said Melvin, "but I think I can get hold of him if y'all want me to talk to him about comin' out and packin' for us for a few weeks to tide us over."

"See if you can get hold of him," said Joe Harper.

"Yeah," said Aubrey. "See if he still feels up to handlin' a melon or two. Go ahead and work your Voodoo on him."

34.

My first load of watermelons in South Carolina consisted of 30 to 35 pound "Crimson Sweets." In spite of the usual company standard of 20 to 25 pound Charleston Grays, supermarkets and consumers in Detroit and Chicago suddenly had a taste for these large Crimson Sweets. It seemed a strange irony that I had finally arrived in South Carolina, the Charleston Gray Mecca, and yet I was starting out by packing a breed of watermelons as different from Grays as anyone could imagine. In fact, it was almost like going from packing watermelons to stacking pumpkins.

Crimson Sweets were round and attractive melons when viewed individually. They were much larger than the round, dark-green melons people in Indiana called "icebox" watermelons. A small Crimson Sweet was the size of a basketball, while a large icebox melon was roughly the same size as a lady's bowling ball. This particular farm raised Crimson Sweets the size of large "medicine balls," the smallest weighing in at around 30 lbs. Dense, round, and uneven to the touch, these melons had wide yellow stripes against a dark green background, or dark green stripes against a yellow background, depending upon one's point of view. Like all watermelons, Crimson Sweets had pale yellow underbellies due to the absence of sunlight. Underbellies were the watermelon equivalent of the bellies of reptiles, with light pigmentation and smooth texture.

Horticultural scientists had developed Crimson Sweets for their marketability, and their best feature was an extremely large and sweet "heart," compared with most other varieties of watermelons. The large size of the heart was attributable to the overall roundness of the melon. The larger and more spherical the outside, the greater the size of the seedless portion at the center. The taste of Crimsons was as sweet as their name, and the rich red "meat" inside was crisp, cool, and inviting to the eye. The fruit of all varieties of watermelons was sweet and crisp if picked just right, but when a Crimson Sweet was dropped and randomly burst open, an enormous chunk of irresistible fruit popped out on one side and weighed at least two or three pounds.

Despite the difficulty of packing Crimsons, there was something I liked about them. I liked the big juicy hearts that could be grabbed and "slurped" for their cool pink liquid inside. Many farmers neglected to provide water for packers, and truckers who normally carried drinking water were usually in the "do not disturb" mode inside of their rigs when the hardest physical work was being done. After my customary two bottles of cool Coca-Cola or Pepsi were gone, I was forced to rely upon the water inside of a Crimson Sweet for refreshment and quick energy. With the Barlow knife I carried in my hip pocket, I would carve a small triangular hole into the rind of a melon, and then pull out a plug of white rind allowing the water to well up inside of the hole. Then, I would lift the melon above my head and drink the juice as it dripped ever so slowly into my mouth. It was like drinking from a round, 35 pound jug, except that the water didn't exactly come streaming out of the melon. It only trickled its way out, so I had to form a tight suction with my lips around the hole and suck hard, causing the juice to run slowly into my mouth in ample amounts to quench my urgent thirst. Then, I would replace the white rind plug and put the melon in a shaded spot, hoping there would be enough water left inside for another drink later in the day.

Crimson Sweets had thinner rinds than many other varieties of watermelons, and even though consumers loved their taste, their ability to travel had not won them early favor among buyers and truckers. Although they showed potential to be better shippers than previously developed round varieties of melons, their thin rinds made it harder for them to travel than the oblong Charleston Grays which had proven to be ideal for long distance hauling and extended cold storage.

Before making the decision to buy, produce brokers always checked melons for ripeness by thumping them with an experienced knuckle or middle finger. The middle finger method was the most common, and consisted of a sharp flicking motion of the finger off the tip of the thumb pad. Thumping was a reliable method of deciding between the four stages of a full-sized melon: not yet ripe, ready for picking and shipping, perfect for immediate eating, and over-ripe. Not ripe enough produced a tight, resonating sound, while over-ripe melons produced a deep "thud" like the sound of a bass drum filled with mud. It was harder to distinguish between the two in-between stages of ready for picking and needing to be eaten, but the experienced buyer could always tell the difference. Joe Harper jokingly compared the feel of a melon to the feel of a prostrate gland to his doctor; "My doctor tells me you can't describe a good one, but you can damn sure tell what a bad one feels like."

The ideal stage for harvesting produce for shipping was five to seven days before it was intended to be consumed. If farmers waited until their melons had reached the "eat immediately" stage, the produce would be ready for the juice man's blender when it arrived at its designated market. The concept of "vine-ripe" produce was a marketing gimmick. True vine-ripened fruits and vegetables were generally sold at discounted prices from roadside stands or local Mom and Pop groceries, a pleasant irony in favor of the people who lived in regions where good produce was grown.

Crops that were shipped and marketed in bulk, like tomatoes, were picked for packing in half-bushel baskets as soon as a small patch of pink the size of a quarter could be seen at the blossom end of the fruit. A half-dollar sized patch of pale red was pushing it, but tomatoes picked for the top dressing of half-bushel baskets were considered all right if they had the larger patch of color.

An experienced melon packer rarely needed to thump a melon for ripeness, because he could tell the split second the melon hit his hands whether it would ship well or not. When it came to handling Charleston Grays, a packer would usually cull several melons out of each load, while farmers stood by and cried foul. With round melons, an expert packer could tell from the look of the outside skin and the roughness of the underbelly whether or not it would ship. Melons with insufficient roughness, and a tight feel to them were not ripe enough, so the packer tossed them aside without a second thought. Melons with the correct amount of roughness were eased into the stack, and melons that were too rough and felt thick the moment they hit the packer's hands were culled out because they were too ripe for shipping.

My favorite story about Slick's near mythical packing skill was about his ability to judge the ripeness of a watermelon by glancing at it in mid-air, as it hurled toward him. If he knew a melon was over-ripe or not ripe enough, he would sometimes shift to one side and let it drop and burst at his feet. However, he tended to reserve this tactic for farmers who were difficult to deal with, or in his words, "flaming assholes!" On one occasion in the early 1960s, Slick was feuding with a Florida farmer over the advanced ripeness of the melons being passed up to him. When Slick finally lost his patience with tossing melons back, he began to let the culls fall and burst next to his feet. As each successive rejected melon hit the floor of the trailer, the accumulating pile of juicy pulp revealed an advanced stage of ripeness. Not missing a beat, Slick ignored the rejects that accumulated at his feet. Within a few minutes, the agitated farmer came up into the trailer and replaced the farm hand in the chain gang closest to Slick. For the remainder of the day, the farmer fixed a cold stare on Slick and personally tossed each melon to him. Without saying a word to Slick, the farmer assigned one of his hired hands to get a scoop shovel and clean up the mess. Knowing full well how an overripe melon felt to the touch, the farmer made certain that he culled them out as he went along, and not a single overripe melon was tossed in Slick's direction for the rest of the day.

* * *

My ride out to the farm in the shiny Mack diesel gave me the best view yet of my new surroundings. I said nothing to the trucker with the exception of the usual niceties as we got underway. The roar of the powerful engine gave me a measure of privacy and I relished the time alone with my thoughts for the time it took to get out to the farm. Besides, most truck drivers reminded me of what I believed was wrong with American society; too many people down on things they were not up on. When they started with their prattle, I usually smiled and feigned agreement. This was OK with them, because they had no interest in anyone else's view of the world besides their own.

The landmark we were told to look for was a mailbox by the side of the road with the name "Stout" written on it in bold black letters. As it turned out, we were on the correct county road because the driver hit his air breaks when he saw the mailbox. The trailer's rear tires made a loud racket as they bounced up and down on the pavement. He then backed up the rig and made a sweeping turn onto a narrow tree-lined dirt road that led to a cluster of distant farm buildings. As the behemoth lumbered forward, the driver grumbled about the ill effects of the dusty road on his shiny new rig.

The farm Joe had assigned me on my first day in Harkensville was like a plantation, straight out of a scene from <u>Gone With the Wind</u>. I would have bet this grower planted a minimum of 500 acres of melons, roughly five times the size of the entire farm my father owned in Indiana. It was safe to say that this would not have qualified as a truck farm back home. This man was a "planter" in the true sense of the southern word! The enormous melon and cotton fields that flanked us on both sides were dotted on the far horizon with small, unpainted farm cabins to our left and right. The cabins appeared much the same as hundreds I had seen during my initial bus ride through the length of Alabama. From my distant vantage point, I could not tell what purpose the cabins served, but I suspected they might be the dwelling places of Stout's sharecroppers.

As we made our way slowly through the fields, the cluster of farm buildings grew closer. Although considerably longer, the winding road reminded me of the quarter-mile lane that led from the blacktop county road to the small farmhouse in which I had grown up. During the summer months, our dirt lane eroded until it formed two parallel ruts that grew deeper as the hot dry sand was hurled into clouds of dust by cars, pick-up trucks, farm tractors, and eventually the semi's that came to haul away our watermelons when August rolled around. In autumn, my dad graded the dirt road with a blade attached to the back of his Ford tractor, and then he added soil to replace that which had eroded during the summer months. In wintertime, the lane turned cold and stiff, then froze solid and became smoother than it was in the warmer months. When it snowed, it took only a few inches accumulation to make the lane impossible to navigate in the family car.

As we neared the cluster of buildings that made up the Stout farmstead, I focused on the large white house with stately anti-bellum columns in front. The look of the place was one of southern style prosperity. A tall, thin farmer wearing loose fitting bib overalls and a wide-brimmed straw hat emerged from one of the freshly painted barns to greet us. He appeared to be around 50 years of age, but he was very fit for his age and moved with the agility of a much younger man. The farmer wasted no time in directing us to the spot where he wanted the driver to situate the trailer for loading. Our designated parking place was under a grove of deep green live oak trees that stood in stately elegance next to the largest barn on the premises. The driver showed off his best maneuvering skills, inching the mammoth rig through the loose sand and into the parking spot.

The shade from the massive trees would provide a cool place for those of us who would be working inside the otherwise steamy trailer, as well as a cool spot for the driver to sleep. He would open the square portholes at either end of his sleeper compartment, and enjoy the relatively cool breeze as it passed over his outstretched body.

The driver pulled his rig forward, then reversed and quickly lurched forward again, twisting and turning until it eventually took on an "L" shape. Surprisingly, each subsequent maneuver took the awkward trailer closer to its designated spot under the trees, and he eventually brought the rig back into near-perfect alignment. Perspiring heavily from manhandling the oversized Mack steering wheel with the chrome likeness of a bulldog in its center, he looked over at me, wiped his brow with a soiled cloth he kept next to him in the driver's seat, and shut down the powerful diesel engine. His truck driver's pride had not allowed him to stop for a rest until the semi was parked to the farmer's satisfaction. I appreciated the driver's accomplishment, and as the day wore on I would appreciate even more the fact that we were beneath the cool shade of the oak trees.

"Shit fire and save matches!" said the driver. "That's like herdin' a fuckin' elephant into the startin' gate at Churchill Downs. My tires was spinnin' like I was caught in a damn snowstorm. That's the trouble with these big rigs—you get 'em off the main road and the tires spin in this sand like they've got fuckin' grease underneath of 'em. And these fuckin' farmers expect you to get it perfect on the first try."

I offered the driver my words of praise for his skill in situating the rig among the oak trees.

* * *

"Mornin' y'all." The farmer greeted us before we opened our doors to crawl down from the cab. His raspy voice, along with the weathered look of his skin, gave him the appearance of an old time sea captain without the yellow oilcloth coat and hat. The driver and I had no doubt why Clarence Stout was in a good mood. He was about to sell his first load of melons from a crop that would net him as much as $50,000 or $60,000. Each time he guided an empty semi into this position under the oak trees, he would pocket another $850 to $1,000. Fifty or sixty semis would park in this same spot before his crop would have given its all. I couldn't imagine a melon farmer making that much money over the course of a few weeks. In a good season, my father would be lucky to net $8,000 to $10,000 from his entire melon crop. I only hoped I would not have the dubious honor of packing out Clarence Stout's entire crop! In fact, I would have been perfectly happy to pack only this one load, and then turn Mr. Stout over to the other packers.

"Y'all are gonna' love these fuckin' Crimsons, packer!" Stout let out an evil sounding laugh, as if warning a young child about a troll laying in wait under the next bridge. "My boys here is ready to throw them fuckers at ya' any time y'all are ready ta' start catchin' 'em!" He pointed toward a group of young black men resting for the moment under the cluster of trees near the back of the trailer. "If'n you do me a good job a' packin' these Crimsons, we'll likely be seein' a lot of each other. Think you can handle fifty or sixty loads a' these babies in three weeks?"

"I'm as ready as I'm ever gonna' be," I said.

The semi driver and I walked around to the rear of his trailer. When we reached the back end, the driver took out a large bundle of keys, and locating the correct one, he opened a sturdy looking padlock that kept the tall double-doors of the trailer secured. The creaking of the tight, new eight-foot high doors signaled the start of a long day's work. As I climbed into the trailer, the driver grabbed a large bale of the farmer's straw from a stack next to one of the oak trees, and strained as he tossed it up into the truck bed. He had not stopped to purchase straw or bring any out from the co-op, because it was customary for farmers to provide straw when drivers came out to them for loading. The driver picked up several more bales, and grunted each time he heaved another one inside the trailer. "You can't use too much straw on these babies," he said breathlessly as he tossed the final bale upwards in my direction. "I heard you was kinda' like an expert at packin' open top trailers back in Alabama. That's why I wanted you for these here Crimsons. I figure anybody who knows how to straw-down an open-top, damned sure oughta' be able to straw down a load of Crimsons so I don't end up drippin' my way to Chicago."

I had no idea how the driver had heard about my packing skills. I jokingly said, "Now who the hell would spread those kinda' lies about me?" I smiled. "All I know is paddin' down these melons is gonna' be my number one job. Then there's the problem of keepin' these round balls from comin' down like a landslide."

The driver nodded agreement as I reached for my pocketknife. With my free hand, I grabbed a 100-pound bale of straw and began to drag it to the front end of the trailer, where I would cut the two parallel strings running lengthwise around the bale. The second the taut twine gave way with its familiar popping sound, the straw cooperated by falling into many large flakes. I took several of the flakes and pulled them apart with both hands, then spread the straw onto the bed of the trailer to form a soft landing surface for the first few rows of melons. I thought about Shorty and how he'd instructed me on spreading, or rather piling up large amounts of straw inside the beds of open-top trailers. Although I wanted to exude confidence, I was painfully aware that the sum total of my experience with Crimson Sweets had been the previous summer in Indiana, where I had packed no more than three or four loads of them in 20-foot straight trucks. But those had been nothing compared with these prize winning South Carolina specimens. The only round, striped melons I had seen this size were the ones 4-H members had entered for judging in county fairs, in the hope of taking home a blue or purple ribbon.

I signaled to one of the farmhands who appeared to be the senior member of the work detail. He told me his name was Jonah; "straight out of the belly of the whale," he said with a friendly smile. He could not have been more than 17 or 18 years of age.

It was time to form a chain gang and begin passing melons out of the wagon that Clarence Stout had pulled perpendicular to the back end of the trailer. Although lean and slightly malnourished, the young men were muscular for their ages, and looked a bit like youth league football players in tattered blue jeans. Their well-developed shoulder muscles and biceps served as evidence that they had done little else but hard physical work during their short lives. The seasonal work cycle began in early spring with the planting of thousands of tiny melon sprouts in the fields. Next came a couple of months of chopping weeds with dull hoes so the young melon plants could flourish with minimal competition for the moisture that was available in the soil. Along with that came the turning of the rapidly growing watermelon vines into straight rows with long pointed sticks, so Clarence Stout could cultivate either side of the rows of melon plants with his specially designed tractor that was nicknamed "the bug," because it bore a slight resemblance to the main character of a popular children's board game known as "Cootie." Finally came the heavy lifting; picking the mature melons and tossing them into wagons, then into trailers to be packed and hauled away. This backbreaking routine had turned many a skinny boy into a muscular young man.

Jonah barked out a pair of quick commands. I tried to understand his words, but I suddenly felt like I'd been dropped into the middle of a foreign country. The dialect these young men spoke to one another was not like any language I had heard before. Maybe, I thought, they were speaking an obscure variation of an African language brought over by their ancestors, or a form of Afro-English that had evolved into a dialect all its own. I suspected the latter was true, because I had read about this phenomenon within immigrant subcultures in various parts of the country. For instance, Southern Italians who settled in South Philadelphia had developed a distinct dialect known as Italo-American, and even published newspapers in their unique new-world language.

In addition to their speech patterns, another thing that fascinated me about these young workers was their thickly calloused feet. I assumed they could easily trample across nettle weeds or thick sand burrs without feeling the slightest pain. The calluses, born of layer upon layer of dried skin robbed of its moisture by hot farm sand, were like naturally-grown shoe soles that took the place of the work shoes these young men could not afford. Some of their calluses were so thick that they developed large cracks in them, like a form of dry rot.

As we began our day's work, it occurred to me that these teenagers had never been given a choice of summer jobs as I had, nor would they be given the option of leaving Clarence Stout's farm. In fact, the rules that governed mainstream American life were completely foreign to them. Their dark skin color, combined with their social isolation and lack of formal education, would keep them from achieving a better life. Some had not been to school of any kind, and their illiterate mothers were in no position to provide home schooling above and beyond family folklore and memorized Bible stories. They were lost among the remnants of Southern slavery from which they had no means of escape, and landowners like Clarence Stout wanted to keep them that way forever.

As soon as we began the business of loading watermelons, I retreated into my own thoughts. Since I didn't understand what the farmhands were talking about, their conversation was like background noise. Surely, I thought, Bobby Leeds had come from a less impoverished background than this. After all, he owned his own home, and while the job of Melon Packer was not the most prestigious employment, Bobby was considerably better off than common farmhands or sharecroppers. Watermelon packers were mobile and able to experience new surroundings, while farmhands were tied to the land as well as to their status as indentured servants. I was not only witnessing first-hand what indentured servitude meant in the 1960s, but I was beginning to learn that varying degrees of status existed among poor southern blacks.

* * *

My first semi trailer load of Crimson Sweets started out better than I had expected. The thick bed of straw I had laid down eliminated the rolling effect of the large round watermelons. Although the melons appeared perfectly round when growing in the fields, the large Crimson Sweets were actually flat underneath. This gave them the ability to nestle surprisingly well into my pyramid-shaped stack.

Mr. Stout's experienced crew passed the melons to me quickly and efficiently, never stopping unless I needed to reach back for more straw, or when I called for a short break to wipe the perspiration off my face or take a drink from my bottle of Coca-Cola. My shoulder muscles strained under the weight of the melons, while the tendons in my wrists and forearms became sore before midday. I soon discovered, however, that the best method of catching these over-sized melons was to hold my arms close together and form a two-handed "basket." By contrast, catching them with my arms spread apart caused intense pain in my wrists and forearms.

The morning hours vanished into a cloud of itchy straw dust, and before I realized what time it was, Clarence Stout offered to take the semi driver and me into Harkensville for the noon meal. We tried to awaken the driver, but he grumbled his displeasure and showed no interest in joining us. Mr. Stout gave me a nod in the direction of his bronze-colored 1965 Ford pick-up truck. I climbed in through the passenger's side door, and he started the engine.

Farm pick-up trucks were notorious for a bouncy ride, usually as a result of worn-out shock absorbers brought on by countless hours of driving with heavy loads over deeply furrowed farm fields. Most pick-up trucks in the late 1960s were built to provide a smooth ride over paved roads, but not for the heavy hauling farmers demanded of them. Shock absorbers rarely lasted more than two years, which was about half of their normal life expectancy. It was obvious that Mr. Stout's shocks were well past their functional limits, but I had the distinct impression that he was a miserly sort and would not invest in a new set any time soon. The soft sand underneath us gave the truck a gliding effect that could almost make a person seasick. I had the feeling that the body of the truck might float right off its frame any minute as we bounced along the winding road that meandered through what was arguably the world's largest watermelon field.

Mr. Stout said, "Wanna' go for a quick drive around the farm?" It was obvious he didn't expect an answer, nor did he care whether I wanted to see his farm or not. He had decided to show me his massive freehold before we ate, as he probably did with every newcomer. Little did I know that his chattel consisted of more than real estate and the usual livestock.

I was hungry, my mouth was dry, and my lips were chapped from the heat. I imagined myself crawling across a desert floor in a French Foreign Legion movie, begging for an oasis with cool, clean water. But my personal discomfort was of no concern to Clarence Stout. As my body struggled to regulate its internal heat, I continued to sweat profusely. The only thing that felt good about the ride in the pick-up truck was the slight breeze that brushed across my right arm and shoulder as we slowly bounced our way through the hot farm fields. The motion of the air felt good, and a secondary benefit of the moving vehicle was that my personal swarm of gnats had finally lost track of my whereabouts. Not even in Alabama had I experienced the swarming gnat phenomenon, but in South Carolina the annoying insects were part of the ambience. I knew that my swarm would find me again once I returned to work, but I would not miss them in the meantime. Along with the gnats, I had spent the morning fighting off the aggressive South Carolina flies. Unlike common barnyard or houseflies, these flies were smaller and darker in color, and truly enjoyed biting into human flesh. They quickly appeared whenever the breeze was relatively calm. A steady breeze would tend to drive them into hiding, but there was never a steady breeze inside a cavernous semi trailer. I was convinced that horses, with their long and wiry tails, had a distinct advantage over humans when it came to dealing with flies and pesky insects. With a wisp of the tail, they instinctively swished the irritating varmints away. People, on the other hand, could not rid themselves of the bothersome creatures as easily.

Clarence Stout said, "Look over yonder at them folks choppin' cotton."

"Yeah," I replied. I looked through the front windshield of Stout's pick-up truck and noticed a small group of black people who were bent over. They suddenly worked a bit faster, since the pick-up entered their field of vision.

"Them's my niggers," Stout blurted out in a straightforward, matter-of-fact tone of voice.

I nodded my head, but tried not to show any other reaction. I was suddenly aware that this was a farm where the laborers were considered the personal property of the owner. These people lived in a world apart. This sudden realization validated what I was thinking all morning about the young men who had been tossing melons to me; this was a microcosm of the past and Stout's so-called sharecroppers were nothing more than latter day slaves.

Stout drove a bit farther down the road, then pointed toward three unpainted wooden shacks as he drove closer to them. These were the small houses I had noticed earlier that morning from my perch in the Mack diesel. Up close, I saw that they were in far worse condition than they had appeared from a distance. Some of the framed windows were missing glass panels, and others were boarded shut. I wondered how these peasant families kept disease-carrying insects away from their children at night.

I knew the answer; they didn't. Flies and mosquitoes had their run of the shacks, and that was probably the least of the occupants' worries.

"See them three shacks over yonder?" Stout said.

Once again, I nodded like a bobble-head doll, indicating only that I had seen the buildings, but consciously trying not to provide feedback.

"Them's *all* my niggers!"

Stout then pointed to a distant spot across the field, where there were five more shacks. "Them shacks over t'other side is my niggers too."

"*My niggers . . . my niggers!*" Clarence Stout's words echoed inside my head. I had no idea what to say to this man, and yet I knew those two words would repeat inside my head for a long time to come.

"Big place you've got here," I said, for lack of anything else to offer. More than ever before, I was aware of my deeply-rooted belief that all people had a right to their self respect. But Clarence Stout's concept of self-respect was limited to whites only, and the black sharecroppers who subsisted out of the kindness of his heart were supposed to be proud of the fact that they were *his* niggers—and not someone else's.

"Damn right, young fella'. I've done right well for myself here. My daddy and my Grand pappy both owned this spread, and a lot a' these nigger families go back generations with my people. Melon farmin's treated us good, and we've always been good to our niggers. I don't beat 'em like my Grand pappy did, but I sure as hell wish I could get 'em to stop drinkin' on pay-day weekends. If I could do that, everything would be perfect.

"Any fella' that pays his niggers more than once a fortnight is just plain shootin' himself in the ass! I pay my niggers good money every other week, and the stupid fuckers (especially the younguns) go out on Saturday nights and spend it all on cheap rotgut booze as soon as they get the money in their hands. Then ya' don't see their sorry asses 'til the next Tuesday, and *late* in the mornin' at that! It takes 'em that long ta' sober up and come down off the hooch. You wouldn't believe what them crazy bastards will drink when they start runnin' outa' money! Hell, I've seen some a' my niggers spend their last 50 cents on a bottle a' drugstore rubbin' alcohol. Then they drink the fuckin' stuff and come close ta' dyin' of alcohol poisinin'. The medics call me from the local hospital and have me come and get their sorry asses in the middle of the night, after they done pumped their stomachs out. I go down and git 'em, and pile 'em in the back end a' this pick-up and haul their asses home. I'll tell you right now, I sure as fuck don't need no niggers dyin' on me. I've got so much work here that I need every swingin' black dick, especially this time a' year!"

What surprised me most about Stout's account of his sharecropper's drinking binges was his paternalistic attitude. He was an erstwhile plantation owner who thought of his slaves as children who needed the protection that only he could provide. In the plantation owner's eyes, this provided ample justification for the treatment he exacted upon his subjects. Stout's decrepit shacks were home to these legally free, yet economically bound people, most of whom would remain here for their entire lives. While Clarence Stout was getting rich from their hard work, his sharecroppers could only look forward to daily survival thanks to his self-righteous benevolence.

Although his so-called sharecroppers were aware of their dubious status as "Clarence Stout's niggers," they were powerless to improve upon it, so their only escape was in the form of a drunken payday binge.

35.

During his *Social Psychology of Race Relations* course, Dr. Andrew Harmon sometimes told stories to his classes about his early days in Nashville, Tennessee as a graduate student. His stories often included examples of racial discrimination he'd experienced first hand. For instance, in the late 1950s he was involved in a two-car accident while driving one evening from the university to his part-time job as a night watchman in a local sausage factory.

While driving down a priority street, Dr. Harmon was broadsided by another car in the middle of an intersection. The white driver who slammed into the passenger side door of Dr. Harmon's car was drunk, and he had run a stop sign just before ramming into Dr. Harmon's car. On top of being intoxicated, the driver did not have a valid driver's license. Despite this, the white policeman who reported to the scene was ready to charge Dr. Harmon in the accident, but Dr. Harmon spoke up in protest.

"Officer," Dr. Harmon reasoned in his finest white man's English, "as you can plainly see, I would have to have been driving my car sideways to cause this accident!"

The policeman was eventually convinced that he should not cite Dr. Harmon in the accident, but issued him a warning ticket for disrespecting an officer of the law. When Dr. Harmon related the story to us in class, he also mentioned that, at the time of this incident he was about to complete his Master's Degree, and had decided to pursue his PhD in France. Stopping and looking toward the class, he paused. "Do you know what a white bigot calls a black man with a Ph.D.?" he asked rhetorically. "Nigger." Dr. Harmon followed this with a hearty laugh.

No matter how many of Dr. Harmon's lectures I attended, nor how many stories he related, he could not have prepared me for what I saw on Clarence Stout's farm that first day. I felt like a time traveler who had stepped into the past. I wondered for a moment if Dr. Harmon was aware of situations like this one, or if this was such an isolated phenomenon that no one in the outside world knew about it? Surely Dr. Harmon knew. How naïve of me to think for a moment that he might not! Nevertheless, when I returned to the university in the fall, I would certainly be ashamed to admit to Dr. Harmon that I had ridden in the same pickup truck with modern day slave owner, Mr. Clarence Stout.

When the day was done, I could not remember my lunch in Harkensville with Clarence Stout, nor could I remember much about the afternoon, except for the steady stream of oversized round melons flying toward me. Every time I closed my eyes that night, I saw the young black men working alongside me. And like a broken record, my mind could not stop replaying the farmer's voice. "*My niggers . . . my niggers . . . . my niggers . . .*"

* * *

As I lay in bed, the voice of Dr. Harmon spoke to me.

"*Kinda' shocked you, didn't it?*"

"Yes," I replied mentally.

"*The thought of one man owning another is foreign to you, but believe me, it's not unusual for men like Stout.*"

"But it sounds so obscene: MY NIGGERS," I thought.

"*Obscene is the correct word for it,*" said Dr. Harmon. "*I would be disappointed if you had not recognized the obscenity of it, because it meets all three of my criteria for being obscene: truly disgusting, abhorrent, and repulsive.*"

"But in 1968, people are supposed to be more enlightened than this!"

I could imagine Dr. Harmon's voice laughing at my naïveté.

36.

Ben,

*W*ell, here I go again! I hope these letters aren't getting too depressing, but it does me good to write them, so I guess you'll have to bear with me . . . like you always do.

Speaking of depressing, I'm still down in the dumps about Shorty's death, and I really miss being around him and Bobby Leeds. Those two guys added a dimension to my job that was truly refreshing. I wish I had gotten to the point where I could have truly called them my friends. I'm not sure what to call it . . . but Bobby and Shorty had something we don't have, and never can have. Don't get me wrong, I like hanging out with the white guys here, but most of what I've learned this summer about the packing business has been from Bobby and Shorty. The good news is that Bobby is going to be OK, but they say he might not be able to work for the rest of the summer. He suffered a serious stab wound to the shoulder . . . which included some tendon damage.

My real news this time is about the huge farm where I packed my first load of melons in South Carolina, or "Sow Calahna" as they like to call it around here. The owner of this place grows ONLY Crimson Sweets. You've packed those before, so you know how hard they are to work with. And it's even worse when each one weighs around 35 pounds! Somehow, they've decided to turn me into a fuckin' Crimson Sweet expert, and I don't think I like that idea! This seems to have grown out of my recent reputation as a pretty good open top trailer packer.

Anyway, the good ole' boys at Quality Melon sent me out to this farm, owned by a man named Clarence Stout. His crew of farm hands, 10 or 12 young black dudes, speak a dialect I cannot begin to understand. Ben, I'm telling you, I could hardly understand a fucking word they said all day! I understood one or two of them a little bit, but only when they spoke to me in their best southern dialect. Best I can figure is that they speak a dialect that's left over from the old days on the plantation, when slaves didn't want their white masters to know what the hell they were saying to each other. I also suspect they might be speaking a version of the Geechee dialect, like Bobby Leeds, only not slowly enough that white ears can understand.

Here's the part you're not gonna' believe. This farmer named Clarence Stout took me for a ride around his farm on the way to lunch, and every time he pointed out a small rundown shack or a group of black people hoeing cotton ('choppin' cotton', as they call it down here), he'd say, "Those are my niggers!"

Ben, this man owns these people! At least, in his mind he does. In polite society down here, whites call black farm workers "sharecroppers." I always thought a sharecropper was like a full-time hired hand that "shared" in the profits of the farm. Stupid me! These people LIVE on his farm . . . lots of them. And they don't get a percentage, nor do they have anything they can call their own. Apparently their "share" is in the form of a shitty little house to live in, and even that belongs to old man Stout. He pays them every other Saturday evening, and says they go into town and spend their weekends getting drunk! He says they come staggering back to their shacks, and don't get back to work until the following Tuesday. According to ole' man Stout, even on Tuesday when they show up for work, "his niggers" are so hung over they aren't any good until late in the day!

Jesus Christ, Ben! I can't believe this shit! These black people on the farms are invisible to the outside world. How has the whole world lost track of them? Surely somebody will find out about them and bring it up on the evening news. (If it has gotten the attention of the media, I must not have been paying attention!) I just can't believe this shit is still going on in 1968!

Well, I'd like to write more, but I'm tired as hell, so I'd better close this thing for now. More soon! Matt

* * *

After my first day in Clarence Stout's little corner of South Carolina, I made it clear to Aubrey that I preferred not to go back out. Aubrey said he understood, but there was nothing he could do. Stout was a very influential melon grower, and in Aubrey's words, "none of the other packers can pack Crimsons worth a shit, except for Bobby Leeds, and Bobby ain't here right now."

I decided not to fight it. And besides, I had no choice but to accept Aubrey's decision. At least, I thought, going out to Clarence Stout's farm got me away from Melvin, the boisterous bigot who drank Cutty Sark all day long, shot craps and said, "7 and 11, and I ain't had you," every time he rolled the dice across the concrete floor of his tiny office building.

Even though I would not have been around Melvin a great deal of the time, the thought of being around him at all was worse than the thought of spending my days at Stout's farm for three weeks running.

Melvin's insensitivity toward Shorty and Bobby was reason enough for me to avoid him like the plague. He impressed me at the outset as a lower form of scum than Clarence Stout could ever be. The good news about Stout was that he, like other successful farm owners, was not in the habit of harming his own personal property. A farmer would take good care of a workhorse or a milk cow. By the same token, Clarence Stout took care of his indentured workers—in his own way. Melvin, on the other hand, saw all blacks as lazy and worthless and took care of nobody except Melvin.

Another thing that would make my trips to Stout's farm tolerable was a simple truth spoken by a faint voice in the back of my mind. The voice, perhaps one and the same as the voice of Dr. Andrew Harmon, was telling me I could learn something from Stout's sharecroppers. I knew if I listened closely I might overcome the language barrier and catch a glimpse of what was important in the lives of Stout's young farm workers. Of course, there was the usual banter about sex, which was on the minds of all young men everywhere. From the few things I had picked up in their conversation on my first day, I already knew that they did more than drink alcohol on payday weekends. It sounded like they spent their weekends in the company of young lady friends, most of whom were from nearby towns. Even these poverty stricken farmhands, who could not afford proper work shoes, dressed up for the occasional trip into town to seek out female companionship. But more than learning about their weekend social activities, I wanted to know what they thought about their lives on the farm, and whether or not they harbored any hopes of escaping it.

Maybe these farm workers knew more about the outside world than I imagined they knew. Perhaps they knew about the struggle for racial equality that was taking place across the South. Perhaps they envisioned a future in which they could play a role. And, most important of all, maybe they saw the real possibility of future independence. The only way I could get the answers would be to listen and learn from them, so I decided to make this a personal challenge.

*   *   *

Dr. Harmon would have found my academic curiosity about Clarence Stout's farmhands rather amusing. The next time his voice materialized inside my head, he would probably ask, *"What do you care about the future of these young people? And why would you want to know how they'll turn out after growing up in a place like this?"*

"I'm not sure," I would answer. "Maybe it's the result of the academic curiosity I picked up from role models like you," I would tell him. "And, as strange as it might seem, a part of me might really care about these young men, after what has happened to Shorty and Bobby Leeds."

Then Dr. Harmon would probably tell me, *"That's admirable, but I think you should keep it simple. You'd be surprised how small talk can make a difference when there is somebody around to admire. My guess is that these young men admire you. To them, you are a man of the world from a far off land that they know nothing about. Talk to them. Talk about anything. Don't bother them with your academic curiosity. You might be pleasantly surprised when they open up to you. And you never know, before your time in Harkensville is finished they might begin to trust you a little. Just don't expect miracles."*

37.

Bobby Leeds made his first appearance at the Harkensville farmer's market early one morning, roughly two weeks after Shorty's death. His arm was in a sling. Indeed his shoulder injury had been worse than he had originally thought. The deep wound was still painful, and it had a long ways to go before it would be completely healed inside. He had sustained serious damage to a tendon, and although the rotator cuff was not torn, his mobility would be limited for some time to come. His earlier optimism about returning to work had come face-to-face with the reality that his melon packing days for the summer of 1968 were probably over.

Bobby's wife had driven him into the farmer's market, and the first thing they did was to slowly circle the perimeter so Bobby could eyeball the entire operation. Then they parked in front of the small cinder block building that served as QM's Harkensville office. Bobby got out to walk inside alone. Luckily, I was there that morning getting another driver assignment and preparing for my morning ride out to Clarence Stout's farm.

Bobby greeted me with a smile, as he did the other packers who were present that morning. I detected a deep sadness in his eyes. He was clearly not the same as he had been before the incident in Holcomb.

Bobby said, "Hey, Matt. I talked to ole' Aubrey on the phone and he say you be goin' out ta' ole' man Stout's farm a lot." He smiled and turned his head slightly to the side, still looking at me out of the corners of both eyes. "You gittin' along alright wit' dat ole' slave driver?"

"It's been OK so far," I said. "He's got a good crew of hard workin' young men out there. I can't believe how hard those kids work for that old bastard. They give him a lot more than he deserves." I laughed, and so did Bobby. I didn't want to say too much about Clarence Stout in front of the others, especially Melvin, but Bobby could tell I had more to say. He and I both knew we'd have to wait until we could talk later.

After visiting with the others for a few minutes, Bobby motioned for me to follow him outside. He stopped halfway between the building and his car.

"Hey Matt," said Bobby, "I wanna' take you over ta' my place for a groun'hog barbecue, then we gonna' go out for the night and have some *real* fun! Jis' you an' me! We gonna' leave momma home."

Bobby looked toward the car where his wife was sitting behind the steering wheel.

"Ole' Shorty, he always be talkin' 'bout you 'fore he done got killed. He always say he wanna' take you out fur some fun wit' da' ladies when we come to Sow Calahna. We ain't got Shorty no more, but my people gonna' take care a' you. Maybe we even git ya' some a' dat fine brown pussy! Ummmmmm, I know you gonna' like dat chocolate stuff! You won't ever wanna' go back to da' white meat . . . . if you know what I mean!"

Bobby laughed his contagious laugh for the first time that morning. It was the laugh I had remembered. I laughed with him, mostly over the irony of our discussion of his plan to get me laid, while his wife sat in the car only a few feet away.

"Sure," I said. I didn't believe Bobby was serious, and even if he was I didn't think it would ever happen. It was one of those things men talked about, but often did not follow up on.

I said, "you go home and finish gettin' healed up, then we'll talk more about your plans to take me out. If we can do it, fine, but if we can't, I'll understand."

I thought that would probably be the end of it, and besides, I wasn't sure how my going out with a black packer would go over with Aubrey and Joe, much less with the local white population. I didn't want a burning cross to turn up in front of our hotel, or at the farmer's co-op, over my spending a night on the town with Bobby, nor did I want one to show up in Bobby's front lawn because of his "dirty work" in corrupting an out of town white boy. But, I had to respect the fact that this was Bobby's home turf, and even if I were advised not to go out with Bobby, I might choose to go anyway. Besides, after Shorty's death I was not so much in the mood to be intimidated. Bobby and I had a new bond of friendship because of Shorty's death. While I was light years short of the moral courage of a civil rights worker, I tried to convince myself that I would do whatever it took to hold on to my budding friendship with Bobby Leeds. Harkensville would be my chance to do that, and maybe to strengthen it at the same time.

* * *

Bobby's family was part of a community that made up the backbone of black society in Harkensville, South Carolina Many of Bobby's friends and relatives owned their homes, held respected jobs, and were well off compared with other South Carolina blacks. Bobby's lack of formal education was the main reason he had not risen above the occupation of watermelon packer. He had only completed 6th grade and was fortunate to have been small for his age, because it took him until he was 14 to advance to the 7th grade. His family had made several moves over the years, and they eventually worked their way to Harkensville. Several of Bobby's friends and family members were preachers, doctors, dentists and lawyers. Others were shop owners who had built their own businesses, or inherited established family businesses. These professionals and business people provided goods and services to the larger black community, which had produced great athletes at college and professional levels, as well as soldiers, civil rights leaders, engineers, and a few politicians. Harkensville had a reputation in the black community of South Carolina as a breeding ground for black talent, and this strength was attributed to the town's ability to build pride and respect among its members. Black people from Harkensville believed in themselves. Bobby Leeds had inherited this belief, as well as the solid foundation of his Geechee heritage. Even so, he was grateful that his family had decided to move away from St. Helena Island, and eventually to Harkensville where he met a good woman and settled down. As his father had always told him, "There ain't nothin' like a good woman ta' make a man what he s'pose ta' be." And this had certainly proven to be true in Bobby's case.

* * *

Each day of the week after Bobby's return to Harkensville, Joe Harper sent me out to Clarence Stout's farm. There was no sign that the crop was near its end, and Stout could barely count his money as fast as it was piling up. Stout put me in mind of the miserly comic book character, Scrooge McDuck.

Each morning, I rode into the farmer's market with Lonny and Don Jr., and each morning I accompanied a different semi driver to Stout's farm to pack more Crimson Sweets. I became the fearless guide, directing truckers who were not familiar with the countryside around Harkensville. Not a day passed in which I did not make at least two consecutive trips to the Stout farm, each time with a driver who was pulling a 40 foot semi trailer that I would fill up with Crimson Sweets, with the help of Stout's young crew of workers.

* * *

I was keenly aware that the time was drawing near for me to meet Bobby's family and friends, and I gradually became more apprehensive about the evening out Bobby had planned. My Midwestern background brought with it a strong conservative tendency, and one consistently nagging question, "What might go wrong?" But Bobby was not a Midwesterner, nor did he take his promises lightly, especially when it came to promises involving his best friend, Shorty. Besides, Bobby was prone to superstition, and it didn't take a great deal of superstition to convince a person that a dead man's wishes must be honored.

The week after I'd spoken with Bobby at the farmer's market, he stopped by again late one evening for a visit. Minutes earlier, I had returned from Clarence Stout's farm after packing my second trailer of the day. At that point, I was up to 24 trailers packed at the Stout farm, but who was counting?

I was not surprised when Bobby said he had set up the plans for our big night out.

"We gonna' have one big time of it, buddy! First, you comin' over ta' my house fur some barbecue dinner, den you and me is goin' out so I can show you what I been talkin' about. You ain't neva' gonna' furgit' dis Saturday night!"

"Are you picking me up at the hotel?" I asked.

"Shore 'nuff, Matt. Shore nuff am! Eight o'clock sharp."

"You want me to dress up, right?"

"Yeah, dress up nice, Matt. No suit, no tie, but nice . . . you know what I be talkin' 'bout. Da Missuz, she wanna' have a big ass barbecue. But after dinner, we gonna' go to a *real* nice place next ta' Orangeburg. Y'all gonna' love deez here wimmin! Y'all jis' gonna' *love* 'em!"

Bobby laughed. He was genuinely looking forward to our night of male bonding.

I had not packed dress clothes for my summer in the South, so I asked Joe Harper for some time off on Saturday afternoon to go shopping. That would mean one load of Crimson Sweets at the Stout farm, rather than two. I needed a nice pair of dress slacks, a dress shirt, and some new loafers so I could properly clean up for the evening at Bobby's.

I knew I could still cancel out, and Bobby would probably forgive me, but it was late in the week and I had begun to feel locked in. If it came down to backing out at the last minute, I could always tell Bobby I was sick with the flu, food poisoning, or some other diet related ailment.

A precept my parents had taught me was, it was never too late to back out on a commitment. Mafia members, soldiers on the field of battle, and rugby players had to stick with their commitments. Midwestern farm boys, on the other hand, could back out at the last minute. This rendered many a Midwestern farm boy (like myself) incapable of taking significant risk, and it was working overtime in my brain.

38.

"Nigger Rich?" Melvin yelled into the telephone receiver. "Nigger Rich, is that you?" Melvin paused for a second and waited for a reply from the other end. "Oh, terrible sorry, Ma'am! I thought you was Nigger Rich!"

Melvin cupped his hand over the mouthpiece and looked at Joe Harper, struggling to keep his laughter silent.

"Is Nigger Rich there, ma'am? He is? Good! Could you carry him over to the phone for me? Thanks, Ma'am, much obliged."

"Hey, Nigger Rich, you sorry mother fucker, what the fuck have you been doin' with yourself lately?" Melvin had the right person on the line this time. He cupped the mouthpiece again and winked at Joe Harper. "You enjoyin' retired life, are ya'? I bet it's boring as hell, ain't it? Fishin? Sittin' around the house? Momma bitchin' at ya' all day long!"

Melvin couldn't keep from laughing at his own cleverness. He paused for a moment and pretended to listen. He felt at his best this time of day, after the Cutty Sark had killed off millions of his brain cells and taken firm possession of the rest.

"I'm sure you done heard about your old friend Shorty gettin' shot and killed, and Bobby Leeds gettin' stabbed. They say bad news travels fast, and I know from experience that kinda' word gets around the nigger community at lightenin' speed." Melvin paused again. "It's just too damn bad what happened to them ole' boys. They was damn good boys, and they never meant nobody no harm. But this whole thing has put us in a fuckin' bind, 'specially with the flood a' melons these growers is haulin' in for us to pack every goddam day. I ain't never seen the likes of it, Rich. You been out to see this year's crop?"

Melvin listened for a moment, then looked at Joe Harper again and winked as he listened to Rich.

"I figure a good ole' packer like you would know all about the crop this year. And I know you ain't ever gonna' git watermelons outa' your blood until they put your sorry ass in a pine box and lower you into a hole in the ground! Shit, ole' Slick's still packin' melons fur us, and that sorry ass fucker looks like he might fall over dead any minute. Must be 100 years old by now." Melvin laughed again, then stopped and listened. Melvin had a real talent for telephone work, and his timing was flawless when it was show time.

"So, whatcha' think, Rich ? You gonna' come over here and help us out, or not? You know us, we gonna' pay ya' damn good, and maybe if you behave yourself, I'll toss in a bottle a'Cutty. Shit, Aubrey done said he'd be ready to pay you $25 a trailer, you bein' the old pro and all. Just don't tell Slick about it, or he'll string me up by the fuckin' nuts! The young boys on the crew probably won't care, cause they know about your reputation, plus they've all got rich white daddies, so they don't really need the money anyway."

Melvin paused, raised his right hand into the air, and crossed his index and middle fingers as a young boy would do behind his back in hopes of getting a "yes" answer out of his parents.

"Sore back?" Melvin yelled. "You big pussy! God dammit! I've got a sore ass too, but I'm still here sittin' on the damn thing every goddamn day! Just get your bad back over here and use it for liftin' some melons. It'll feel fine once you work up a sweat and work the kinks out of it! It's rustin' up on ya' is all! After a few loads a' melons, you'll be back to fuckin' the old lady like a young buck! She'll like the money, and she'll damn sure appreciate the extra meat in her diet!"

After a final pause to listen for Rich's reply, Melvin yelled out, "Fuckin' ay! I knew you'd find it in your heart to help us out, you ole' stud horse! Have your ass in here at 6:30 in the mornin', and we'll start ya' wit' your first load a' melons! And like I said, it's $25 a trailer, just for you."

Melvin slammed the receiver down so hard he nearly broke the brittle black plastic of the cradle, and then he quickly bounced up out of his creaky office chair with an expression of sheer glee on his face. "Damn, I'm good! I've still got it, Joe, and you know it! That's why you fuckers keep my sorry ass on the payroll."

Joe Harper had taken it all in. He shook his head and smiled. "What's this line of bullshit about Aubrey saying he'd pay Rich $25 a trailer? You know that's a bald faced lie!"

"Fuck," said Melvin. "Aubrey wanted him a packer, and I got him a packer. I know goddam well Rich will do a fine job, and it sure as hell won't break the QM bank to pay him for it."

Joe slowly walked outside, still shaking his head. Of Melvin's undesirable qualities, and there were many, his over-blown ego was the most annoying to Joe. But, as Aubrey was prone to say about Melvin, "The sorry fucker can close a deal over the phone when he's drunk, better than most of us can in person when we're stone sober."

Melvin followed Joe outside, lighting a cigarette as he walked. "Joe, Nigger Rich'll be here with bells on, first thing tomorrow mornin'. I sure as fuck hope he can handle a coupla' loads a' these big fuckers a day. Even I'm smart enough to know, we damn sure need him! And if Aubrey's too fuckin' stingy ta' pay him $25 a load, I'll pay the extra $5 outa' my own pocket."

Joe said, "If I know Rich, he would have told you up front if he couldn't handle it. Your job was to get him hired, now it's my job to keep him busy and keep an eye on him once he gets here."

It was mostly out of respect for his old friend Shorty that Rich had agreed to come back to work, certainly not out of any respect for Melvin, or to help Melvin through a workload crisis. Within the network of black packers from the South, Shorty had been one of the most respected, not only for his humor and hard work, but because he was a decent human being. Richard Saunders and his wife shared many of the same interests as those of Shorty and his wife. This was an aspect of black community life that was completely unknown to the likes of Melvin, who would rather go on believing that most "niggers" sat around waiting for social welfare programs, or benevolent white people to get them through the tough times.

39.

Saturday evening arrived, and as he'd promised, Bobby arrived at the hotel to pick me up at 8:00 P.M. sharp. I had taken a fair amount of kidding from Lonny and Don Jr. over my plans to spend a Saturday evening with Bobby and his family and friends. They both liked Bobby, but they had a tendency to think of him as a funny little man who could not be taken seriously. And although they had not been too mean with their harassment, I had the impression that neither of them believed I would (or should) go through with it when the time came. But I didn't need to apologize for my decision to go out with Bobby. I simply told them the truth: that groundhog barbecues were not uncommon in southern Indiana, and every summer for as long as I could remember, my dad had taken me with him to a groundhog festival sponsored by a local Black Baptist congregation. I explained that the taste of barbecued woodchuck was not overly gamy, and it was only a little bit greasier than regular pork barbecue. Still, they didn't seem convinced that I would go through with it, especially because they knew that the evening was not *only* about eating groundhog barbecue!

When Bobby picked me up that evening, he had a passenger in the front seat with him. I got into the back seat of the late model Chrysler. The car was smaller than Shorty's Buick, but certainly large enough to qualify as a luxury sedan by automobile standards in the late 1960s.

Bobby introduced the other man in the front seat as his friend, "Rich Saunders." I knew immediately that this was none other than Nigger Rich! Saunders looked back over his left shoulder and said, "I'm shore you heard ole Melvin at da' packin' house talkin' 'bout Nigger Rich! Well, dat be me, in da' flesh! I bet you be expectin' Nigger Rich ta' be some old shriveled up muthafucker, didn't ya'? I been heppin' out at the co-op several days now, but I damn shore ain't seen you around. Bobby tells me ole' Joe Harper be sendin' you out early to ole' man Stout's place damn near ever day."

"Nice to meet you, Rich," I said. "Melvin's been braggin' ever since he sweet-talked you into coming out to help us. And you're right, I've been out at Stout's place every day, and I haven't been around the co-op except to meet up with my semi drivers early every morning. At the end of the day when I'm finished, I come in only to catch a ride to the hotel with Joe Harper, so I guess that's why we haven't crossed paths at the farmer's market. How are you holdin' up so far?"

"I be holdin' up OK," said Rich. "Don't rightly know if 'dees ole' bones gonna' hold up fur too many more loads a' melons, but I do what I can do. B'sides, da' Missuz, she says she need a new 'fridgerator, so I don't guess it's a bad time fur me to make a few extra bucks right about now."

* * *

Changing the subject, Bobby's voice became very emotional. This was a side of him I had not seen before. He began to tell Rich and me about Shorty's funeral, and the huge crowds of friends and family who attended. Most of the people in attendance lived near Ocala and had known Shorty for their entire lives. Bobby described the funeral service as a loud affair with a full choir of robed gospel singers who were led by a flamboyant director with "James Brown Hair." Bobby said the fiery preacher talked about Shorty "like a saint." Bobby described a scene in which there was a great deal of screaming and wailing, especially by Shorty's wife and mother, who had been overcome by grief. Bobby described the scene at the burial site, where Shorty's mother, a large woman in her 70s, had completely lost control and hurled herself atop the casket just before it was to be lowered into the grave. She then lay on the casket, screaming for 15 minutes or more. Nobody knew whether she would live through it. Finally, relatives helped her down from the casket and escorted her back to the limo that was designated for the immediate family.

After the burial service and dinner were over, Shorty's wife regained emotional control and explained to Bobby that she had no idea her husband was such a popular man, particularly since he had been away much of the time with his melon packing job. She also told Bobby that she wanted him to have the Buick that had been impounded in the Sheriff's storage lot back in Holcomb, Alabama. She tearfully explained that the car would "bring her nothin' but bad memories of Shorty dyin' in that terrible way." Because of this, she did not want the car.

Without giving it much thought, Bobby promised her that he would return to Holcomb for the car. And later, when he had time to think about it, he realized that the car meant a lot to him as well. In fact, as Bobby spoke, I could tell that he really wanted Shorty's car, if only for its value as a memento of the best friend and melon packer he'd ever known.

I said, "Those fuckers in Holcomb won't let you take Shorty's car, especially if you show up down there without everything being greased by somebody like Joe Harper or Aubrey ahead of time."

"Da' way it usually woiks, if'n I go ta' Holcomb, dey gonna' think I jis' there to start somethin', or dey be thinkin' I'm some kinda' lazy nigger wantin' somethin' fur free. But here be somethin' you don't know, Matt. Shorty's wife, she give me da' car papers, and I damn shore forgot my name was on 'em. I be half owner a' Shorty's car, so dey gotta' give it ta' me if'n I got da' papers. Do I be right, Matt?"

"Really?" I asked. "You and Shorty were joint owners of the car? If you've got the papers to prove it, they should give you the fuckin' car. You might need a copy of Shorty's death certificate, but his wife probably has that by now."

"Shit, Matt, dey be da' one's dat killed Shorty. Why da' fuck dey need proof ole' Shorty be dead?"

"They might not," I said, "but when it comes to legal matters, they might want to see a death certificate to clear the release of the car to you. And what if they tell you they're holding Shorty's car as evidence?" I asked. "I mean, they could tell you they still need it for the investigation, and you'd never know if they were tellin' the truth or lyin' through their teeth! Shit, they might be plannin' to sell it off at the county Sheriff's auction so they can pay for the strippers at the Sheriff's stag Christmas party."

Bobby said, "You damn shore full a' fuckin' questions, Matt! You ever think about bein' a fuckin' lawyer?"

I looked at Bobby's eyes in the rearview mirror of his wife's car, and smiled.

"I bet dey jis' love fur me ta' not show up," said Bobby, "den day jis' sell dat Buick at da' county auction and pocket da' money. But maybe if'n you and me go ova' ta' Holcomb together wit' da' papers I got, we might could git them muthafuckers ta' let me carry da' black beauty home. Think about it, Matt? What da' fuck you gotta' lose, except a day or two a' packin' Crimsons for ole' man Stout. I know you could use you a little break, and I damn shore could use a white man's hep once't I gits to Holcomb. If'n I walks in and tells them muthafuckkers I's there ta' pick up a car, an' I ain't got no white man standin' next ta' me when I says it, I damn shore could be in deep shit. A black man can't jis' show up claimin' no right ta' nuthin' in a place like Holcomb."

"Do you have a driver's license, Bobby? I mean, I know you're driving your wife's car right now, but do you have an up-to-date license to show those assholes in Holcomb once we would get there?"

"Shit, yea, Matt! I got me a' Flawdy license, *an'*a Sow Calahna one too! Dey gotta' let me drive my car! I be legal as a fuckin' Eagle man, but even if I got two licenses, I shore as hell can't drive two cars at da' same time, so I need y'all wit' me ta' drive one of 'em back here. Fact is, I'll be real nice and let ya' drive Shorty's big ass car. It handle slick as shit on da' open road, Matt!"

"What the hell, Bobby? I guess I could take a day or two off before headin' up north. After we got back here, I could get one of the truckers to drop me off in Indiana on his way up to Chicago. I'd pay for the ride by packin' a nice load a' melons for him!"

"Sure! Why not?" I said.

"Let's do it. But then I've gotta' move on and pack some more a' them beautiful Charleston Grays back in Indiana! Damn, I'm lookin' forward to bein' back home! I'm lookin' forward to some hard days of melon packin' and some long nights with my tall, blond Indiana honeys! It's been a long summer, especially with all the shit that's happened with Shorty and you. What a fuckin' piece a' shit this turned into!"

"It damn shore ain't been no fun fur me neither, Matt! It be da' worst summer a' my sorry-ass life. When ole' Shorty and me was packin' as a team every day, da' summers flew by. We damn shore had fun—an' we made some money too! But dis' summer be all fucked up! I miss ole' Shorty, and I ain't had no fun!"

Rich said, "Bobby tells me you done turned into a damn good packer, an' you be a damn good fella on top of it. If Bobby say it, I damn shore believe it! But I tell ya' now, ain't nobody met a better man 'den ole' Shorty! Before 'dis young fella sittin' here next ta' me come along wit' his packin' magic," Rich nodded towards Bobby, "me and Shorty was a team fur many years, and we be sittin' on top a' da' melon packin' world! Axe any a' dees here buyers and truckers. We damn shore had some good summers togetha'. An' you can believe me when I say da' fuckin' melon bidnuss be changin'. Ain't never gonna' be like it was when Shorty an' me, or Shorty an' Bobby was first teamin' up. First, dey starts off wit' dat fancy shit dey be usin' over in Alabama, an' nex' thing ya' knows dey be loadin' melons in big ass wood boxes, and drivin' 'em right in da' trailer wit' a fuckin' forklif'. You mark my words. Da' fuckin' melon packer is gonna' be outa' bidnuss in a few years."

It wasn't long before Bobby pulled up, directly in front of his own home. I had not paid attention to the route he had taken, but I knew we had meandered our way through a sizeable black neighborhood. I was also aware that I was the only white person within several blocks, but somehow that didn't matter. I had once ridden a city bus in Indianapolis, and having fallen asleep for at least 30 minutes, I found myself at the end of the bus line in the middle of a totally black part of the city. As a white kid straight off the farm, I had been extremely uncomfortable to find myself all alone in a non-white area. That was scary, mainly because I had heard too many of my father's stories about growing up on the "rough" south side of Chicago in the 1930's.

Here in Harkensville, South Carolina, it didn't bother me in the least to be the only white man in the neighborhood, because I knew I was a welcome guest of Bobby Leeds and his family.

Bobby's home was a small, four-room wood-frame house, and at least twice the size of the narrow shotgun style shacks that passed for family homes on Clarence Stout's farm. Bobby's house was painted white, with a green-shingled roof and dark green shutters flanking either side of screened windows. Some of Bobby's window screens had small but noticeable holes in them, but they were generally in good repair, much better than the sorry excuses for screens at Smitherman's restaurant in Holcomb.

On the front of the house was a small porch with a screen door. Most of the neighboring homes were similar in size; almost cookie cutter patterns out of the post-WWII National Homes blueprint book. Most black people in Harkensville were too poor to afford fancy houses, and black families who could afford it dare not violate the unwritten laws of the social order, which dictated that they live in modest homes in all black neighborhoods. Even if a fancy home were located in the black section of town, there could be problems. If a wealthy black family opted to build a large home, that home might not stand for long before jealous whites came into the neighborhood at night to "teach the uppity niggers a lesson." The so-called lesson would come in the form of a "house warming party," and the uninvited guests would likely be dressed in white sheets with tall, pointed headgear.

The black community of Harkensville accepted the social limitations placed upon them by white society. They had little choice. If they could afford a few of life's luxuries, they would usually settle for a fancy car. Whites didn't mind if a black man had a fancy car, as long as there was no danger it would be permanently parked in front of a home in a white neighborhood.

Bobby's home had no garage, but a gravel turnaround in front that served as a parking space large enough for two cars. None of the neighboring homes had garages, despite the presence of many large and expensive cars. Perhaps a garage would have defeated the purpose of owning a fine looking automobile. Dr. Andrew Harmon called this social phenomenon "compensatory consumption," a term of art used by Social Scientists for the practice of buying one thing to make up for the lack of another. For instance, a black man often bought a big car to compensate for his lack of social status, or the lack of a luxurious home. He might also dress in gaudy and expensive clothes when going out on the town, to give others the impression that he was financially well to do.

There were at least ten cars parked around Bobby's house, including a few in the side yard and one or two in the back yard. A thick plume of white smoke wafted over the roof of Bobby's house. The sweet aroma of the smoke had the familiar and inviting smell of barbecue, causing an instant release of digestive juices into my stomach. I had not smelled the enticing aroma of meat cooking on a grill since my dad had cooked steaks for the family the weekend before I left Indiana. I was hungry, yet I tried not to think of the fact that some of the tiny particles entering my nostrils had flown off a thick, South Carolina version of Punxsutawney Pork.

"Matt, dis gonna' be a fine groun'hog barbecue party! You gonna' love it."

Bobby led the way toward the back yard, and Rich and I followed closely behind. I had genuinely looked forward to this part of the evening. Although apprehensive about our plans for later in the evening, I didn't let on to Bobby that I was the least bit afraid of going beyond the point of social fellowship and the evening meal. But Bobby needed to regain a sense of control in his life, and if a commitment of friendship on my part would help, I was determined to go through with it.

As the three of us entered the back yard, I saw at least 25 people gathered there, all speaking the same dialect that Bobby spoke. While I had begun to understand Bobby's speech pattern, zeroing in on any given sentence from his crowd of guests would be a challenge. It felt a bit like a movie scene, and the words being spoken were merely background noise, not necessarily a conversation in which I would be expected to participate.

Although mine was the only white face in the crowd, a few people in the group had skin only slightly darker than mine. Bobby and Shorty had explained to me how easy it was for a black person to spot another black person who had white blood, and light brown people were automatically afforded a higher status within the black community.

Light tan people were common in the South, dating back to the days of slavery when white plantation owners had their way with young slave women. Many prominent white Americans, Thomas Jefferson included, had fathered children with slave women. Since the Civil War, thousands upon thousands of the lightest skinned blacks had "passed" into white society, abandoning their biological families for the chance to have what they perceived as a better life on the socially privileged white side.

Bobby politely took the time to introduce me to his friends and family. He seemed proud to have me as his special evening guest, and I suddenly felt embarrassed from the special attention.

"Matt, dis' is my wife, 'Lizabeth.'"

"Nice to meet you," I replied, turning on my best Indiana charm. "I'm honored that Bobby invited me to join in on your family barbecue."

"You like groun'hog, Matt?" Elizabeth was smiling with her eyes, and revealing her nearly perfect white teeth at the same time. She was short and a bit stocky, and her skin was decidedly darker than Bobby's. She wore a green and yellow, full length dress with a bright green bandana over her straightened hair. I was fascinated by the fact that dark skinned people like Elizabeth looked so attractive in bright colored clothing that would look completely overdone on white people.

"I've tasted groundhog a few times, and actually liked it. But what I smell here is better than any I've smelled before. The secret must be in your barbecue sauce." I was going out of my way to be polite to my hostess, almost to the point of feeling insincere.

"You don' have-ta' eat dis' stuff if'n ya' don' want to," Elizabeth laughed. "Ole' Bobby, he be puttin' ya' up ta' dis,' I jis' know he has. But I got some real nice barbecue pork ribs here, an' some fine chicken barbecue if'n ya' don't want dis' here groun'hog. I works in a butcher shop in Harkensvul, so Bobby an' me is lucky enough ta' do lotsa' barbecuin' at home. You ain't never had the kinda' barbecue y'all gonna' taste here' tonight. But dis' here grounhog is jis' a little somethin' ta' remind us of da' hard times. We used ta' call it 'panic pig,' 'cause dat's all da' meat folks had ta' eat back in da' panic days in da' 1930s. I s'pose white folks calls it the Depression. But whatever you calls it, it's good ta' remember da' hard times da' old folks had ta' suffer through, before folks like us could git aholt a' white people meat," said Elizabeth. "I guess you could say Bobby an' me be eatin' high off da' hog dees days, and we sure be thankful ta' the good Lord."

"I'll try a little bit of everything, even the groundhog. It all smells so good, and that smell has made me real hungry!"

I had convinced myself I was telling the truth when I told Elizabeth that I wanted to try the groundhog, but she knew I would prefer the pork ribs and chicken, without my saying so.

"Bobby tell me he done ax'd y'all ta' go wit' him ta' his card game after we's finished here! When he not be on da' road, he can't seem ta' stay home on a Saturd'y night, at least not since he be goin' ta' dat' card game a' his over by Orangeburg! But now, with his arm in a sling, you might need ta' hold his cards so he can play 'em' tonight." She laughed.

*   *   *

A handsome man, who looked a bit like Bobby, expensively dressed and a bit taller than Bobby, came up to us as Elizabeth was telling me about Bobby's weekly card game. The man said, "Yeah,' ole' Bobby, he be hooked on dat' Saturd'y night *card game*!" He laughed playfully around the words as he spoke them, moving his shoulders up and down, just as Bobby did when he laughed. "I don't know what Bobby would do if'n he didn't go out and play dem' cards!"

Turning to the man, Bobby grabbed my forearm. "Matt, dis' here is my crazy-ass brotha', Charles. He be laughin' an' carryin' on all da' time. He worse den me! Don't pay him no mind!" Bobby put his arm on Charles' shoulder and laughed, leaning heavily toward Charles, as if he were about to fall over, all the time maintaining perfect body control.

I got the point of the two brothers' laughter, as well as their exaggerated body language. They talked about playing cards on Saturday nights for the benefit of Bobby's wife, who was probably aware that their "card game" involved more than cards. There may have been cards played, but low stakes gambling was very likely secondary to other forms of play.

Guests began milling around near a long wooden plank table that had been set up to accommodate a large number of people and a tremendous amount of food. One end of the table was no more than ten feet away from a red brick barbecue grill where Elizabeth was cooking the taste-tempting cuts of meat. It looked like the meat was about done, and the smell in the air was making everyone hungry by now.

The long table was filled with bowls of extra barbecue sauce and ample supplies of fresh baked cornbread, grits, okra, and black-eyed peas that female guests had been carrying out from the house.

Elizabeth provided the meat from her place of employment, and the invited guests had carried in the "fixin's" to accompany her barbecue feast. Soon, she began to fill large serving trays with groundhog meat, slabs of pork ribs, and juicy pieces of chicken.

Bobby quickly finished introducing me around before he invited me to take a seat at the table. I was intrigued by Bobby's smoothness in dealing with the crowd of people. Not an educated man by formal standards, Bobby was very polite and well mannered. His introductions were gracious and natural. I had been taught that an educated person was one who knew how to treat other people, and Bobby's actions that evening proved to me that he was an educated man. He'd had "good upbringing," as my grandmother would have said.

It suddenly occurred to me that Bobby's family was similar to my own in its love of the large, backyard social gathering. We, like most middle class midwestern families, loved overflowing portions of rich food, eaten to the accompaniment of loud conversation and out-of-control laughter. A noticeable difference between Bobby's family and mine was the loudness of the conversation. I never would have guessed that any group of people could out-yell my family at a barbecue, but Bobby's family and friends took the prize in that category! My eardrums were overwhelmed with sound, and it became difficult to discern individual words that were aimed at me. I began nodding and smiling knowingly, just as I would have as a guest in a foreign country where I did not understand a single spoken word.

After everyone gathered around the table and Bobby led us in the blessing, he then reached for a bottle of dark red Thunderbird wine. As the special guest for the evening, I was the first to receive my glass of wine. Then, Bobby continued pouring wine until everyone at the table had enough to hold up for a toast. By the time he finished, Bobby had opened and poured four full bottles, and every adult at the long table had a half glass of wine.

Bobby raised his voice as he raised his glass.

"To my good friend, Matt. He's been a friend ta' me, an' he was a friend to ole' Shorty. He's a damn good melon packer, fur a white boy."

Everyone around the table enjoyed a loud and extended laugh.

"Matt be a good man, and a good friend. Let us all drink a toast ta' Matt!"

Everyone raised their glasses and took a sip, as if I were a true celebrity. Even the kids toasted along with the adults, holding their glasses of sweet tea or lemonade in their small hands and clinking them playfully against each other's.

Captured by the spirit of the moment, I stood up at the table and said, "I would like to offer a toast to Bobby. To the best friend anyone could have, a man who would give his *life* for a friend, and probably the best watermelon packer I've ever known. Here's to Bobby. Thank the Lord we still have him with us to share this evening."

Everyone at the table raised their glasses and took another sip of their liquid of choice. I knew that everyone present agreed with my sentiment, especially the part about being lucky to have Bobby with us.

Despite the outward acceptance, I continued to feel a bit awkward among Bobby's family and friends. For a second, I was a little embarrassed that I'd offered a toast, but Bobby and the others sensed that my toast was heartfelt. They had raised their glasses and drank, and they seemed to appreciate my gesture of respect towards their good friend and family member.

With the social formalities out of the way, we began passing serving bowls and trays around the table and filling our plates. The live oak trees overhead shaded the back yard like a lush, green umbrella, and the cool evening breeze was pleasant to the ear as well as soothing to the skin. The biting flies miraculously stayed away. Perhaps it was the heat and humidity in midday that made them irritable.

It was the kind of peaceful summer evening that makes a lasting impression; a moment one can return to in the future by closing one's eyes and listening for the rustling of leaves overhead.

I filled my plate with more food than I'd had in front of me all summer. I took large slabs of pork ribs and chicken, and avoided the groundhog and okra for the first serving. I told Bobby I needed "side-boards" on my plate, like the ones on the melon wagons at the farmer's market. If only I had sideboards, I'd have room for some groundhog. Bobby liked the analogy, and laughed along with me as I expected he would.

We ate, drank, talked, laughed, slapped knees and shoulders, and enjoyed each other's company throughout the meal. When everyone seemed to have his or her fill of food and friendship, Elizabeth asked Bobby and his brother Charles to accompany her into the house to help carry out the desserts. After a few minutes, the two brothers emerged from the back door of the house, each carrying a tray of warm sweet potato pies. I sighed under my breath, thinking of how much I had already crammed into my stomach, and wondering how I would find room for dessert. It was 9:30 P.M., and that would normally have been too late in the evening for pie. But this evening was just getting started as far as Bobby was concerned, so I assumed we had plenty of time to enjoy dessert.

I'd decided for at least the 10th time that evening that I would ask Bobby to take me back to the motel following the barbecue. Despite his enthusiasm for sharing the entire evening with me, I didn't feel I was ready for the sort of after dinner entertainment Bobby had in mind. But, as soon as the guests had finished their pie, Bobby gave Rich and me the nod, signaling that it was time for us to move on. Both men said their goodbyes, and I lingered for a minute or two to thank Elizabeth again for the wonderful meal. I thanked her for the southern barbecued groundhog, which made her laugh. I would have been happy to stay and help her with the dishes.

Elizabeth yelled after Bobby as he started around the corner of the house on his way to the car.

"Bobby, you never done told me Matt here was quite the young politician. Maybe some day he'll be famous, an' we can tell folks we done fed him some barbecue in our own back yard before he done got famous. Maybe he'll be the President some day, a regular John F. Kennedy."

"Well, 'Lizabeth, you let your little Mr. Kennedy come with me now. We gonna' show him a good time, and he can worry about bein' President some other time."

As I crawled into the back seat of Bobby's car, I felt the pressure of the huge meal pushing against the walls of my stomach. At that moment, what I needed most was to loosen my belt and stretch out on the double bed in my cool motel room. I said, "Bobby, you've gotta' take me back to the motel. I think your wife got me too full for me to enjoy any partyin' tonight!"

Bobby laughed as he turned the ignition key.

"Shit, what you mean, Matt? A man ain't never got too much in his belly to enjoy some sweet lovin'! Y'all damn sure not passin' up what we done set up fur you young ass tonight!" Bobby and Rich laughed again. Rich, who had consumed several glasses of wine with his dinner, laughed so hard his entire body rocked back and forth in the front seat of the car. Had it not been for the locked car door to his immediate right, he could easily have tumbled out onto the pavement.

"You ain't never seen the kinda' sweet lady ole' Bobby done lined up fur ya', Matt! Fact is, I ain't too damn shore you ever seen a woman naked, close up! But 'dat be you bidnuss."

Rich was no help to me in my feeble effort to thwart Bobby's plans, so I eventually gave up trying. The simple fact was that I was outnumbered, and Bobby was literally in the driver's seat. The moment I had stepped into Bobby's car at the motel, I had made the commitment to see the evening through. Ready or not, I would soon be introduced to my first black prostitute. In fact, it would be my very first experience with a prostitute of any color.

Rich said, "You gonna' love dis place! You ain't never seen so many black an' white muthafuckers with money ta' spend, all havin' a good time under da' same roof. An' I damn betcha' you won't see anything like it ag'in. Color don't matter here, an' it's all 'cause da' pussy be sooooo damn fine. An' all 'dat pussy be black an' tan! White dudes don't even mind hangin' out wid' us at dis place. Nooooo, brotha'! Y'all don't wanna' pass up dis' night, Matt! Dis here is part a' you education 'bout da' *real* South. Dis be somethin' you ain't NEVER gonna' read in no book, and you ain't never gonna' forget about it, either!"

For me, second thoughts were a chronic affliction. But Bobby was on a personal mission to carry out his plan, and I could tell that he was not prone to second thoughts once he'd made up his mind. Neither was Rich.

* * *

Dr. Andrew Harmon's voice refused to render judgment. From a barely lit corner deep inside of my brain, I heard him laughing. When he stopped laughing, I heard him whisper . . . *"It probably won't hurt you."* Then the light went out.

40.

Bobby drove for what seemed to be 30 or 45 minutes, and the back seat of the car was so dark I couldn't see my watch. When his headlights illuminated a small green sign along the side of the road that read "Orangeburg 5 Miles," I recalled he had mentioned that the place we were going was near Orangeburg. We must have been getting close.

"Hey Matt," said Bobby, "you still awake back there? I gotta' tell ya', man, you ain't seen no watermelons like these you about to see tonight! These is the soft kind, and they be real easy on you hands." Bobby and Rich both laughed. They were truly enjoying the anticipation of introducing me to recreational sex.

I was reminded of the times my college friends in Indiana had tried to introduce me to the ladies of "Little Harlem," an all-black brothel located on Highway 41 in the heart of Terre Haute, Indiana. Terre Haute, locally referred to as "Sin City," was a mere hour's drive from Elmwood. A small group of my fraternity brothers had gotten into the habit of making Saturday night trips to Little Harlem, but I had steadfastly refused to go along. I always had a date with a girl friend, which I thought was infinitely more wholesome than visiting a whorehouse. But wholesome living left me naïve, and I now wished I had gone along with my friends at least once. An ounce of experience might have made this evening a lot easier.

Bobby began to slow the vehicle down, and then he made a quick right-hand turn onto a tiny dirt road that felt like the road to Clarence Stout's farmhouse. He and Rich had been laughing so hard after his last comments, that he'd almost missed his turn off the main road. In a few seconds, I discerned the outline of a large and secluded brick house.

"Fasten your seatbelts for the final approach," I thought.

The house had the look of an antebellum mansion, complete with its stately white columns in front. I had trouble focusing on the building because of the darkness, but the two lamps hanging in front illuminated it enough that I could make out the basic structure. There were no lights in the windows, and they appeared to be covered from the inside with dark, pull-down shades or European style roll-down shutters. Bobby drove past the front of the house, and parked around back next to the other cars.

There were at least 25 cars in the parking area, and all seemed to be shiny late model luxury vehicles. The clients at this establishment included those who had money, and those who wanted to give that impression.

We parked next to a white Cadillac that was so big it would take a man a half a day to walk around it. I wasn't sure whether I was excited or just nervous, but I could feel a million butterflies floating upwards inside my stomach as I got out of the car. I was sure this was due to my heightened sense of awareness, but the place also had a distinct air of sensuality.

"Matt, da' ladies here is tall an' got long legs dat go all da' way up ta' make an ass outa' deyself!" Bobby and Rich laughed. "And guess what, Matt?" Bobby asked rhetorically, "Dey wants you ass, man! You gonna' have da' night of you life, Matt!"

"I'm not so sure about this, Bobby. Maybe I'll just play cards this first time."

"What y'all not sure of, Matt? Not sure you can make one a' dees ladies happy? Jis' remember, you day job is packin' melons when da' sun shine, and da' lady's job here is makin' young men like you happy when da' sun go down! Dey gittin' paid to make us men happy, and you ain't got ta' do nothin', jis' lay back and let it happin'."

"Shit, man" said Bobby, "a big strappin' young man like you? I bet ya' ten dolla' you gonna' git da' job done!"

"The only thing I'm afraid of is that I might get the job done before she does anything!" I laughed.

*   *   *

The three of us walked toward the back door of the house, and when we arrived, Bobby rang an illuminated doorbell that was shaped like the trademark Playboy bunny. There was no immediate response, so Bobby rang again. Eventually a long-legged, mocha-skinned woman answered the door. She was easily three inches taller than Bobby; her breasts were large, perfectly shaped, and barely contained within her red "Teddy" camisole. The way she and Bobby reacted to the sight of each another, I could tell they were *very* good friends.

Bobby said, "Hey Brandi, how y'all doin' tonight, sweetie?"

Brandi leaned forward and kissed Bobby on the forehead. "I's fine, sweetie, and I damn sure been worried about you ever since I heard 'bout dat shootin' over in Alabama." Brandi greeted Rich, giving him a friendly hug around the shoulders. She was careful not to touch either of the men with her unusually long nails, for fear of breaking one off.

"Hey, who's your handsome young white friend, Bobby? He be a *fine* hunk a' man!" Brandi laughed, and then went into a deep cigarette cough. I sensed that she already knew what I had only suspected; that our liaison was pre-arranged.

"'Dis here be Matt! He be a melon packer 'dat woiks wid' us. Me an' ole' Shorty decided he need some lovin'. An' you know ole' Shorty usually gits what he want! I damn shore wish he was still wit' us so he could see da' look on dis young white boy's face right now!"

I was slightly embarrassed, but Brandi's long legs and perfect tan skin quickly took control. She had a presence that put me at ease, and the perfect shape of her body had an almost hypnotic effect.

"Come right in gentlemen," said Brandi in a deep velvety voice. She extended her hand to me and led me across the threshold into the house. The symbolism of the neophyte being led inside by the experienced woman was not completely lost on me. I had fantasized about a moment like this many times, after my friends tried to convince me to go with them on their Little Harlem outings. Now I followed Brandi like a child who was entering his first haunted house on Halloween; breathing fast, heart pounding harder with each step. I could have likened my excitement to Mount Etna, just before a major eruption. I felt it all the way down to my stomach, and even lower.

Shortly after Brandi led us inside, we entered a large open area with a rotunda style ceiling that could easily have accommodated a hundred-person reception with cocktails. Above us hung an enormous crystal chandelier that would have been at home in the White House. In front of us were two carpeted staircases about 20 feet apart. The room had an intoxicating scent about it, and my heart pounded at the realization that exotic women who were available for sex on demand surrounded me.

Brandi said, "Y'all comin' with me, Matt?" She pointed to the staircase that led up to our left. Her soft voice melted my fears, and her smile could have melted a block of ice at the North Pole during the month of December. For the moment, I was content to take in the atmosphere, and I was in no hurry to ascend the stairs to the erotic world that awaited me.

Bobby and Rich nodded in the direction of the stairway, making it clear that it was time for me to go upstairs and enjoy the woman's body. They had the look of two young boys who had put a friend up to something that was guaranteed to get him into big trouble.

Looking back towards Bobby, I had the urge to stall for time. Was I really supposed to go upstairs with Brandi? I should ask. But I already knew the answer. It was all part of the deal, and even though I was surprised at how fast things were moving, the time had come for me to lose my virginity.

Bobby laughed his quick boyish laugh. "Dis' here is what Shorty had in mind. Dis is on me, so y'all go up and enjoy Miss Brandi. Go on! Y'all have fun. Ole' Bobby and Rich, we be waitin' fur ya' when y'all gits done. We ain't gonna' leave ya', big fella."

I looked at Brandi again. This time, my eyes took in her sexy lingerie and her long legs in a much brighter light than I had seen before. I was shaking, but at the same time I was becoming more and more aroused despite my jitters.

As she led me across the open area beneath the enormous crystal chandelier, I noticed there were two large, walnut-paneled parlors, one to the left of the large foyer and the other to the right. Smoke-borne laughter billowed out in generous amounts from both sides. The parlors were nearly identical, with over-stuffed oxblood leather chairs one might expect to see in a high-class men's athletic club. Some men were seated with women on their laps, and others with women next to them, draped over the arms of their leather chairs. All of the men in the parlor to the left of the staircase were white, and the men in the parlor to the right of the staircase were black. All were dressed like southern gentlemen in nice summer wear. A few of the women in the room to the left could nearly have passed for white women in the outside world, but the women in the parlor to the right were dark skinned with distinctly African features.

"Separate but equal, even in the sex industry," I thought to myself. But in this case, whites and blacks seemed to happily co-exist. Everyone who was there had entered on nearly equal terms, and all had come in through the same door, the *back* door. I thought it ironic that white customers would have been insulted if relegated to the back entrance of most southern establishments, and yet they were content to use the back door here. It was also ironic that, had this been a restaurant, the rules would have been completely different. But in this magical place, all of the clients were having the time of their lives under the spell of these beautiful black and tan women. Whites made the rules outside of this building, but whites and blacks enjoyed the same leniency in this secret world of erotic pleasure. Everyone benefited, nobody got hurt, and the barriers that applied to life outside these walls made little sense inside. Perhaps its ability to demonstrate that all men were truly created equal was the happy irony of the world's oldest profession.

I wondered for a moment how many of the white men present that evening were KKK members. In 1968, the simple law of averages dictated that somebody in a crowd of this size was a Klansman. But even the authoritarian ideologue could enjoy himself in this place, as long as there was a clear distinction between the light skinned girls who serviced whites only, and darker skinned girls who serviced blacks.

Brandi, who appeared to be a very good friend of Bobby's, would not be able to sit with him in this place. In fact, she had probably been walking a thin line when she greeted him and Rich at the back door, but the fact that I was with them made it all right.

Brandi took me by the hand, and the warmth and softness of her skin took me to yet another level of arousal. She led me to the base of the stairs with their plush red carpet, gold gilt handrails, and walnut banisters six inches apart from each other. My knees were about to buckle as Brandi slowly led me up the staircase. My heart pounded as she neared the bend, halfway up the staircase, and I glanced back over my right shoulder at Bobby and Rich. Bobby gave me the thumbs up sign, and I winked at him nervously.

I looked at the soft brown skin on the back of Brandi's neck, then my eyes focused on her gorgeous ass. I took a deep breath and let it out slowly. My excitement reached a new peak at the thought of my hands feeling the soft skin underneath her sexy red bikini briefs. I could not believe that something this exciting was really happening to me. Before now, my only fantasy of making love to a black woman was the sleazy, hardcore porn version. As I lie awake in the hotel, late at night after an exhausting day, I would sometimes have visions of it happening to me around twilight after everyone had gone from the farmer's co-op. It would take place on the floor of a semi trailer, atop a bed of prickly straw that still held its warmth from earlier in the day. In theory, being a watermelon packer could have led to that sort of chance encounter, but my raging 20 year old hormones had never come close to conjuring up a vision like this!

Brandi led me by the hand to the top of the staircase and down a long hallway. She came to a large oak door on our left with ornate gold leaf decoration around its frame, and then she led me inside the room. She pointed to the queen-sized four-poster bed that was adorned by a plush red velvet bedspread. The room was elegantly decorated, and smelled clean and fragrant with a slight scent of coconut oil. I had the urge to playfully hop onto the bed, like a little boy waiting for his mother to read him a bedtime story. Brandi kicked off her high-heeled shoes and gave me a shove with her hand against my chest. I played along and fell onto my back, my head landing against a plush pillow. Had she used a feather, her effort to push me over would have been equally as effective.

Wasting no time, yet careful not to hurry my youthful arousal, Brandi straddled me as I lay on my back, and then she lowered her shoulder straps to reveal two full mocha colored breasts with nipples the color and size of Hershey's Kisses. As she lowered her soft feminine body over mine, I began to suck her nipples like a half-starved infant. As I kissed and sucked, I could feel them tighten and stand up firmly between my lips. The feel of her soft breasts, and her aroused nipples between my moist lips made my cock stiffen into a full-blown erection. Even though I wanted to suck on Brandi's nipples for hours, my lack of experience gave me a sense of urgency. I wanted to make love to her right away, and it didn't matter to me whether it lasted thirty seconds or thirty minutes.

Brandi moved her body with the motion of my hands as I stroked her back. I could feel the warmth between her thighs moving softly across my pants. As I continued to kiss her breasts, slowly alternating between the two, I reached down and felt her soft buttocks through her panties, and then moved my hands around to the front of my lower torso to loosen my belt. Brandi interrupted and moved my hands back to the soft skin of her butt, then took over the task of undoing my belt and zipper. She moved her body downward over mine and lowered my pants until they were completely off. Then she eased her body back up to resume her sitting position on top of me. The feeling of her warm body against my hot cock, through my briefs and her bikinis, brought me to the greatest level of anticipation I had ever experienced.

As I massaged Brandi's soft buttocks with my hands inside of her panties, I continued kissing her breasts. Brandi reached behind herself and slowly and gently massaged my balls. The soft, warm palm of her hand made them roll in response to her touch. My cock was rubbing up against her pussy through thin pieces of cloth, one mine and one hers, and I was more than ready to ease into her wetness at any moment. I knew I would not last long once that happened, so I was happy that she continued massaging my testicles a bit longer.

Suddenly, Brandi slid her body gracefully toward the foot of the bed, gently pulling down my briefs as she moved. She removed them as smoothly as she'd removed my pants a few minutes earlier. Leaving her panties on, she slowly began to move her wet mouth toward my cock. I throbbed harder than ever with anticipation. I was about to get the first oral sex of my life, and I could not imagine anything better than getting it from Brandi's full, warm, sensuous lips. She reached up and gently cupped my balls in one hand, then eased her lips over the head of my steel-hard erection. I moaned with pleasure, and she responded by taking her lips off my cock. She slowly kissed her way down one side of my throbbing member, then back up the other side. Brandi not only knew how to please a man, but she also knew how to make his pleasure last.

I tried to divert my attention away from my intense pleasure by thinking of my surroundings in the beautifully appointed room. I stared at the ceiling with its ornate crystal chandelier, attempting not to think of the intense pleasure that was building inside my swollen penis. Despite my efforts, Brandi was in complete control. Had she taken me into her warm and wet mouth, I would have cum in a matter of seconds. I moaned again and asked her to come up next to me so I could hold her and kiss her for a while longer. I wanted my intense anticipation to last as long as it could, so Brandi stopped kissing and came up to lie beside me. She gently rubbed my tight stomach muscles.

I looked into her beautiful eyes, and then kissed her soft neck. I reached down with my left hand to feel the small of her back, and continued kissing her neck. Gently massaging her back, I moved my left hand to feel her naked skin. Moving my left leg upward between her long lean thighs, I eased my thigh as high as it would go to feel the warmth and moistness of her pussy. I carefully reached around to her soft buttocks, pulled her closer and pressed my left thigh tighter against her. I kissed her nipples, and noticed how hard they felt against the soft skin of my lips. The middle finger of my left hand felt her wetness and I was once again ready to explode. Brandi knew it was time, so she stopped and said she would help me put on a condom. She pulled one from a small nightstand next to the bed, removed the wrapper, and eased it slowly over the mauve colored head of my penis.

Once the condom was in place, Brandi took off her panties and positioned herself on her back in the middle of the bed with her legs spread and her knees upward. As she reached to pull my body toward hers, I looked at her in all of her tan and sensual glory. When I saw the beauty of her eyes, with their greenish-gold glow that rivaled the beauty of a stained glass window, my throbbing shaft could wait no longer. Easing down over Brandi, I kissed her breasts again and gently probed her warmth and wetness. Easing into her and stroking gently, I made love to her with a passion that was more suited for a young bride than a prostitute I would never see again after this night.

In less than a minute, I came hard. I moaned and bucked, as I looked down and smiled at Brandi. If I was not in love, it was certainly close enough that I would remember it forever.

41.

Bobby and Rich were both on beer number four when Rich remembered the cigars he'd left inside the glove box of Bobby's car. Rich asked Bobby for the car keys, so he could go out and retrieve his smokes, then he exited through the back door of the house. Once outside, he noticed it was considerably darker than before. Perhaps, he thought, the security lights had been turned off or a bulb had burned out. He remembered the general area where Bobby had parked, so locating the car would not be a problem in the dark.

After consuming four beers, on top of the wine he'd enjoyed at Bobby's earlier that evening, Rich could not resist the thought of a nice stogie. He whistled as he crossed the dark parking lot, and he arrived at Bobby's car in less than a minute's time. He took the keys from his pocket and fumbled for a second, then tried one of the keys in the locked door. When the first key failed to open the door, Rich moved on to the next and the lock turned easily. As the car door opened, a bright dome light came on inside, enabling Rich to see the glove box. He found the cigars—all three of which were sealed in individual metal tubes to preserve their freshness.

* * *

Night watchman, Charlie Boggs was filling in at "The House," and was making his first rounds of the evening. He knew what went on inside, and he didn't approve of such activities, but working part time as a security guard was easy money and it helped to support his fishing habit; night crawlers and spin casting lures weren't getting any cheaper. At a place like this, customers came and went quietly and discreetly, and there was very little work for a security man to do. During the major portion of his six-hour shift between 8 P.M. and 2 A.M., Charlie sat in his car, sipped coffee from his thermos, and listened to baseball games on his small SONY transistor radio. He had found that, on a clear night, he could pull in games from states farther west, and although it was late at night he could listen to major league games from as far away as St. Louis. Sometimes he would close his eyes and take a little catnap during ballgames, but he was careful not to doze off for too long at any one time.

At age 68, Charlie often referred to himself as a "card carryin' World War I veteran," a label that gave him a lifelong lease on courage. He remembered how to handle a loaded weapon, and that was the only qualification he needed to work in the security field. His wife, Sophie, worried about him when he was at work. She told him he was "too damned old" to be walking around in the dark with a loaded pistol, and he would probably end up shooting somebody by accident or shooting himself in the foot. Sophie knew Charlie's eyesight wasn't what it used to be, especially at night when the eyes of a younger person could quickly adjust, but those of a man over 60 were far less adaptable. His eye doctor had explained to him that the liquid inside the lenses of his eyeballs had become stiff and slow to adjust to light variations.

For his part, Charlie didn't pay much attention to his wife or the eye doctor. He liked getting out of the house of an evening, and he truly enjoyed the $20 cash he was paid for each shift he worked. He also liked to stop off at the truck stop outside of Orangeburg on his way home in the middle of the night, where he would drink a cup of black coffee and eat a slice of apple pie with a scoop of vanilla ice cream.

The dome light of Bobby's car was the only thing that seemed unusual to Charlie Boggs as he walked around from the front of the house to the back parking lot. As Rich had noticed a few minutes earlier, Charlie could tell that the security lights were not working properly on this particular evening.

"Strange," Charlie thought to himself. "Maybe I'd better ring the doorbell and see if there's something I can do to get the lights back on." It wasn't a big deal, but it was something for Charlie to do, and it might help the customers later on when they began to trickle into the parking lot to return home to their wives.

* * *

Rich found his cigars, but he had trouble closing the glove compartment. He gave it a hard push, and as it closed, the top of the little door caught the smallest finger of his left hand. "Mutha' Fuck," cried Rich as he rose up instinctively to distance himself from the pain. He hit his head on the inside of the door frame. "Shit, you goddam muthafucker!" Rich was upset with himself. His finger throbbed, and the back of his head felt like it might be bleeding from the blow it had just taken. The only thing that hadn't gone wrong was the fact that he had retrieved his cigars. He now held all three of them firmly in his grip.

Rich backed away from the car, far enough that he could stand up. His frustration erupted as he kicked the door shut with his right knee. The door slammed, the dome light went out, and Rich turned toward the back of the car. The cigars were in his right hand, which he now held at waist level. He could see the shiny tubes reflecting the distant light from the full moon above him.

* * *

Charlie Boggs heard the noise when Rich slammed the car door, and as he turned back in the direction of the car, everything was totally dark. The dome light he had noticed just a few seconds before was no longer lit, and he was certain that what he'd heard was the sound of a car door slamming. Using the techniques of scanning and off-center vision he'd remembered from his days in the Army, he could only make out the car's general outline. His heart skipped a beat, and he instinctively reached for his service revolver with his right hand and his flashlight with his left. "Who goes there?" Charlie bellowed.

There was no sound. Charlie became a bit frightened now because he had expected an answer of some sort. Any answer would have calmed him.

"I said, who goes there?"

Still no response. It seemed quieter than ever now, and things were getting a bit eerie.

Rich froze in his tracks, afraid to make the slightest noise after hearing the night watchman's voice.

Charlie Boggs, flashlight firmly in his grip, quivered from his adrenaline rush. He flipped the switch to turn on the powerful flashlight beam, and the first thing he saw (not 30 feet in front of him) was the reflection of the cigar tubes in Rich's black hand.

As Rich tried to raise his hands to indicate he was neither armed nor a potential threat, Charlie reacted in the worst possible way. The sight of a black man so close to him with a shiny metal object in his right hand caused Charlie to react. His reaction blasted forth in the form of a gunshot from the barrel of his revolver. The shot sounded louder than Charlie had expected, and it was followed by a howl of pain, as Rich grabbed his left shoulder and fell backward several feet against Bobby's car. Fortunately for Rich, the bullet from Charlie's handgun had only grazed him.

Just then, the security alarm went off at the back of house, and a confused and distracted Charlie Boggs turned his attention to his primary function, customer and staff security. He broke into a dead run toward the house.

* * *

Brandi led me from the guest room where I had fallen in love, and she had completed a business transaction. We ambled slowly toward the large open area between the two party rooms below, each of which was filled with customers and cheerful working girls. When we reached the bottom of the stairs, we looked to our left and saw Bobby Leeds sitting in a large, wing-backed leather chair with his feet propped up on a richly upholstered ottoman. He was taking a sip from his beer glass, and enjoying the company of a dark-skinned young lady. When he saw Brandi and me at the foot of the staircase, he excused himself and got out of his chair to walk over and greet us in the area between the two men's lounges.

Bobby said, "Damn, you shore be smiling,' Matt! Looks ta' me like Brandi done made you a happy man!"

I said nothing, but laughed and playfully pulled Brandi closer to me with one arm.

"Ole Rich, he done gone out to da' car to git' us a coupla' cigars. But wit' you bein' done and all, maybe we best be gittin' you back home. It damn shore be gittin' late."

I said, "Yeah, I could use a bit of sleep. Brandi's worn me out here! I'll be sleepin' like a baby tonight, and half the day tomorrow. Good thing it's my day off!"

Just then a white man came, half-staggering, into the area between the two staircases with a beautiful tan skinned woman on his arm. He saw me with Brandi, and then he looked at Bobby and did a double take.

"Hey, you know what?" the man said. "I think I seen that chick together with that there nigger in Orangeburg one night. I damn sure know it was them. Ain't that against the fuckin' house rules for the girls that sees the white men in here to date niggers?" He looked at Brandi. "You're gonna' mess around and lose your job here, little missy!"

With complete disregard for the sling on his arm, Bobby flew toward the drunken white man with lightning speed. Bobby used his one good arm to land a solid punch to the man's mouth. Blood spurted from the man's lower lip as he hit the floor. Hearing the fracas, several other white men came pouring from the left side lounge, and blacks stormed toward them from the other side of the house. Brandi ran to the security alarm by the back door and pulled it. In a matter of seconds, Charlie Boggs stormed through the back door of the house. Although Boggs was out of breath, he was moving like a man half his age. He drew his pistol, fired a shot into the ceiling and yelled at the top of his lungs, "Somebody call the fuckin' Sheriff, now!"

Nobody reacted, so Boggs, panting heavily and appearing to be on the verge of a heart attack, yelled out again. "Goddammit, I said call the fuckin' Sheriff," looking at Brandi. "The number's written on the wall next to the phone."

Boggs again fired his revolver, this time into the chandelier. Slivers of glass flew in all directions. He motioned toward the phone with his weapon, and then toward the back door.

"Get the fuck outa' here, every swingin' dick, if you don't want your goddamm names in tomorrow's papers!"

To escape the melee, customers grabbed their hats and rushed for the back door. Every customer in the house wanted out, and not only out but far away from the place before any lawmen appeared. Despite the fact that the County Sheriff and Orangeburg police were well aware of what went on at this place, none of the customers wanted to be seen except by the working girls and their trusted partners in crime. One never knew what might end up in the newspapers if law enforcement officials were forced to file a formal report. Careers, happy families, and political ambitions could be in shambles. Worst of all, the infamous house near Orangeburg could be forced into closure.

When Bobby and I reached the car, Rich was in severe pain and still bleeding.

Rich didn't know whether the bullet had lodged inside his shoulder, or merely grazed the muscle and left him bleeding and in pain. He opened the back door of Bobby's car and slid across the back seat, assuming the prone position. He held a handkerchief to the wound and asked Bobby to get him home as soon as possible.

"No fuckin' hospitals, OK, Bobby?"

For an instant, Bobby's thoughts flashed back to Holcomb, Alabama, and the agonizing moments he'd spent in the back seat of Shorty's car.

"No fuckin' hospitals," he promised Rich.

"What the fuck happened to you?" Bobby asked.

"Just git in the car, Bobby, and let's git the fuck outa' here!" Rich yelled. "Some old muthafucker with a flashlight and a gun tried ta' kill my ass!"

As Bobby sped away from the house in a thick cloud of dust, I couldn't help wondering how he could watch his good friend Brandi going up the stairs night after night with white men. Perhaps he really was seeing her on the side, as the drunken white bigot asserted. Bobby must have seen Brandi's work at this place as strictly business. Even so, I wondered how he could sit in the black customer's lounge and watch a woman he loved entertaining other men.

42.

Ben,

    Do not let your bride read this letter! If she does, I'll be embarrassed to face her for the rest of my life. But I can't wait until I get home to fill you in on what happened to me last night.

    Bobby Leeds invited me to his house in Harkensville for a groundhog barbecue. The food was great. I even had a small piece of groundhog, then made a complete pig of myself on the barbecued chicken and pork ribs. Those baby backs were delicious! Bobby's wife is a really nice lady and a damn good cook, and his family made me feel right at home. Maybe I was a novelty; the only white boy in that part of town! But whatever the reason, they acted very natural and I felt like I was really supposed to be there. (I wonder if our family would welcome a black face at the table as freely!)

    After dinner, the most amazing thing happened! Bobby and his friend Richard Saunders (a.k.a. "Nigger Rich") took me to a whorehouse! Bobby and some of his buddies go to this place every Saturday night. When they talk about it in front of Bobby's wife, they refer to it as their "Saturday night card game." I'll tell ya' Ben, these folks know how to play cards down here! (Ha! Ha!) This place was like a mansion out of <u>Gone With The Wind</u>. Anyway, a tall slinky black woman named Brandi greeted us at the back door. She was obviously a good friend of Bobby's, but for the evening Brandi was mine, compliments of Bobby and Shorty. Bobby kept insisting that Shorty had decided to fix me up with "some fine black pussy," and he claimed he was only fulfilling Shorty's wishes.

    I've gotta' tell you, Ben, this place was filled with rich looking black guys AND rich looking white guys, and the only thing that separated them was a big smoky foyer. The house had two carpeted staircases—one for white customers and one for black customers, and an enormous crystal chandelier that hung over a huge open area. I'm not the world's greatest fan of this "separate but equal" shit, but I gotta' tell you this place was a damned good example of a separated "facility" where everyone seemed to be treated equal and everybody seemed happy with that arrangement! All of the customers seemed to be getting equal treatment from gorgeous women, dressed in skimpy teddies and guaranteed to give a dead man a hard-on! Of course, the unwritten rule was that the light skinned chicks entertained only white guys, and the dark skinned girls were only allowed to consort with the black clients. But I didn't see any of the customers objecting to the arrangement, no matter what their skin color.

Ben, I can't believe I did it, but I actually went through with the plan Bobby had laid out for me, so to speak. The hour I spent with Brandi was incredible. I think I'm in love! I'll fill you in on the rest of the details when I get home. I gotta' get going for now.

Love, Matt

P.S. *This might be my last letter. I'll be home in a week or so.*

43.

The next few days around the Farmer's Co-op were a buzz of activity. Every melon farmer within 20 miles of Harkensville dragged in whatever melons he could find in his fields, in the hope of squeezing out the last several hundred dollars from an already outstanding crop. It wasn't easy to keep up with the workload, especially with Rich out of the line-up and Bobby still on the mend. Somehow farmers, buyers, and packers worked together and managed to keep up with each other's demands.

Aubrey announced that the crew would be pulling out of South Carolina and heading north on Wednesday afternoon. Unlike the farmers in Holcomb, Alabama, the Harkensville farmers were not angry over the pullout announcement. In fact, Aubrey had told them in advance. They had all made more money than anyone had made from a single melon crop before. One farmer commented that the crop of 1968 had been a "50 year crop," and several were talking about buying new cars, giving end of season bonuses to farmhands, and planting more acres of melons for the 1969 season. If there was one thing I had learned from growing up on a farm, it was that farmers who talked about buying new cars were coming off good crops.

Lonny, Don Jr., and I would follow the crop to Indiana, but Bobby would stay home in Harkensville. Quality Melon would need to recruit new packers when we arrived up north, because they had lost the services of their two best packers.

I would try to talk my brother Ben into leaving his cushy office job in favor of doing some *real* work for the last few weeks of his summer.

* * *

By the middle of the week following Bobby's Saturday night barbecue, we were putting the finishing touches on the South Carolina melon crop. Things were going more smoothly than they had at the end of the crop in Holcomb, and I was ready to depart for Indiana with the rest of the crew. I knew, however, that Bobby was serious about needing my help, and I had made a commitment to travel back to Alabama with him to retrieve Shorty's Buick. My experience over the past several weeks would not have been the same had I not met Bobby, and while some of it was tragic, it had changed me in ways that no previous events had.

When Bobby came to pick me up at the co-op on Wednesday, most of the semis had already pulled out and I was free to leave. Aubrey and Melvin had departed after closing up the small brick office building and turning in the keys to the co-op manager. Melvin would not be going to Indiana, and the crew of packers was happy to see the back of him. Joe Harper would remain behind for a day or two to finish up a few details and coordinate last minute business between truck drivers and farmers. Buyers from other companies were leaving town, and the co-op was taking on the look and feel of an abandoned circus camp.

44.

It suddenly occurred to me that the risks in making the trip to Holcomb with Bobby may be real. Local authorities in Holcomb needed little excuse to turn against a black man, and they would be highly skeptical of a black man and a white college student traveling together. This would cancel out whatever benefit Bobby might accrue by having me along with him when he arrived in Holcomb.

A lot had happened in recent summers involving northern college students and blacks working together in the South. Adding to the potential for Holcomb hostility would be the memories triggered by the sight of a black man who had been involved in an incident in which a white man ended up dead. Bobby had not been implicated in the drunken white man's death, but his best friend had wielded the knife.

I tossed my suitcase into the trunk of Bobby's car and got in. We left for Alabama at approximately 1:15 P.M. The scorching afternoon sun beat down without mercy on the remains of the South Carolina melon crop. The beautiful fields that had been green and lush a few weeks earlier were wilting with age. The vines had become leathery from sacrificing their moisture to the steady growth of thousands of melons, and the sun had greedily sucked out the remaining moisture. The last melons would be picked in the next few days, or left to sunburn and rot in the fields.

I had not noticed on the Saturday evening before when Bobby drove us to the Orangeburg area, but the air conditioning system in his wife's car was long overdue for a recharge. In fact, what came out of the vents felt hotter than the air outside. We soon gave up and rolled down our windows to allow the warm breeze from outside to circulate through the car. This provided little comfort because the temperature outside was well over 100 degrees!

"Bobby, you fucker," I said. "I think I'm in love with Brandi! I haven't thought of anything but her since Saturday night. I know she wasn't impressed with my skills in bed, but I could sure use some more practice with her! She's so damned beautiful! Why did you do that to me?"

Bobby laughed, but it was not his usual contagious laugh. "Dat's normal fur you ta' be in love. I bet she was da' first woman you ever had. But hey, it's jis' a lil' piece a pussy, man! You don't need ta' be makin' weddin' plans! Brandi damn shore be cute, but you gotta' go back home now. Plus, she be my little sumthin' on da' side, an' now I have ta' be careful after dat white fucker done say he seen me wit' her in Orangeburg! I damn sure can't be messin' wit' her at her place a' bidnuss, and I don't wanna' be seen wit' her in town either. I could git my ass skinned alive."

"So that asshole was not just making that up about seeing you out with Brandi?"

"He was mos' likely tellin' it da' way he done see it. But it wouldn't a' made no fuckin' difference if he done made it up. Everybody gonna' b'lieve a white man, an' a black man jis' gits use' ta' 'dat kinda' shit. But bein' use' ta' it damn shore don't make it go away. It be jis' like I tell ole' Joe Harper about Shorty bein' better off dead. If he be alive now, da' white folk in Holcomb be wantin' ta' lynch his sorry ass 'cause he done stab hisse'f a white man. An' even if Shorty got scared, an' stab da' fool in self-defense, day still wanna' hang him up in a fuckin' tree! Best he'd a' got off woulda' been choppin' weeds along da' highway in a chain gang, wearin' dat orange color 'Bama Pajama' for da' res' a' his born days."

"I suppose you're right, Bobby. But next time, I want you ta' fix me up with a fat ugly woman. Then I won't be in love! You hear me?"

Bobby and I both laughed.

"OK," said Bobby. "I might could find you a fat ugly one da' nex' time, if a nex' time come along!"

* * *

Many white motorists overtook us along the highway. Upon noticing that Bobby was driving, and I was in the passenger's seat, some made obscene gestures or their passengers spat out of their car windows in our direction. Bobby figured he'd seen enough violence for one summer, so he tried to ignore the rude gestures. Besides, we would soon be traveling under the cover of darkness.

Had Bobby been wearing a black cap and bow tie, and I had been riding in the back seat of a limo with dark tinted windows, the whole scenario would have been acceptable. It was all right for a black man to drive *for* a white man, but not *with* a white man.

As we drove through Georgia, a redneck trucker made an obvious attempt to force us off the highway. Bobby hit the breaks quickly and steered sharply to our right. Despite the truck driver's evil attempt, Bobby was able to stay in control of the car.

"Surely he wasn't a watermelon hauler," I said. "One of 'our' drivers would never do that to us."

Bobby smiled. "I wouldn't be too shore about dat, Matt! I know a few of 'em that would damn shore love ta' do it."

* * *

Try as I might, I could not help wondering why the act of traveling from one place to another was such a racially charged issue. Perhaps it was the sense of unease over free black people moving about the country, no longer tied to a single location of white society's choosing. The uncertainty over where people of color were going, and where they would end up, must have been threatening to many whites.

Our last fuel stop was in south-central Alabama, about an hour before we would reach Holcomb. Bobby pulled into a roadside gasoline station and got out to pump $10 worth of high-octane fuel. I got out of the car and went inside to pay for the gasoline. The man behind the register gave me a dirty look, which quickly evolved into a Cheshire cat grin.

"Who the fuck do you think you are, college boy? You ain't one a' them goddam civil rights hippies, are ya'?"

I gave no answer, but put a $10 bill on the counter, wanting only to complete my transaction and get away from this man as soon as possible.

"If y'all's one a' them nigger lovin' civil rights freaks, I need to tell ya' that around these parts, we like to give 'em a night to remember. I guess you could say they's the only breed around here that we treat worse than we treat our niggers. That's mainly to teach 'em a lesson, since they ain't welcome around here. Our niggers around here was jist fine until all these fuckin' civil rights white boys showed up down here a few years ago. Ya' see, this here kinda' shit gives us a huge fuckin' pain in the ass, 'cause we done lost the Civil War once. We don't wanna' lose this here thing they be callin' the Civil Rights War. What a fuckin' joke! It's jist another Civil War, no matter how they dress it up in fancy TV lingo. So, if I was you, white boy, I'd be gettin' the fuck outa' this county real fast. It's gettin' nigh on ta' nightfall, and you and your little nigger friend might run into a few problems if'n ya' try and stay around here."

When I got back into the car, I said nothing to Bobby about the gas station attendant's remarks, but Bobby recognized immediately that something was odd about the way I was acting.

"What's da' matter, Matt? Cat got you tongue? You catch a little hell inside 'dat gas station about you choice a' travelin' buddies?" Bobby laughed.

"Wasn't nothin', I'm just a little scared," I said.

"Da' fear don't go away, Matt. If ya' think it be scary bein' a white man *ridin'* with a black man, you oughta' try *bein'* a black man. Now, 'dat can be some scary shit!" Bobby laughed.

I found it difficult to believe that anyone who had endured what Bobby had that summer could see the humor in life. I now saw first hand that Bobby was a man with a strong sense of who he was and where he had come from. Both his humor and self-esteem were deeply rooted and backed up by a community of people who knew and loved him. His sense of self-worth did not teeter on the attitudes and actions of a handful of bigoted whites. He was from a place where blacks had a sense of pride that no white bigot could take away. And somehow that sense of pride, like the pride of Martin Luther King, made it possible for men like Bobby Leeds to rise above the fear. I was beginning to see for the first time how a lesser man than Bobby could easily lash out at a man like the one I encountered in the gasoline station.

45.

It was twilight when Bobby and I arrived in Holcomb, where the next morning we would attempt to pick up Shorty's car. He had offered to drop me off at a hotel in Dothan, and come back and pick me up the next morning. I told Bobby I preferred to see the trip through to Holcomb.

"We can pull into the co-op parking lot and sleep in the car," I said.

"I be thinkin' way ahead a' ya', Matt. Fact is, I done decided 'dat's e'zackly what we gonna' do. I don't think you an' me gonna' find a room togetha' in Holcomb anyway!" Bobby laughed. "Besides, dis be one quick night. We be seein' Mr. Sheriff early in da' mornin' about pickin' up Shorty's car. Soon as we do dat, we gonna' git da' fuck outa' here!"

I remained skeptical about our chances of leaving Holcomb with Shorty's car, and I couldn't help noticing Bobby's sudden shift from the notion of "getting Shorty's car" to that of "seeing about" getting Shorty's car. Until now, he had spoken with confidence about taking the car back with us, but now I wondered if he had a plan in the back of his mind for this trip that he had not mentioned to me. We had come all this way, and I didn't want him to think I had lost hope of success. Besides, if Bobby believed there was a chance that one of us would be driving Shorty's Buick back to Harkensville the next day, then maybe he was right. He was wiser to the ways of the South than I was.

* * *

The evening air was cooler than Bobby and I had expected, and that would be in our favor when it came time to sleep. Although we were not in friendly territory, neither of us felt it completely unsafe as long as we could hide Bobby's car well behind the large co-op building before attempting to settle in for the night. If a Holcomb cop or sheriff's deputy happened along behind the co-op in the middle of the night and found a black man and a white man together in the same car, it could spell trouble. But we calculated it was highly unlikely that any local authorities would be patrolling the co-op, especially now that the Holcomb melon season was over and the machinery had been mothballed until next year. Even the large panels that resembled oversized garage doors had been lowered, and the co-op had taken on a "closed-for-business" appearance.

"Too bad the Sheriff's storage lot is locked up at night," I said. "I'd love to get Shorty's car and get the fuck outa' this hell hole tonight! This town gives me the fuckin' creeps. Wouldn't it be nice to get outa' here tonight and be back in Harkensville for breakfast? I'd be happy to drive all night to make that happen."

Bobby knew I was wishing out loud for his benefit, and we both knew that even if the storage lot were open at night, no one except the Sheriff could authorize the release of a car.

"Matt, les' git' some wine so we be able ta' settle down an' git some sleep! Dat's what me an ole' Shorty use ta' do. We'd say, 'let's git us some air conditionin' juice!' Den, soon as we drunk us a bottle or two, we be sleepin' like a fuckin' baby, and forgit all about it bein' hot outside."

"Good idea," I said. "I'm not sure I can sleep without something to help me along a little bit."

"Dat wine'll damn shore hep' ya', Matt. We gonna' fix y'all up wit' a big ole' bottle a' Mad Dog 20-20, or T-Bird. Den y'all be in good shape come mornin'!"

Bobby drove into Holcomb past the restaurant where Shorty had lost his life. Seeing the place was depressing as well as disgusting for both Bobby and me. "Kwick, Klean Kitchen." Neither of us had anticipated that the sight of the place would affect us as it did. The events of the past few weeks had been a powerful lesson for me in how difficult it was for a black man to get an even break. No matter how many marches, freedom rides, and peaceful protests, the South would cling to its time-honored system of keeping blacks in their social "place." No matter that the Williams of the world were not man enough to pack a decent load of watermelons, they were successful in keeping blacks at the back door of places like Smitherman's.

Shorty had saved Bobby's life by stabbing the drunken white man and scaring off his companion. The white men who started the trouble that day could have killed Bobby and, no matter how drunk they were, the Sheriff and Judge would have believed their story. Bobby was correct in what he'd told me earlier about the trouble Shorty would have faced had he lived. "Self-defense," the white men would have pled, and both would have gotten off with little more than a legal slap on their wrists. Shorty might have spent the rest of his life in jail.

Bobby could not put his profound sadness into words, so he said nothing as he drove past Smitherman's. He tapped the breaks and hesitated, as if to pull over, but thought better of it and kept driving. What would be the point of stopping?

* * *

Every structure of significance in Holcomb, including a large percentage of the residential housing, was clustered along the main road in a classic example of what urban geographers called a line settlement. Holcomb was very quiet at this time of evening, and a slight green cast had fallen over the sky. It was the rare sort of evening sky that had always put me in a dark and foreboding mood.

About a quarter mile past Smitherman's, we drove past a black man who was staggering his way through town. Bobby had to swerve to the left to avoid hitting him. "Shit, mutha'fucker!" Bobby yelled. "Dat ole' fucker done been around here as long as we been comin' ta' this town, but I never done see him drunk enough ta' walk out on da' road like dat! He dam shore gonna' git his ass killed!"

"Maybe that's what he wants," I thought out loud.

"Shit, you might be right, Matt," said Bobby.

A few blocks later, we pulled into an alley next to the Holcomb liquor store. The pink neon sign over the front door of the tiny structure flashed, "HOLCOMB TOWN LIQUORS." Bobby knew he had to pull around to the back of the building, rather than take one of the convenient diagonal parking spaces in front.

Like most other establishments in town, the liquor store had a separate entrance for blacks, in the back. Bobby got out of the car and shut the driver's side door, then went inside to purchase our evening's supply of wine. The owners had nothing against blacks coming in as long as they obeyed local etiquette and entered through the back door. A goodly portion of gross wine sales were to blacks, so the store stocked Mogan David's "Mad Dog 20/20," Thunderbird and Ripple close to the rear entrance for black customers. This had the extra benefit of keeping black customers toward the back of the store. Boone's Farm, Gallo, and the funny shaped bottles of Mateuse Rose were stocked toward the front to suit the more "refined" tastes of white customers. The front of the store was carpeted, while the back end consisted of a bare concrete floor. The cash register was located in the middle of the store, with one counter that faced the front and another that faced to the rear. These psychological barriers were effective in separating the customers along racial lines.

Bobby reemerged through the rear door of the cinder block building with a brown paper grocery bag in his hands. The bag contained two magnums of wine. The owner neither recognized nor hassled Bobby. Although it had been the talk of the town for the past few weeks, the incident behind Smitherman's had blown over, and Bobby's picture never appeared in the local papers. Conventional wisdom chalked up the incident to a simple case of a drunken white farm hand clashing with a couple of out-of-town blacks. One drunken white for one black watermelon packer; the closest thing to an even tradeoff in the eyes of respectable locals. There was no grieving period, little discussion after a few days, and nothing new to hold against local blacks. One of the blacks involved was dead, and the other had moved on with the rest of the watermelon crew.

"Let's git back to da' co-op, Matt. I gotta' git' some a' dis' here wine in me! Bein' back here is damn shore makin' me feel bad! I wish you woulda' talked me outa' comin' here!"

Bobby and I both knew that I could not have talked him out of making the trip, no matter what argument I had used. For my part, I realized the moment he'd asked me in Harkesville that the mission to Holcomb was etched in stone. His promise to Shorty's wife had taken on a life of its own, and there was nothing left to do except play it through . . . whatever the cost.

Bobby drove toward Smitherman's, but this time he didn't drive past. He made a left turn into the sandy front parking lot, and drove around to the back to have a closer look. It was obvious that he needed to see the back of the building one last time in order to achieve some sense of closure. Bobby swung the car around so he could shine his headlights toward the rear of the restaurant, then sat quietly and stared at the back of the building. I looked over and noticed that Bobby's eyes were filled with tears. Soon, his forehead fell downward until it rested atop his hands at the summit of the large steering wheel. After a couple of quiet moments, he drove back toward the front of the building, then made a left onto the blacktop road and drove the short distance back to the co-op.

We drove around behind the group of co-op buildings in search of a secluded spot. As soon as Bobby turned into the sandy parking lot, he shut off his headlights. Familiar with the layout of the lot, he picked out a spot where drivers of passing cars could not see us. The perfect spot was behind the large stack of hay bales left over from the melon season, and covered with an enormous black tarpaulin.

Bobby and I opened one of the large wine bottles and poured two paper cups full. He raised his cup and looked at it for a moment, then took a large inaugural gulp. We proceeded to drink and talk until we forgot we were back in Holcomb on a serious mission. For the moment, we were two men getting drunk together and nothing else mattered. The warmth and humidity of the evening no longer bothered us, nor did the fact that we were in enemy territory. Our sense of danger was left behind after our second glass of wine, but the memories of Shorty remained intense. After we began to feel the effects of the alcohol, it seemed appropriate to summon his spirit.

"It damn shore feel like Shorty's ghost is still here in Holcomb. Dey say ghosts stay around 'til dey be finished wit' bidnuss. I don't know what bidnuss Shorty's ghost got here, but I damn shore feel he still be here!"

"I have no idea how that works," I said.

"I know I probl'y been sayin' dis before, Matt, but I gotta' say it ag'in. Dis' woulda' been a damn fine melon season if'n Shorty wouldn't a' gone and got his ass killed. Shorty and me was havin' a good time packin' an' laughin' an' jokin'. We was makin' good money, an' we was gonna' turn you young ass into a fine melon packer! We damn shore was. And I was only followin' up on Shorty's promise when I done fix you up wit' Brandi. It was all Shorty's idea. He had a heart a' gold, ole' Shorty. Yessir! He had him a big ole' watermelon heart. Ain't any bigger heart dan da 'one Shorty had,' sep mine when I let you young ass take Brandi upstairs." Bobby laughed.

"I know things got all fucked up when Shorty got killed," I said. "But I've gotta' tell you that you and Shorty made me into a better packer than I ever thought I could be. In fact, you made me a better man. Thanks, Bobby! And thank you, Shorty!"

I held my paper wine cup outside the car window, raised it high above the roofline of the car and aimed it at the beautiful full moon that appeared that second. Offering a toast to Shorty seemed appropriate, so Bobby looked out of his window, stared at the moon and lifted his cup. "Ta' Shorty!"

We gulped large amounts of wine, then refilled our cups again.

It must have been near midnight when I crawled into the back seat of Bobby's car and went to sleep. Several minutes after I fell asleep, I heard Bobby step out and walk around to the back of the car. I quickly dozed off again, oblivious to the fact that Bobby had lifted the trunk of his car and taken out a large can of gasoline.

46.

Bobby walked around to the front of the co-op building, staying close to the large structure so the outline of his body could not easily be detected. He then walked down the road towards the center of Holcomb. There was no movement in town, and only one car drove past him as he walked toward Smitherman's restaurant. At a passing glance, the driver of the lone car might have thought Bobby was a stranded motorist carrying gasoline back to a car he'd parked along the roadside ahead.

The wine no longer made Bobby feel happy, but instead it brought on a deep wave of depression. He had achieved no real sense of closure an hour or so earlier when he had stared at the back of the building from the front seat of his car. Tears welled up in Bobby's eyes, as he walked toward the back of the restaurant where he and Shorty had been treated so badly by Smitherman, and where Matthews and Braslow had randomly confronted them. He was overwhelmed by the memory of that day, and the grief came down on him worse than anything he had ever experienced. He felt as though he were still lying in the back seat of Shorty's car, helpless, as Shorty fought off his attacker. He knew at that instant that he could never again stand the sight of Shorty's car. If the trip back to Holcomb was only for the purpose of retrieving Shorty's car, it had been a complete waste of time. It had not been about the car at all. Bobby knew now why he had returned.

As he walked toward the back of the building, he was startled by a rattling sound where he and Shorty had been served their meals. Shorty had not eaten a single bite off his plate that day. Bobby was about to hand it to Shorty as Teddy Braslow's car had come flying around the corner. It was to have been Shorty's last meal, and he never had a chance to enjoy it.

Bobby cast a startled look in the direction of the garbage cans, his heart pounding inside his eardrums. A raccoon looked back at him, holding what appeared to be a partial ear of corn-on-the-cob. Bobby smiled, and spoke to the animal.

"We be two coons here tonight!" Bobby staggered to keep his balance. "You don't even got ta' pay fur you garbage, do ya' little fella'? Shorty and me, we had to pay." Bobby laughed out loud, as if he and the raccoon were sharing an inside joke, and the irony of the scene struck him again as he spoke. "A fuckin' coon eatin' his midnight snack at da' coon's back door! Ain't that somethin'?"

Slowly, Bobby eased toward the back door until he arrived at the spot where the overweight, sweaty Smitherman had grudgingly served him day after day. He closed his eyes, then stood and thought for a moment. As if he was saying a prayer, he mouthed some words and a slight whisper came through his lips. "This is fur you, Shorty, ya' big dead nigger! Why did you have to go and git you ass shot?"

Bobby opened the gasoline can and began pouring generous amounts of the cool liquid against the door, and all along the building's foundation. He quickly emptied the contents of the container, and became so caught up in the task that he didn't notice he had gotten one shoe and one pants leg soaked with the volatile liquid.

He then put the gas can down, looked up at the building and staggered backward as he searched in his pocket for the Zippo lighter that Shorty's widow had given him on the day of Shorty's funeral. He had not seen the fancy lighter before that day, because Shorty never brought it with him for the melon season. His father who had died of lung cancer had passed it down to Shorty.

Bobby flicked open the shiny metal top of Shorty's lighter, then pressed his right thumb firmly against the friction wheel and turned it a half rotation. He smiled at the site of the perfect blue and gold flame that shot upward, and held it over his head for a moment. The flame shot at least two inches high and glowed brightly against the dark Alabama sky. Bobby lowered the flame and leaned over to touch it to the gasoline that had soaked into the aged dry wood, just above the building's concrete block foundation. He knew exactly what to expect, yet it still sent an enormous thrill through his stomach. The flames spread like a whirlwind across a desert floor, and soon the entire building was engulfed. Bobby's smile spread across his face as tall orange flames lapped over the gray siding and greedily swallowed the structure in front of him.

The terrified raccoon was not interested in staying around for the festivities, so it bolted out of the garbage and scampered across the sand parking lot and into the safety of the small wooded area behind the building.

This was the moment in which Bobby's anticipation became action. His plan had only come together after he'd arrived in Holcomb, but it was a good plan. Everything from here on would be downhill. For a brief moment, he enjoyed himself immensely as he watched the hated structure turn into a massive conflagration before his eyes.

Whoooomp! The flames shot upward and Bobby stood back to admire his handiwork. But as he expected, his moment of triumph was brief. Torching the back door of the building where he and Shorty had been treated with all the dignity of stray dogs brought with it an intense catharsis. The sheer joy of watching the place in flames was all he could think about. He felt a rush of adrenaline as he stood and watched the building burn, and he savored the sweet crackling sounds, like thin slats of kindling in a pot-belly stove on Christmas Eve.

Suddenly Bobby felt an intense heat building against his legs, much greater than the reflected heat from the burning building in front of him. Looking down, he was startled to see that a billowing flame had engulfed his pant legs. The wine he had drunk clouded his thoughts. This was a cruel reversal of fate, considering the drunken state of the white farmhands who had assaulted Shorty and him a few weeks earlier. Bobby had acted out with the courage he had drawn from the bottle, but now it was his turn to panic and flee from the scene.

Without thinking to remove his burning pants or bury his lower extremities in the deep sand of the parking lot, Bobby ran towards the back of the parking lot to seek shelter in the woods as his little raccoon friend had done a few minutes earlier. His only thought was that he desperately needed to find water, perhaps a small pond or a spring, in which he could douse his flaming clothes and burning legs. He thought he'd seen a small stream inside the woods when he and Shorty had once gone into the woods to urinate. But in the dark, a small stream would be next to impossible to find.

As Bobby ran towards the trees, the light from the flaming building reflected off the shiny green leaves in front of him. He could hear the faint sounds of sirens in the distance as he plunged himself into the woods. His pants grazed against a thicket of dried underbrush, which instantly began to burn.

Bobby's priorities were badly distorted. At first, he looked frantically for a source of water, but now he only wanted to hide from the law. Black men were shot at the scene or lynched by angry mobs for much less than what he had just done. A black man bold enough to destroy a white man's place of business had less chance of surviving than a caterpillar crossing a four-lane Los Angeles highway during rush hour.

The fire he had set off in the dry underbrush spread quickly, literally blazing a trail behind Bobby's gasoline-soaked trousers. The sirens were those of local police and Sheriff's department cars coming to check on the restaurant, not those of fire trucks. No fire fighting vehicles were within earshot, as Holcomb's fire service came from a volunteer squad five miles away, from the opposite side of town.

Police and Sheriff's vehicles arrived at the scene quickly, and one of the men noticed flames spreading along the edge of the wooded area. The policeman swung his car around to the back of the building and pointed his search light into the woods where Bobby lay burning. The Holcomb cop jumped out and grabbed a double barrel shotgun from the trunk of his cruiser.

Bobby could see the spotlight filtering through the trees, and he heard the slamming of the police cruiser's trunk. The cop ran toward the wooded area, where he followed the burning brush trail to Bobby, who lay screaming in horror at the smell of his own burning flesh. Had he only stopped for a few seconds to smother his burning pants legs under the deep sand of the parking lot, he would not have ignited the underbrush, and he might have bought himself enough time to escape into the darkness . . . at least until the bloodhounds came looking.

The burly cop looked down at Bobby Leeds, smiling cruelly as if he had just tracked down a wounded animal. Bobby looked up and saw the policeman's eyes. He noticed the cop had the small stub of a cigar hanging from the corner of his mouth.

Spitting the soggy cigar stub onto the ground, the policeman continued to stare at Bobby. "You fuckin' niggers will never change! Always think you can get away with somethin', don't ya'?"

Bobby looked up and screamed again in pain.

"Don't worry. I'm gonna' put you outa' your misery, you sorry little fucker!"

The sound of the shotgun rang out. Bobby felt no pain at first, only a general numbness that might have been caused by the blunt end of a 30-pound Charleston Gray watermelon against his chest. He was aware for a split second that he no longer felt the pain from his burning legs.

* * *

Sheriff Rufus Lane had not gotten out of his car, but radioed back as soon as the policeman returned from the wooded area and gave a verbal report. "Nigger shot dead at Smitherman's. Call the funeral home in Dothan. Have 'em send a hearse right away."

* * *

I was sleeping soundly in the back seat of Bobby's car with the help of several paper cupfuls of cheap wine, but I stirred for a brief moment. Having slept through the sirens, I heard what sounded like a shotgun blast, but I didn't surface from my deep sleep. I knew Bobby was as drunk as I was, and by now he was probably passed out in the front seat of the car.

"Coon hunters," I thought, as I drowsily drifted back to sleep. "I wonder why their dogs aren't barking . . . ."

EPILOGUE

Harkensville Examiner—Obituary Page

"Robert E. 'Bobby' Leeds, age unknown, of Harkensville, died of gunshot wounds on Wednesday evening in Holcomb, Alabama. Local police and County Sheriff's authorities pursued Leeds, who was suspected of arson in connection with the burning of a Holcomb restaurant. According to official reports, Leeds gave chase and threatened officers at the scene. Officers shot and killed him in self-defense. The incident is under investigation by Holcomb authorities. His wife Elizabeth, of Harkensville, and several local relatives survive Leeds. He was employed as a watermelon packer by Quality Melon, Inc., of Florida."

* * *

When I awoke on Friday morning in the familiar hotel room in Harkensville, I felt as though I was waking up from the worst nightmare of my life. For a brief moment, as I lie in bed getting my bearings, I was not sure whether I had really gone back to Holcomb with Bobby or not. Bobby could not be dead, could he? Had I really been awakened 24 hours ago by a steady tapping on Bobby's car window from the knuckles of Sheriff Rufus Lane? Surely, he had not asked me to accompany him to the County Jail for questioning about my possible role as an accomplice in an arson case? There was no way he had asked me to accompany him to a morgue in Dothan to identify the shotgun riddled and partially charred remains of Bobby Leeds.

"How absurd," I thought. I could not have driven Bobby's car back to Harkensville the evening before and delivered it to Elizabeth Leeds, along with the tragic news of her husband's death. As I stared at the hotel room's ceiling, I slowly but surely accepted the fact this nightmare had been real. Of all the strange dreams I'd had that summer, this was the one that *had* to be real!

Within seconds of opening my eyes, the clock radio alarm next to my bed went off. I was suddenly aware that there was still a *real* world, and I was part of it. I would need to be at the Harkensville farmer's co-op in one hour from now, where I would offer to pack one last load of melons to pre-pay for a ride back to Indiana. Even though the Harkensville farmer's market was officially closed, there were truckers hanging around and last minute loads being packed.

It seemed impossible to crawl out of bed and start a new day. What was the point? Why had I been spared, when Bobby and Shorty had been killed? Bobby's life had ended as abruptly as Shorty's, but at least Bobby's had ended more or less by his own choice. I had yet to fully understand what had happened, let alone deal with my own feelings about it. Part of me felt unworthy—even unwilling—to move on to another so-called "normal" day of life.

As my feet hit the floor and I sat on the edge of the bed rubbing my sleep-encrusted eyes, the phone beside the bed rang. I picked up the receiver, and the voice at the other end was Joe Harper's. I was surprised, yet glad to hear from him.

"Joe," I said, "I didn't think you'd still be in town. I thought this would be a trucker calling for me to pack a load of melons in exchange for a ride back to Indiana."

"Well, you know how it goes. Aubrey asked me to stay around here for a couple of days to finish out a few loads of Crimsons for 'you know who.'"

"Ole' man Stout and 'his niggers'?"

"You got it, big fella'. He's the biggest grower of Crimsons in South Carolina, and damn sure not one of my favorite people either. Even so, Aubrey caters to him so he won't go with another broker next season. All things considered, he's only about half as hateful as Aubrey's cousin, Melvin." Joe laughed. "Anyway, we loaded five trucks at Stout's farm yesterday, and I was out there until 9 P.M. last night. I don't mind tellin' ya'—I'm beat!"

"Who'd you get to pack those puppies? Didn't all of the packers take off when Bobby and I left for Holcomb?"

"They sure did, but ole' man Stout had a couple of his young sharecroppers do the packin' for us. After watchin' you all month, they picked up a few tricks of the trade, and that's good on you. All in all, they didn't do a bad job. In fact, I might consider puttin' a couple of 'em onto the payroll as packers next season when we're here in the area. Anyway, at this late stage of the season, you kinda' take what you can get when it comes to packers. Plus, I stuck around and added handfuls of straw when they were needed. I'm sure the trucks we loaded out will make it to the markets just fine." He paused.

"Changing the subject, I'll be driving you to Indiana after we get some breakfast, so get ready as fast as you can and we'll be hittin' the road."

"Damn, I appreciate that Joe. How did I get so lucky?"

Joe laughed on his end of the phone line. "Well, if you insist on *earning* a ride home, we've got ole' Doris Dickman comin' down to be loaded out later today. He's pickin' up a load of Grays at one of the smaller farms, then he's headin' back toward Indiana later this evening. You remember him, don't you?"

"Of course, I remember him! But my ride from Elmwood down to Huntsville was all I needed of Doris Dickman for one summer! He's your typical gasbag trucker. Thinks he knows it all, and then some!" Joe and I both laughed.

"Well, I'm not gonna' charge you for the ride, or make you pack a load of melons. I can use your company for the trip to Indiana, plus I need some help with the drivin'. These old eyelids of mine get a little heavy after a few hours on the road." Joe said, "What time d'ya get in last night, anyway?"

"I'm not sure. I know it was after midnight. I feel like I've got a goddam hangover, and I didn't drink a thing. At least not yesterday."

"So, did you and Bobby get Shorty's car back out of Holcomb?"

I paused, and there was total silence on the line.

"What's wrong?" asked Joe.

"I can't think of anything that isn't wrong, Joe. We got over there Wednesday night. After we found a place to park Bobby's car for the night, we both drank some wine to help us sleep. It was pretty hot, and not all that comfortable sleeping in the car. But we cracked open the wine and cracked the windows to let in some cool air, and before I knew it I was out like a light."

"What about Bobby?"

"Joe, let me get my shower and I'll meet you at your car in 15 or 20 minutes. You're still here at the hotel, right?"

"Right, Matt." I sensed the concern in his voice. He knew that what I needed to tell him was too painful to say over the phone. I knew he suspected the worst about Bobby.

"My car is parked outside the registration office. Take your time. I'll grab a cup of hotel coffee and a paper in the lobby and wait for you in the car."

* * *

When I got to Joe's car after stopping at the motel office to return my room key, I sensed that Joe already knew. I opened the car door and immediately saw that he had been reading a copy of the local Harkenville newspaper. He leaned over and pointed to the obituary page.

"So, you know?"

"Goddammit! What the fuck happened, Matt?"

"I can't say for sure, Joe, but the best I can tell, something inside of Bobby snapped when we drove past the place where Shorty was killed. I don't think Bobby planned it out that way ahead of time, but after we got to Holcomb he felt something inside that even *he* didn't expect. I could tell it. I think he decided right then and there that Shorty's car didn't really matter. What mattered to him was getting his revenge against Smitherman even if it cost him his life, and once he had some wine in him there was no turning back."

"Why the hell didn't you try to stop him? Bobby might have listened to what you had to say."

"Joe, I swear to Christ, I didn't know he was gonna' do it!" Unexpected tears stung my eyes, and I suddenly felt like a guilty schoolboy who was being scolded by his teacher. "Bobby got up and left me three quarters drunk and sound asleep in his car. I woke up once and thought I'd heard something like a shotgun going off, but I was in a deep sleep by then. I remember thinking it was coon hunters, so I rolled over and closed my eyes again. I just *knew* Bobby was sound asleep in the front seat of the car the whole time. Honest to God, Joe, I thought he was still in the car with me!"

Joe sighed heavily. "This fuckin' summer has been a disaster from start to finish. We've had one of the best money makin' seasons ever, but two of the best goddam packers that ever came down the pike are dead. Maybe it's time for me to get outa' this fuckin' racket. It seems like there's a war goin' on here and I don't wanna' be part of it. I already put in my time in the Marine Corps. Back then, at least you knew where the enemy was, and *who* he was."

As Joe started his car, it occurred to me that I was hitching a ride with the most decent men I'd ever had the pleasure of working for. And yes, my friend, Dr. Andrew Harmon still lurked inside my head, ready to keep me company when Joe and I were not talking. I told Joe I needed a bit more sleep, and I closed my eyes.

* * *

Dr. Harmon's voice was loud and clear inside my head, and this time it carried a tone I'd never heard before.

"I'd hate to think that your two favorite packers died for nothing." Dr. Harmon's voice had turned judgmental.

"What have I done to deserve this judgmental attitude?" I asked.

"You want to know what you've done?" Asked Dr. Harmon.

"Yes! I replied. "I'd like to know!"

"Nothing—that's my point," said the voice. *"You have proven to be a non-committal white boy. You've been the same all summer! I have to tell you Matt, as I told you after Shorty was killed, I'm disappointed. In spite of your so-called faith in humanity, you were not committed enough to your two black friends to make a difference. You went along with the program, made no waves, and let it all happen as if you weren't there. My point is that you freely chose not to have an impact on any given situation."*

"That's not true! I showed them that not every white man is a hate-filled bastard who's out to get them! What exactly would you have expected me to do differently?"

"Think!" Said Dr. Harmon's voice. *"Have you learned nothing about commitment? What have I taught you about the dedication of people like Rosa Parks and Martin Luther King, and the young civil rights workers who died in Mississippi in the summer of 1964?"*

"You've taught me a great deal," I said. "But you're a social scientist, not a civil rights activist. I thought my obligation was to become aware, and to think more deeply about things. I thought that would be enough to help me understand and appreciate the actions of others. Isn't that what being a social scientist is all about?"

Dr. Harmon laughed. *"Of course, I'm a student of human behavior, but there are times to study and there are times to drop the academic façade and become a human being. You have to know the difference. Social Science does not exempt a man from taking action when action is called* for! You students talk about values, but I wonder whether you feel the obligation to internalize them. If we are to be human, we must act like humans."

"Oh, give me a break," I thought. For the first time I felt Dr. Harmon's voice had become too critical. I wanted to open my eyes and talk to Joe Harper to drown it out.

Andrew Harmon's voice persisted. *"You pretend to be a Christian, and you say you live by the message of a man who was willing to lay down his life."*

"OK, just a second," I thought. "Are you trying to tell me, as you strongly suggested after Shorty's death, that I should have intervened or risked my own life?"

Dr. Harmon's voice replied, *"I'm saying you should have cared enough that it might have entered your mind to help. You might have spoken up on their behalf, rather than sitting on the sidelines. You might as well have been watching this entire summer on television, for all the difference you've made. When is it going to turn around in this country? When are white people going to get the message that violence eventually comes home to roost? Violence begets violence, and as long as you are unwilling to make a real difference, you will remain a part of the silent majority that protects the status quo."*

"But," I said, "the problem is obviously too big for one white college student to tackle. In fact, it's so big that I can't see why most blacks don't give up the struggle."

"It's not human nature to give up. You've got it all wrong. We'll never give up. As long as we have leaders of great wisdom and courage like Frederick Douglas, Booker T. Washington, and Martin Luther King, we'll never give up. As I've told you before, we will win this civil rights war, and in so doing we'll demonstrate to people the world over that there is a better way."

"I sincerely hope you're right, Dr. Harmon."

* * *

I had eventually dozed off despite the stern admonitions from the voice of Dr. Harmon, and I had no idea how long I'd been asleep or how long Joe Harper had been driving. All I knew was I'd fallen asleep, partially from mental exhaustion and partially out of self-defense against Dr. Harmon. My inner struggle over what I had witnessed in the course of this summer had become more than I cared to deal with, and Dr. Harmon's voice in my head had become that of a judgmental uncle. Would he really be this harsh in his assessment in person, or was I just doing this to myself?

Joe nudged me with his elbow. "You want to stop and get some dinner?"

I knew he meant lunch.

"Sure," I said. "Any time you're ready. I can drive afterwards if you want."

"That's not a bad idea. It's 11:30 already. You dozed off for over two hours."

"Damn," I said. "I guess I was more worn out than I realized. It's not always the physical work that wears us down in life, is it, Joe?"

"No, it's not the physical work. It's a combination of things. The years show on the outside, but I've never really felt old on the inside before now. I always kept myself in decent shape and ignored the gray hair, wrinkles, and extra pounds. But I can tell you I'm startin' to feel old. Yes, young man, somethin' inside of me is feelin' old."

I looked at Joe, and for the first time I studied his aging face carefully.

I said, "Well, I can't blame it on the number of years I've racked up, but I sure don't feel like the carefree college kid I was a few weeks ago."

We were both silent for a few seconds.

"You know what? Joe?" I asked rhetorically. "I'm not sure if this summer will ever end for me. Something my black professor once said keeps coming to mind. '*Life is a journey, not a destination.*' If that's true, then maybe my trip down here was just the beginning of a journey."

"One thing I hope is true," said Joe. "I hope the memories of Shorty and Bobby Leeds are with you for a good long time, wherever you go."

"Don't worry, Joe, they *will* be with me, and I hope the people of Holcomb, Alabama will remember them every time they drive past that sorry pile of ashes that used to be Smitherman's restaurant."

* * *

Joe reached into his shirt pocket, pulled out a postcard and handed it to me. "Sorry I forgot to give you this earlier," he said. "It came for you back at the hotel."

I smiled when I saw that the front of the card was a photograph of the student union building on the Elmwood University campus. I knew immediately that the card was from my brother, Ben. "Dear Matt," he began. "Don't worry, your letters have not been depressing, but I have learned a few things about you by reading them over the past several weeks. For one thing, I'm impressed by your compassion for your fellow packers, Shorty and Bobby, and for the so-called sharecroppers you've met in South Carolina. Knowing you the way I do, I'd be willing to bet you feel a bit guilty that you haven't been able to wave some sort of magic wand and make their lives better. But keep in mind that you have probably given something back to each one of them in your own way.

Hang in there, buddy. I can't wait to get you back in Indiana. I want to hear all the details about your summer with the melon boys.

Ben"

I smiled again.

CPSIA information can be obtained
at www.ICGtesting.com
Printed in the USA
FSHW022055240619
59392FS